"I HAVE A SOLUTION
I SUGGEST MARRIAGE. THE SOONER, THE BETTER," HE SAID FIRMLY.

It was a moment before she could speak.

"You must be mad, Nick Brannon! That's your solution? Marriage? You know what I think of marriage—of becoming some man's property! Knowing that, you'd insult me?" She leaped to her feet and marched angrily to the door.

He grasped her shoulders from behind and spun her about.

"An insult, you say? A man offers you marriage, and you call it an insult? By God, Audra, I'll teach you what an insult is."

In one swift movement Nick jerked her robe open and pulled it down to her elbows, effectively rendering her immobile. Then his angry mouth cut off her gasp, crushing her soft lips. Audra sagged against him helplessly.

Only then did he lift his head. His eyes, glittering with sparks, bored into hers. "Consider yourself insulted," he said brusquely. Then his voice became dangerously soft. "And just so you know the difference . . ."

Too late, she realized he wasn't finished with her yet. . . .

Priceless

DONNA SCHAFF

Toe Rose —

Cousin from Belfield —

Thanks for coming.

Donna Schaff

7/13/98

A Dell Book

Published by
Dell Publishing
a division of
Bantam Doubleday Dell Publishing Group, Inc.
1540 Broadway
New York, New York 10036

ISBN: 0-440-22586-8

Printed in the United States of America

Published simultaneously in Canada

August 1998

10 9 8 7 6 5 4 3 2 1

OPM

For Dennis,
who fed me popcorn and wouldn't let me quit;

For Tom, Tanya, and Thane
because they believed;

And especially for Todd—
Never forgotten, always loved.

Prologue

"$\mathcal{A}$re ye daft?" McKee sputtered. "London is no place for a bonnie lass alone. Ye canna go!"

At any other time, Audra would have laughed at his mulish expression and his lapse into the thick Scots brogue. But not this time. She'd planned her strategy too carefully. "I won't be alone. Jack and Dan Murphy are to go with me."

McKee snorted. "Ha! Even together those two canna figure which end of a bucket to piss in."

Despite her efforts, Audra couldn't keep her grin to herself. "I agree they carry more brawn than brain, but no one will dare approach me with them at my side." And though she didn't say it, she was counting on the fact that the cook's two sons would be able to ask questions without arousing too much suspicion. They were utterly devoted to her, and would keep mum about what she was up to. But first, she had to convince McKee that she should go.

Indicating the papers scattered over the top of the

desk, she spoke quietly. "Look at the figures for yourself. I've worked the sums until they've begun to dance in my head. There's simply no way to squeeze another pound from the meager funds my stepfather left."

"I ken that, lass. Dinna I help you search his room and his things?" McKee knew only too well that the few coins they'd found among William's possessions had already made their way to the village shops, and that Sheffield was still in arrears. "But I dinna like the idea of ye traipsing off to London. Is there no other way?"

She met his gaze. "You know the alternative. There's the arrangement William made with Lord Cowan . . ."

The desk was massive, made of mahogany and heavy enough to require the strength of half a dozen strong men just to lift, yet it shuddered under the sudden impact of McKee's fist. Audra practically jumped out of her chair. Anticipating McKee's fury was one thing; experiencing it was another.

"No! Never! I'll kill that auld bastard afore I'll let him touch a hair on your head!" McKee shouted, leaping to his feet. "Dinna even think about it!"

Knowing him almost as well as she knew herself, Audra wisely remained silent as she watched him pace the study in his odd bowlegged stride. The drumming of her ink-smudged fingers upon the desk was the only sign of her tension.

Only a few inches taller than herself, McKee nonetheless had a powerful build, with broad shoulders topping a brawny torso and long, thick arms with hands as big as hams.

But the color of his eyes had faded to a soft blue over the years, his curly reddish brown hair was graying at the temples, and he had a slightly crooked nose which gave him an air of vulnerability.

In her younger days, she'd teased him often about that

nose in the hopes of learning just how it had been broken, but he'd steadfastly refused to divulge his secret.

Audra loved every hair on that grizzled head. Like his father before him, McKee was Sheffield's steward, but more than that he was her friend, her protector, and— excepting her father—the only man she'd ever loved and trusted.

McKee came to a sudden halt, only to turn his penetrating glare upon her before returning to rest his palms on the desk. " 'Twas a low trick to play on an auld man, wee lassie," he said grimly.

Audra had the grace to flush. "I'm sorry. But truly, McKee . . . do you have a better idea?" she asked earnestly. "It's now been a month since William's burial, and three days since we received the letter from that so-called business manager," Audra muttered to herself as she dug through the papers on her desk. "Ha! Isn't that also what William's crony, Silas Norton, called himself? God knows he was just as much a blackguard as William. Ah! Here it is. It's from a Peter Winters, who writes to inform us that William's will leaves the Manor to his male heir, *Nickolas* Brannon, who will 'make a determination as to the disposition of Sheffield Manor' and advise us of the same 'in due time.' " Audra waved the letter in the air before tossing it down in disgust and pushing her heavy chair away from the desk.

Walking over to the window, she spoke more to herself than to McKee. "He expects me to just sit and twiddle my thumbs while he carelessly decides our fate. Dispose of my home, will he? Ha! In a pig's eye! How dare he? God knows one Brannon was enough! This one has no more moral right to Sheffield Manor than William ever did." Her long mane of black hair twined about her as she whirled to face McKee. "He has to agree to return Sheffield Manor. And since this Brannon hasn't come to us, I have no choice but to go to him in London." Audra returned to the desk and perched on the edge of it. "And you must stay, for someone has to watch over Mother and keep Lord Cowan's men and the bill collectors from the door." Then she played her trump card. "You and Mother are all I have left, dear McKee," she said softly. "I trust no one else."

McKee sank back into his chair. "Aye, your mother. And what will ye be telling her, then?"

An expression of sadness crossed Audra's face. Her mother was still very ill. The recent birthing of a stillborn son had sapped all her strength. Despite assurances from the doctor that she would recover, her mother seemed to have lost her will to live.

"Only that there are legal matters to attend to." Audra's mouth tightened. "I haven't had the heart to tell her about William's will. I may not have to if I can convince Brannon to give the Manor back to us."

"Aye. If anyone can convince the mon, ye can, being the stubborn, prideful lass ye are."

"Of course I am. I learned from you."

That brought a rueful smile to his face. "Och, lass that sweet tongue will lead ye into trouble someday," he said gruffly, but his smile broadened. "Ye know the right words to touch a man's heart, ye do."

Relieved she'd finally won, Audra returned his smile and patted his cheek fondly. "Let's hope I can touch Nickolas Brannon's heart—if he has one." Then she sobered. "I'll be fine, McKee. I'm no longer a 'wee lassie,' you know."

McKee pierced her with a stern look. "Aye. I do know, and that be what bothers me," he grumbled.

Audra grinned. "Then it's settled. The boys and I will take the morning coach." Other than horseback—which would have been preferable but not even an option since

Sheffield no longer had suitable mounts—it was the only way, for the railroad didn't reach their small village of Stanly.

"Ye'll be sure to keep the Murphy boys with you at all times?"

"Of course. Don't worry so, McKee. Nothing will go wrong."

Chapter 1

Everything was going wrong.

Audra muttered an unladylike curse as she snatched a pillow and crammed it over her head, then lay perfectly still. It didn't help. Those embarrassing and disgusting sounds were still coming from the next room.

Blazes! Were all Brannon men debauched?

William had almost never spoken of his family, but one evening when he'd been in his cups, he'd let slip that he had an older brother. Since William had been fifty-five when he'd died almost a month ago, that meant that his brother—who was now enjoying himself so noisily and thoroughly next door—had to be nearing sixty!

Lord, where did a man of his age find the stamina? Especially since the Murphys reported that he spent most of his time aboard a ship, the *Maryanna*, and that he did common seaman's labor.

Which in itself was odd, for the address on Mr. Winters's letter had led her to a suite of offices with *Brannon*

and Benedict engraved on a brass plate on the door. Audra
had been taken aback to discover that Nickolas Brannon
appeared to be a man of some importance, so she'd sent
the Murphy brothers into the streets to glean what information they could about him. They'd not only returned
with the name of the inn he was staying at, but also with
the surprising information that he was part owner of the
Maryanna.

Not that she'd set her own eyes on Brannon yet. But
she'd obtained a room at the Crown and Arms for herself
and, with a little more maneuvering, had managed to en-
sure that her room adjoined Brannon's.

But that had been two days ago.

The unexpected discovery that he had a paramour had
led to a delay, which was necessary but nonetheless frustrating, for Audra didn't intend to carry out her plan in
front of any witnesses. She'd been forced to drag her feet
for two days—and two interminable nights . . .

It was a well-kept inn but, like most, the walls were
thin. For the past two nights, she'd suffered those awful
sounds of mingled pain and pleasure. Gasps and moans.
Masculine groans and feminine squeals.

Audra tried not to think of what the two people in
that room were doing every night. For one thing, it confused her. It also gave her a queasy feeling in her stomach
and brought back ugly memories.

She closed her eyes, not wanting to remember the
muffled voices—one angry, the other softly pleading—
that she'd occasionally heard coming from her mother's
rooms. Nor did she want to recall the ugly bruises that
sometimes marred her mother's delicate skin, or how her
mother had become a shadow of her former self, quieter
and thinner as the months of her marriage to William
Brannon had worn on.

Oh, yes. Audra was familiar with the sound and sight of pain.

What she didn't understand were the spurts of laughter coming from the room next door. How could there possibly be anything *pleasurable* about what they were doing?

Frustrated, Audra punched the pillow and threw herself onto her back. She suddenly realized that the sounds had ceased. Everything was quiet.

Thank God!

She didn't know how much more of this she could take. The waiting was driving her mad! She was worried about her mother and anxious to get back to her. And McKee would be fretting.

Audra smiled at the thought. McKee worried too much. And if he'd known what she really had planned, he'd never have let her come to London.

Not that she wasn't a little frightened about it herself. Doubtless, it was even against the law. Still, the thought of losing the only home she'd ever known frightened her even more. She didn't know what else to do.

A woman's high-pitched giggle interrupted her thoughts.

A man's deep laugh, followed by a strange masculine growl.

The rhythmic creaking of a bed.

Oh, God! Not again! she thought, turning over again and ducking her head beneath the pillow.

Standing in front of the narrow full-length mirror attached to the inside of the armoire in her room, Audra smoothed down the skirt of her new suit. Initially, she'd worried that the color would make her look dull, but now she was convinced that the pearl gray ensemble made her look mature and confident. And the saucy hat with the black feather made her feel stylish.

Heaven knew she'd hated to part with the money to buy anything for herself, even if several years of hard-learned bargaining had resulted in the dressmaker's lowering the price. Still, if she was to achieve her goals, she needed something other than the old gown and threadbare cloak she'd arrived in. And it *had* made a difference, for Mrs. Garvey, the innkeeper's wife, had assumed that Audra was a respectable young lady who, along with her two companions, was awaiting passage on a ship.

Sadly, she'd had to sell her magnificent emerald to fund this little venture. It had almost broken her heart to do so, for her father had given her the pendant on her sixteenth birthday—only days before he'd been killed when his stallion had spooked and his pistol had unexpectedly discharged. It was precious to Audra for that reason alone. But it was also the only thing of value she and her mother had left, and their needs were so pressing.

For herself, she didn't care. She could find some means of support—as governess, companion, anything. But her mother . . . Audra would do anything to protect her and make her well again.

Audra couldn't help being a little excited at the prospect of a new dress. Even as a young girl, she'd loved beautiful clothes, and heaven knew she had few left. Especially since she'd burned the gowns that William had bought for her.

She'd hated them! Just as she'd hated how they'd made her feel so . . . so tawdry! Like a prize filly on display for auction. She now knew she *had* been.

But she wasn't going to think about that anymore, she decided as she left her room and went down the hall. She was going to take a walk, find a bookstore, go to a market. *Anything* to get out of her room. She'd turn into a blithering idiot if she had to spend another day just sitting and waiting.

Audra turned the corner to the stairs and walked smack into the tray carried by the maid, Millie, who was looking back over her shoulder instead of where she was going. Millie's head whipped about, and she shrieked in surprise.

The tray tilted. A full decanter tipped, balanced momentarily, then tipped again as Millie made an attempt to recover and overcompensated. Audra's hand flew out, but she was too late. The red wine spilled, splashing over the front of Audra's new suit.

They both froze, Millie's eyes wide with shock, her mouth agape. Audra stared at the large stain now covering her bodice and the front of her skirt, and wanted to cry.

Her suit! Her lovely new suit!

Millie's face crumpled and she began to wail loudly.

"What is it? What . . . Oh, my!" The feminine voice came from behind Audra.

Audra lifted her forlorn gaze from her ruined suit and turned. Coming down the hall was another woman. A mass of auburn curls surrounded a lovely, heart-shaped face. It wasn't until she neared that Audra saw the fine lines at the corners of her light green eyes and realized that the woman was older than she first appeared.

Then Audra's gaze fell lower and her mouth dropped almost as far as Millie's had. Good Lord! The woman's milk white bosom—of which there seemed to be an awful lot—was practically coming out of her green silk gown! And the scent she was wearing . . . Audra's nose twitched. It was too powerful. Cloying.

"For heaven's sake, Millie, stop that caterwauling!" the woman ordered sharply. "It isn't doing a bit of good." Millie's crying instantly abated. "That's better. Go downstairs and get a large clean cloth. Be sure it's soaked in cold, clear water. And bring more dry towels. Hurry!"

As Millie scampered off, the woman circled Audra, her curls bouncing as she shook her head. "I'm afraid that lovely suit is ruined, luv." She clicked her tongue. "Servants can be such fools at times, but Millie *is* discreet, which is so important in a servant, don't you agree?" The woman took Audra's arm. "Come along, now. Into my room with you."

Too startled to say anything—not that she'd yet had the chance—Audra found herself being propelled back down the hall, like a puppet on a string. "You'll have to remove those clothes. I hate to say so, my dear, but you reek of wine," the woman said.

Audra knew it was all too true. Even the woman's scent was now overwhelmed by the smell of wine. Audra wrinkled her nose as she held the sodden skirt away from herself.

"My name's Delia Jones, by the way. Just call me Delia," the woman informed her. "Do come in. You can change out of those wet clothes and borrow some of mine."

About to declare that she had her own room, with other clothes, Audra looked up and suddenly realized that they were standing in front of the open door to—

Nickolas Brannon's room!

So *this* was the woman that old degenerate was sleeping with! Audra forgot all about her ruined suit, for it occurred to her that if she saw his room, she would be able to carry out her plan more easily.

"I'm Audra," she said quickly, deliberately omitting her last name. "Thank you. I'll need something only until my clothes dry."

Once inside, Audra couldn't help but gape. The room was nothing like her own utilitarian one. This one even had a tub of its own, peeking out from behind a screen near the fireplace. And more furniture than hers—a large dresser, two armoires instead of one. Several trunks lined the walls. And the bed . . . Audra tried not to stare at the huge four-poster bed. Tried not to think of the creaking noises, or the other sounds that had come from it. . . .

Delia caught her stare and laughed. "Nicky does like his comforts." She waved her hand. "The Garveys allow him to furnish his own room since he stays here often on business. Not that they'd refuse, considering what he pays them for the convenience. Now, let's get your clothes off."

Millie had returned with towels, and with her and Delia both helping, it took only moments. As her sodden skirt fell away, Delia's "Oh dear!" chagrined Audra. Sure that Delia was referring to her much-mended underclothes, Audra almost regretted not giving in to the dressmaker's attempts to sell her the new petticoats and the beautifully hand-sewn camisole and drawers.

But Delia wasn't looking at the mending. "You don't wear a corset," she said with some surprise.

"No . . . I . . ."

"Never mind. I've got several. Not that you need one," Delia added as she eyed Audra's waist enviously, "but all my gowns require a corset. Hm . . ." Delia stood with her hands on her hips, measuring Audra. "You're more slender in the hips, but I'd say we're almost the same height and much the same proportion in the bust."

Embarrassed and uncomfortable to have her body examined, Audra was nevertheless amused at Delia's last observation. Her gaze inadvertently went straight to Delia's bosom, which seemed to expand enormously whenever the woman took a breath. The comparison was ridiculous, Audra decided. She'd never achieve Delia's proportions!

But after washing with Delia's heavily scented soap,

after being pushed and squeezed into the corset, after being helped into Delia's clothes and led to stand in front of the full-length mirror, Audra found she was wrong.

Her mouth fell open. She blinked and looked again. It was no flaw of the mirror. The red gown was cut daringly low and the corset lifted her breasts so high that . . . Good God! Were those the dusky tops of her *nipples*? Heavens! If she breathed too deeply or bent too low, her breasts would pop right out!

Apparently, it wasn't a concern of Delia's. "Beautiful, my dear," she gushed. "It's your color, don't you think?"

Audra nodded weakly. She had to admit that the ruby color was startlingly attractive on her, but . . . Audra bit back her protestations. Delia had been more than generous and her pleasure in Audra's appearance was obvious. Audra didn't have the heart to hurt the woman's feelings. She would, after all, have to wear it only as far as her own room. She sighed. Unless she changed into her ragged old clothes, she would have to spend the day in her room. Again.

Delia clapped her hands in delight. "Oh, I wish Nicky could see you! I'd give anything to see his face when he did."

Immediately, Audra's hands clapped over her generously exposed bosom. No way on earth was anyone going to get even a glimpse of what she had just seen in the mirror! Especially not "Nicky"!

Delia was still talking. "It's a shame I'm leaving."

"You're leaving?" For the first time, Audra noticed that an open trunk, almost full, sat at the foot of the bed.

"Shortly, yes. Charley's due home today, so, unfortunately, my time with Nicky has to come to an end. In fact, the lads should be up in just a minute to take this trunk down. Be a love and hand me those clothes from that chair, will you?" Delia began to carelessly stuff more gowns into the trunk.

Audra's heart beat faster. At last! Brannon would be alone. Alone and completely unsuspecting.

"Luv . . . ?"

"Oh! Sorry." Absently, Audra scooped up the clothing from the chair. "Who's Charley?" she ventured to ask.

Delia was gathering more toilet articles and dumping them into a valise. "My husband, of course!"

Husband? Delia was a married woman?

Audra's mouth tightened. She'd been right not to trust Nickolas Brannon. He was even more debauched than she'd thought. Just what kind of man was he, for heaven's sake—to keep a married woman as a mistress? And what kind of woman was Delia, to *sleep* with one man while being married to another?

Delia sorted through the clothing in Audra's arms. "Those stay. They belong to Nicky."

Audra realized, belatedly, that she was holding a pair of men's breeches. She quickly let them fall back upon the chair. "But what about your gown?"

"Keep it, luv."

"Oh, no! I couldn't possibly . . ."

"Of course you could. It was a gift from Nicky, so I'd only have to explain it to Charley, the dear man." At Audra's perplexed look, she laughed. "You must think me mad. Well, Charley *is* a dear, sweet man and he's wild about me. But he's not very exciting, if you follow my meaning, whereas Nicky is so skilled, so . . ." Delia sighed expressively before tossing Audra a coy glance. "Nick fills his breeches wonderfully, while poor Charley . . ." Delia shrugged. "Well, a woman can't always have everything in one man, can she?"

Audra's cheeks burned at Delia's rather blunt assessment of Nickolas Brannon's charms. Surely he had to be older than *Charley*? Audra's head buzzed with unasked questions, but Delia was already standing before the mirror, tilting her hat just so before shoving pins into it. "Ah . . . here are the lads," Delia said as she threw a cloak over her shoulders.

Two young boys had come into the room. They stopped short, both gaping at Audra in fascinated awe. Suddenly aware just where their blatant stares were focused, Audra felt her face grow warm. Instinctively she crossed her arms over her chest.

Deliberately, Delia stepped in front of her. "Here now, get a move on with that trunk," she ordered, reminding them why they were here. Abashed, they quickly lifted the trunk and carried it out. Delia turned to Audra. "They can't help staring, you know. You're very lovely, and I daresay most men would lose their senses and do the same." A thoughtful expression crossed her face. "What rotten timing," she groused. "I have a feeling that introducing you to Nicky would be a most interesting occasion. Most interesting. Too bad." She sighed expressively and pulled on her gloves. "Time to go, luv," she announced as she stood by the door, waiting for Audra to exit.

Audra did so, though she desperately longed to look through Brannon's things. Well, at least she knew how the room was laid out. Good thing, too, for she'd assumed that it was similar to hers. She could see it now—herself and the Murphys tripping over furniture and trunks in the dark!

The last Audra saw of Delia was a hastily blown kiss and a wink, accompanied by a "ta ta, luv."

Back in her own room, Audra threw her arms into the air and pirouetted to the bed, elated. It had cost her a suit but she'd learned a few things about Nickolas Brannon. And the price had definitely been worth it.

At last. Tonight! It would be tonight.

Dizzy with relief, Audra flopped onto the bed. Immediately, she was floundering like a fish out of water as she gasped for air.

The blasted corset was squeezing the breath out of her. And now that she thought of it, how in blazes was she going to get out of it?

Chapter 2

$\mathcal{N}$ick pulled open the door to the Crown and Arms and was immediately assailed by the din and the smoky atmosphere. He didn't know which he was beginning to hate more: living in the hubbub of busy hotels and inns, or going home to an empty and silent house.

Maybe Delia was right. She'd noticed his restlessness and had been insisting that it was time he found a wife. Had children. Lived in a house he could really call home. . . .

Nick had accepted her nagging with good grace only because they'd been friends for over ten years—from the time he'd taken command of his father's shipping business and Delia had been a struggling actress who'd soon learned that her talents were better suited to a more intimate form of entertainment than the stage. Their relationship was one of easy camaraderie and mutually satisfying sex, and was renewed whenever Nick came to England, despite the fact that she'd found a husband some years back.

At least, Nick thought wryly, Delia had managed to achieve her goal in life—security and a measure of respectability. And she'd be damned careful to hold on to both, Nick knew, even if she'd never be faithful to her poor Charles.

She laughingly justified taking lovers by claiming that she was saving her much older husband from herself, but in actual fact, Delia had no conscience when it came to her sexual appetite.

Last night, after they'd made love and Nick had hoped to finally get some sleep, damned if she hadn't insisted on giving him an "appropriate farewell." She'd disappeared under the covers to torment him, and when she'd climbed on top of him . . . well, things had just proceeded to their natural conclusion.

Nick chuckled at the memory. Maybe Delia had a point. Maybe she *was* saving her Charles from a too-early death!

Just as well she'd returned to her spouse and respectability today. Nick was looking forward to having peace and quiet tonight.

Unfortunately, his bath and bed would have to wait, for some of *Maryanna*'s officers had spotted him and were even now beckoning him to their table. Resigned, he stopped to have a word with Mrs. Garvey before joining the men.

"So," the first officer, Mr. Jacobs, asked as Nick pulled up a chair, "the *Maryanna*'s set to sail in two days, is she?"

"Yes." Nick nodded his thanks to the barmaid who had just slipped a pint of ale before him, but he left the drink untouched. Earlier, he'd shared his captain's dinner along with a bottle of fine French wine, and there was another bottle—brandy, this time—waiting for him upstairs. "I've only to see to her papers and tie up a few other loose ends.

I'm afraid it's all desk work for me tomorrow, at the office with Peter Winters," he added.

Which is where he should have immediately gone when he'd first returned from the country several days ago, Nick knew, particularly in light of the increasingly urgent messages he'd received from Peter. But discovering that some of *Maryanna*'s crew had eaten bad food and had taken ill, Nick had decided that readying her for sailing took priority over his uncle's estate, so he'd spent the time helping to load his own cargo, instead.

"I, for one, will be glad to get back to the States. My wife is expecting our second child in two months' time, you know," Mr. Jacobs proudly informed everyone.

"And how could we not," Chief Engineer Daley hooted, "what with you tellin' us every day since we left?"

Nick listened with half an ear and gazed about the room as the others good-naturedly teased the first officer. Jacobs was a lucky man. He had a family to go home to.

Nick's gaze suddenly focused on a dim corner. Two burly men—boys, really, for all their size—dwarfed a table as they sat facing him, nursing mugs of ale. Their gazes were averted from him, yet Nick was positive that they'd been staring at him only a moment before. Now that he thought of it, he'd swear that he'd seen those two on the docks in the last few days.

Nick frowned. Because of its proximity to the water-front—which was why he stayed here, himself—the Crown and Arms catered to ships' crews and passengers. But these two didn't fit either category; they looked more like farmers. Then he shrugged it off, for that wasn't really unusual. Many a new sailor had come straight from shoveling manure.

Belatedly, he realized that someone was speaking to him. "Sorry. What was that?"

"I wondered whether the ale wasn't to your likin', Mr.

Brannon?" one of the men asked, indicating Nick's un-touched mug.

Nick grinned as he pushed the mug over to the man. "I've already overindulged tonight," he said lightly. "But knowing your fondness and capacity for the brew, Mr. Darten, I have no doubt that you can handle it for me." Amid the laughter, he shoved back his chair. "I'm off to bed. Good night, gentlemen."

As he reached the foot of the stairs, the two farm boys suddenly left their chairs and headed in his direction. One almost cut him off, rushing up the stairs before him. The other collided with Nick, who banged his elbow painfully into the banister while the farmer reeled back. Recovering his balance, the boy touched the brim of his cap and mut-tered an apology. Nick rubbed his elbow and eyed him narrowly.

"After you, sir," the boy said respectfully.

Just a clumsy oaf, Nick thought. But just in case, he deliberately reached inside his jacket to make sure that his pocket wallet was still there. The boy flushed and stepped back. Nick nodded then turned to ascend the stairs.

Inside his room, the gas lamp next to the door wouldn't light for some reason. It didn't matter, for Mrs. Garvey had, in her usual efficient way, ordered a fire lit in the grate and—he was glad to see—his tub had been pulled in front of it and was filled with steaming water.

After pulling off his boots and emptying his pockets, Nick reached around to pull the Colt revolver out of the waistband of his breeches, where he always kept it while on the waterfront, and set that, too, on the table before peeling off his clothes. Once naked, he poured himself a generous splash of brandy and climbed into the tub, his back to the door. Resting his elbows on the sides of the tub, he leaned back. Ah, bliss!

Just then, someone tapped on his door. Irritated, he sat up. "Who is it?"

A muffled, feminine voice replied. "It's Millie, sir."

Nick frowned. So that it wouldn't get cold before he was ready for it, Millie usually didn't bring his water for rinsing until he'd been in his room for a good half hour. They must have gotten busier downstairs, and Mrs. Garvey had decided to send it up now. "Thank you, Millie. Just slip the bucket inside."

Nick lit a cheroot as the door opened. Brandy in one hand, smoke in the other, he leaned back again.

A footstep alerted him. One that was too heavy to be Millie's. What the hell . . . ? He started to turn his head.

"Wouldn't do that if'n I was you," a gruff voice said.

The order was hardly necessary, for the press of cold steel against his temple had frozen Nick into place.

Damn! He should have been more wary. He should have known.

As if to confirm his suspicion, the door opened again and someone else slipped into the room. He'd bet his last dollar they were the "farmers" from downstairs.

"All clear. Rest of 'em are below, drinkin'," another said.

"Good. Stay near the door, Jack, just in case. Dan, I want Brannon at the table," a different, softer voice ordered.

This new voice was younger than the others'. A little hesitant and oddly breathless, he noted. It sure as hell didn't sound like any burly farmer's voice. And it meant that there were three of them, not two. A cold fury built up inside him. Caught naked as a jaybird. Helpless. His Colt revolver—damn it to hell—was out of reach.

"Stand up and turn around, Brannon. Keep your hands in front of you. Do it slow or this pistol just might go off."

Nick slowly set his glass on the floor and tossed his

unsmoked cheroot into the fireplace before he complied. "I don't suppose you'd at least extend the courtesy of allowing me to put some clothes on, would you?" he asked casually as he turned carefully to face them. At first, he saw only two. The one holding the pistol—Dan—was the same young man who'd bumped into him earlier, and the one by the door was his companion from downstairs. Then, from behind Dan's back, the third figure emerged. Nick was surprised to see that this one was both slighter and shorter than the others. Then, to his utter astonishment, the scrawny one caught sight of Nick, gasped, and suddenly turned his back.

His hands moved in agitation. "Boys . . ." he said hoarsely. The three moved together for a whispered consultation. As the gun in Dan's hand didn't waver, however, Nick remained still. He picked up a few mumbled words. "Didn't plan . . . naked . . . !"

Despite his fury, Nick almost laughed. Obviously the threesome hadn't expected to find him dressed in nothing more than bathwater up to his knees!

There was a shuffling of feet. "Do you have a robe, Mr. Brannon?" The voice was distant, as if the speaker still had his back turned.

"On the bed."

"Get it, Jack."

It was thrust into Nick's hand. Stepping out of the tub, he slipped into it and knotted the tie.

"'E's decent now."

"Did you bring the rope from next door? Good. Bind his hands," the shadow ordered in that odd voice. "In front. He needs to be able to sign his name."

Nick suddenly realized that the smallest of the three was the ringleader. "What's this about?" he asked, annoyed, as Jack jerked his hands before him. There wasn't any sense in fighting them. Not yet, anyway. He had no idea if and how the other two were armed.

"I would advise you to keep quiet, Mr. Brannon. If so, we won't hurt you. Jack, what's taking you so long?"

"Nothin'. I got it now." Jack pushed Nick to the table, pulled out a chair, and shoved him into it. "Sit. And just to make sure you don' get ideas you ain't s'posed to have . . ." Jack picked Nick's Colt up and held it out. A hand came out of the shadows, a slim finger looped into the trigger guard, and gingerly took the Colt before setting it back onto the edge of the table, out of Nick's reach.

He was so astounded at this delicate handling of a firearm that he didn't even realize that the table lamp had been lit until the wick was turned up. The light flickered, then burned brightly, blinding him for an instant before it was dimmed again. When his eyes adjusted, the lamp was almost under his nose and all he could see across from him was a small, indistinguishable face, dominated by big eyes that stared at him from under the brim of an oversized hat.

Nick almost laughed. "Christ! You're only a child!"

The dark eyes glittered momentarily. Suddenly the urchin pushed the lamp closer to Nick, causing him to squint. "Who in blazes are *you*?" he asked.

Nick's brow went up. "Pardon me, but isn't that supposed to be my question?"

"Damnation!" The urchin jumped to his feet. "You've got the wrong man, boys. This can't be Brannon."

The gun next to Nick's face wavered. "What?" Dan's alarmed face suddenly appeared in front of Nick's. "He sure as hell is!"

"Yeah," Jack agreed. "He's the same man we been watchin' these last days. He were pointed out to us by more'n one sailor."

"It's not possible! Boys . . ."

A sudden shuffling of feet, and again, three heads came

together at the other side of the table. Another whispered consultation. Nick considered making a grab for his revolver, but the thug with the gun was still watching him. Presently, Dan reclaimed his position behind Nick, Jack went back to the door, and the urchin sat down to stare at Nick again. "You're an impostor. Who are you really?" he demanded gruffly.

Despite his anger, Nick was beginning to find amusement in the situation, and it showed in his voice. "At this moment, I'm beginning to wonder myself. Who do you think I am?"

"Why, you are . . . are . . ." The urchin made an exasperated sound. "Blazes . . . what does your name matter? You don't even sound British. Where's Nickolas Brannon and why are you in his room?"

Nick leaned back. This was getting interesting. A gang of confused thieves? Hardly. "You're partly correct. My mother was American, my father very much British. As to my name, I'd think it matters a great deal. However, if you're looking for the man I think you're looking for, I'm afraid you're in the wrong county."

"I beg your pardon?"

Hm. A very polite thief, Nick thought. "Suffolk County. I buried him myself, just last week. There's been no time for a headstone as yet, but . . ."

Another gasp. "Nickolas Brannon is dead?"

Nick's mouth tightened. Though his father had been ailing for some time, his death had still been an unexpected blow. "I'm sorry to say that he is," he said quietly. "However," he added, "his son is very much alive. Perhaps we should start over," he suggested. "Nick Brannon the Second at your service," he intoned seriously, bowing his head in an exaggerated manner.

That bit of news left the urchin speechless. For all of

five seconds. "But he . . . he can't be!" he sputtered, and this time, his voice was a high, immature squeak.

Nick smiled grimly. Clearly, the advantage was now on his side. "I assure you, he is and I am. Now, perhaps you'd like to tell me what this is all about. It's obvious you're not here to rob me." A nod of his head indicated his watch and wallet, still on the table, untouched by any of them. "What *do* you want?"

The brat seemed to gather himself, for he reached into a pocket of his jacket and pulled out a paper. "Unlike some I could name, we're not thieves. All we want is your signature," he said as he passed it over to Nick.

Nick managed to conceal his surprise. But he hadn't gotten this far in life by simply signing everything that was put before him. "Signature on what?" he asked.

"Your father . . . you, now . . . recently inherited a small parcel of land. The property consists of a narrow wood and a run-down manor house. Since it appears that you have resources of your own, it can't be important to you. But it is important to . . . to others. We're here to protect their interests and get it back. You have only to sign this deed to return the property to William Brannon's widow."

Nick was utterly incredulous. "That's it? That's what this is all about?"

"Yes."

It could only be the Sheffield property. Damn! He should have responded to Peter's messages immediately. At least he'd know where he stood. All he knew right now was that his uncle had gained a small manor house with his marriage. The brat was right; it couldn't be that important or valuable. But damned if he was going to be forced to sign anything at gunpoint.

"Why the hell didn't the Sheffields just ask me for it?" Nick asked, suddenly tired of this little game.

"Because you're a Brannon, and Brannons don't have hearts! Your actions in this room the last few nights prove you're no more to be trusted than William was!"

"My actions . . . ?" What the hell was the brat talking about now? Could he possibly be referring to Delia? "What does what I do in the privacy of my own room have to do with . . . ?" Nick came to an abrupt halt, for even in the poor light, it was obvious that the brat was blushing, for God's sake! Just like a young girl who—

It hit him, then. The voice, the almost delicate stature.

He leaned back in his chair, deliberately conveying an impression of relaxed casualness. "And just what do you plan to do if I refuse to sign?" he asked, grinning maliciously. He nodded at the Colt lying on the table. "Shoot me? Go ahead. The noise will bring everyone flying up here. Then where will you be?"

The brat blinked, recovered, then extended her hand. Dan—or was it Jack?—slapped an evil-looking blade into it. "Does this answer your question, Mr. Brannon?"

"Ah. I see. You'll slit my throat. Before or after I sign the deed?"

The brat shrugged. "After, of course."

"I see. What about witnesses? My signature will need to be witnessed."

The grin faded. "I know that. The boys will do it."

"Really? They actually know their letters?"

There was a muffled curse behind him. "Want I should give 'im a little tap on the noggin?" Dan asked eagerly.

"No! Of course not! He . . ."

The unexpected knock on the door startled them all. "Mr. Brannon? I've brought your water."

Jack, who was guarding the door, stepped forward quickly, but he wasn't fast enough. It flew open, striking him hard, and he lurched forward into Dan's arm.

The pistol went off with a deafening blast.

Millie shrieked as she stumbled into the room. She took one startled look and tossed the bucket, splashing Jack and Dan with hot water before she shrieked again and fled.

"Jesus, Mary, and Joseph!" Jack hollered.

"Ow! Blimey!" Dan yelled.

"Damnation!" the brat shouted, jumping to her feet.

Nick couldn't believe this comedy was happening, yet he had enough presence of mind to recall that his own revolver was still sitting on the table. . . .

He slowly got to his feet. Glanced at the brat.

For a split second they locked gazes before, in unison, their glances fell to the Colt.

They both dived for it. But clumsy in her haste, the brat knocked the lamp over and was startled into making a grab for that, instead. She managed to catch it before it fell to the floor, but the wick had been doused. In another lightning-fast move, Brannon had come behind her to slip his still-bound hands over her head and around her. The Colt pressed against her heart as he coldly ordered Dan to drop his pistol.

It clattered to the floor just as footsteps came pounding down the hallway.

"What the hell's going on in here, Nick?" First Mate Jacobs pushed his way through the door, and crowding close behind him were a number of other officers.

"Just a gang of hoodlums," Nick replied coolly. "A rather inept gang of hoodlums." The brat, captured within Nick's arms, made a sound of disgust. *She* hadn't liked that little insult.

Too damned bad! She was going to be a lot unhappier before this night was through.

"Want we should call the authorities?"

"That won't be necessary." Nick nodded toward Jack

and Dan. "But you could take those two and . . . I believe they have a room next door. Take them in there, and tie them up for now."

"Want one of us to stand guard over them? What about that one? Jesus, he don't look like much more'n a kid."

Nick gave the slight body a little jerk and felt it stiffen. "This one," he said slowly, "is mine. And as long as he stays with me, those two won't need a guard. They'll behave and stay put. Isn't that right, lads?"

There were chagrined sounds of compliance from Dan and Jack.

"And while you're in their room, Jake," Nick added, "take a look around." He waited until the others left before he turned his attention back to his captive. "You," he said, lifting his arms, "get that knife off the table and cut my bonds."

Slowly, her eyes dark pools of unease as they stared at the Colt, Audra reached for the blade.

"Carefully. This pistol has a touchy trigger." Nick waved the Colt in warning.

Still mute, she complied. As the ropes fell away, Nick stepped in front of her and extended his hand. Cautiously, Audra turned the hilt forward and pressed the knife into his palm. Placing it on the table, Nick reached down to pick up Dan's discarded pistol and checked the chamber. His brows went up in surprise. "Only the one cartridge?" he asked, shaking his head in disbelief.

As the girl was standing with her back to the fire, Nick still couldn't clearly make out her features, but he could see in the dim light that her eyes were huge round circles. That, and the way she'd gingerly handled the Colt, made Nick realize that the girl had no love for firearms. Still, he wasn't going to let her off that easily. The brat was going to pay for this little contretemps.

He retrieved the knife and bounced it in his palm, almost playfully. Her eyes grew even bigger, if possible, but still she remained stubbornly mute.

"Lost your voice, have you?" Nick asked. "Fine. We'll just wait and see what my men come up with, shall we?"

It didn't take long. "Didn't find anything but a valise with some woman's clothes," Jacobs said in a puzzled tone when he returned. "And this." He tossed a small bag to Nick, who deftly caught it.

"Thanks, Jake. You and the others can go now. I'll handle it from here." He waited until they'd left again before he shook the bag questioningly. "Spoils of another theft?"

The girl flew at him. "It's mine!" she shrieked. "Give it to me!" She tried to snatch the bag from him.

"Ah," Nick said with satisfaction, holding it out of reach. "*She* speaks!" And with another of those swift movements, he pricked her cap with the tip of the blade and flicked it aside. Her hair came unpinned and fell in a long braid down her back.

Audra chewed her lip as she backed away.

How could things have gone so wrong?

Damn those Murphys again! Why hadn't they told her the inn was filled with Brannon's friends? Why hadn't they told her he was much younger than William? And why hadn't they listened to her when she'd told them the pistol wasn't to be loaded? She'd counted on Brannon's being cowardly enough to be able to bluff. Who would have thought that he'd turn out to be . . .

Audra squeezed her eyelids shut. For a moment, the incongruity of the situation struck her. She was in a strange bedroom with a strange man who was clad in nothing more than a robe. Silk, by the feel of it. Hysterical laughter bubbled in her throat, and threatened to spill over. She tamped it down and opened her eyes. He was staring at her speculatively, the firelight gleaming off that blade he was playing with. She had to get out of here!

She took a tentative step to the right. Brannon stepped to his left. She feinted to her left. He copied her movement.

She suddenly realized that with each step, he'd been stealthily advancing toward her. His robe was coming loose, revealing a chest that looked as hard as granite. She backed up slowly.

"Who are you, and what did you hope to gain with this farcical little drama?" he asked, his voice cold and dangerous.

Audra suddenly became aware of the heat on her backside. She sidestepped swiftly, came up against a wall. With nowhere else to go, she pressed her damp palms against it and took a deep breath, striving for calm. "Who I am is no concern of yours."

"Wrong answer. You damned well made it my concern when you and your cronies shoved a pistol to my head." Slowly, he walked toward her.

"It wasn't supposed to be loaded!" It was a feeble apology, and Audra knew it. He had a perfect right to be angry. He had a right to be furious, actually. But now that her plan had become a fiasco, she'd die before she told him her name! If he found out who she was, he'd find a way to punish her and her mother. Just as William always had. He was a Brannon after all.

Now he was standing so close to her that the flickering light from the fireplace touched the planes of his face and reflected gold in his eyes and burnished his hair. "I'm a man of little patience, and what little I have is fast disappearing," he said softly.

"Go to hell!" she replied defiantly.

He flicked the blade at her shirt. A button hit the wooden floor with a small pinging sound. Audra gasped.

"Your name?" he repeated, the tip of the knife touching the next button.

Audra's eyes were glued to the wicked point. He wouldn't!

The second button hit the wall behind her. Before the blade could touch the third button, she was moving.

But he'd been prepared, been waiting for it apparently, for his arm suddenly encircled her waist and, in one smooth motion, she was off her feet and flying through the air.

She landed on the bed, on her back, her breath knocked out of her, confused and . . .

Her face was suddenly pressed up against a living, beating heart . . . and over that heart was warm flesh. Skin and curling hairs that tickled her nose. A clean piney soap scent . . . Oh, God! She was going to faint! "Off! Get off!" she gasped.

"What was that?"

"My . . . corset. Can't breathe."

In a flash, he'd hauled her upright, stripped the jacket away, ripped the shirt off her, and flipped her unto her stomach. She was too shocked to do more than lie there gasping, still struggling for air, until she felt several tugs on her corset stays. In less than a moment, the hated contraption fell onto the bed and cool air brushed her naked back.

He flipped her again, as easily as if she were a dead fish, then pinned her to the bed with his body. She lay helpless, sucking in deep drafts of air, despite the fact that she now wished she would faint.

"Well, well. It appears you're not the child I first thought you were."

Her eyes flew open. The silhouette of his head was

raised above her as he scanned her body. Her fingers scrabbled on the bed for her shirt, but came away empty. She clutched her arms over her breasts, hoping it was too dark for him to have seen anything. "Get off me, you rotten, degenerate, Brannon bastard!" she hissed.

"Now, now. Be nice. Didn't I just save you from suffocation?"

"Ohh!" She struck out with her balled fist. Right on that nicely firm chin of his.

"Ouch! Damn it, that hurt!"

Audra heard a thud as the knife landed on the floor. Truly afraid now, Audra went wild, her blows landing anywhere and everywhere on him. He parried them easily, so she grabbed two fistfuls of his thick hair and pulled hard.

"Stop that, you little hellion! I don't want to hurt you!"

Ha! In a pig's eye, he didn't!

Her next blows glanced off his immovable chest, after which she tried pushing him off her, but was forced to draw back immediately, for the feel of his heated flesh beneath her fingertips shocked her.

Her hesitation only gave him the opportunity to capture her wrists in one large hand and pull them above her head.

Audra lifted her head to spit at him, but he twisted her thick braid around his free hand, effectively holding her head immobile. "Give up?" His breath fanned her skin. She smelled expensive brandy and tobacco. And something else—something completely undefinable to her and disturbing, because it wasn't unpleasant.

Frantically, she tried to jab him with her knee. Her unsuccessful attempt only resulted in his knee being immediately jammed between her thighs to press down upon her. That hard knee—bare and almost touching that very private part of her through nothing but her thin breeches—was a second dose of shock.

"That was a foul move, sweetheart. And it calls for retaliation."

And he effectively brought the battle to a swift conclusion by suddenly, stunningly, covering her mouth with his.

His lips were hard, but soft. Demanding, yet . . . Audra's head spun as they slanted over hers, moving languorously, as if he were tasting her. Dazed, she was aware of nothing but the taste of brandy and the heat of that mouth. . . .

Ohh! The rotten, dirty swine. She no longer cared if she touched him. In fact, she intended to hurt him if she could—anything to get free of him. And then she'd kill him!

But she could barely breathe, much less move. Instinct told her that her best chance was to go limp, so she did. The instant his mouth began to leave hers, she clamped her teeth over his lip and bit down—hard—and tasted blood.

Instead of rolling off her, as she'd hoped, he only tightened his hold and swore viciously. "God's blood! What the hell did you do that for? I'm bleeding, damnit!" His voice held more perplexity than pain.

"Good. I hope you bleed to death, you pig! How dare you attack a lady?" Her voice was raspy with anger.

"Lady! Ha! Don't make me laugh, sweetheart."

"Hell's bells! Don't call me sweetheart! I'm not one of your . . . your paramours, you stupid oaf! Do you have so many, then, that you can't tell one from another?"

There was a momentary silence, and then, to Audra's surprise, he laughed. It was a low and throaty sound which, for some unfathomable reason, made her stomach quiver.

"If you don't free me, I'll scream!" she threatened.

"You can try, sweetheart. But I don't think you're going to get the chance."

Warning bells went off in Audra's head. It *was* time to scream. But she barely had time to draw breath before his mouth—that damned warm mouth!—was upon hers again. This time, he devoured her lips, seeking capitulation. Her senses swirling, she felt his tongue parting her teeth. At the same moment, she felt his hand stroke her shoulder, then move downward.

Her wildly beating heart lurched in frenzy when that hand covered one of her breasts. She geared herself, expecting him to paw her unmercifully, expecting his strong fingers to pinch cruelly.

But his thumb found the tip unerringly and trailed across it ever so gently, surprising her, forcing it to rise involuntarily. Waves of new, strange feelings washed over Audra.

They frightened her more than he did. She capitulated. "I . . ."

He raised his head. "Yes?" he asked softly.

"Stop!" she said breathlessly. "Just stop. I'll tell you what you want to know if you get off me and . . . and let me put my shirt back on." Just because she'd had to give in didn't mean she had to do it gracefully.

"Promise?"

"I promise, damn you!"

He tilted his head, as if considering, and Audra suddenly became aware that a certain part of his body which had been pressed against her thigh was—

She squeezed her eyes shut. "Please . . . ?"

He laughed again, softly, before rolling off her.

For an instant, Audra couldn't believe he'd actually done it. When she realized she was really free, however, she wasted no time in finding her shirt before scooting off the bed to lunge to her feet. She struggled into the shirt, realized it was too torn to be of any use, so had to scrabble around again for the jacket.

Unfortunately, she'd landed on the far side of the bed and he was between her and the door.

She quickly slipped into the jacket, hoping that the heavy pewter pitcher was still on the table behind her, as it had been when she'd been in the room with Delia. It was. *He* was on the other side of the bed, bending over slightly. "What are you doing?" she asked as she tightened her hold on the weapon.

He straightened. "Getting my trousers. Or would you prefer that we have our discussion before I put on my clothes?"

Audra didn't bother to reply, only closed her eyes helplessly. Though she couldn't see him clearly, the thought of watching while a man . . . while *this* man stepped into his trousers was altogether too much. The whispers of cloth seemed outrageously loud to her ears. "What's taking you so long?" she asked impatiently.

"I beg your pardon. I seem to be having some difficulty fastening my trousers. Need I explain that a certain part of my anatomy . . . ?"

Her face flamed. Thank goodness he couldn't see it in this dim light. "Don't be absurd," she retorted irritably, her embarrassment giving rise to petulance. "I'm not entirely ignorant about men!"

His warm chuckle told her that he'd said it deliberately, perhaps just to goad her. "I should point out that you're not . . . ah, shall we say . . . quite fully dressed, either."

Audra's eyes flew open, and her startled glance fell to her bosom. Oh, good God . . . her jacket was gaping!

Her indrawn breath covered the almost silent, swift move he made toward her, but a sixth sense alerted her at the last instant. Too late, she realized that he'd only been distracting her with his outrageous remarks. Startled into panic, she hurled the heavy pitcher at him.

He ducked just in time. The weapon thudded harmlessly against the far wall, but it slowed him down long enough for Audra to recover and rush at him, arms outstretched.

Unprepared for the force of their collision, he was thrown off balance, crashing into a chair. It toppled under his weight, his long limbs tangled within the wooden legs, and he lost his balance completely. His head struck the hard wood of the bedpost.

Nick saw bright, flashing lights, then a blurred vision of the woman as she snatched her small bag off the table before darting out the door, her long dark hair flying behind her. Then, there was only blackness.

Chapter 3

"*N*ow remember, Jack . . . Dan . . . not a word to anyone," Audra cautioned as soon as they'd dismounted from the coach that had whisked them out of London. "Especially McKee! He'll have our heads if he finds out."

Dan nodded mutely. Audra had already blistered their ears half the night, regarding the loaded pistol. God forbid they'd have to face McKee's wrath, too.

"Aye," Jack said as he glanced over Audra's shoulder. "Which is why we're leavin' right now."

Turning, Audra saw McKee sauntering toward them with his rolling gait. As she waited for him to come to her, she knew she'd never be able to tell him the truth of what had happened in London.

She was still finding it difficult to believe it herself. If McKee had been along, he would have beaten the daylights out of Brannon! McKee would have killed him for her!

McKee *would* have, she realized with a jolt. And then he would have been imprisoned or hanged! Bad enough that she'd already made him a conspirator in one death.

At least she wouldn't have the death of *this* Brannon on her conscience! She knew that because after she'd freed the Murphys and sent them down the back stairs before gathering her things, she'd crept back to his room. She'd had one frightening moment when she'd seen that he was still lying on the floor. She'd stood for several minutes, torn in an agony of terror and despair. Not again! Surely, God wouldn't be that cruel to her!

To her immense relief, she'd heard a soft moan. The growling curse that immediately followed it, however, had sent her spinning on her heels.

No. She couldn't tell McKee. She couldn't ever tell anyone about what Brannon had done to her in that room.

Thank God she'd managed to escape.

"Now where are those two off to?" McKee stood beside her, frowning suspiciously as he watched the Murphys slink away.

"They have some errands to run and said they'd find their own way back to the farm," Audra replied dismissively. Since Sheffield no longer had any work for them, the Murphy brothers had found employment on a neighboring farm and came to the Manor only occasionally to visit their mother, who was Sheffield's cook.

"Hm. They look like two mongrels who've just stolen the dinner roast," McKee observed. "What took ye so long? I came every day to meet the coach and was beginning to worry about ye, lass."

"Unavoidable delays," Audra said shortly. "How's Mother?"

Assuring her that her mother was no worse, McKee

helped her collect her things. "Did ye see Brannon, then?" he asked as they walked to the cart.

"Yes."

It was said in such a clipped tone that he leaned over to peer into Audra's face, but she'd turned away. "And is he anything like William?" he persisted.

"He's even more despicable!" Audra sputtered as she tucked her packages into the cart.

McKee grasped her upper arm and turned her about. "And what's that to mean? Did he harm ye, lass? Only tell me, and . . ."

"No! No, McKee, you're not to worry." She gave him a weak smile. "It's just that . . . I'm afraid I couldn't get him to sign over the deed. He, uh, he said he needed time to think it over."

"So, lass, do we just wait?"

She'd thought it over during the miserable coach ride this morning. Calmly and rationally.

She'd fled without accomplishing one positive thing. Instead, she'd lost the deed, ruined her new suit, and probably . . . no, *definitely* antagonized Nickolas Brannon. Not that he'd been any kind of gentleman to begin with!

Still, Brannon really hadn't hurt her. She'd managed to get away and she didn't think he'd even seen her face clearly. He didn't know her name. He was sailing to America in two days. She had enough money left over from the sale of the emerald to see them through several months.

There! It had only been an embarrassing situation, and it was over. She'd simply forget it.

"No," she told McKee. "I'm going to write to Father's former solicitor. Mr. Pemberly will know what to do. Besides, I'd prefer that he deal with any Brannons in the future." Audra sighed deeply. "Good Lord, but I've had my fill of them! Now, let's go home."

McKee frowned at her as he helped her climb into the cart, but she never even noticed.

It wasn't like the lass to be so short, McKee thought as he tapped the old horse with the reins. And Audra looked even more exhausted than when she'd left. In fact, they'd gone only a short distance before her head began to nod, despite the rough bouncing of the cart. Finally, she stopped resisting and took advantage of the comfortable and sturdy pillow his shoulder provided.

McKee studied her face. The smudges under her eyes only accented her creamy skin, which to his way of thinking was much too pale. All due, no doubt, to the nightmares.

Audra had no idea that he knew she'd been having them since William's death. Letty had told him how she'd twice gone into Audra's room after hearing the screams. "I tried to shake her awake, Mr. McKee, and she fought me like I was the devil himself, she did," the maid had confided.

Now McKee had to smile as Audra issued an inelegant little snore. Transferring the reins to one hand, he tightened his arm protectively around her. She wasn't much more than a wee lass, and if he could, by God, he would gladly take the burden those slim shoulders carried. But he couldn't. There wasn't a thing he could do about the past. He'd tried, God knew, but William had threatened to run him off Sheffield land if he ever interfered. But he was damned, McKee was, if he'd ever let anyone else hurt Audra or her mother again.

At the thought of Serena, McKee's mouth tightened. The day she had married Edward Sheffield, McKee had stood in the church along with the other guests, and he hadn't been able to take his eyes off the new bride. He'd fallen in love with Serena's gentle golden beauty himself, but it had remained his secret. Never, neither in word nor deed, had he made his adoration known. And when Serena had given birth to Audra, all the love and fierce protectiveness he'd felt for the mother had been transferred to the little black-haired baby girl who was now a lass of almost twenty years.

McKee remembered no home other than Sheffield, for he'd been a motherless boy of three when his father became steward to Edward's father. McKee being two years older than Edward, the boys had been close enough in age to grow up together as friends. And when, at a young age, Edward had inherited the estate, McKee had become his right hand, working alongside him to make Sheffield prosperous.

He'd tried to do the same for Audra.

The week after Edward had been killed, Audra had released her tutor, put away her schoolbooks, and turned her attention to managing the estate. She'd been only a month past her sixteenth birthday. Still, she was fully capable, for from the time she could walk, Audra had been her father's shadow, learning all he would teach her about the estate. After his death, she took on the task with all the confidence and vigor of youth. It hadn't been easy, but they'd managed, he and Audra. McKee had been as proud of her as her own father would have been.

But the actual work took all their time and energy. Neither he nor Audra had time to devote to a grieving Serena, and neither had paid enough attention to what was going on between Serena and William Brannon, who'd one day appeared at the estate claiming an old friendship with Edward. Even in the beginning, Audra hadn't particularly liked William, but he'd made a grieving Serena smile again, and for that alone, Audra had been willing to accept him.

But within a month of Serena's marriage to William, none of them was smiling, for William had shown his true colors. By then, he'd coerced Serena into signing over all she owned, to him.

McKee glanced at the sleeping Audra again and shook his head in wonderment. She'd had too much sadness for a lass her age. What would happen to her now? What would this new Brannon be like?

He could only pray that the new owner of Sheffield Manor would be of softer persuasion than William had been. And that the lass would be able to bear another disappointment, if it came to that.

"Bloody hell!"

Young Peter Winters winced.

He'd been working for Brannon and Benedict for just over a year, and the sudden vision of his bright future dissolving into nothingness made his hand itch to delve into his pocket and remove his handkerchief to swipe at his brow.

Before him sat his employer—the man who had placed an enormous amount of trust in Peter when he'd hired him as his assistant—the employer who was now barely restraining his . . .

. . . *Laughter?*

Peter blinked. He'd expected anger. Instead, Nick Brannon was sitting there, his head thrown back in unrestrained laughter!

Peter stared in complete bafflement.

Nick certainly didn't look wealthy or important, dressed as he was in a seaman's cap, a pea jacket over a rough shirt, and loose britches tucked into boots. It was those boots, custom-made and incongruously polished to a high sheen, which made one question whether he was only a common sailor.

He wasn't.

He was, in fact, the most demanding, the most exacting, the most impatient man Peter had ever dealt with. The man wanted everything done yesterday, and he had no time for fools or incompetence.

But Peter had also come to learn that Nick's drive and vigor were tempered by an ingrained integrity and fairness that had to be respected. One always knew where one stood with him. He was also generous. Peter was handsomely rewarded, both in praise and money.

"Damn bloody hell," Nick repeated softly, still chuckling.

"I don't understand, sir . . . eh, Nick," Peter stammered. He still wasn't accustomed to addressing an employer by his given name. But Nick had insisted on it. Peter supposed that this informality was the result of Nick's parentage. He knew that Nick's father had once owned a small shipping business, and had met and married Nick's mother, the daughter of a ship's captain, in Boston. Nick had actually been born there. "I assumed," Peter explained, "that this would come as more unwelcome news."

Of course Peter didn't understand, and Nick wasn't about to explain. Yet one side of his mouth insisted on tilting wryly. He'd just spent a sleepless night dreaming of an elusive woman whose hair smelled of roses, had determined that he was going to find her again, and here she was—practically tossed into his lap.

Well, nearly so. He straightened his shoulders and made an effort to control his amusement. "I'm sorry, Peter. It's a private joke. On me. I'm laughing at the twisted humor of fate."

"Yes," Peter said. "It *is* rather a coincidence that your father and uncle both passed away only weeks apart, and before I could even notify your father of this unexpected development."

Nick nodded noncommittally, not bothering to explain the true reason for his humor. "If I learned anything at all during the War Between the States, Peter, it's that Death sets his own clock, and the hell with those left to deal with it."

And deal with it he would have to, for the majority of what Peter had just told him wasn't promising. It appeared that what Nick had actually inherited was a mountain of debts, a very small and deteriorating estate, a widow, Serena Sheffield Brannon, and . . . ah, yes, the stepdaughter, one Audra Sheffield. No doubt the very same wildcat who'd tried to make him sign over the property to the widow. Audra "Smith," Mrs. Garvey had said when he'd asked her the name of the young woman who'd been occupying the room next to his.

Nick leaned back and tented his fingers under his chin. "Tell me," he demanded, "all you know about the girl."

"It appears that your uncle was involved in a number of nefarious schemes and questionable investments, and was forever seeking capital. To this end, he often entertained wealthy guests at Sheffield. Your uncle's stepdaughter acted as his hostess."

"Why the girl and not his wife?"

"Apparently, Mrs. Brannon has suffered from poor health since their marriage. It's hindered her participation."

"I see. Go on."

"It's a delicate matter. . . ." Peter's hesitation and high color indicated his discomfort.

"Yes?" Nick prompted.

Peter cleared his throat. "The majority of the guests also had, shall we say . . . dubious reputations? It's rumored that the entertaining was often uninhibited. Further, your uncle made no secret of the fact that he was seeking a wealthy protector for his stepdaughter. In fact,

I've learned that an agreement had been reached with Lord Cowan only the day before William Brannon's untimely death."

Nick's brows rose. "An agreement. I presume you aren't referring to an offer of marriage?"

"I'm afraid not."

Nick didn't bother to hide his distaste. "My God! Lord Cowan! That old lecher? His propensity for young girls got him thrown out of society years ago. Married only once. Wife died without issue. Had a number of young mistresses since—all well-bred virgins before he took them under his 'protection.' I take it the Sheffield girl *is* a virgin?" Nick asked bluntly.

The question took Peter by surprise, and his struggle to regain his composure almost had Nick laughing again.

"As to . . . the state of the Sheffield girl's . . . er, virtue, that is . . . I, of course, have no knowledge," Peter stammered. "However," he continued manfully, "I can make discreet inquiries—"

"Not necessary. I'm quite capable of gleaning that information on my own," Nick replied blandly. "What else?"

Peter was clearly relieved to forgo more comments on *that* subject. "It happens that I have the acquaintance of a junior member of the legal firm Lord Cowan retains, and I learned that the sum Lord Cowan settled *was* considerable. Moreover, William Brannon cashed the draft. Unfortunately for the Earl, however, the money seems to have disappeared and Miss Sheffield refuses to honor the agreement. She's claimed no knowledge of any moneys, and has turned away all the Earl's representatives. Needless to say, the Earl is most perturbed."

Nick almost grinned. "Rather impertinent of her, wouldn't you say? Old he may be, but Lord Cowan is still a powerful man."

"Exactly. I, for one, would not care to cross him."

"Inform the Earl that circumstances have changed. The young lady is no longer available . . . to him." Nick didn't so much as blink as he gave his instructions.

Peter blinked twice. "I beg your pardon? Did you say . . . ?"

"Send him a draft for the amount of the settlement," Nick said calmly. "If he balks, remind him that I own a fourth of his railroad stock. I may decide to sell, very quickly."

"Yes, sir!" Nick could do it, Peter knew. And it would throw the other investors into a panic.

"Now," Nick continued. "About my uncle's debts . . ."

Peter ruffled papers until he found the ones he wanted, which he passed over to Nick. "I received these from your uncle's business manager, one Silas Norton. As you can see, while there are a number of jewelers' and dressmakers' receipts included in the list of your uncle's creditors, there are also a number of gaming debts. Your uncle, I'm sorry to say, seems to have been a poor hand at cards. Incidentally, I understand that the holders of these notes were pressing him for payment, hence the arrangement with Lord Cowan.

"Also, among those bills and receipts is the one from Norton himself. He claims that your uncle owed him a substantial amount for his services. However, Norton was either unable or unwilling to produce any receipts or itemization of those services."

Nick leaned back in his chair. "You did well, Peter, in the short time you had." Nick was sincere in his praise. Peter had proven more than capable of managing Brannon and Benedict's British interests. Nick was suitably impressed by the young man's ability and intelligence.

"Unfortunately, I've already put off the *Maryanna*'s departure once. I can't do it again. I'll have to let her sail without me, I'm afraid, and delay my own return while I go to Sheffield Manor and see for myself how things stand." Nick stood. "I have no idea how long I'll remain, but until you hear otherwise, you may reach me there. And Peter . . . don't bother to let them know I'm coming."

"As you wish." Peter rose as Nick made signs of departing. "Shall I settle your uncle's debts in the interim, or do you wish to review this accounting more thoroughly?"

"Peter, I have full confidence in your ability. If I didn't, I wouldn't have employed you. See that all legitimate debts are settled from my personal funds." Nick's mouth tightened. "As to Norton, inform him that I won't see him, then offer him a third of the amount he claims due him. Make it clear that it's either that or he can wait for his claim to be settled through the courts. I think you'll find that he'll be only to happy to accept my offer."

"I'll start on it immediately," Peter affirmed.

In a few short minutes, Nick took his leave and was in his rented carriage and on his way back to the docks.

Despite his decision to stay in England for a longer period, this new complication had come at the worst possible time.

It had been a hectic year for him and his partner, Alex Benedict. They'd moved their headquarters from Boston to Central City in Colorado Territory, as many of their interests and investments were now located in the territory. Alex was there now, for their arrangement was that one of them would always remain at the home office while the other was traveling on business.

Because Nick still had family ties in England, he was the one who handled their British affairs. In the past, he'd always looked forward to visiting England, but he'd felt differently about this trip. This time, he'd been eager to take care of business quickly and return to the States, for in the past year, he'd found himself questioning the forces that drove him to channel all his energy into creating a business empire.

At first it had been a challenge. From his mother's father, Sebastian Hunt, Nick had inherited a love of sailing. From his father, a talent for business. And from both men, a stubborn will to succeed and conquer. When his grandfather had insisted that an eager Nick was old enough, at twelve, to accompany him on his voyages, Nick's father had reluctantly consented only after obtaining a promise from his father-in-law that when Nick was older, he would return to Boston to attend university.

Unfortunately, Captain Hunt's ship had been lost at sea while Nick was receiving that education, and so the Captain had never seen his grandson graduate. But he'd left Nick his only assets—two ships. It was a beginning. A way for Nick to expand his father's business. He'd only lacked the capital, and that need was met when Alex, his fellow graduate and best friend, insisted on investing his personal wealth in the business. They'd become partners, and Brannon and Benedict had come into being.

They'd just begun to show a modest profit when conflict, secession, and finally, war reared their ugly heads. Alex had returned home to join the Confederate cavalry and Nick had left the business in his father's hands while he spent the next years as a naval officer for the Union.

Though he and Alex fought on different sides, they retained their personal friendship and respect for one another, which, as it turned out, was a damned good thing. Because when the truce was signed and Alex was paroled, he no longer had a home or land to return to, and the only family he had left was a younger sister. He'd desperately needed an occupation and an income.

Ironically, Brannon and Benedict had prospered

greatly during the war, and continued to do so in the following years. The truth was, Nick and Alex had succeeded far beyond their wildest dreams.

But now Nick was becoming restless, and he'd begun to wonder what purpose he found in his ambition.

What he *had* found was an affinity for the staggering mountains of Colorado Territory. Despite their wildness, or perhaps because of it, they promised peace and contentment, something he'd never felt a need for until now. He'd been looking forward to spending the next several months of spring and summer surrounded by those silently brooding sentinels.

Unfortunately, it would now have to wait. When he'd gone to see Peter this morning, he'd fully expected to be told that his uncle had left some small estate which he, Nick, would have gladly returned to the widow. It should have been a simple matter safely entrusted to Peter.

Damn! According to Peter's account, William Brannon should have married well and found security as a member of the landed gentry. Instead, he'd gone through his wife's inheritance in less than three short years. And by the sound of it, he'd had some help. The woman he'd married had obviously not objected to William's squandering of her money and property, and the daughter had played hostess to William's debauched friends—and had let herself be sold to an old man.

Or had she?

Nick touched his sore lip. Her name was Audra.

He knew that much about her. And he knew that she hated him—hated all Brannons. And that she was daring enough to try to force him—at gunpoint, no less—to sign over the deed to what had once been her home. Daring enough, or desperate enough?

Nick rubbed his chin thoughtfully. As much as he enjoyed women and their charms, experience had taught him that they could be the most devious creatures God ever made. Particularly when they wanted something.

Which was Audra Sheffield? Innocent virgin or seasoned trollop?

Nick chuckled to himself. Damned if he cared! She owed him. He *wanted* her.

And he was going to have her, even if he had to double Lord Cowan's offer.

She wouldn't turn him down. He was, after all, not quite in his dotage, unlike Lord Cowan and his ilk. He was extremely wealthy—a fact that he'd never found to be a detriment. And most women seemed to find him decently attractive.

Nick's mouth curled wryly. He'd never claimed modesty as one of his admittedly few virtues, but the plain truth was that in his experience with the opposite sex, he was more often the pursued than the pursuer.

Yes, he'd go to Sheffield Manor. A few weeks—one month at most—to straighten out the mess his uncle had made and convince one scheming little vixen that she'd be foolish to turn down his offer. More foolish, still, if she thought she could buffalo him again.

She'd started the game, and he intended to finish it.

But damned if he wasn't looking forward to playing it!

Chapter 4

$\mathcal{A}$udra bolted upright, her hands flying to her neck. Something was wrapped around it, becoming tighter and tighter, squeezing all life out of her. Her fingers clawed at her throat, but she couldn't loosen it.

"Land's sake, Miss Audra! Are you all right?"

Audra filled her starving lungs with air and looked up. Letty was staring down at her, a concerned expression on her face. Confused, Audra glanced about and saw that she was in her own room, in her own bed. She leaned back against the pillows and closed her eyes. A nightmare. It had just been another nightmare.

But she could still hear the echoes of William's malevolent laugh. And remember his eyes . . . eyes that had burned like fire, red as the blood pouring down his face. He'd been grinning spitefully. *"You'll like what I have for you, Audra. I'll make you like it, by damn!"* he'd said. He'd been holding a rope, and when he'd jerked on it, the noose around her neck had tightened.

"Miss Audra?"

Audra took a shaky breath. "Just a bad dream. I'm sorry I frightened you, Letty. I didn't wake Mother, did I?"

"I don't think so," Letty said as she pulled the scattered bedding back into place. "I didn't hear you myself until I came into your room. I made sure to close the door real fast-like."

Audra breathed a sigh of relief. "Thank you, Letty. Bring my mother's tray to me, won't you? I'll take it in to her."

"I'll be back in a flash." Letty eyed Audra doubtfully. "I've set your tea on the table. Are you sure you're all right now?"

Audra nodded. "I'll get over it. Go on and get Mother's breakfast now." With a last worried glance, Letty left.

Ignoring her tea, Audra rubbed her temples with trembling fingers. God! Would she never be rid of the dreams?

Would she never be rid of William?

"Mother, *please* won't you eat this egg? Mrs. Murphy cooked it just the way you like. And she's made your favorite raisin buns."

Serena turned a weary gaze to Audra. "I'm sorry, darling, but I'm just not hungry. Perhaps later?"

Audra's face creased with worry. Her mother wasn't getting her strength back. Not surprising, since she hardly ate enough to keep a bird alive. She was still so thin that her cheekbones stood out prominently and fine blue veins were clearly visible through her translucent skin.

Audra sighed in frustration. Damn William! He'd been so determined to have a son, an heir, and he'd ruined her mother's health in the process. The irony was that he wouldn't have had anything to leave to a son, since he'd spent or lost it all, anyway!

"All right, Mother," she conceded, as she removed the tray. "I'll be in the garden. You'll ring for Letty if you need anything, won't you?"

"Yes, dear," Serena murmured. She didn't even stir when Audra smoothed her hair back from her forehead and kissed her on the cheek.

Back in her own room, Audra washed and dressed quickly, then stood gazing out her open balcony door as she brushed her hair. It was the kind of clear, sharp morning that heralded an unusually warm day and an early spring. From her bedroom on the second floor, she could look out across the front lawn, past the now empty pond, to rolling countryside broken only by hedgerows. At one time, all of it had been Sheffield property. How she loved it all! And how it still hurt to have lost it.

When she'd first discovered that William was selling the land, she'd confronted him and railed at him angrily, threatening to go to Mr. Pemberly. William had only laughed, and she'd quit the study in frustration and anger, still determined to stop him.

She'd failed. He'd intercepted the letter she'd written to the solicitor and become enraged, punishing her by selling her mare, Fantasy's Lady. Even that wouldn't have quieted her, but she'd already learned that each time she defied him, he took his rage out on Serena. So Audra desisted, and watched in helpless dismay as her father's work and their livelihood disappeared.

Audra sighed as she shut the balcony doors. How she missed those early mornings with her father—riding across those same hills and fields and pastures, laughing with the sheer joy of being with him, of being alive, of being here, at Sheffield.

How long had it been since she'd felt like laughing?

Not since William had come into their lives. Perhaps not since her father's death. And God knew there was nothing to laugh about now.

Audra sighed again. Responsibility weighed heavy on her slim shoulders. It took all her energy to will her mother to get well, to keep everyone fed and look after the house. Not to mention the worry about whether they still had a home.

Oh, blast! Now she'd gone and brought Nickolas Brannon to mind. She didn't want to think about him.

Still, she couldn't help but be curious about him, for he had been the first man to—

The sudden warmth on her cheeks wasn't all due to the warmth of the day. This was ridiculous! After witnessing William's abuse of Serena, Audra had vowed that no man would ever touch her in that way, nor would any man rule her life, so why was she thinking about Nickolas Brannon at all? It was just that the incident at the inn kept popping into her mind at the most unexpected moments, despite her desire to forget it.

Not that it really mattered. Chances were, she'd never see him again, for it had been three days since she'd returned from London. It was clear that he didn't give a damn about Sheffield, either. No doubt he was too busy with *Delia* and other selfish pursuits! Besides, by this time, he should be on a ship bound for America.

And she and her mother were still here, weren't they? Since she'd only just sent her letter to Mr. Pemberly, Audra was convinced it would be weeks—months even—before he'd be able to track Brannon down. In the meantime, they had nothing to worry about.

Audra quickly braided her hair, pinned it up, and left her room. She was not—absolutely not—going to give Nickolas Brannon another thought!

She spent the next hours in the garden, digging, turning the soil with more force than was necessary. Gardening, she'd learned, was an excellent remedy for the anger and frustration she'd been forced to subdue during William's sojourn at Sheffield. But more than that, she enjoyed it, for nursing Serena and helping to take care of the house left her little time to be outdoors.

Ruefully, she had to admit that even if William hadn't sold her mare, she'd be hard-pressed to find time to ride.

Audra dropped the last of the seeds into her neat row, then patted the rich earth over the seeds. Done! At least they were assured of fresh vegetables and herbs this year.

She stood and stretched, arching her back and rolling stiff shoulders. It was time to go in and check on her mother.

About to gather her garden tools, Audra paused to tuck a stray curl back into the old kerchief she'd tied over her head. She was wearing one of her father's old shirts, the top two buttons unfastened, and her skirt was hitched up between her legs and tucked into her waistband in complete unconcern about her display of black-stockinged legs. Who was likely to see her anyway? Almost no one came to Sheffield Manor these days. Strangely enough, even Lord Cowan's people had finally stopped badgering her.

Suddenly she froze, the prickling awareness at the back of her neck alerting her to the fact that she was being watched. Spinning about, she confronted the strangest-looking man she had ever seen. He was leaning against the brick wall of the house, and as she turned he abruptly straightened and removed his hat.

They stared an one another.

He was tall. Very tall and powerfully lean. His skin was touched with bronze, his hair as black as midnight, as hers was. His eyes were a startling pale blue against all that darkness. Despite the fact that he appeared to be hardly older than herself, there was a taut, predatory look about his features.

And his clothes! He wore the most unusual trousers, which fit his legs snugly, a checked shirt such as she'd never before seen, and a bright kerchief tied around his neck. The broad-brimmed hat he was holding looked as if it had been stomped upon unmercifully.

This strange apparition, in turn, was staring at her much too boldly. When his gaze moved to follow the contours of her body in open speculation, she came to her senses. "It's rude to stare," she pointed out, ignoring the fact that she'd been doing the very same thing. "Particularly when we haven't been properly introduced."

He blinked at her imperious tone. Then he grinned, suddenly looking boyishly innocent. Striding toward her with catlike grace, he offered his hand. Surprised, she took it, and found her own being shaken firmly.

"The name's Rafe, miss . . . Rafael, actually." His voice had an unmistakable drawl, which was as foreign as his clothing.

Enlightenment dawned. "Why, you're an American! You're one of those . . . those cowmen!" she blurted.

"The word's *cowboy*, ma'am," he corrected. "But I'd prefer it if you called me a wrangler."

"Whatever!" she agreed impatiently. "What are you doing here?" she demanded, hands on her hips.

"Why, ma'am, I'm here with my boss," he offered. "Now it's my turn. Who are you?"

His question made her suddenly aware of her grubbiness. She swiped at her damp cheeks, realized that she was only transferring more dirt from her encrusted hands, and gave up the attempt as hopeless. "That, sir, is none of your business." She grabbed her tool basket and stomped past him.

She stopped short as she went through the back door

to the kitchen, for all she could see of Mrs. Murphy were the skirts that covered her ample bottom. The cook's upper torso had disappeared somewhere out the doorway to the entrance hall. Audra thumped the basket onto a large table, startling Mrs. Murphy, who whipped about, letting the door swing shut behind her. An expression of relief passed over her face when she saw that it was Audra.

"Oh, miss, thank goodness. We didn't know what to do, and . . ."

She was interrupted by Letty's voice, and another, masculine one, both coming from the hall. What in the world . . . ? Audra didn't wait for Mrs. Murphy's explanation. She marched to the door and shoved it open just as the cowboy, who must have slipped in the back door, caught up to her. He tapped her shoulder. "Wait a second . . ."

The door to the entrance hall gave way as she jerked away from him. Losing her balance, Audra stumbled through it and immediately slammed into a solid barrier that shouldn't have been there. Her hands came up to brace herself. Just at the instant she realized that her palms were pressed against a gleaming white shirt, a pair of hands came around her slim waist and steadied her.

Her wide-eyed gaze slowly traveled up the masculine chest within that shirt, up to a firm square chin, past full lips. Up. Up to a straight, arrogant nose and to a pair of gold-flecked eyes. *Heavens!* Audra thought in mindless wonder. *I had no idea they were so lovely!*

Nor had she known his hair was a rich brown, streaked with gold. No marble statue, but a golden god, she thought, bemused. Only he was real. Too real.

She groaned and closed her eyes to send up a silent prayer. *Please . . . please don't do this to me, God! Make him go away!*

Unfortunately, God ignored her plea.

"Do you suppose, young lady, that I could have my shirt back?" asked that deep voice she'd hoped to never hear again.

Audra blinked. Belatedly, she realized that her fists were clenched about handfuls of shirt. Cheeks flushed with mortification, she released it and took a cautious step back, brushing at her skirt. Oh, Lord! It was still tucked into her waist. She jerked it down. From the corner of her eye, she saw Letty scurrying off.

"I hardly expected a warm reception," Nickolas Brannon said ruefully. "On the other hand, I was hoping for something more than . . . dirt." He then proceeded to deliberately brush at the two dirty blotches upon his otherwise pristine shirt. "What's your name?" he asked, suddenly glancing back at her.

"I . . . ah . . ." For the life of her, Audra couldn't seem to think of a sensible thing to say.

"Not you, too!" He tossed an exasperated look over her head, toward Rafe. "Lord, a houseful of speechless children."

Children? *Children?* Why, the arrogant, pompous fool! The . . .

Then it suddenly sank in. He thought she was a child. He'd given his name . . . and asked hers.

Was it possible he *didn't* recognize her? Or was he simply playing with her? Testing her?

There was no hint in those amber eyes.

Audra breathed another silent prayer . . . of thanks, this time.

"Sir!"

Everyone turned. Hurrying down the hall was McKee, his face redder than usual. Letty was tagging behind him.

"At last, Rafe," Nickolas Brannon said. "Someone with authority. Someone with a *voice*."

"Sir, I've just been told of your arrival." McKee ex-

tended a hand, and the two men shook. "I'm Fergus Mc-
Kee. Steward of Sheffield, or what's left of it."

"Nickolas Brannon. Perhaps you've been expecting
me?"

McKee threw Audra a baleful glance. "No, can't say as
we have. 'Twas our understanding that ye'd left England."

"Hardly. As you can see, I'm here. I was just about to
ask this little moppet here . . ." Brannon turned back to
Audra. "What did you say your name was?"

Audra's mind had been working frantically. She'd truly
not expected this arrogant, demanding man to show up in
person. But he was here now, and he didn't seem to know
who she really was. . . .

What if he thought Serena had no one to care for her
except the servants? Despite the fact that he was a Brannon, he surely wouldn't force a sick woman from her bed.
If he had any decency at all, he'd at least let her mother
stay until she regained her health, wouldn't he?

Swiftly, before she could change her mind, Audra
bobbed into a clumsy curtsy and, head down, scuffed her
worn shoe on the floor. "Agnes, sir."

Letty gasped, then stuffed her apron into her mouth.
McKee crossed his arms over his chest and narrowed his
eyes at Audra.

"Well, Agnes. I was just about to ask to see Mrs. Brannon."

"That isn't—ain't possible. 'Fraid you cain't see 'er."

"No?" His eyes glittered dangerously.

Audra shook her head soberly. "No. My m . . . er
. . . me mistress be sick. Bless the puir, sweet lady. She
ain't strong enough to see anyone but the doctor. Puir
thing don't know nuthin' aboot you. You'd be a shock to
her."

He frowned. "I wasn't aware of the severity of her ill-
ness. However, I believe there's a daughter?" At Audra's

nod, he continued. "If someone would inform her of my arrival . . . ?"

"Ain't possible," Audra repeated. "See, Miss Sheffield is . . . ain't here." Letty gasped again, and Audra threw her a warning look from beneath her lashes. "Gone away, she has."

Nickolas Brannon didn't appear the least bit surprised at this announcement. "When is she expected back?" he demanded.

Audra hoped her expression held the right amount of humility. "Don't rightly know, sir. She just packed up and left." His piercing gaze made her want to flee, but she held her ground.

"Didn't she give anyone any indication of where she's gone or when she's expected to return?" he demanded.

" 'Fraid not. Miss Audra, she's always been a flighty thing. Told us she was . . . ah, fed up playing nursemaid, and . . ." Audra was improvising as she went along. "Ah, being a prisoner in the country. Aye." Audra nodded solemnly. " 'Twas the way she put it. Off to London, she was. Maybe, she'll never come back," she added.

"Are you saying that she's simply abandoned her seriously ill mother?" he demanded.

Audra shook her head and shrugged, as if it wasn't any concern of hers. Nickolas Brannon looked as if he wanted to throttle someone. He threw a questioning glance at the others, in turn.

Letty bobbed her head, became confused, then shook it frantically. Mrs. Murphy bit her lip. McKee simply continued to wear a reproachful expression as he stared at Audra.

"Rafe, see to the horses, and keep an eye open for the wagon. Once it's arrived, bring the bags in."

Audra caught her breath as Rafe nodded, tipped his strange-looking hat, and left. "You can't mean to stay!

Surely—" At Brannon's sharp look, Audra changed her tone. "That is . . . *are* you staying?" He looked down his straight nose at her again—a look that told her exactly what he thought of having mere household help question him. "Sir?" she tacked on belatedly.

"Having just arrived, I don't have any inclination to ride all the way back to London today."

Audra almost danced in relief. "We're not . . . we ain't prepared for guests," she said meekly. Now that she knew he wasn't staying long, she could be just a bit charitable. "We'll need time—"

"Just what is your position here, Agnes?"

"Why, I . . . er, I'm . . . ah, maid-of-all-work, sir. I do the outside work—the gardening and the dairy. Oh, and I help take care of m . . . Mrs. Brannon. She likes to have me tend to her."

"I see. Well, Agnes, as I'm not precisely a guest, I'll make do with whatever accommodations are available." With that, he simply dismissed her and turned about. "Mr. McKee . . ."

"Just McKee will do."

"McKee, then. I'd like to inspect the property. We'll start outside, if you don't mind."

McKee glanced at Audra, who nodded almost imperceptibly at him, but the look on his face promised an interrogation later. Audra shrugged. It couldn't be helped. She could never explain all her reasons to him.

She watched Brannon follow McKee, relieved to see him go. He'd taken only a few steps when his voice came back to her.

"Agnes!"

She almost jumped. "Sir?"

"I hope you intend to wash before you see to Mrs. Brannon. Being cared for by a dirt-covered urchin can't do much to improve her health."

Audra stared daggers into his broad back while resentment washed over her. The nerve of the man! He hadn't even bothered to turn around and speak to her directly.

Hands on her hips in belligerent exasperation, Audra muttered under her breath. Urchin, was she? Wash her face, indeed! What did the man think she did in the garden—sing lullabies to the vegetables? Of course, *he'd* probably never touched a hoe in his life. Probably didn't even know what one looked like, she fumed as she stomped toward the stairs.

She stopped as she came to the full-length mirror in the hall. Good Lord! No wonder Brannon had been so easily convinced of her lower status.

The face staring back at her bore little resemblance to the one usually reflected. There was indeed dirt smeared across her cheeks and nose. On her forehead, too. What wasn't concealed by grit was red from the sun, for she hadn't been able to find her hat this morning. Her cotton shirt was as streaked as her face, with the addition of embarrassingly damp patches here and there.

A satisfied smile suddenly brightened Audra's face.

It hadn't been a bad disguise. A few embellishments . . . Now that she thought of it, there were still some old maids' dresses and aprons in storage from the days when Sheffield had been fully staffed. And mobcaps, of course.

She stepped closer to the mirror. Too bad there was no way to disguise her eyes, but nothing would hide that deep blue, nor those long lashes. Grimacing at her reflection, she decided there was no help for it. Dirt would have to be a part of her daily toilette.

It would only be until Brannon left. Surely he wouldn't stay long. He was a young man who likely had vast interests and requirements that Sheffield Manor couldn't possibly satisfy. No amusements. No *Delia*!

Oh, yes. She could do it. A few days—a week at most—then that insufferable man would be gone.

Audra and Letty spent the next two hours dusting, scrubbing, and airing out William's rooms for the new Brannon. They had just finished when McKee appeared in the doorway. Seeing the thunderous expression on his face, Letty quickly made an excuse, and left Audra to face him alone.

He stood, his arms crossed over his brawny chest, his blue stare relentless. "Explain to me, lass, how 'tis ye forgot to tell me that Nick is a braw young mon, and why 'tis he dinna know ye," he demanded grimly.

"Nick? Already he's *Nick?* He's only been here two hours!"

"Aye. Nick. He insisted. Dinna change the subject."

"I . . . he . . . it was very late when we met, McKee, and dark," Audra floundered. "We didn't even speak very long."

"Aye," McKee said dryly. "Yet there was enough time for ye to decide he was even 'more despicable' than William. Those were yer words, were they not?"

Audra waved her hand carelessly. "It was a mistake, as I said. Suffice to say, he didn't know . . . *doesn't* know who I really am, and I intend to keep it that way. He won't be here long."

McKee sighed in defeat. Obviously, it was all she would tell him. But what *he* had to tell her wouldn't be welcome. His expression softened. "Ye be wrong, lass. Not only does he intend to stay for a time, but he plans to put Sheffield back in order."

"He's staying *indefinitely?*" Audra squeaked in dismay.

"Aye. That he is," McKee affirmed. "Even now, I'm to go into the village and bring back more help."

Audra's eyes widened, as she sank helplessly onto the bed.

McKee well understood her distress, for he'd had the same sinking feeling himself as he'd struggled to keep up with Brannon's rapid-fire questions and watched the new owner's expression become more and more thoughtful. The man wasn't ignorant of estate matters, McKee had realized. More, Brannon was clever, discerning, and to the point. A dangerous man to cross; he wouldn't suffer fools easily, nor would he enjoy being played for a fool.

McKee told Audra so, now. "Ye'd best confess, lass. Admit ye made a mistake, for it won't be easy to pull the wool over this man's eyes."

"No. I intend to continue as Agnes," she retorted.

"Are ye daft, lass? Ye cannna let this deceit go on. I dinna think he's a callous man. Hard, yes—but not hard-hearted, such as William was. If ye confess now, he may be understanding."

"Ha! He's a Brannon, and an American, to boot. Why should he care what happens to Mother—a British woman he doesn't know, hasn't even met? You saw his arrogance. And did he mention a wife? No? Well, do you think that if he has one, she'd care to have a strange woman and her daughter living in her home, or under her husband's protection? I will *not* wager on Mother's well-being. No, McKee. It's better that we go on this way," she argued stubbornly.

McKee groaned inwardly. He was a man unused to deceit, and extremely uncomfortable with it. He'd already found it necessary to lie to Brannon. After they had completed their inspection of the Manor, Brannon had invited him into the study to partake of a brandy and—as it turned out—to question him about the staff.

"There's only meself, Mrs. Murphy, and her grand-daughter, Letty. Her sons, Jack and Dan, worked here until last year, though they sometimes come to help with heavy work," he'd explained.

"Ah, yes. The Murphy boys," Nick had murmured.

"Ye've met them?" McKee asked, hoping for some insight into the London excursion.

"Not really. But you can be sure I intend to," Nick said, thus disappointing McKee and only adding to his curiosity. "What of Agnes? Does she belong to Mrs. Murphy, also?"

"Er . . . no. A . . . Agnes be . . . her mother be unable to care for her." McKee had swallowed a big gulp of the brandy to help wash down the partial lie.

"And her father?"

"Ed . . . Er, her father died some years ago." McKee silently cursed his slip of the tongue.

But Brannon had said "I see" in such a contemplative manner that McKee knew the man had immediately caught it, and was already wondering whether "Agnes" was Edward Sheffield's illegitimate daughter.

Instead of being angered, McKee was amused. It was no less than Audra deserved for her playacting. Particularly since she'd just informed him of her intention to go on with it. He knew her willful nature only too well. William may have subdued it for a time, but now it seemed to be coming back in full force.

Still, he tried. "Ye be making a mistake, lass." He raised a hand to forestall her as she opened her mouth to retort. "I'll say no more. Only remember, 'tis ye who will pay for yer actions."

"So be it. I'm willing to pay the cost—whatever it may be—to keep Mother safe," Audra replied as she rose. Then she suddenly remembered. "Dr. Hargrove is coming tomorrow. I don't suppose you'd consider stopping off and warning him . . ." She flushed guiltily as she caught Mc-

Kee's glare. "Of course not. I'm sorry. I'll waylay him myself and ask him not to give the game away. He'll do it for Mother," she added confidently.

McKee groaned as she left the suite.

Chapter 5

$\mathcal{N}$ick stood before the desk in the study, scanning Peter's letter. It contained a summary of matters requiring Nick's attention, and ended with a brief paragraph stating that the detectives Peter had hired had been unsuccessful in finding so much as a trace of Audra Sheffield in London. She hadn't returned to the Crown and Arms, nor had she boarded a ship. She'd simply vanished.

Nick wasn't really concerned that something untoward had happened to her, not with those two muscled companions she'd had, but where the hell was she? Was it possible that the chit *had* absconded with Lord Cowan's money and was now living in careless luxury?

Rubbing the back of his neck in frustration, Nick dropped the letter onto the desk and went through the adjoining door to the library. His gaze fell on the portrait above the fireplace. The fragile air of the light-haired woman painted onto the canvas portrayed Serena faithfully. There was no doubt in Nick's mind that the artist's rendering of the young child sitting at Serena's feet was just as accurate. Despite the young age portrayed, the dark-haired girl showed signs of promising beauty.

Her blue eyes stared innocently back at him, revealing no hint of the bold young woman desperate enough to attempt to force him to sign the deed. No hint that she was callous enough to leave no one to care for her mother but the servants.

According to Dr. Hargrove, whom Nick had met on his second day at Sheffield, Serena was a very ill woman. And the doctor had been downright blunt about who was to blame. According to him, William had accorded Serena no consideration. The strain of miscarrying two babes in less than two years and the recent delivery of a stillborn son had all been too much for her. Her heart had been weakened.

It was as Nick had feared after his first meeting with Serena. Her fragility had moved him to sadness, and made him more determined that he'd do all in his power to make her comfortable and content.

And if that meant dragging her daughter, kicking and screaming, back to Sheffield Manor, so be it. But first he had to find the girl.

What would she think, he wondered, of the changes he planned?

Walking out the French doors and onto the lawn, Nick stood, hands clasped behind his back, as he surveyed the view.

Sheffield was more run-down than he'd expected. Fences were leaning, the bricks of the buildings needed scrubbing, and the wood, new paint. Gardens were overgrown and wild with untrimmed shrubs and weeds. The pond in front of the house was choked with weeds and scummy rainwater. The only outside area that looked like it was being cared for was the vegetable patch behind the kitchen—which probably accounted for little Agnes's grubby appearance!

The Manor itself wasn't large by nobility's standards, but the three-story Georgian house had stately grace and charm. Nick had admired the fine oak paneling, but it had been dull from lack of polish. The walls of the hall and most of the rooms had been almost bare—he'd seen lighter areas where paintings had once hung. The furniture was of excellent quality, but there were few ornaments or clocks on the tables or the fireplace mantels. The few remaining carpets had been worn.

He'd hired an army of workers and repairmen. The exteriors of the buildings were being scrubbed and polished, the roofs were being repaired. The pond would be cleaned out, filled again, and would be home to a pair of nesting swans. The grounds would be back in order in no time.

Nick kept Rafe constantly going back and forth to London with lists and instructions to Peter, the result of which were almost daily arrivals of wagons filled with goods. Slowly, Nick was replacing those items that had disappeared during William's sojourn.

Nick was satisfied that, once he was done, the property would look much as it had when Edward Sheffield had been alive. A veritable little treasure of the English countryside. It almost made him want to reclaim his English roots. A pity his uncle had been too damned self-absorbed to see that Sheffield would have provided him, his wife, and his stepdaughter a good living.

Behind Nick, someone cleared his throat. Turning, he found the roofer standing, cap in hand, waiting to be acknowledged. "Good morning, Mr. Jackson. What can I do for you?"

"Mornin', sir." The man's face held a look of mingled chagrin and frustration. "It be the girl. Agnes, that is."

Agnes! Nick should have known. He'd already received half a dozen complaints about her interference. In
her ridiculously overlarge mobcap and ill-fitting clothes,
and with curious eyes in that still-grimy face, Agnes
seemed to be everywhere and wasn't afraid to let her views
be known.

Not that he'd seen much of her himself. In fact Agnes
avoided him like the plague, disappearing around corners
whenever he appeared, staying a good distance away from
him as she watched the workmen, arms crossed over her
chest and looking for all the world as if she were biting her
tongue.

Nick sighed. "What's she done this time?" he asked.

"Ain't what she's done, Mr. Brannon. 'Tis what she's
doing." Jackson stepped aside, giving Nick a clear view of
the west side of the Manor. At first, all Nick saw were the
painters, and over their heads, the roofers, hammering
nails.

A flutter of dark cloth caught and narrowed Nick's
gaze. What the bloody hell . . . ?

"Agnes! Come down from there!"

The girl only stared down at him from the veranda
roof. "*Now*, Agnes. *Don't* make me come up after you."
Nick's tone was implacable, as was his expression.

"Oh, for heaven's sake," he heard her mutter before
she cautiously made her way across the slanted canopy.

The roofers grinned at one another before turning
away.

Nick almost shouted again, thought better of it, and
held his breath, instead, as Agnes quickly scrambled down
the tall ladder with no apparent fear. Good God! It was a
wonder she didn't break her scrawny neck. Her ugly black
skirt fluttered about her legs, revealing what looked suspiciously like men's trousers beneath it. At least she'd had
enough sense to retain some measure of modesty!

Agnes hopped onto the ground, whereupon she primly smoothed out her skirts. "Goodness! You didn't have to shout," she calmly informed him.

"What in bloody hell were you doing up on the roof?" he growled.

Agnes raised her brows and tossed him an innocent look. "*Someone* had to point out the places where the roof leaked."

Nick blew an exasperated breath and shook his head. He'd been wrong. The girl had no sense at all! "Come with me," he ordered, and turning about, headed toward the French doors, leaving no doubt that he expected her to follow.

Audra took her time, noticing that the painters had all stopped working and were watching her in gleeful anticipation. She had a childish urge to stick her tongue out, but glared at them, instead. She knew exactly what they thought—that she was an obnoxious pest.

"Oomph!" She'd slammed right into Brannon, not realizing that he had come to a sudden halt and was waiting for her by the door to the study.

The ensuing cloud started them both coughing.

"Good God!" he choked. "What have you been doing . . . rolling in the dirt?"

Some imp of mischief made her shake her skirts again. "No," she replied, waving away the residue floating before her face. "More like ashes. Bates set me to cleaning grates earlier." Bates was the new footman and he irritated Audra no end.

Audra heard Brannon mutter something which sounded suspiciously like ". . . certainly chose the right person" before he stepped aside to let her pass.

Once inside, he walked around the desk and slid into the leather chair. Audra stiffened. It still hurt to see another man seated in her father's chair, using her father's desk. Whenever William had been in residence at the Manor, she'd entered the study only when it had been absolutely necessary.

Nick glanced up to find Agnes hesitating at the door. There was no help for it. The room would simply have to be dusted again after she left. Wordlessly, he pointed to the chair opposite him.

She came in and sat gingerly, then just stared at him with those big eyes. "Tell me . . . do you ever bathe?" he asked.

Though she was obviously startled at the question, he could swear he saw her mouth curl before she turned an innocent look his way. "O' course. It's been, oh . . ." She frowned in thought as she counted on her fingers. "It's been only three weeks since I washed in the stream."

"Three weeks!"

"Oh, aye. And I ain't due for another bath for another week." She sat back and grinned at him in satisfaction.

At least, Nick thought absently, she took good care of her teeth. They were absurdly white against that grimy face.

Oh, hell! Short of throwing her into a tub himself, he didn't see how he was going to get her cleaned up. And he didn't have the heart to punish her. He had almost no experience with children, but Agnes seemed vulnerable and, despite her brashness, almost fearful of him. Damn! He wasn't an ogre, for God's sake. The last thing in the world he wanted to do was hurt the girl.

Deciding that handling her was going to take more diplomacy than he'd thought, Nick got to his feet and, hands clasped behind his back, paced . . .

Audra lowered her head and smiled to herself. At least she'd managed to disconcert him for a change! Served him right! After all, he was an interloper who'd already outstayed his welcome. . . .

Her gaze focused on a pair of shiny shoes peeking out from beneath fawn-colored trouser legs. He'd come to a halt, right before her.

Slowly, her gaze traveled up. And up. Lord! He was taller than any other man she knew. Taller than her father had been. Lean, but well built. Narrow flanks and strong limbs . . .

Audra tried to disappear into her chair, blushing furiously. She'd been taking inventory, as if he were a stal . . . a horse.

Thank God he hadn't seemed to notice, for he backed up and perched on the edge of the desk. "I've been here two weeks, Agnes, and in that time I've received at least a dozen complaints about you," he began.

She looked startled. "Complaints?"

"Complaints," he affirmed. "I've let them go until now, but after seeing you . . . Was it really necessary to go onto the roof?"

"Yes. As I told you, I was pointing out the leaks."

"Why couldn't you have done it from the attic?"

"The roof seemed the most exped . . . er, the simplest way."

"You won't do it again. Is that understood?"

Her eyes flashed, but she only shrugged indifferently and said nothing.

"The well diggers tell me you argued with them about where the new well is to be dug." One eyebrow went up in inquiry.

"That was a mistake. I've since decided they know what they're doing."

She'd decided? Nick almost smiled at that. "Bates is quite upset with you, also. He informs me you're disrespectful, and that you ignore his orders to use the back stairs. Is this true?"

"I never used the back stairs before he came, and I

ain't about to start now. As to being disrespectful—all's I said was that he pranced about the Manor as if he's got . . ."

Nick raised his hand to stop her, afraid of what she'd say.

"I was only going to say," she went on in an injured tone, "as if his nose was trapped in a cloud."

"His nose. I see." Nick pinched his own nose in an effort to conceal his smile. "And the gardener's assistant? Is it true that you threatened to use your garden shears on his toes if he so much as stepped into your vegetable patch?"

"Not true."

"Not . . . ? Are you saying he lied?"

She nodded solemnly. "It wasn't his toes I threatened. It was another part of his anatomy altogether. You see . . ."

"Enough!" God only knew what the girl would say next. He didn't know whether to laugh or to lock her in a room until the repairs to Sheffield were completed. Trying to suppress his amusement, he got to his feet.

Audra relaxed as Brannon walked to the open French doors and stood, staring outside.

Blast! She'd managed to keep out of his way until now. He *would* have to catch her several feet above ground, where she hadn't been able to sneak away!

And then he'd scolded her as if she were a child. The least he could have done was let her finish explaining about the gardener's assistant. The boy—and he wasn't much more than that, with his pimply face and oscillating voice—had tried to pull her behind a tree and kiss her. Boy or not, he'd been strong. She'd threatened him only *after* she'd been forced to smack him over the head with a spade handle and push him into a pile of manure.

What would Nick Brannon say to that? Even more,

what would he say if he knew that the boy had really insulted Audra Sheffield?

"There's another matter I'd like to discuss with you."

Audra glanced up to find that he was now sitting behind the desk. Discuss? He was actually going to discuss and not *demand*? "What is it?" she asked warily.

"I'd like to hire a trained nurse to care for Mrs. Brannon. Since you've been her primary caretaker up to now, I thought it only fair to ask you, first."

Audra stared at him suspiciously. He was *asking* for her permission? It had to be a trick—like one of William's nasty little games! Oh, she knew all about those! William had fooled them all in the beginning, too, with his charming manners and his eagerness to please. It had lasted only until he'd gotten what he wanted, that being Serena and her prosperous estate. Then he'd changed completely, into a cold and callous despot.

It was difficult to believe that Nick Brannon would be any different. Still, to be fair, in the two weeks he'd been at Sheffield, he hadn't taken anything from it. It appeared that he was, in fact, giving much back.

Why? He really had no obligations to either her or her mother, so why was he doing it? A sudden thought had her sitting up in alarm. "My . . . Mrs. Brannon's not getting worse, is she?" Audra gasped.

"Quite the contrary. The doctor tells me that her general health is improving daily."

Audra was relieved. Still, she persisted. "Then why can't I continue to care for her?"

"No one can deny that your care has been exemplary. But you're only a . . ." Nick thought better of saying "child." "It's an enormous responsibility," he amended. "You want what's best for Mrs. Brannon, don't you?"

Audra winced. "Of course," she replied reluctantly.

"Good. Also, the woman Dr. Hargrove has in mind is

more than a trained nurse. She held the position of house-keeper in her last situation." Audra watched as Nick raked his fingers through his thick hair. "God knows we need one. I don't have time to tend to all the household problems."

They did need one, Audra knew. Badly. The current situation was awkward. She was able to issue orders only by implying that they came from her mother. Still, the new servants resented it.

Actually, they resented *her.* McKee had wisely chosen strangers, but Bates had aspirations of becoming a butler, and he looked down his nose at her. Rose, one of the new maids, had even had the nerve to giggle at "Agnes's" scruffy appearance until Mrs. Murphy had blisteringly chastised her. Thereafter, the new girls eyed "Agnes" curiously, making it plain that they considered themselves above her. And still Rose constantly whispered behind her back to the other maids, leaving no doubt in Audra's mind that she was being ridiculed. There was nothing she could do about it short of boxing the girl's ears—and how would she explain her motives for doing such a thing to Nick Brannon?

"I'll make a bargain with you, Agnes," Nick said, suddenly bringing Audra's focus back to him. He was watching her closely, she saw, which made her itch to swipe at the grime on her face.

"What kind of bargain?" she asked suspiciously.

"I'll give you an opportunity to meet the woman before I hire her," Nick said. "If you don't approve of her, I'll have Dr. Hargrove look for someone else."

He'd let *her* choose? Despite her surprise, Audra had to admit that it was a generous gesture. Still . . . "And in return?"

"In return, you'll bathe at least weekly. In a real tub."

That was it? That was all he wanted? But if she did

that, her disguise would be ended, and her true identity disclosed.

But . . . Audra thought quickly. The result of the bargain was up to her, wasn't it? All she had to do was withhold her approval. No nurse-housekeeper, no bath. What did she have to lose? It wasn't as if she didn't bathe each night, anyway.

Of course, Brannon didn't know that. And what he didn't know couldn't hurt her. Biting her lip to hide her smile, Audra looked Nick square in the eye. "I agree. You've got a bargain."

Nick was congratulating himself on a brilliant idea—coming up with the idea for the "bargain"—when it occurred to him that Agnes had left the room wearing a smug little smile.

Damned little scamp! He just knew she was up to something.

What a contrary child she was! She switched from brashness to acquiescence in a flash. From unwashed urchin to haughty lady with refined speech, particularly when she became angry. Yet she wore an air of vulnerability that convinced him she'd been hurt badly in the past. It only confirmed his suspicions that she was Edward Sheffield's illegitimate daughter.

Strange that Peter hadn't discovered her existence, for it was hardly a kept secret. Stranger still, how everyone reacted so oddly at the mention of both of Edward's daughters. Dr. Hargrove hemmed and hawed. McKee became defensive, and Serena would, whenever someone spoke the name Agnes or Audra, gently change the subject.

Agnes's situation was extraordinary. Why hadn't Edward Sheffield planned a better future for the girl, legitimate or not? And damned if he could fathom why Serena not only kept Agnes on, but actually seemed fond of the dirty little hoyden.

Then he chuckled. Maybe it wasn't all that difficult to understand, after all. Despite the grime she wore like a shield, there was something appealing about Agnes.

When she'd been sitting, watching him so boldly, he hadn't been able to help but notice that her lashes were so long, they brushed her cheeks. And despite the grubby face and hands, what he could see of her hair gleamed with health and cleanliness. What secrets were hiding under all that grime? he wondered.

He smiled to himself. He had no doubt that he'd soon find out, for the woman Dr. Hargrove recommended had once lived here. Had, in fact, been Audra's nurse until she'd left the Sheffields to care for her ill sister some eight years ago. Dr. Hargrove had assured Nick that Agnes, too, had been very fond of the woman.

Whether in business or his personal life, Nick never made a bargain without knowing that he'd come out the winner.

Agnes didn't know it, but she'd already lost.

Chapter 6

"*B*last and damn!"

Audra kicked at a stone, stubbed her toe painfully, and swore again as she hopped about on one foot.

She hated, hated, *hated* Nick Brannon!

Oh, he was so sneaky!

Who would have thought that he'd bring her beloved Bertie back?

Not that Audra wasn't happy about it. She was. Bertie—Roberta Hauson—had always been a second mother to her, and Audra loved her dearly. And she couldn't deny that Bertie's presence had made an immediate difference in Serena's spirits.

But now it seemed that the only useful thing left for Audra to do was milk the cow. That, and the upkeep of her kitchen garden, which she'd been able to hold claim to only under dire threats to the head gardener and his assistants.

It was all so frustrating, and she was bored silly. She

was also tired of dodging Nick Brannon, of sneaking up back stairs, of taking lukewarm sponge baths. She was tired of how everyone else fell all over themselves to please Nick Brannon!

They all thought that the sun rose and set on his orders. McKee, who had refused to do anything specifically for William, was always coming and going for Nick these days. Letty, when she wasn't mooning over that cowboy, Rafe, doted on him. Mrs. Murphy, who thought she'd died and gone to heaven because her larder was once again lavishly stocked, cooked to please Nick. Dr. Hargrove eagerly shared a brandy with him each evening.

Even her mother was charmed by him! Just last evening, Audra had gone into Serena's room and found Nick sitting at her bedside, reading to her in his deep, melodious voice. The pleasure on Serena's face had been obvious. Audra had quietly slipped back out of the room before either of them had so much as noticed her.

Audra tried not to be hurt by it, but it was hard not to be. For so long, she'd been the one to keep things together at Sheffield Manor, the one who'd done the fretting and worrying and the planning. Now *she* felt like the outsider.

She was sick of it. She'd made herself a prisoner. She didn't dare even venture out to the fields, or go into the village, for it had been put about that Audra Sheffield was in London, and she couldn't take the chance that she'd be recognized. What if word got back to Nick Brannon?

But the worst—oh, the very worst of it—was that they were all so indebted to him. Who would have thought that William's heir would be so vigorous and incite so much activity? Or that he'd be a wealthy man in his own right?

Very wealthy, Audra amended. She hadn't needed the letter Mr. Pemberly had sent to tell her that. The letter had also confirmed that William had left nothing but debts, and informed her that Nick Brannon had already settled those. He'd closed by saying he was confident that she and her mother would be in good hands.

Audra still wasn't convinced of that. Yet, despite her misgivings, she couldn't deny that Sheffield was now in much better hands than it had ever been in William's. In the six weeks Nick Brannon had been at Sheffield, he'd already managed—with the help of his vast fortune, of course—to overcome reluctance from the neighbors who had purchased Sheffield land. He'd not only replenished almost all the original holdings, but was even now negotiating the purchase of some of the neighbors' land. Sheep grazed the newly green pastures once again and there was now a fat herd of dairy cattle.

Audra sighed. To be perfectly honest, she had to admit Nick had his merit, for she could find no fault in his consideration for her mother, in the way he treated the staff, and in his ambition to restore the estate. In fact, as she'd grudgingly admitted to McKee, it was almost back to perfect. Despite her grumblings, Nick Brannon had done everything as she would have done herself, if she'd only had the funds.

Most certainly, she would have purchased the horses.

Ah! Those beautiful horses!

Rafe went back and forth between Sheffield and London often, and each time had returned with horses. The last time, he'd brought two beautiful Arabian mares. Almost as fascinating were the strange-looking saddles that Rafe and Nick used. They seemed ugly and cumbersome, but there was no denying the superb craftsmanship of the leather. Audra would have loved to try one, but much more than that, she longed to ride the horses.

She was delighted with them, and spent so much time in the stable crooning to them and feeding them treats

THE NOVEL PLACE
PRAIRIE HILLS MALL
1681 3RD AVENUE WEST
DICKINSON, ND 58601-3025
(701) 225-1052
Transaction No: 84789
07/13/98 18:33:43   CLERK:BS

1 @   5.99 0440225868   5.99
   PRICELESS
SUBTOTAL   5.99
TAX @ 6.000%   0.36
TOTAL   6.35
CASH   20.00
Total Tendered $ 20.00
CASH Credit   13.65

THANK YOU!
EXCHANGES & RETURNS NEED A RECEIPT OR

OUR BARCODE LABEL

I'e 3.99 0440225060   8.99
PRICELESS
                        SUBTOTAL   3.99
                   TAX @ 6.000%   8.36
                           TOTAL   6.35
                            CASH   20.00
           Total Tendered $ 20.00
                     CASH Credit   13.65

that the two new stable boys had begun to eye her suspiciously.

Audra didn't want to be petty or resentful. Most of all, she hated feeling sorry for herself. She longed only to be herself again—as she had been before William had come into their lives. Before her father had died. Would she ever be that carefree again?

Audra sighed again as she headed for the woods.

Lying in a small clearing, under a huge oak, Audra watched a noisy, cavorting family of squirrels. When the creatures suddenly quieted and stood on their hind legs to scan their territory, she realized that something had alarmed them. She cocked her head to listen. There! The sound of snapping twigs and a horse's bridle.

Audra peered around the trunk and saw a large shadow moving down the path. Thinking it was McKee, she was about to call out when the stealth of the movement arrested her. McKee wouldn't be creeping behind her. He would have called to her by now.

She waited until the shadow moved into a patch of sunlight. Recognition drew a gasp. Silas Norton—on foot and leading his horse! What was he doing sneaking around in her woods?

She'd disliked him on sight when he'd first come to Sheffield Manor with William. Tall, slender, with blond hair and eyes of an indeterminate pale color, he might have been considered handsome by some women, she supposed. But Audra hadn't liked the perpetual sneer he wore. Nor had she cared for the way his eyes roved over her in a manner that made her uneasy.

Her instincts, as it turned out, had been right. Each time Norton visited Sheffield with William, she'd had to fight his crude innuendos and grasping hands. It had all come to a stop, surprisingly, when William had come upon them and severely chastised Norton. *"I've got better plans for the girl than for you to ruin her,"* he'd said. Audra hadn't understood his meaning—until the day he'd told her that she'd been *sold* to Lord Cowan. Audra didn't trust Norton. He'd come to Sheffield several times since William's death, but she'd refused to see him, except for one time, and for one reason only—to plead for funds from William's estate to care for her mother. Norton had insisted that there were none, but implied that he'd help if Audra was willing to repay his generosity.

Audra still shook with anger whenever she thought of that incident. There had been no mistaking Norton's insinuation. She'd called for McKee to escort the man out and let him know in no uncertain terms that he was no longer welcome at Sheffield.

So why was he here now?

"Audra! Where are you? I know you're here because I watched you come into the woods. Answer me, damn it!"

Audra held her breath as she pressed against the tree trunk. Where could she go? Norton was still some way down the path, but if she tried to leave the clearing, he'd surely see her. A sudden rustling brought her head up. The tree!

Quickly, she lifted the front of her skirt and reached between her legs to bring the back hem forward and tuck it into her waistband. One agile leap, and she was able to grasp the branch above her and swing over and onto it. Praying she wasn't making a racket, she climbed higher, until she was sure she was well concealed within the foliage. Just in time. Peering below, she saw the top of Norton's head as he passed below her. She grinned as he let out a string of frustrated curses.

She kept still, sitting on one branch while her feet rested on another, until she could no longer hear the horse clipping along the path. Just as she wrapped her arms about the trunk in preparation to slide down, she heard the horse again. Blazes! Norton must be retracing his path. Quickly she scrambled back to her perch. An angry squirrel suddenly appeared and nipped at her hand. Startled, she jerked away and lost her grip. Her feet slipped. Then, everything seemed to happen in slowed motion.

She lunged for another branch, missed, and slid down the trunk, her feet scrabbling for a hold. Her cheek scraped painfully, and she lost her mobcap as her hair caught on a protruding branch. Her toes touched something solid, slipped, and to her horror, she lost her grip completely. Squeezing her eyes shut, she let out an involuntary scream as she fell through the branches and down . . . down . . .

Her breath escaped in a loud whoosh as she landed on something hard, but giving. A growling curse, a horse's whinny, and she felt herself lifted into the air again, yet she was being held securely and reassuringly.

She opened her eyes and saw Nick Brannon's face only a few inches from hers. Somehow, she'd landed smack in his arms, but he was astride his horse, Ulysses, and the stallion was rearing and fighting him. Precariously positioned, Audra didn't have any other choice but to throw her arms about Nick's neck while he calmed the startled animal.

Even as she clung to Nick, Audra had to admire his masterful handling of the stallion. In a few seconds, Ulysses was under control, though he continued to stamp his hooves and toss his head fretfully.

"Quiet, boy! That's it . . ." Once the horse was settled, Nick turned his attention to the girl.

She was staring up at him with those huge, dark blue eyes, but he saw no indication of fear. As usual, her face was grimy, but mixed in with the dirt was a thin line of red. "Are you hurt?" he asked in concern.

She blinked, as if just realizing where she was, and swiped at the blood on her cheek. "No," she replied breathlessly. "Just a scratch." Perfect white teeth flashed as she grinned at him. "I daresay I was saved a number of bruises by your timely arrival."

"Damn it, moppet! What are you doing falling out of trees like that? You could have been killed!" He shook her slightly.

Moppet, was she? Audra couldn't resist. Her grin widened. "Ohh! Don't let me fall, Mr. Nick, or the big beastie will trample me!" She wriggled and clung tighter.

Nick stared down at her. When she'd came flying out of the trees in a flurry of skirts and petticoats and long, slim legs, he'd been just as startled as Ulysses. But he was even more startled now as he held her squirming body against his. He'd first learned the feel of a woman's body when he was fifteen, and he'd only perfected that knowledge in the years since. Beneath Agnes's loose, high-necked dress and enveloping apron was a woman.

His fingers tightened about a slim waist, pressed against a full curved breast. Most assuredly, a woman's body. His eyes narrowed. "Exactly how old are you?" he asked.

Audra hadn't missed his sudden stillness, nor his warm hand against her breast. "Too old to be on your lap . . . and too young for what you're thinking," she replied tartly as she pushed away from him. "Let me down."

Reluctantly—he had to admit he was reluctant, for he'd just discovered another of her secrets—Nick allowed her to slide down Ulysses' flank.

The second Audra's feet hit the ground, she backed away. The stallion snorted, shook his head, and leaned down to nuzzle at her apron pocket, forcing her to step back again. She pushed him away. Ulysses came at her again, his great head almost knocking her off her feet. She swatted him lightly on the nose. "Stop that, you beggarly beast!" she ordered affectionately.

Nick eyed this byplay in astonishment. "It appears to me that he's searching for something." Enlightenment hit. "Agnes, you haven't been in his stall, have you?" he asked sharply.

Audra flushed guiltily as she gave up trying to shove Ulysses away and patted his huge head, instead. "He likes me," she hedged.

"Damn it, Agnes! It's far too dangerous. Ulysses is extremely high-spirited. He almost killed his former owner. You are not—I repeat—*not* to enter his stall alone. Ever. Do you understand? No . . ." Nick raised his hand to forestall the argument he saw she was about to begin. "There will be no discussion. I want your promise on this."

Audra's disappointment was keen. Blast! There went her only joy. The stallion wouldn't hurt her, but . . . Nick looked utterly implacable. Perhaps it would be wise to use a little discretion just now. She nodded reluctantly. "If that be all . . ."

"For now." But Nick made no move to leave, Audra noted. In fact, his gaze had moved from her face to her hair.

Too late, Audra remembered her lost pins and mobcap. Her braid was unraveling. Damnation! Self-consciously, she shoved her hair back behind her ears and tried to edge around the stallion, but Nick was suddenly standing in her path. He'd moved as silently and swiftly as a cat and had dismounted.

"Frightened, Agnes? Are there wolves in these woods?"

It suddenly occurred to Audra that Nick was riding in

the direction Norton had gone. Lord, she hoped he didn't meet up with Norton! What if Norton told him he was looking for Audra Sheffield, whom he'd seen in the woods only a short time ago?

Nervously, she twisted a strand of her hair around her finger. "Ain't seen any," she replied, then almost jumped as Nick reached behind her ear.

His lips twitched as he brought his hand back in front of her face. "Strange. I thought trees produced leaves, not grass," he said, opening his palm to reveal several blades of grass. Audra stared at the evidence he'd removed from her hair. "Perhaps it wasn't a true wolf at all; perhaps it was more the two-legged variety," he suggested.

Those amber eyes were staring at her speculatively. Rattled, she retorted, "And what if it was? Surely my free time is my own. If you don't feel I'm earning my keep, you could always purchase another milk cow or two!"

His mouth straightened abruptly. "I'm not concerned about you earning your keep, Agnes. But perhaps I should be concerned about *how* you earn it. You're far too intelligent, and under that grimy appearance, I suspect you're far too attractive to be a maid all your life." He ignored her gasp of indignation. "In fact, there seems to be more to you than one would first suspect."

"I don't know what you mean!" she hedged.

"Why don't I believe you?"

Audra flinched as he reached out and, with his thumb, rubbed at the dirt on her cheek.

"And you've reneged on your end of the bargain," he continued. "You're a sore loser, Agnes."

"I am not! I bathe every day," she admitted reluctantly.

His raised brows told her he didn't believe her. "What shall I do with you, little Agnes? Hm . . . Yes, I think it's time I gave some thought to your future." He ignored her startled gasp as he easily vaulted back onto his saddle, dipped his head, and turned Ulysses toward the Manor.

All the frustrations of the last weeks—no, the last months and years—suddenly came to a head. What was *he* going to do with *her*? Determine her future, would he? Ha! In a pig's eye! No man—particularly a Brannon—was *ever again* going to control her life.

Needing to vent her fury, Audra grabbed a broken branch lying at her feet and drew her arm back to throw it.

It was a mistake. She should have waited until Nick was out of sight. She'd intended for it to go into the woods, hadn't meant to strike him at all. But it slipped from her grasp. The two-inch-thick branch hit Nick right between his shoulder blades.

She froze as he brought Ulysses to a halt. He sat unmoving, unspeaking, but Audra could swear she saw his entire body expand as he gathered himself. In another moment, he would be . . . He *was*! Audra backed away as he turned the stallion and came back to her. One look at the golden blaze in Nick's eyes and she lost courage. Turning, she fled.

It was ridiculously hopeless, of course. He caught up to her, simply reached down and scooped her up into his arms again, then turned Ulysses back toward Sheffield.

She tried bravado. "Put me down!" she demanded.

"Like hell, you stubborn brat! You're a precocious child with no discipline who needs a lesson in manners."

"Like hell!" she mimicked. "I'm not a child and I don't require a lesson in manners from you! I'm not the intruder here. You are!" Audra could have bitten her tongue, particularly when she saw a muscle in his cheek twitch and his expression turn grim. Alarmed, she struggled against his unyielding hold.

She gasped as his large hand and forearm clamped securely around her waist. "Keep squirming like that, and you'll not be able to breathe," he warned in a deadly serious tone.

Audra knew she had no choice but to obey.

The ride seemed interminable. She was afraid to move, almost afraid to breathe, so uncomfortable did she feel in such close proximity to Nick Brannon. The feel of his strong fingers against her waist, even through her clothes, stirred strange, confusing feelings within her belly. It didn't help that he smelled wonderfully of leather and horse, and that piney soap. Or that his chin was at her eye level, and his mouth . . .

Audra was never so relieved to see the Manor come into sight. Thinking he'd simply drop her, she straightened in preparation, but he clamped down on her, holding her more tightly than before. To her astonishment, he pointed Ulysses straight toward the pond. Bringing the horse to a halt, Nick swung his leg over the saddle and unceremoniously pulled Audra down with him.

"Your mouth needs scrubbing," he said. Audra immediately heard the note of amusement in his voice. "As does the rest of you," he added.

It took a moment for Audra to comprehend. "No!"

He tossed her into the pond, as easily as if she were a sack of flour. She had time only to see the swans scatter in startled disarray before she hit the water. She barely got her mouth closed in time.

She struggled to her feet, sputtering and spitting water, half blinded by her straggling hair, so furious she wanted to tear Brannon's eyes out. Pulling her hair away from her face, she saw him standing with his fists on his hips, grinning. "Oh!" she cried furiously. "You rotten, horrible man! How dare you treat a lady like this?" she sputtered.

"Lady? Ha! Don't make me . . ." Nick dropped off in mid-sentence, for it suddenly struck him that they'd flung these same words at one another somewhere, sometime, before.

His eyes narrowing, he stared at Agnes. Her hair had come loose and now cloaked her almost to her thighs. Gone were the smudges of dirt, and though ire flagged her cheeks, it couldn't fully conceal creamy, fine skin. Generous dark brows, delicately arched, accented shimmering blue eyes.

And then he knew.

He was so enraged that he actually stepped forward to walk into the pond. Damned if she didn't deserve to be drowned!

But then he looked into her eyes again, and saw that they were brimming with hurt and outrage. He halted. "Erin!" he called.

The stable boy, who along with the others had been watching this drama with avid curiosity, came running.

"Take care of Ulysses," Nick ordered. And without another word, he turned his back on Audra and stalked to the house.

Nick paced the study in agitation.

Agnes. Audra.

How could he have been so utterly, stupidly blind?

"Eyes like jewels," Mrs. Garvey had said.

He'd been struck by those incredible sapphire eyes from the moment she'd slammed out of the kitchen and into him. A man would have to be blind not to be.

And *"hair down to . . ."*

Under that ridiculous maid's dress was a sweetly curving bottom and perfectly formed breasts. He could still remember what she'd felt like at the Crown and Arms.

Audra Sheffield. What a cunning little actress she was! Then Nick's fury suddenly died. Damned if he didn't admire her spunk. It wasn't often that anyone—much less a little bit of a woman—got the best of Nick Brannon.

What the hell was he going to do with her? He couldn't decide if he wanted to spank her, or kiss her. Or both.

Yet he thought he understood why she'd done it. She was embarrassed about the incident in London, and she didn't trust him. Could he really blame her, knowing what he now knew of William?

Audra Sheffield was full of contradictions. She seemed fragile, but was stubborn and strong-willed. She was witty, and despite the fact that she could be a hellion, he suspected that once she was *really* cleaned up, she'd look like an angel.

She was a challenge, but he'd never backed away from one yet. Besides, it would be interesting to see just how far she was willing to go with this game.

And how long it would take before she realized that he was a master at bluffing and that he was about to change the stakes to be damned certain that they were all in his favor.

Chapter 7

$\mathcal{A}$udra spotted McKee going to the wine cellar and decided this was her opportunity to tell him about Norton.

She'd not been able to speak to him before this because Nick had given Bertie orders that "Agnes" was to help serve dinner, so for the two last days, Audra, scrubbed and dressed in a new maid's uniform and with her apron tied snugly around her slender waist, silently helped Letty serve. It should have been an easy task. It wasn't. Not with Nick's gleaming eyes constantly following her and watching her every move—as if she were some odd but interesting specimen. Worse, he made no effort to conceal his observation.

It didn't help that Bertie and McKee were completely unsympathetic and clearly amused at her predicament. Audra retaliated by keeping them on tenterhooks, for they were only too aware that she was capable of deliberately overturning the soup tureen onto Nick's lap.

Rose had complained and pouted mightily about Agnes's change in status, until she'd been told that her own would be upped to that of upstairs maid. Still, she threw hateful looks at Agnes every chance she got.

More irritating still, whenever Nick needed a maid to bring something to him or perform some task, he always called on "Agnes." Audra was convinced that he was doing it to torment her.

"Why doesn't the man get a valet?" she grumbled, as she followed McKee down the stairs into the cellar.

"He says he prefers to do for himself," McKee explained over his shoulder. "Told me he wasna used to having people fetch and carry for him all the time."

"Oh, he said that, did he?" Audra sputtered, hands on her hips. "Then why is it, pray tell, that I seem to be doing all his 'fetching and carrying' these last days? It's been 'Agnes, do this,' and 'Agnes, do that!' And all the time, he's watching me with those damned laughing eyes. The man is driving me mad!"

McKee chuckled. "Well, lass, ye have to admit that ye do look a tad better without all that dirt on yer face. Can the poor man help it if he's blinded by yer charms?"

Audra's snort of derision was anything but ladylike. "Charms, indeed! He's playing some game with me. Well, I can hold out longer than he can. But, oh, how I wish he'd return to America and leave us all in peace!"

"Well, as to that, I dinna know what his plans are." McKee's voice became muffled as he disappeared behind a tall rack. "He hasna told me. But I sense that he may be getting restless, so mayhap it willna be much longer."

"Do you really think so?"

McKee's grizzled head reappeared. "Do I think what?"

"That he's becoming restless?"

McKee grinned at the frown creasing Audra's forehead. "Aye. That he is. He's a man used to action, and now that things seem to be in order here, 'tis only natural he would become . . . bored."

"But surely, there's still much for him to do here." Audra bit her lip. "I've seen him working in the study, trying to get the ledgers back in order. And there are the new lambs to sell and fields to . . ." She broke off, confused by the sudden realization that she was finding reasons for Nick to stay.

"Do ye want him to stay then, lassie?"

Audra focused on McKee. "Of course not!" she denied hotly. "Didn't I just say the man was driving me mad?"

"Aye. So ye did," McKee said as he found the bottle he was looking for and came to her.

"I did," she said firmly. "But I didn't come down here to speak of him." Swiftly, she told McKee of her brief encounter with Norton. As she'd expected, he was aggravated.

"What's the scum skulking about for? He has no business on Sheffield land." McKee frowned. "He may be staying in the village. I'll find out tomorrow, lass. If he's about, I'll take it upon myself to change his mind about any plans he may have about seeing ye. Dinna worry yer bonny head about him."

"McKee, you don't think he knows anything about . . . ?"

"No! How can he when he wasna here the night William died? 'Tis only the two of us who know. Ye dinna tell Bertie?"

"No. Bertie has an understanding heart, but she never knew William. She couldn't possibly understand what a monster he really was. No, McKee—I alone have the burden of guilt to bear. Oh, if only I could forget William!"

McKee patted her on the shoulder. "Lass, I know ye canna forget. But none of it was yer fault. Keep that thought in yer head. William came to his end through his own folly."

"I know," Audra agreed despondently. "I can't be sorry he's out of our lives. I'm only sorry about the way it happened."

"As am I, Audra lass. But only because he deserved a more fitting end—such as having his neck stretched!" Seeing the shadows in her eyes, McKee wrapped a comforting arm over her shoulder and led her toward the stairs. "Come along, now. Enough of this! Nick's waiting for his brandy and here we are mooning about something we canna change. Here," he offered, putting the bottle into her hands, "do ye want to take it to him?"

Audra's expression was one of horror as she shoved the brandy back into McKee's hands. "Are you daft?"

Audra waited at the top of the stairs until McKee had locked the door again, then turned to leave the kitchen. Letty was just coming in. "Oh, here you are, Miss Audra. Mr. Nick is fretting for his brandy. He says you're to bring it to him in the study."

Audra rolled her eyes at McKee and reluctantly accepted the bottle back from him.

Grinning at her frustration, he asked, "What's a maid for but to fetch and carry?" He backed off from her threatening hold on the bottle, but added, as he retreated through the outside kitchen door, "And dinna ye be pouring it all over him now, ye ken? Ye came close enough with the pudding at dinner."

After sticking out her tongue at McKee, Audra prepared to do battle, if necessary, with Nick. She still hadn't decided whether to forgive him for that little dunking in the pond.

Yet as she knocked on the study door, she couldn't help experiencing a swift frisson of excitement. Struggling with the effort to maintain an air of aloofness, she entered at his request and carried the tray to the little table beside the fire. She had no need to look his way to know that he was watching her from behind the desk. She straightened swiftly. "Will that be all, sir?"

He glanced at the tray. "No, I need a fresh glass."

"Oh! I'll be right back."

He put his book down. "No. Ring for Letty to bring it."

Puzzled, she did as he asked, then went to door to tell Letty what was required. "Yes, Miss Audra."

"Not Audra. *Agnes!*" Audra hissed under her breath.

Letty glanced over Audra's shoulder. Her eyes widened in dismay. Clapping her hand over her mouth, she scurried off.

"Do you have something you want to say to me?"

The voice came from right over Audra's shoulder. She gasped and spun about. Nick had moved swiftly and silently, and was now only inches away, looking down at her intently with those tawny eyes. Had he heard Letty's slip?

But his face revealed nothing, so Audra assumed she was still safe. "I have nothing to say to you," she replied haughtily.

"Really? Then I was under a misapprehension at dinner. I had the distinct impression that you were bursting with the desire to tell me something. Particularly when you served the pudding."

He was grinning at her, the infuriating man! Yet she found herself smiling back. "That obvious, was I?"

Nick laughed. "You were." Then he sobered. "Tell me, Agnes . . . do you intend to spend the rest of your life at Sheffield? Don't you long for something better than serving others?"

She turned her face away. If he only knew! She

wanted to wear bright colors again. She wanted to ride
Ulysses—or any horse.

Her eyes unexpectedly welled, and she was horrified to
find that she'd almost sniffled. She wouldn't cry! She
would *not*! She'd not cried since the night she'd first seen
the bruises William had put upon her mother's face. And
she'd vowed that no one—no *man*, would ever make her
cry again.

Nick's keen eyes missed nothing. So, he thought, she's
not all that happy with her charade, either. What would it
take to get her to come clean?

"I could help, if you'd let me. You seem to be a bright,
young woman, Agnes. You're even passably attractive."
He almost grinned. If looks could kill, he'd be a dead man.
"I have friends and connections in London," he continued
blandly. "I'd furnish a suitable wardrobe and send you to
them, as my ward. They'd introduce you to the right people. It's not impossible that you'd catch the eye of a serious
suitor. I'd even furnish a dowry . . . as a gift from the
Sheffield estate for all your years of dedicated service to
them and your care of Mrs. Brannon." He expected her to
refuse, of course.

Her reaction was all he'd hoped. And more.

Fury shot from her eyes. "Marriage?" she flung at him
derisively. *"Marriage?* I've seen what a miserable state that
can be. Wedded and bedded? Becoming some man's property for life? Unable to say yea or nay, to have no freedom?
You're mad if you think I'd willingly suffer the pain of
bearing his heirs year after year or, for that matter, to even
submit to his offensive desires. Ha!"

"Desires? Just what do you know of men's desires?"
Nick asked sharply.

"Enough to know that men aren't to be trusted, for
they only use a woman for their convenience and don't

give a damn for her feelings or for her well-being!" Audra paused, only because she needed to take a breath.

"My word! That's quite an opinion. And you expressed it so fluently. Why, Agnes, I do believe you've lost your charming brogue." Nick suppressed a grin as her marvelous eyes widened in confusion, then fear. Good! A little fear wouldn't hurt her, he thought. She had it coming— for London; for her clever little masquerade. "It makes me wonder whether there isn't even more refinement and intelligence hidden behind that nice, clean face of yours. Hm. If I'd known, I might have tossed you into the pond sooner."

Unexpectedly, he stepped forward to grasp her chin in one large hand and turn her face from side to side, taking his time as he subjected her to a silent and thorough scrutiny that, to Audra's chagrin, made her cheeks burn. "Perhaps you'd like to examine my teeth, also," she suggested sarcastically.

"No need," Nick said smoothly as he released her chin. "Yes, I do believe you have his look."

Audra's anger gave way to confusion. "Whose look?"

"Why, your father's."

"My . . . ?"

"Yes. Edward Sheffield's. Come now, Agnes. I've seen his photograph next to Mrs. Brannon's bed. You have the same coloring, the same intense eyes. There's no doubt in my mind that you're his daughter."

Audra paled. Blazes! He knew!

"There's no need to look so stricken, Agnes," Nick said gently. "Being born out of wedlock is not the child's blame."

Audra's mouth opened, then snapped closed. Her face turned a deep crimson. Suddenly, to Nick's consternation, she covered her face with her hands and lowered her head. Her shoulders shook.

Bloody hell! He'd pushed her too far! If there was one thing that made him feel completely helpless, it was a crying woman.

He murmured an apology. Her shoulders convulsed even more, but she appeared to be trying to regain control, for her silent sobs changed to gasps. Not knowing what else to do, Nick quickly backed her into a chair and went to pour a small measure of brandy and bring it to her. "Drink this," he ordered as he knelt beside her.

Audra was giddy with relief. And disbelief. Oh, heavens! Nick had discovered she was her father's daughter all right, only he thought she was his *illegitimate* daughter! Audra tried desperately to suppress her laughter, to no avail. So when Nick pushed the glass at her, she grasped it eagerly with both hands and swallowed it all. Immediately, her throat was on fire. She choked and sputtered helplessly. "You could have warned me," she croaked indignantly. "I thought it was water."

It took Nick a moment to realize that she hadn't been crying at all. In retaliation, he slapped her back soundly, causing her to double over. She gasped and coughed and waved her hands feebly. "Sorry," he said with false solicitude. "I meant to help. Better now?"

"Yes!" She sat up and eyed him warily, looking for all the world as if she was prepared to smack him back if he dared do it to her again.

Nick's mouth quirked. "I'll have to give you lessons on how to drink brandy," he told her. And then he couldn't resist pushing her even more. "Agnes, I didn't mean to upset you," he said as he took the chair across from her. "But surely you realize that it isn't so unusual for a married man, even your father, to have a mistress. In fact, it may sometimes be a necessity."

"My father . . ." About to deny there had ever been a mistress, Audra quickly changed her mind. What did it

matter if Nick thought her father had been unfaithful? But
. . . oh! Someday she'd make him pay for his insulting
assumption! Still, perhaps a little revenge was called for
now.

"And what of you, Mr. Brannon? Do you have a mistress that you keep happily dressed in fancy clothes and
jewels?" She kept her tone carefully innocent and hoped
she looked the same as she peeped at him from under her
lashes.

Nick's eyes narrowed. Damned if the little minx wasn't
baiting him! She needed a lesson on more than drinking
brandy! He shrugged. "Like all men, I have certain basic
needs. Only I have no wife. As to the fancy clothes and
jewels—since you ask, I prefer to see my women dressed in
nothing but the jewels," he drawled.

Already warmed by the brandy, Audra's cheeks red-
dened even more at this blunt disclosure. But she wasn't
about to admit defeat. "Really? You've been at Sheffield
for many weeks now. As I recall, you brought no *woman*
with you—dressed or otherwise. Pray tell, where is this
happy creature? Can it be that she's so happy with the
gifts you give her that she doesn't miss *you*?" She saw that
the barb had missed its target, for his grin only widened.

"I have no woman, happy or otherwise, whom I call
my own. I do have a female friend in the States, however,
who seems to be quite happy with whatever gifts I bring
her."

Audra's eyes widened, for she'd been thinking of Delia.
The fact that he had another woman in America . . . a
friend, he'd called her. Ha! More likely another mistress!
The thought filled her with angry distaste. "I'm sure she is.
What will it be this time . . . some shiny little bauble, or
perhaps a ruby-colored gown or two?" she asked sarcastically.

His retort came swiftly. "The substance of the gift

doesn't matter. I'm quite sure that Brenda has managed to console herself elsewhere these months I've been away."

"As I'm certain *you* have," Audra snapped.

Nick's eyes narrowed speculatively. What a sharp little tongue she had! "As you pointed out, there's been little time for consolation, not to mention the lack of a consoler. Also, I'm very fastidious in my choices. You wouldn't happen to be interested, would you?" Nick asked with an exaggerated arch of his brow.

Audra's mouth fell open. The man was being deliberately crude. Suddenly tired of the game, she jumped up from her chair and stood over him, hands on her hips. "Absolutely not! How dare you! This entire conversation is insulting. If I were someone else . . . if I were Audra Sheffield, you would never dare to speak to me this way!"

Nick got to his feet, too, and stood before her. Audra found herself craning her neck to look up at him.

"Does that bother you, little Agnes—not being her?"

Her eyes shot sparks at him as she drew herself up proudly. "Of course not," she lied. "I'm quite happy just as I am." She turned to leave, but had taken only a few steps before she was brought up short by his hand on her shoulder. She arched a delicate brow at him. "Was there anything else, Mr. Brannon?" she asked coolly.

"Yes." So saying, he stepped forward, so close that his breath touched her cheek. She stiffened warily and took a step backward. He stepped forward. She retreated farther until the wall pressed into her back. Trapped, she squared her shoulders. She would *not* be a coward!

Audra gasped as he placed the palm of one hand against the wall near her ear and leaned forward. His eyes, his mouth, were only inches away, close enough for her to smell the brandy on his warm breath. Her heart suddenly tripped over itself—a feeling strangely akin to anticipation of something wonderful about to happen.

"Are you quite sure," he asked softly, "that you wouldn't like to reconsider? *Both* of my offers still stand."

Audra blinked. For just a moment, she'd been entrapped by those golden lights, but now she saw that he was laughing at her again! She almost stamped her foot in frustration. "You certainly didn't expect me to take your proposition seriously, did you?" She faked a gay laugh that she knew didn't fool him for an instant. In fact, it deepened that dangerous smile, making Audra's palm itch to slap that male smirk off his face. Gritting her teeth, she continued. "Even if I had, you'll soon be returning to America. What would your 'protection' do for me then? After all, one can hardly eat baubles or gowns, can one? Thank you *so much* for your *kind* offers, but no thanks," she concluded scornfully, "I have no need of anything from you. Of that you may be certain." She took a tentative step sideways. To her surprise, he let her go.

"Ah, well," he drawled, "as I don't have any immediate plans to leave Sheffield, I may yet change your mind."

"Oh! You're not leaving, then?"

Nick tilted his head and studied her thoughtfully. She was standing quite still, her wonderful eyes bright with eagerness. Which was she hoping for—that he would, or that he wouldn't? "Would you be sorry to see me go, little Agnes?" he asked softly.

Audra feigned insouciance and shrugged. "Why should I be? You give yourself too much credit, Mr. Brannon. The truth is, you're completely irrelevant to my well-being." She deliberately raised her nose in the air as she flounced out of the room, caring little if she looked overly dignified, or not dignified at all. But just as she closed the door behind her, she was almost certain she heard his deep laugh.

He was, Audra decided, the most arrogant, the most annoying and frustrating man she'd ever had the misfortune to know! And just when she was beginning to like him, too.

Still, he couldn't possibly have been serious when he'd made that ludicrous proposition, for she could swear he'd been laughing at her the entire time. Almost as if he'd been testing her.

Now, why would he do that?

Comfortably seated before a cheery fire, his feet on a foot-stool, Nick opened the brandy bottle and leaned back to savor the liquor and enjoy a smoke as he thought about Audra.

He may have gotten a bit carried away, but sparring with her was too entertaining to resist. And she gave as good as she got.

Stubborn, little minx! Not only was she unafraid of him, she enjoyed defying him.

Then he had to chuckle. Audra was as unpredictable as the weather in the mountains of Colorado Territory. He'd always enjoyed their sudden summer storms; they came with unbidden violence and power, and sometimes left just as suddenly, leaving the air peaceful and content afterward.

Unbidden came the thought, that was exactly what making love to Audra would be like. Despite the fact that he was now convinced that she was an innocent, he'd also discovered that she had a passionate nature. Of course, she was completely unaware of it herself.

It was going to be a pleasure to teach her.

Audra was in Serena's room, reading to her mother, when the door opened and Letty, her finger over her lips, tiptoed inside. She stepped aside to admit a beaming Mrs. Murphy, who was carrying a huge cake. Bertie and McKee followed.

"Damned foolish to be acting like thieves," McKee grumbled as he lifted a wide-eyed Audra out of her chair in a huge bear hug. " 'Tis only for ye I'd agree to sneakin' up the back stairs."

"Shh," Bertie warned. "We don't want the others to know we're having a birthday party for 'Agnes.' "

Audra was touched to know that they hadn't forgotten, even if she had! They had a quiet celebration, and she was happy and content for the first time in ages. This was her family—the few people she cared about.

But Serena still tired easily, so the others stayed only long enough to have their cake and present Audra with small gifts before taking their leave.

"That was sweet of them," Audra commented as she helped her mother prepare for bed. "I only wish . . ."

"What, dear?"

"I just wish things could be the way they were. When Father was still alive," she said wistfully. "I expected that he'd always be dancing at my birthday parties." She sniffed and a tear ran down her cheek. "Remember the lessons? You would play the pianoforte while Father twirled me about the room." She laughed softly. "He was so patient, though I must have flattened his toes each time."

Serena reached over to push Audra's hair behind her ear. "I wish it could be so, also. But we can't change the past, nor can we decide how long our lives will be. That's as it should be. Still, I'm sorry you aren't dancing tonight. Perhaps you would have been if it weren't for this ridiculous masquerade you insist on playing."

Audra swiped at her cheeks. "I know." Leaning over, she laid her head in her mother's lap. "Oh, I'm sick of being Agnes! I wish I'd never begun this ridiculous farce!"

She sniffed. "I felt like a nobody when William was alive, and now I feel even more so."

"Then stop it, Audra," Serena murmured as she stroked Audra's hair. "You have only to confess to Nick. Dear, I know you thought you had good reason, but surely you can see that he's not like William. Nick has shown only kindness and consideration. Why, he's even assured me that Sheffield will always be my home."

"He has?" At Serena's nod, Audra snorted inelegantly. "Well, of course he's kind to you, Mother, because he likes you. But he thinks I'm only a . . ." Audra turned away, her cheeks pink.

"A what, dear?" Serena prompted.

"A bastard! Mother, he thinks 'Agnes' is Father's illegitimate daughter!" Audra's voice revealed her disgust and scorn.

Serena made a strange choking sound. Audra turned back to her in alarm, afraid the shock had injured Serena in some way. To her surprise, her most proper mother was doubled over with laughter.

"Mo-*ther*!"

"I'm sorry, dear. It's just . . . well . . . to think that your father . . . Oh, it's too much!"

A reluctant grin broke out on Audra's face. "I reacted the same way. And Nick thought I was crying because he'd insulted me."

Mother and daughter laughed together until Serena finally sobered. "Really, Audra. Can you blame the poor man for thinking that? He never knew Edward, after all. And I change the subject each time he says the name 'Agnes,' for I'm frightened to death I'll give you away."

"I'm sorry, Mother. But you may not have to worry much longer. McKee seems to think that Nick is becoming restless. Perhaps he'll be returning to America soon. If so, I'll be able to forget 'Agnes' ever existed."

"Why, oh why, did I permit Edward to let you become so willful?" Serena shook her head. "I only hope you won't come to regret it. Now, that's my last word on the subject," Serena promised as she yawned delicately, then snuggled into her pillow.

"Good night, Mother," Audra murmured as she kissed her mother's cheek. But after closing the door softly behind her, she leaned against it instead of going directly to her own room.

Why hadn't she admitted the truth to Nick today? Her mother was right, she thought. Nick wasn't even remotely like William.

Perhaps that was the problem. Nick made her feel things that confused her, and want things she couldn't understand, much less explain. Even to herself.

Chapter 8

"$\mathcal{H}$ow do I look, Miss Audra?"

Letty twirled before Audra, her skirts flying out around her. She and the others were all going to the village to attend the evening festivities of the two-day fair which annually heralded the official beginning of spring. Tonight there would be dancing and games. Almost everyone in the county attended.

"You look very pretty, Letty. The young men won't be able to take their eyes off you."

Letty's face flushed in pleasure. "But will Rafe like it?" Then she frowned. "That silly Rose will try to keep Rafe to herself."

"Does Rose like him, too?"

Letty sniffed in disdain. "Rose likes *all* men. She's a terrible flirt, but if you ask me, the one she's really set her cap for is Mr. Nick. Can you imagine that?"

Audra could. She'd heard the other maids whispering about how attractive Nick was. But what had Letty heard that she hadn't? "How do you know?" she asked sharply.

Letty snorted. "She says since he's American, he's not as stuffy as an Englishman, and doesn't care about class. And she's always making excuses to be in his room much more than she has to be. She spends *forever* up there."

This was news to Audra. Since Rose didn't like her, Audra had almost no contact with the maid.

"Here you two are." Bertie had just come in. "Letty, you look very nice. But Rafe is already waiting for you below."

"Oh!" Letty was suddenly all flustered. She smoothed her skirts down nervously, and took a last peek in the mirror. "Do you think he likes freckles?" she asked as she tried vainly to brush them off her nose with her fingers.

Audra exchanged an amused look with Bertie. "As long as they're on a feminine face, I rather think he does." Rafe didn't hide the fact that he appreciated anything in skirts. Audra only hoped Letty knew it, too. She wouldn't want to see the little maid hurt.

"I hope she realizes that Rafe will never be a one-woman man," Audra said worriedly after Letty left. "He flirts with all the maids. He's too devilishly handsome, and knows it."

Bertie quirked a brow. "He doesn't flirt with you, does he?"

"Heavens, no!" Now that Audra thought of it, why not? With her, he was merely polite and, lately, almost deferential. Which was odd, for though Rafe worked for Nick, he was no man's servant, and Nick gave him the courtesy and respect due an equal. But then, Nick never looked down on others. A rather enlightened American habit, she supposed.

"Are you sure," Bertie was asking, "that you won't change your mind about going to the fair? I could stay with your mother."

Audra shook her head. "I can't. Someone will be sure

to recognize me, and Nick is going. My secret won't last a minute."

Audra's wistful tone didn't pass Bertie's notice. "You could solve that problem by revealing your identity to Nick. Really, Audra. You're carrying this too far."

"I know," Audra agreed, sighing. "But William deceived us in the beginning, also. Once he got what he wanted, he changed."

"And you think Nick will change?" Bertie asked, then shook her head when Audra nodded. "Just what is it that you think he wants?"

"I don't know," Audra said in frustration.

"He doesn't need Sheffield as he doesn't intend to stay in England. He has a business to run in America. He has wealth of his own," Bertie pointed out. "What else could he possibly want?"

"I don't *know*, Bertie! I only know that he's a man, he disturbs me, and I don't trust him." Audra got up and moved restlessly to the door. "I'm going to check on Mother," she tossed over her shoulder as she left the room.

Bertie pursed her lips in thought. Audra had always been frightfully stubborn, but she'd also been willing to listen to reason. Until now.

And the comment she'd made about Nick disturbing her—Bertie wondered if Audra even realized what she'd admitted.

Peeking in on her mother, Audra found that Serena was already asleep, so she settled on the chaise longue in her own room with a book. Half an hour later, she'd turned only two pages. Setting it down with a sigh, she got up to glance out the windows, then paced the room restlessly. She felt suffocated. The brooding silence of the house was almost more than she could bear.

Suddenly, she stopped pacing. It had just occurred to her that, for once, she could do whatever she wished without fear of running into Nick, or having one of the maids or Bates look at her strangely. Laughing, she whirled gaily about the room. It was a heady feeling—this freedom. She had the entire house to herself. The entire estate, for that matter. She could go anywhere on it, do whatever she pleased.

Audra stopped short again. Another lovely thought had just come into her head. McKee had said that he and Nick would be taking Bertie to the fair in the buggy, which meant that Ulysses . . .

Did she dare?

Excitement coursed through her veins. It had been so long. It was a beautiful, warm night, the moon was full, and her mother never woke until morning.

She rushed to the wardrobe, stripping off her clothes and scattering them haphazardly. Quickly, she pulled out a shirt and a pair of men's britches. In a few short minutes, she was running down the stairs, tying her hair back with a scarf as she went.

The stable doors had been left open on this warm night. As she lit a lamp, one of the cats circled her feet and rubbed against her. She picked him up. "Hello, baby," she said, nuzzling his nose with hers before tucking him into her elbow.

Ulysses tossed his head as she approached his stall, then greeted her with a low snort when she spoke quietly to him. He turned his head to look at her when she placed her saddle on his back, as if to ask what this unfamiliar contraption was. Audra would have loved to try one of the western saddles, but she didn't dare. Someone might notice that the stirrups had been adjusted.

He was an enormous horse, so Audra led him out of

the stable to the mounting block in the yard. In seconds,
she was on his back. Ulysses pranced nervously.

"Shh. Easy, my boy," she soothed, patting him on the
neck. "Easy. We're going to have a lovely ride together."
The horse quieted, and obeyed her wordless command to
go forward.

Once out of sight of the house, she urged Ulysses into
a trot, cautious enough not to give Ulysses his head. She
knew every inch of this land and was dying to gallop
freely, but there would be hell to pay if she brought him
back injured. But Ulysses was big and powerful, and he
fought her for the reins, so she finally gave in and allowed
both herself and the stallion the pleasure of a short run on
flat terrain. Thereafter, she kept him at a trot.

She had no idea how long she rode, but finally, reluctantly, she turned him home. She unsaddled him in the
dark, brushed him down quickly, then pulled his head
down to give him a hug. "What a lovely, lovely brute you
are, Ulysses," she whispered in his ear. "Thank you."

A powerful arm suddenly snaked about her waist and
dragged her out of the stall. Shrieking in surprised fear, she
was lifted, then easily tossed through the air to land
facedown on a pile of fresh straw. A hard body fell on top
of her, knocking the breath from her.

Her face itched where it was pressed against the straw,
and she was being crushed. Gasping, she struggled for air.
Suddenly, she was flipped over onto her back, and was
finally able to breathe again. The stable was too dark to
make out more than a dark shadow above her, but that
silhouette was unmistakable.

"Get . . . off me, damn you! Get *off*!"

"What the . . . ? Audra?"

She'd just had the breath and the life scared out of her,
but she was too angry to care that Nick had just called her
by her real name. "Who did you think it was—Mrs. Mur-

phy? Get off me, you big oaf!" She wriggled in a futile attempt to get out from under him, until she became aware that he was only pressing her farther into the straw. She stilled.

"Well, well. If it isn't Miss Sheffield," he drawled. "We meet in the most unexpected places, don't we?"

There was a pause from the still figure beneath him. Finally, her voice came out of the dark, stiff and tentative. "I don't know what you're talking about."

Nick grinned in the dark. Initially, when he'd heard the sound of hooves going into the stables, he'd suspected a horse thief. How convenient that it had been Audra, for she had played right into his hands. "Really?" he mocked. "What a poor memory you have, Audra Sheffield. Perhaps a little reminder . . . ?"

She divined his intention too late, for his mouth was already upon hers. Instead of the rough assault she expected, however, his lips played against hers in soft feathery strokes. She was surprised into acquiescence, too bemused to do more than just lie there, until he lifted his head and said, "Remember now?"

"No! I . . ." She turned her head aside, but his hand slid up to thread his fingers into her thick hair and hold her still.

This time he deepened the kiss, and when his tongue forced her lips apart and she felt his, warm and wet within her own mouth, she could only gasp in outrage. Or was it . . . excitement?

It seemed an eternity before his mouth left hers again. "Now?" he asked again.

Damn him! "No," she whispered hoarsely.

"Hm. I suppose I'll have to change my strategy." His fingers slid out of her hair and down her cheek, over the pulse beating wildly in her throat. . . .

She held her breath. He wouldn't dare!

He would and he did. One hand covered the fabric over her breast and squeezed gently. With the other he began unbuttoning her shirt.

She yanked his hair to tug his head away. "Yes!" she yelped.

He was off her and on his feet instantly, pulling her up with him. He held her arm in a tight grasp as he dragged her out of the stable and along the path to the house.

"Nick, slow down!" When he ignored her, she dug in her heels. He responded by jerking her forward and tossing her over his shoulder as easily as he would his jacket.

Too late, she realized that the muscles bunched under her were tense with anger. She supposed he had that right, considering that she'd just been caught riding his stallion—not to mention the fact that he'd just discovered her deception. And then she realized that he hadn't been surprised at all that "Audra" was at Sheffield—only that she'd been in the stable. She lifted herself from her waist, straining away from him to pound on his back with her fists. "You bastard! You knew who I really was!" she accused. "You've been playing with me! How dare you?"

"Don't *you* play the affronted party with me, Audra. Or do you prefer to be called 'Agnes'? You certainly seemed to enjoy carrying out your own deception!"

He carried her directly through the open veranda doors of the library. Once inside, he simply bent over and dumped her onto the divan, where she landed with a bounce. She sat up quickly to glare at his back as he walked away from her. "You're supposed to be at the fair," she accused, then wished she'd kept her mouth shut as he suddenly whirled to face her.

"And you, Miss Sheffield, are supposed to be in London." His eyes glittered dangerously. "Come here," he ordered brusquely.

"What?" Her eyes were wide with confusion, but Nick

only pointed to the floor at his feet, and waited. That he would wait for as long as it took, Audra knew without a doubt. Hesitantly, she stood up and went to him. But then her anger flared again.

"You beast! You already knew who I really was when you insulted me the other day. How dare . . . ?"

"Hold your tongue, Audra," he warned in a dangerously soft voice. "You're the one who owes the explanations. For one thing, you rode my horse without permission."

"You kissed me without permission," she retorted.

His steady gaze pressed on.

"All *right*. I'm sorry I rode Ulysses without asking," she apologized. "I shouldn't have done it, I know."

"You broke your promise to me."

"I most certainly did not," she responded quickly. "I promised not to go into his stall alone and I didn't. I took one of the kittens along."

Nick stared at her for a moment, his eyes shooting golden sparks before he lifted his head, squeezed his lids together, and took a deep breath. "One of the kittens," he repeated prayerfully.

"Yes. Not only do the cats keep the stables free of mice, but they keep the horses calm. They play at their feet all the time. Ulysses hasn't hurt one yet."

It hadn't been the cats he'd been concerned about. His initial anger had come from the thought of what Ulysses could have done to *her*. "First carrots, then kittens," Nick said helplessly. He opened his eyes and regarded her as if she were some strange creature. "You've turned my stallion into a four-legged pansy."

"Of course I haven't," she replied indignantly. "That would be a terrible thing to do to a marvelous creature like Ulysses."

"He's also dangerous. I assume you're a good horse-woman?"

Her chin went up proudly. "No. I'm an *excellent* one. My father was the best horseman in the county. He began to teach me to ride when I could barely walk," she replied quietly.

"Why don't you have a mount of your own?"

"I did. But William sold Fantasy's Lady when I . . ." She fell silent and glanced away.

"Yes?" Nick prompted.

"I made him angry. He sold my mare as punishment," she said bitterly, and refused to say more.

Nick raked his hand through his hair. He would pursue that particular revelation at another time. "Did you deliberately set out to make a fool of me? Been having a good laugh at my expense?"

Audra's eyes widened. He sounded almost . . . hurt. Her defiance fled. She'd never considered that he would think that. "Oh, no! It wasn't like that at all."

"Why did you do it, then?" he pressed. "I want explanations, Audra, and I mean to have them."

Audra dropped her gaze. "I . . . I was afraid," she finally admitted. "I . . . we didn't know you, and we only had our experience with William to guide us. I thought . . . if you were like William, you might throw us out. . . ." Audra shrugged her shoulders helplessly. "You know how ill Mother was. We no longer had a home or an income. . . ." She chanced a glance at him. His gaze was penetrating, but she couldn't interpret his expression.

"That's not good enough. Have I ever given any of you reason to think I'd do such a thing to your mother? *Have I?*"

"All *right!* I was ashamed and embarrassed about what happened at the inn," she admitted. "I'm truly sorry. You have a right to be angry with me, but it wasn't anyone else's doing," she said softly. "Punish *me* if you must, but please don't take it out on any of the others." She stood proudly, bracing herself as if expecting a blow.

God! Did she actually believe he would strike her? To reassure her, he tucked his hands into his pockets. "All right. I'll accept that," he said quietly. "But what the *hell* did you think you'd accomplish by trying to force me to sign that deed?"

Audra's cheeks turned bright red. "No one had come here to claim Sheffield, you see, and I was desperate." She shrugged helplessly. She was humiliated enough; she couldn't tell him about Lord Cowan.

"More secrets, Audra?"

She only looked at him mutely, her eyes deep, dark pools of misery.

"All right. Keep your secrets. For now." She looked so forlorn that if he didn't do something with his hands, he'd probably take her in his arms. He went to his desk and removed a cheroot from a silver case, instead. "But I warn you—never, *never* lie to me again, Audra. I won't tolerate it," he said quietly as he walked to the fireplace and bent to light a sliver of wood.

Audra stared in astonishment. He was peering at her over the flame, his brows raised in inquiry. Surely he wasn't finished with her? "Is that all?" she asked apprehensively.

"Yes," he affirmed. "I understand that you thought you had a genuinely good reason for doing what you did." Nothing he'd heard about his uncle had been good, but now he was convinced that it was worse than he knew. He would probably never learn it all if he couldn't gain her trust.

Audra felt the tension drain out of her. She didn't deserve his calm acceptance, or his understanding, she knew. Yet she was grateful. Her relief was reflected in the beaming smile she gave him. "Thank you, Nick." She let out a deep sigh. "I did so hate the name Agnes!"

Nick practically dropped his cheroot. Then he broke out in a booming laugh. "Ever humble, I see," he finally said, coming to stand before her again. His mouth curved softly as he peered down at her, then crooked his finger under her chin to lift her face. "While I have no intention to punish you, I *do* expect to exact a penalty," he said, sobering. "You owe me, sweet."

She didn't even hear his endearment. Her eyes narrowed. "Owe you *what?*" she asked suspiciously.

His teeth flashed white again. "I haven't decided yet. But rest assured—I'll let you know when I do."

The next morning, Nick and McKee weren't at breakfast. Bertie knew only that they and Rafe had left early for London, and claimed she had no idea why, or when they would return.

Audra felt an unexpected pang of disappointment. She told herself she didn't care where they'd gone, or that she hadn't been informed. Besides, she had her hands full dealing with the servants when she appeared as Audra Sheffield, and not Agnes.

On that first day, the entire staff, which now numbered a dozen indoors and out, were thrown into mass confusion and consternation. By the next day, they were falling all over themselves in an attempt to right any wrongs—real, imagined, or implied—they might have done to "Agnes." All except Rose. She took it as a personal affront that the maid she'd so gleefully ridiculed was now someone she'd have to take orders from.

By the third day, Audra was convinced she'd had more freedom as "Agnes." Desperate to get away from fawning servants, she finally escaped to her room, but soon found herself pacing restlessly and growing more irritated that Nick had left so mysteriously. She told herself it was silly, it was ridiculous. Why, she should consider herself blessed that she had no infuriating, disturbing man to aggravate her!

That evening, Audra and Serena were having dinner in Serena's room. They had just finished when the door opened and Letty, face flushed with excitement and her mobcap askew, rushed in.

"Oh, ma'am! Miss Audra! Rafe's back and . . . oh! Wait 'til you see what he's brought!"

Audra's heart unexpectedly jerked. If Rafe was back, then Nick was back, too. Trying to appear nonchalant, she got to her feet. But before she'd taken even one step, Rafe, his arms full of boxes, came staggering into the room. His handsome face peered over the top. "Ah, there you are, ladies," he said with obvious relief. "Where do you want these?"

"What in the world . . . ?" Audra began.

From the bed, Serena replied quietly. "You may set those on that bureau, Rafe. Letty, clear it for him, please."

Audra was too surprised to do more than watch as Rafe did as requested. He then brushed his hands with satisfaction and walked to the door. "That's all of it, ma'am. Nick said to tell you he hoped you'd like them."

"He hasn't come back with you?" Audra asked absently, her eyes still glued to the stack of boxes.

"No. But he'll be coming along later tonight."

"Oh. What's in the boxes?"

Letty, still excited, replied for Rafe, who was already slipping out the door. "Clothes, Miss Audra! And there's more. Boxes and boxes of them already in your room."

"My room? But . . ."

Serena calmly answered the question in her daughter's eyes. "Nick pointed out that since William had never seen fit to replenish our wardrobes, he felt it was his responsibility to do so. He asked my permission, and I agreed, dear."

"But, *Mother* . . . !'

Serena just smiled softly. "Why don't you go to your room and see what your boxes hold while Letty helps me with mine?"

Audra walked to her room in a daze. When she opened the door, she gasped. Boxes and parcels of every size and shape covered her bed and overflowed onto the floor. She stood and stared at the intriguing parcels in indecision. Finally, she couldn't stand it any longer. Eagerly, she tore the first one open.

It was a day dress; a soft cotton with short puffed sleeves and yards of skirt. Shades of pink blossoms which made her think of spring. Tossing it aside, she lifted the cover off another box. Then another. By the time she'd opened all the larger boxes, her eyes were sparkling with sheer delight. Three other simple dresses of varying hues, then a classic gown of pure ivory. A more sophisticated evening gown of red silk that shimmered softly. And in the last box . . .

Audra reverently lifted out a sapphire blue riding habit. There was a matching hat and scarf, too, and two pure white silk blouses. How lovely! She pictured herself on Fantasy's back, the feather on the hat bouncing as she rode.

She opened the heaviest box, and gasped. A pair of riding boots made of leather so soft and supple, they would fit like a glove! How wonderful!

For someone who had always loved clothes, the dresses were delightful. But it was the riding habit Audra clutched to herself as she danced before the full-length mirror. Oh! She knew it would be perfect on her!

She opened the smaller boxes. Slippers of varying

hues. A pristine white satin robe. Nightgowns of the softest lawn. Even softer chambray chemises. Petticoats . . . Audra blushed furiously, even though there was no one to see her. What in the world was Nick doing, purchasing *underclothes* for an unmarred woman?

Oh, the clever blackguard! He'd asked her mother's permission. How was she to refuse this wonderful gift without appearing petty?

Torn between laughter and chagrin, Audra couldn't resist slipping into one of the dresses. At first, she was pleased, then dismayed, to find that it fit her perfectly, for she was now even more tempted. Then, she couldn't resist trying on a red silk, and this time she was shocked at her appearance. The first gown had been modest, but this one . . . Why, it was almost as bad as Delia's ruby gown! It made her look like a . . . a wanton. Like some man's mistress!

That was it! Why, the rake! The scoundrel! It was precisely the kind of dress a mistress would wear. Damn the man!

Resisting the urge to try something else on, Audra carefully put the clothes away. But her fingers caressed the fabric of the habit lovingly. What she wouldn't give to be able to put it on and ride away on Fantasy's back. She sighed as she turned away. She no longer had Fantasy, so it really made no difference.

"Is anyone still about?" Nick asked as he handed his damp cloak and hat to Bates.

"I believe Miss Hauson just went up to her room, and Ag . . . er, Miss Sheffield went up some time ago, sir."

Nick nodded as he slicked back his fog-dampened hair. "If any of the servants are still up, I'd like a hot bath. And send a tray up to my room in about half an hour. Sandwiches will do nicely."

"I'll see to it, sir." Bates didn't reveal any expression at Nick's polite request. Like the rest of the staff, he had finally become accustomed to Nick's consideration of them all. Despite the fact that the master of Sheffield expected his high standards to be met, he seldom demanded, and for that reason alone they were all willing to go to any lengths for him.

A glass of brandy was just the thing to take the edge off the chill, Nick decided as he made his way to the study. It had been a cold and damp ride from London.

Yes, a glass of brandy, a hot bath, some food—it was satisfying to have a real home to return to again, Nick thought as he sipped his brandy and glanced through the letters which had come while he was gone. It gave him something to look forward to.

How much of that anticipation was due to seeing Audra again, he wasn't exactly sure. A great deal, he suspected.

Would she be glad to see him? It was difficult to know. She was so damned defensive, and she wore it like thick armor. How much longer would it take him to break through?

Fifteen minutes later, Nick was upstairs in his dressing room, his head resting against the back of the tub, the brandy bottle sitting on the floor beside him, when he heard the door to his suite open. "Just put the tray on the bed," he called out. There was no response, only the sound of the servant's footsteps and a door closing behind her.

The thought of Mrs. Murphy's cold beef sandwiches— and if he was lucky, a slice or two of her seed cake or fruit pie—brought him out of the tub. Grabbing a towel, he dried himself as he walked into the bedroom.

Surprise froze him to the spot. He'd thought she'd already gone.

"I brought your dinner. Thought I'd wait to see if there's anything else you . . . need," Rose said coyly as her gaze traveled over his wet, glistening body.

Nick finally recovered enough to snatch his robe and quickly shrug into it. "Out!" he thundered as he hastily knotted the belt.

Rose's smile faded. "I just thought . . ." He grabbed her arm and dragged her to the door. His hand didn't leave the knob as he held it open. "Don't think . . . just get out. Now!" he roared.

Rose frowned. This wasn't the reaction she'd expected at all. At the first house she'd served in, the master had thrown up her skirts every chance he got—until his pinched-face wife had discovered what was going on and let her go, without a reference.

She'd learned her lesson. The last time, she'd not only wheedled some nice little trinkets from the master, but had made him write a reference.

Mr. Brannon was wealthier than the others. And he was a man, wasn't he? It was a sure thing that he hadn't had a woman in all the time she'd been at Sheffield. Servants talked among themselves. One of them would have known.

She'd thought this would be her chance, but he wasn't having any of it. Still, she wasn't ready to give up. When he flung her arm away in distaste, she turned back and stepped closer, deliberately brushing her breasts against him as she did so. "Just remember," she said, "any time . . ."

He wasn't even looking at her, but behind her. Rose spun about. Audra Sheffield was standing in the doorway of her room, staring at them in shock. For an instant, they were all frozen in place. Audra's gaze locked with Nick's.

Rose glanced from one to another. So that was it! Mr. Nick was panting after a woman, all right, and from the looks these two were exchanging, it wasn't too hard to tell which one he wanted! The thought infuriated her. Even when she was pretending to be Agnes, the snobbish Sheffield girl had airs. Always acting like she was better than everyone else!

"You're a fool, Mr. Brannon," Rose said spitefully, already knowing there would be no reference here. "Miss Prissy Stick-in-the-Mud Sheffield ain't gonna give you what you want." She laughed derisively. "Look at her. She looks like a bloody nun. She wouldn't know what to do with a man if her life depended on it!"

Audra blinked and slowly turned her eyes toward Rose, as if just realizing that she was still there. "Pack your things, Rose," she said calmly. "McKee will take you back to the village in the morning. Early."

Rose's face hardened. "You can get rid of me, all right, but you'll be sorry. And you'll never be able to please him the way I can . . . the way I *did*!" Throwing an exaggerated wink at Nick before flashing a malicious smile at Audra, she turned and sauntered toward the rear stairs.

Audra silently stared after her.

"It isn't what you think," Nick said as he walked toward her with his hand outstretched.

She slapped it away. "Don't bother to explain, Mr. Brannon. This is *your* house, and you can do what you want. After all, I have it on good authority that most men require a mistress," she spat, her face flaming.

Damn it! She *would* use his own words against him! Nick grasped her upper arms. "I'm not that desperate," he said through gritted teeth. "Even if I'd been so inclined, there was hardly time. It hasn't been fifteen minutes since she came up. Hell," he muttered, releasing her, "at least give me credit for being a better lover than that."

Her face turned a brighter red. "I wouldn't know what kind of lover you are, Mr. Brannon. Nor would I know how long you require . . ." Audra's voice dropped off. It was none of his business what she knew or didn't know. "Frankly, I don't care either way. Only tell me how many more maids you've had your little trysts with. I'd just as soon dismiss them all at the same time."

Nick didn't know whether to laugh or curse. Rose was almost right. Audra *would* resemble a virginal princess, with that wonderful midnight hair against the pure white of her robe—the robe *he'd* bought for her, he noted with no small pleasure—if only her eyes weren't shooting blue sparks of fury at him.

But then he noticed something else. Behind that burning gaze of hers was a hint of . . . hurt.

She backed away when he stepped forward, but the only place to retreat was into her room. She stepped sideways, and came up against the wall. It was a mistake, for Nick effectively trapped her by placing his palms against the wall, one on either side of her head.

"Jealous?" he asked mildly.

Her mouth fell open, then snapped shut.

"There's no reason to be, sweetheart," he continued in the same smooth tone as he fingered the smooth lapel of her robe. "The last woman I touched intimately"—his gaze fell to where the robe parted, just above the curve of her bosom—"was you."

Her sharp gasp told him she remembered, too. Then she ducked under his arm, her hair and robe swirling madly as she spun about and fled into her room. The door slammed loudly behind her.

Audra had taken only two steps into the room when the door crashed open and hit the wall with a crack like thunder.

She spun about in alarm. Blazes! Why hadn't she locked it?

Nick stalked toward her, his eyes glittering dangerously. She retreated, step by step, trying to keep a safe distance between them. He advanced.

The back of her knees hit the bed. She collapsed upon it, staring up at him in trepidation, but an instant later, he'd put his hands on her waist and hauled her to her feet again. Or rather—off her feet, she realized as her toes scrabbled for a foothold and failed to find one.

Her breasts flattened against his unyielding chest, the heat of his groin pressed against her belly. Through the thin fabric of their robes, she felt his masculinity. It occurred to her that Nick wasn't wearing anything under his robe. Audra's stomach fluttered. She suddenly felt weak as a kitten. She couldn't have moved if she'd tried.

Amber eyes stared down at her. Helpless, she stared back.

"I wasn't finished. There's something else I wanted to clarify," Nick said softly. "The next woman I touch will also be you. And just to make it perfectly clear . . ."

She'd expected his mouth to be harsh, but he was surprisingly gentle. Unlike his kisses in the stable, he demanded nothing, took nothing. His lips, slanting over hers, nibbling on her bottom lip, were only sweet promise. And unexpectedly, the longer he kissed her, the more she wanted it to go on.

Her mind whirled with confused thoughts, confused feelings. What was happening to her? Why did she feel as if her blood was singing? As if she were melting?

All too soon, he set her on her feet. It was a good thing the bed was just behind her, for her knees refused to hold her up, and Audra found herself sitting on the bed, dazed, her trembling fingers over her mouth, watching as Nick walked to the door.

Just as he got to it, he glanced back. "One other thing, sweet . . . Don't ever make the mistake of confusing me with my uncle again." His voice was deceptively soft.

A slow flush began to creep into her cheeks. Finally, for the first time since he'd entered her bedroom, Audra found her voice. "I think," she whispered, "that I hate you, Nickolas Brannon."

He grinned at that. "Only think? That's an improvement."

Her head jerked up. "What's that supposed to mean?"

His teeth flashed again. "Give it some thought, sweetheart. It'll come to you." And with those enigmatic words, he closed the door softly behind him.

She did hate him! She *did,* Audra vowed as she kicked her slippers into oblivion and climbed into bed to punch her pillows ruthlessly. He made her feel weak and helpless, and . . . and other things—things she didn't want to feel. Like excitement, and yearning for something . . .

Audra gave her pillow one last jab. Maybe she didn't exactly hate him, after all. And perhaps she *had* overreacted, for she believed him when he'd said he hadn't touched Rose. Somehow, she knew that he wouldn't lie to her.

Oh, what if he had? Why did she even care whom he took to bed?

But if he thought it was going to be *her*—as he'd so boldly hinted—he was badly mistaken. Just let him try!

Chapter 9

$\mathcal{N}$ick glanced up from his late breakfast to see Audra standing in the open doorway. "Good morning," he greeted cheerfully.

Audra mumbled something that sounded suspiciously like "that's what you think" before seating herself and absently pouring a cup of coffee instead of her usual tea. Pointedly ignoring him, she then proceeded to spread jam on a piece of toasted bread.

Nick watched for a while. "Is that all you're going to have?" he finally asked.

"Not hungry," she mumbled, refusing to meet his gaze.

"Still in a snit, I see."

That brought her head up. She glared at him. "I am *not* in a snit!"

"Perhaps you'll feel better after I've introduced you to a friend of mine."

That caught her attention. She wasn't aware that he'd brought anyone home with him the previous night. But she wasn't about to admit to curiosity, so she feigned disinterest. "No, thank you," she said coolly as she licked jam off her fingers. "I don't think I care to meet any of *your* friends."

She looked up in alarm as Nick scraped his chair back noisily. Her eyes widened as he stalked toward her. The toast fell to the table as he took her arm and pulled her out of her chair, past a wide-eyed Letty and to the front entrance.

Audra gasped and attempted to pull away. "What are you doing? Where are you taking me? Let go of me this instant, do you hear me, Nick Brannon?"

"Yes, I hear you. *Everyone* can hear you," he pointed out. "Nonetheless, you're coming with me. Now . . . will it be peaceably?"

"No!" she muttered resentfully, rubbing her arm. "You could try asking me nicely. . . . Oh!"

"Hell! Here we go again," Nick muttered as he bent to wrap his arm about her knees. "It seems there's only one way to get you to obey." She was up and over his shoulder before she'd had time to take another breath, and by the time she did manage to pull air into her lungs, they were out the front door and down the steps and Nick was striding toward the stables. With her stomach pressed onto his shoulder, she managed to mumble, just loud enough for him to hear, "Of course. Where else would a friend of yours be but in the stable?" She earned a light tap on her bottom for that remark, and decided it might be best not to make another. Just yet.

He carried her to the door of the stable, then stopped. Just as she was going to ask him—nicely, of course—to put her down, he spoke. "Is the lady inside, Rafe?" he asked.

Lady? What lady? "I should have known," Audra groused. "Another of your many women. It doesn't surprise me that she prefers the stables. . . ."

A quick peek around him showed her that Rafe was grinning, apparently not in the least surprised to see her lying over Nick's shoulder. "Yup," he told Nick. "I've given her a good rubdown. She settled right in. Knew she was where she belonged." Rafe chuckled. "Can't say the same for that devil Ulysses. The minute I brought her in, he started sniffin' and snortin'. He's a little excited."

"Who can blame him? Well, bring her out."

Audra craned her neck around for another peek, but Nick turned about just far enough to keep her facing backward. When she twisted the other way, he shifted again. "Keep still!" he ordered. "One more move out of you, and I'll put you over my knee."

"You wouldn't dare!"

"Oh, wouldn't I?"

She sputtered helplessly, but finally gave in, feeling silly perched on his shoulder.

But shortly, he bent forward and slid her down his shoulder and arm so that she was finally on her feet facing him, her back to the stable. His hands on her shoulders kept her immobile. "Patience is not one of your virtues, is it, sweetheart?"

"I never claimed it was," she retorted, but she wasn't looking at him, and she didn't really hear what he'd called her, for over his shoulder, she saw McKee and Bertie coming from the house. And they were both wearing the silliest grins. "What . . . ?"

"If you look right now, you won't have to wait any longer," Nick said as he turned her about.

Audra's look of puzzlement was replaced by incredulity. And then, her face was illuminated with joy.

"Fantasy's Lady!" she cried. Pulling free from Nick, she ran to the mare. "Oh, Fantasy. It really *is* you!" The mare whickered softly and blew into Audra's face.

Audra wrapped her arms around the horse and buried

her face in her warm neck. It was true! It really was her horse! And Fantasy hadn't forgotten her. Oh, blessed angels!

She clung tightly. Joy filled her heart. So much joy that she trembled with it. She couldn't seem to stop.

When at last she raised her head and stared wonderingly at Nick, tears were trickling down her cheeks. He was just standing there, watching her with a look of triumph on his face, his mouth curved in satisfaction.

Suddenly, for the first time in a long time, Audra felt lighthearted and gay. Throwing her head back, she laughed.

Nick stood transfixed. Those wonderful eyes of hers were misted, her cheeks were flushed with pleasure. It struck him that this was the first time he'd ever heard her laugh. Joyously. Rapturously.

An unexpected and invisible boot kicked him in the stomach, followed immediately by a feeling of tenderness so overwhelming his knees actually quaked. And in that moment, as he stared at Audra's laughing face, he knew that he was lost. Completely, for his heart simply . . . melted.

God, but she was beautiful! And God, he wanted to be the one to give her more laughter! For him . . . with him . . . at him. It didn't matter. If it took him all his life, he desperately wanted to give her joy for all of hers!

Walking on weak legs, he went to take the mare's bridle from her hand. "Which would you prefer . . . a ride, or finishing your breakfast?" he asked, surprised that he had his voice at all.

Her smile grew even more beatific. "The ride, of course!" she breathed eagerly. "I'm dying to. No, wait!" She stopped him as he was about to take the saddle Rafe had just brought. "Just give me a hand up and I'll ride her barebacked."

Nick raised his brows. "Astride?"

Her peal of merriment shook him to the very soles of his boots. Praying she wouldn't feel his hands trembling, he placed them about her waist and lifted her onto Fantasy.

"I've been riding astride almost all my life. Father wouldn't let me use a saddle in the beginning. He said I had to learn the feel of a horse, first."

"Very wise of him. Rafe, bring Ulysses out . . . unsaddled." Nick saw that Audra was barely restraining herself. "Go ahead," he said gently. "I daresay I'll catch you before you get too far."

Laughing again, Audra wheeled Fantasy about and used her knees to prod the mare's sides. Fantasy needed no further urging. She knew this human on her back. Tossing her head, she took off immediately.

Nick leaped onto Ulysses and they immediately raced after the receding figures. It took only a few moments to catch them; the stallion seemed as eager to get near the mare as Nick was to get to Audra.

He came alongside and she turned her head to flash another smile at him before she urged Fantasy on.

Nick took note of her flushed cheeks and the glow in her eyes, and rejoiced. He'd had no idea if he would be able to find Audra's mare; he'd known only that he had to go to London and try. With Peter's help, he and McKee discovered that William had kept a mistress in London, and so Nick had taken a chance that the horse had gone to her. He'd gone to her house, only to learn that the woman had unexpectedly left for Paris immediately after William's death, leaving behind confusion and an angry, bitter brother. After questioning the man, Nick was convinced that Lord Cowan's money had gone with her. Fortunately for him, however, the woman had left Audra's mare behind, and the brother was only too happy to sell her back to Nick—for a much more substantial sum than she was worth.

Now, watching Audra, Nick knew he would have gladly paid a hundred times the amount to see her this happy.

They reined the horses in alongside a stream finally, and Nick lifted Audra down. The horses found sweet grass to nibble on while Nick led Audra to the shade of a large oak.

Audra had almost been loath to dismount. She couldn't remember ever feeling so free. The warm sun on her face, the wind blowing through her hair, had given her an exhilaration she'd sorely missed.

She sat with her legs crossed under her skirt. "You can't believe how wonderful this is. Except for my ride on Ulysses, it's been over two years since I've ridden." She looked away suddenly, her cheeks burning. "Thank you, Nick. Not only for Fantasy, but for . . . for . . ." She halted, stammering.

"I'm only trying to return what was yours, Audra."

Audra frowned. Her fingers nervously tore apart stems of grass. "I can accept Fantasy's Lady, then, for William had no right to sell her. But the clothes . . ."

"Audra," Nick said with careful patience, "the clothes are nothing. You and your mother are now my responsibility. No . . . don't say a word, for I can already see the storm clouds building in your eyes. If it makes you feel easier, consider the clothes my birthday gift to you."

She glanced up in surprise. "Who told you?"

"McKee, of course. If I'd known sooner, we would have had a celebration."

She waved a hand dismissively. "No matter. I no longer celebrate birthdays. Too many horrible things have happened. . . ." She broke off. "Besides, Mrs. Murphy baked a cake and there were small gifts. We just didn't tell anyone. . . ." She shrugged. "I was still 'Agnes,' after all."

Nick sighed. This learning of patience was a struggle. Was she ever going to trust him fully? "I only want to make things better for you and your mother," he told her quietly, "and to return what my uncle took from you."

"Can you return my mother's health?" she countered quickly.

"No," he replied honestly. "But I *can* make her very comfortable. And I can help you make her smile again. I am *not* William! If you'd let yourself know me, you might discover that for yourself."

Audra glanced at him and frowned. "What do you mean?"

"You refuse to let yourself trust me. You test me constantly. I realize you think you have good reason, but can't you bring yourself to at least give me a chance? I'm not trying to win your trust with gifts, Audra. Anything I may choose to give you is given freely, without expectation. To believe otherwise is to insult me."

She stared at him. "Oh! I'm sorry. I never meant . . . I never thought of it that way."

"You'll always look at me as an interloper, won't you?" he finally asked quietly as he stared at the fields. "I suppose I can't blame you. Other than a legal one, I have no claim here."

There was only silence beside him.

"Perhaps I've asked too much of you," he continued smoothly. "You believe that, as a Brannon, I'm not deserving of your trust, don't you?"

Audra's head flew up. How did he *know*? She sighed. It was difficult, this giving of trust. But in all fairness, he deserved a chance. She leaned forward and touched his sleeve. It was a tentative touch, but the first voluntary one she'd given him.

Nick glanced down. She was staring up at him, her gaze open and earnest. "Please understand. It's been difficult, and Mother's been so unhappy. . . ." Audra fell silent as she considered.

Her mother. Nick ached for what Audra must have gone through herself, yet she hadn't spoken of her own unhappiness, only of her mother's. "Try," he said softly. "I won't rush you, but I'd like for you to try. I promise I'm worth your trust." He *wouldn't* rush her, but he wanted her trust so damn bad it hurt. Still, he kept his tone neutral. "That's all I ask."

"I will try," Audra promised. "When you first came, I was convinced you would be another William. I apologize again. I had no right to judge you on another's merits, or lack of them."

Until this moment, Nick didn't realize he'd been holding his breath. It was a small victory, but it was a beginning. "Thank you. I can't tell you how much those words mean to me. Now . . . I think it's time we get back, don't you?"

They were silent as they remounted and turned the horses back toward the Manor. Nick could see that Audra was deep in thought. Finally, just when he'd decided she wasn't going to speak at all, she lifted her head and gave him another of those radiant smiles. "If I must learn to trust you, then I should know more about you, don't you think?" she said impishly. "I know you're American by birth, but your father was English. I know that you're . . . wealthy, unmarried . . ." Her voice fell off. She wouldn't bring Delia up, or ask him about the woman called Brenda. She *wouldn't*! "There's not much else I really know about you, is there?" she finished lamely.

Nick wanted to shout with joy. It was the first time she'd ever expressed any interest in him. That she was aware of him as a man, he already knew. But she was wary of that knowledge, confused. He had no doubt that he could seduce her. But he didn't want only that. He wanted her heart, her soul forever entwined with his. He'd give her as much time as she needed.

And so he told her about his childhood and his love for the sea, learned from his American grandfather. About Alex Benedict, and what they had built together.

"At the present time we're expanding our railroad lines into the mountains, and developing mining claims. It won't be long before the territory of Colorado receives statehood. Its potential has barely been scratched. Denver City is located practically in the center of the United States, and someday it will be an important business center. Right now, we're headquartered in Central City, and probably will be for a few more years."

"Tell me what it's like."

"It's beautiful, Audra. Tremendous, wondrous mountains, such as you've never seen. Cold, crystal-clear rushing streams and green meadows filled with wildflowers of every hue. We have a ranch in the foothills. It's one of my favorite places. I only wish . . ."

"What?"

He gave her a whimsical smile. "I'd like to have someone to enjoy it with. Sometimes, it seems I'm building an empire for nothing."

"But family, Nick? Don't you have any family left?"

"I have a sister. Cleo is ten years younger. She's married to a minor noble, and they live in Yorkshire. I see her whenever I come to England, but it's never long enough." He tilted his head and gave her a considering look. "I think you'd like one another."

"Is she anything like you?"

"Much prettier."

Audra's laugh pealed out. But she sobered quickly, and her glance skittered away. "You're really *not* like William, you know. You're . . ." She hesitated, then lifted her face to look him steadily in the eyes. "I owe you more than a promise to try to trust you, Nick." She rushed on, before her courage deserted her. "I haven't been very kind to you, and at times I've even been abominably rude. It's not the way I was brought up, and I ask your forgiveness." The sober look left her face and was replaced by mischief. "I certainly haven't shown you any of the ladylike manners my mother taught me, have I?"

Nick threw back his head and laughed. Eyes crinkling, he looked at her, and immediately another roar of laughter came forth. Audra looked at him, perplexed.

"Well, really!" she finally said in vexation. "Here I am, attempting nicely to apologize to you, and you're laughing at me."

"Sorry," he choked out, and made an effort to control himself. "It was just that your remark about being ladylike . . ." His gaze traveled meaningfully to her legs.

Audra looked down. Oh, Lord! Here she was, trying to convince him of her "ladylike manners" and her skirt was riding up over her knees, showing a shocking length of white-stockinged leg. Chagrined, she attempted to regain her modesty, but found it difficult in her present position. She couldn't pull her skirts down without pulling the fabric out from under her buttocks and the only way she could do that was to repeatedly bounce up and down on Fantasy.

She glanced at Nick in embarrassment. He was desperately attempting to restrain his laughter. Finally, she gave up and stopped bouncing. Meeting his gaze, she joined his laughter.

"Well, I *try* to be ladylike. I must admit, Mother had to give in and let me wear breeches when I rode astride. She agreed that it was more modest than skirts. Obviously, she was right."

"No! I'm truly shocked, Miss Sheffield! A lady wearing breeches! In England!"

She frowned at him. "Why do you say it like that? Do women in America wear breeches?"

"Some do. Particularly in the territories. You'd be surprised how much more freedom our American women have. I can see that the riding habit won't do. It won't allow you to ride astride."

"Oh, no, it's beautiful!" she hastened to correct. "I *do* have a sidesaddle, also, for those times when we're entertaining, or visiting. . . ." Her voice dropped off. "We haven't done much of that . . . not for a long time." She frowned.

He let that pass. "I have an idea about the riding habit. If you give it to me when we get back, I may be able to find a solution to the problem," he said just as they arrived back at the stables. He dismounted easily as Rafe appeared to take Ulysses' bridle. Walking to Audra, Nick raised his arms to help her down.

She sat on the horse, smiling at him and oblivious to the fact that Rafe was looking at every inch of her exposed legs. "Nick, it was glorious. How can I ever thank you?" She placed her hands on his shoulders as he lifted her off Fantasy. He held her close, her feet dangling above the ground.

Ignoring Rafe, Nick grinned at her wickedly. His voice was so low, only the two of them could hear. "I'll think about it. There must be *some* way you can show your gratitude."

"I . . ."

"Not what you're thinking," he added swiftly. "My intentions are strictly honorable."

Her brain refused to come up with an appropriate reply. He was teasing her, surely. Of course he was. Averting her gaze, she glanced frantically about and saw that Rafe was watching them. She began to struggle, and hissed, "Put me down! What will Rafe think?"

"He can think whatever he damn well pleases. Certainly he's used to me by now." Nevertheless, he finally set her on her feet.

Audra winced as her muscles protested. Nick was immediately alert to her distress, and gave her a hand. "You may change your mind about thanking me and curse me instead in a few hours. We shouldn't have ridden so long. I daresay you'll be stiff and sore for the next day or two."

Gingerly, Audra tried her legs. Her buttocks and thighs ached, but she was still too elated to complain. "You forget. I rode Ulysses the other night. Besides, I don't care. It was worth every ache." Turning to Fantasy, Audra gave the mare an appreciative pat. "I'll see you tomorrow, you lovely girl, you."

But she was stiffer than she thought, so they walked to the Manor slowly in deference to her muscles. She didn't even think of protesting when Nick's arm came around her waist, but leaned against him gratefully. But as she was about to mount the stairs, Nick's arm tightened around her. Surprised, she glanced up at him.

"If I beg nicely, do you think that you could force yourself to wear one of your new gowns to dinner tonight?" he asked.

She could tell by the gleam in his eyes that his words had been meant to tease, not censure. Suddenly forgetting her aches, she skipped up the steps and turned to face him. "Well," she drawled thoughtfully, "I'll have to check with 'Agnes' first. She may not want to part with any of them."

And with that, Audra entered the Manor with the pleasant sound of Nick's rich laughter following her.

Chapter 10

"Mother, you look positively beautiful!"

Serena looked, in fact, almost as she had in earlier days, when she'd been married to Edward. She was wearing a new gown, one of those Nick had given her. The soft rose flattered her fairness. Bertie had washed and brushed her hair to a gloss, then pinned it up. Serena's cheeks were flushed and her eyes bright with excitement, for Dr. Hargrove had finally given permission for her to have dinner downstairs.

"Thank you, dear. You look lovely yourself."

Audra blushed, for she, too, was wearing one of Nick's gifts. The decision to do so had made her giddy with delight. New clothes! No more drab, maid's dress! No more outdated clothing that was either threadbare, too small, too girlish—or all three!

Nick carried Serena downstairs for dinner, which became the most pleasant one the Manor had seen in years. Conversation and laughter filled the dining room. Sitting at Nick's right, Audra couldn't seem to stop smiling. It was wonderful to throw aside all pretensions and just be herself again!

After dinner, the entire party adjourned to the drawing room. Serena was allowed one cup of coffee, and she sipped it slowly, savoring it, while the others conversed.

Audra, still basking in happiness, was oblivious to how carefully Nick was observing her mother until he suddenly got to his feet, took the cup and saucer from Serena, and lifted her into his arms. "Time for bed, Mrs. Brannon," he told her gently. Audra glanced at her mother and saw that, indeed, her eyelids were drooping. For the first time, she recognized that Nick's thoughtfulness went much deeper than mere courtesy.

He was, she realized, a kind man. And she was immediately awash in shame. He was right. She hadn't given him a chance.

She blinked as Nick stopped before her. "I'd like to speak to you when I return in a few minutes. In the library." Audra nodded.

Nick carefully placed Serena onto her bed. "May I say, Mrs. Brannon, that you look ravishing tonight?" he said, grinning.

Serena smiled. "As ravishing as my daughter?" she asked.

Nick glanced at the picture of Audra that had mysteriously reappeared in its proper place on Serena's bedside table, then back at Serena. He appeared perplexed at how to answer her question, so she took pity on him. "You're not required to answer that, you know. It's quite obvious to me that you're very . . . intrigued by my daughter," she said, laughing.

Nick gave her a wry look. "And I thought I was being

so circumspect, so cautious and very careful not to . . ." He hesitated.

"Frighten her off," Serena finished for him. "She's very vulnerable right now. My fault, of course. I made a ghastly mistake when I married William. And once we were married, he was always so *angry*. He was particularly disappointed that I couldn't give him a son. Audra and I both paid a terrible price for it." She sighed deeply. "And my poor daughter is still paying." She glanced at Nick. "There's something I should explain. Something that Audra doesn't even know. The only person I've told is McKee. And now, you."

"Serena . . . if you'd rather not . . ." Nick took her hand gently.

"But I do." She took a deep breath. "I would never, never have freely signed away Audra's birthright. But William called me into the study, almost before the ink was dry on our marriage papers. Silas Norton was there, also. And William told me . . ." She hesitated, until Nick squeezed her hand reassuringly. "William told me that if I didn't sign all the property over to him, he would marry Audra off—after he gave her to Silas Norton." Serena's eyes filled with tears. "Norton sat there, with this sly, gloating expression on his face. . . ." Serena shuddered delicately, and Nick could see that it took effort for her to continue. "I reminded William that Audra was barely seventeen, but he said that it didn't matter . . . that she was old enough to keep a man's bed warm. He said other things, too. Even cruder and uglier. It made me ill. But I had no one to send her to. No one to protect her, so I signed. I gave everything to William, and I've been worried since that I still failed." Serena smiled softly at Nick. "But I don't have to worry now, do I?"

"Not," Nick said with complete sincerity, "if I have anything to say about it."

"You have only to be patient, and give her time, Nick. She's stronger than ever I was. She'll recover, for I've already seen the signs. Turn your hands over."

Baffled, Nick presented his palms. Serena studied them carefully. "They're strong and sturdy . . . not afraid of labor, yet capable of gentleness. Not at all like William's, just as you aren't at all like him. Yes, Audra will be in good hands."

Nick reversed their grasp, holding Serena's hands gently. "I'll do my best. And I'll try to never hurt her."

"I believe you, Nick. Thank you. Now . . . if you wouldn't mind sending Bertie in . . ."

Arms wrapped around herself, Audra paced the library as she waited for Nick. There was a fire burning brightly in the hearth, but she ignored it.

This had once been her favorite room. She had spent hours sitting before the fire at her parents' feet. Her father would read aloud, while her mother sat in the small chintz chair, doing her needlework. It had been so pleasant, so peaceful.

Now Audra avoided being in the room alone. It was filled with too many ugly memories. Of William. Of that last day . . .

She'd never hated him so fiercely as she had then. She'd listened to her mother's screams as she'd struggled to birth his son, while William had closeted himself in this room and had not even bothered to ask anyone how his wife was. And when Dr. Hargrove had gone down in the late afternoon to tell him that his son was stillborn, William had become furious and had gotten even more inebriated. He'd raved and ranted, and had called her mother worthless. . . .

"Here you are."

Audra looked up to see that Nick was just entering the library. In his hand was a parcel, wrapped in brown paper.

"Why are you standing way over here?" he asked as he took her hand to lead her to the fire. Then he stopped and studied her. "Are you ill? Your hand is like ice."

"I'm feeling fine. Really. Just a little cold."

"We'll take care of that in a moment." Pulling her to the small chintz chair before the hearth, he urged her to sit. After setting his package on a table, he knelt at her feet to take her hands in his and chafed them slowly. "Would you like a brandy?"

"Ugh! No. I'm fine now. Really." And she was. Somehow, with Nick in the room, the bad memories had dimmed. Self-consciously, she pulled her hands free.

Nick studied her for a moment longer before getting to his feet. "Well, then. Do you mind if I have one?"

"Of course not. A smoke, too, if you like. I could never understand why men have to adjourn to a separate room for their drinks and cigars after dinner. I like the smell of tobacco." Then she laughed. "I've always wondered if they do what the women do."

"And what's that?"

"Why, gossip about the opposite gender, of course."

Nick joined in her laughter as he took his brandy and went to stand before the fire to light a cigar. She looked so damned beautiful tonight, wearing one of the gowns he'd picked for her—a deep blue one that matched her eyes and made her glow. He'd barely been able to keep his eyes off her all evening.

Still, when he'd entered the library, she'd seemed . . . haunted.

Whatever memories had upset her, he wished he could erase them from her mind. He wanted desperately to tell her that he could—would—give her new memories. Better memories. Wonderful, unforgettable memories. If only she would let him.

Patience, Nick. More patience, he reminded himself. He was a former naval officer, for God's sake. He knew when to advance, when to go in for the kill. And when to retreat.

Resting one elbow on the mantel, he said, "I wanted to tell you that I'll be going back to London in a few days."

"Oh. I was hoping . . ."

"What?"

"I thought I'd go riding with you in the mornings. If you'd like, of course," she replied hesitantly, but her eyes were filled with eagerness.

Nick smiled. "I'd like. Very much. Which reminds me . . ." Swallowing the brandy in one gulp, he set the snifter on the mantel and came back to her. "I have something for you." He retrieved the package and ripped it open to reveal her riding skirt. "Stand up," he ordered.

Puzzled, Audra did as commanded. He held the skirt to her waist. "Ah, yes. This should do nicely. What do you think?"

Audra looked down and saw the seam down the front. Taking the skirt from his hands, she examined it carefully. "Nick! How clever! It separates, almost like trousers."

He chuckled. "I had a little trouble communicating my wishes to the village seamstress, and even after she understood what I wanted, she kept shaking her head in perplexity." He didn't add that he'd practically stood over the woman for the two hours it had taken her to do the work.

Audra laughed. "It's wonderful. I'll have to show Mother. She'll be grateful to you for making it possible for me to ride in a more ladylike manner."

Nick joined in her laughter. God, but when she laughed like that, it was damned difficult to keep his hands off her! He wanted to grab her and hug her tightly.

Actually, he wanted to do more, much more, but he would have settled for a hug.

"Incidentally, I neglected to tell you that you look lovely in that gown."

She'd already seen the approval mirrored in his eyes as she had come down the stairs for dinner, but it was nice to have him say it. "Thank you. You'd make an excellent modiste," Audra teased as she folded the skirt. "Not only do you know about the sewing of women's garments, you seem to have an unusually accurate eye for sizing." She peeked at him from under her lashes.

The minx was teasing him. "Hm . . ." Nick looked her up and down thoughtfully. "I do at that. I also have a very good memory," he added. Her pink cheeks told him that she knew very well that he was referring to the night at the inn.

Caught in a trap of her own making, Audra was vexed enough to fight back. "Hm . . ." She pursed her lips and mimicked his actions, deliberately scanning him as he had her. "But your memory isn't as perfect as you believe, for as I recall, it was you who left the most indelible memory," she retorted.

At her reminder that he'd been buck naked, Nick had to laugh. "Touché. In future, I'll only try to remember that your tongue is as quick and sharp as a rapier."

"And I'll remember that you've had considerable practice—discerning women's shapes and sizes, that is."

"Ah, but I've had more than one occasion to hold you in my arms. If I remember correctly, it was you who so obligingly threw yourself at me the first moment I arrived at Sheffield."

Audra gasped in indignation, and brought their parrying to a sudden end. "I most certainly did not throw myself at you. I had no idea you were even behind that door."

He gave her a wicked grin. "You're forgiven for slamming into me and almost knocking me off my feet, but only if you pay your debts to date."

"What debts?"

Nick shook his head mournfully. "Ah, how fast women forget! Let's see . . ." He ticked them off on his fingers. "There's the penalty for the night you rode Ulysses. Your promised payment for your ride today. The skirt. Did I mention that I'd find a suitable manner of compensation?"

"Oh. I'd forgotten." She looked at him suspiciously. "What payment are you asking?"

He pretended to consider carefully before he finally replied. "I'll accept a good-night kiss. Fair, don't you think?"

The memory of his other kisses burned in her mind. She couldn't—wouldn't—kiss him like that! However, she thought perhaps there were kisses and then there were kisses. . . .

Restraining her smile, she moved to stand in front of him. He was so tall! How was she going to manage this?

"Lean over," she ordered.

"I beg your pardon?"

"Bend. I can't reach you from here."

Taken by surprise, he lowered his head. She still had to stand on tiptoe and grasp his shoulders to keep her balance. Shyly, she pressed her lips to his cheek, then quickly removed her hands and tried to step back.

Only then did she realize that his arms were about her waist. Now they tightened. "Oh, no, you don't," he warned. "Since I hold the debt, I claim the right to accept or refuse the worth of payment. That so-called *kiss*, my sweet, was not sufficient."

She had no chance to protest as he pulled her closer. She had no time to wonder at the sudden exhilaration leaping through her veins as she felt his warmth and his strength. She had no time to breathe before his lips came over hers.

One of his hands slid up her back and under the fall of her hair to grasp her nape. The other circled her slim waist so tightly she thought her ribs would crack.

Then she forgot everything but the sensation of his warm, moist mouth on hers. His lips moved slowly, languorously, as if savoring her flavor before leaving to advance along her cheek, touch the corner of an eye, follow the length of her throat. He advanced again, his teeth nibbling on the lobe of her ear, causing a shiver of pleasant anticipation to go through her. Just as she was beginning to enjoy the sensation, his mouth came back to hers. This time, it was more urgent. Demanding. She made a small sound of protest, and his lips softened again. His teeth grazed her lower lip just before the tip of his tongue followed its contour.

It was shocking. It was thrilling. It left Audra weak and breathless.

She hung limply in his arms, so that when he suddenly released her, she almost fell. He held her loosely, then reluctantly took his hands away and bent to retrieve the riding skirt, which had fallen, forgotten, to the floor between them.

Draping it over her arm, he said softly, "*That*, sweet, is a proper kiss of payment. And now I think we'd better say good night, or I'll be sorely tempted to continue the lesson."

Still bemused, she made no objection when he took her arm, led her to the door, and gently pushed her into the hall. He was smiling as he closed the door behind her.

Audra leaned against it weakly. Good heavens! Just how many ways were there to kiss?

She made her way up the stairs dreamily. By the time she reached her room, she was smiling secretively. Perhaps she *would* need more lessons. It seemed she had a lot to learn, after all.

She was still smiling as she fell asleep thirty minutes later.

The following days passed in a haze of enjoyment for Audra. She and Nick breakfasted together early, and then went riding. In the evenings, they read to one another, played chess, or just spent the time in companionable conversation and laughter, particularly when Audra recounted numerous childhood escapades. Nick, in turn, told Audra more about his life in America.

Each night, Audra went to bed with a sense of peace and security. And best of all, her nightmares had ceased. It was a blessed relief.

At the end of a week, Nick had to leave. The morning dawned dark and dreary. The sun tried to break through the clouds, but as rain seemed imminent, he and Audra forsook their morning ride in order that he and Rafe get an early start to London. Nick didn't want to be caught on muddy or impassable roads.

Audra roamed the Manor restlessly after their departure, her spirits as low as the weather. Unaccountably, she felt lonely, and blamed it on the fact that McKee and Bertie had also left, having gone to the village. McKee would return with some supplies, but Bertie was planning on spending the night with an old friend.

She finally settled in Serena's room for a long visit before lunch, but once her mother dozed off, she was at loose ends again, so she threw her cloak on and wandered to the stables to waste away an hour or two with the horses. By late afternoon, it had turned unusually cold outside and rain was pouring down unrelentingly and noisily. Audra thought her mother might be up from her nap, so she got a book from the library and took it upstairs to read to her.

She pushed open her mother's door, and was surprised to feel a draft of cold air. Serena was still asleep in an armchair near the balcony doors. The rain had pelted in and had pooled in a small puddle at her feet. Audra rushed to close the doors, then shook Serena's shoulders gently, and was alarmed to see that the hem of her robe was damp.

Serena awakened groggily. "Audra. Good heavens, I was sleeping so soundly." Her voice was raspy.

"Mother, it's freezing in here. Let me help you to bed. Your gown is damp. I'll get a fresh one. For goodness' sake, why were your balcony doors open?"

Serena leaned against Audra as they slowly made their way to the bed. Serena had just begun to walk a bit in her room each day, but her strength was still poor.

"Oh, dear, were they still open? I opened them just a little after lunch—you know how I like to watch the rain, but I fell asleep. The wind must have blown them . . . Ah-*choo!* . . . wider."

"I can't believe the thunder didn't wake you," Audra said as she helped Serena out of her gown. "And where were the maids?" she muttered as she dried Serena's feet with a towel. "If they'd been doing their duties, one of them should have been up here to close the doors when the rain started."

Audra bundled Serena in a blanket and dashed to the bellpull and yanked on it. Then she rummaged through Serena's bureau until she found a warm flannel nightgown. She pulled it over Serena's head just as Letty entered the room.

Audra quickly gave instructions to stoke up the fire and bring something for Serena's feet, and Letty rushed to comply. "How do you feel now, Mother?" she asked as she tucked Serena under the covers. "Are you warmer?"

"Yes, I feel . . ." Her voice broke as she coughed. "I do feel warmer now, dear."

Audra placed her palm on Serena's cheek. She did feel warm. Too warm, or was it only her worried imagination?

Letty returned with a heated brick wrapped in cloths. Audra placed it under the covers, against Serena's feet. Sending Letty downstairs for hot tea, she sat on the bed and took Serena's hand. Thankfully, she didn't cough again, but she seemed very tired, even though she'd just napped. Audra coaxed her to drink the tea, which was laced with lemon juice and honey, then sat beside the bed while Serena dozed off again. When Letty peeked in again an hour later, Audra was satisfied that Serena was sleeping peacefully, and her skin felt no warmer.

Conferring in whispers, they agreed that one of them would stay with Serena throughout the rest of the day and the night. The rain, though desisting somewhat, was still coming down steadily. Audra fervently hoped it wouldn't get worse in case McKee had to fetch Dr. Hargrove.

But shortly after midnight, Serena awoke to a fit of uncontrollable coughing that wouldn't be soothed. McKee was roused and sent on his urgent mission.

It took him until the early hours of morning to return with the doctor and Bertie, whom he'd also roused and brought back. Audra and Letty had spent that time bathing Serena with cool, wet cloths, to no avail, and the struggle was turned over to Dr. Hargrove with relief.

Bertie coaxed Audra downstairs and into the drawing room, where Audra drank several cups of tea and spoke little, her eyes going to the door continuously as she awaited the doctor's verdict.

When he did finally did come down, he was blunt.

"Your mother is very, very ill. She has extreme congestion of the lungs. As you know, she has great difficulty breathing, and this is putting more strain on her heart."

"What can we do? There must be something we can do for her!"

"My dear, we are already doing it. I've given her some medication for the congestion, and a small amount of laudanum to help her sleep. We've moved her into a sitting position to help her breathe, and are still attempting to lower her temperature. We can only wait and see."

"She has to get better . . . she must!" Audra sank back into the chair, her hands over her face. "It came upon her so fast. She seemed to be fine when we put her to bed, except for a slight fever and cough."

"Audra, these things often come on suddenly. You did exactly what you should have done for her. The rest is up to me. I promise I'll do my best." He stood and patted her on the shoulder. "I have to get back upstairs now. You should get some rest."

"I can't rest, Doctor. And I'm coming up with you," she said firmly. "I need to be near her."

The hours dragged as she and Bertie and the doctor fought Serena's fever. For all that day, and into late morning of the next, they bathed her constantly and coaxed liquids down her throat, and yet Serena's fever continued. When she wasn't fitfully sleeping, she was racked with violent coughing spasms.

The three watching over her took turns resting for short periods and nourishing their own bodies, and by the end of that second day, they were all exhausted. But the fever had finally gone down a bit, and Serena seemed to be resting better; even her breathing was less labored.

Audra sat beside the bed, watching her mother as she slept. She looked up at Bertie and Dr. Hargrove, who were standing on the other side of Serena's bed. "She seems to be sleeping more peacefully. She'll be all right now, won't she?" She leaned over Serena to gently brush back a stray lock of hair, and didn't see the look exchanged by the other two.

Bertie came around the bed and coaxed Audra out of the chair. "We're going downstairs," she said firmly. "It's been hours since you've had anything to eat. Come, love. Your mother would be upset if she knew you weren't taking care of yourself."

Now that Serena seemed to be sleeping peacefully, Audra let herself be led downstairs and into the drawing room. Within a short time, Letty appeared with a full tray. "Mrs. Murphy said you're to eat everything," she announced primly. Audra smiled weakly. She still wasn't hungry, but she nibbled slowly and drank several cups of tea. Bertie sat watching quietly, until Audra's lids finally began to droop. Within a few minutes, Audra's head fell back against the chair and she was asleep.

Bertie carefully removed the empty cup and saucer from Audra's lap. Gently, she brushed a strand of glossy hair from the pale cheek. Her heart overflowed with pity for the young woman. She'd borne so much, and it wasn't yet finished. How much more could she bear?

Bertie gave strict orders that there should be no noise, no chatter, for she knew Audra would need all the rest she could get. The servants went about their duties speaking in hushed whispers, and tiptoed as they passed the drawing room door.

Chapter 11

$\mathcal{N}$ick was tired and hungry, and glad to be back. In London, he'd sent Alex a long cable regarding some business matters, and had held meetings with business associates. Finally, he'd worked with Peter for twenty hours straight clearing up paperwork in his eagerness to get back to Sheffield Manor and Audra.

He entered the house, and was immediately struck by the pall of silence and gloom.

McKee and Bertie were standing at the bottom of the stairs, speaking together in low tones. They both turned as he stepped inside, and waited until he came to them.

"It's Serena," Bertie told him without preamble in response to the alarmed inquiry on his face. "She's taken ill. Her heart becomes weaker by the hour. Dr. Hargrove has said that it's only a matter of time."

"Audra . . . ?"

"Doesn't yet realize. She's convinced that her mother will recover. She's asleep in the drawing room. She's had almost no rest for these three days. . . ."

There was a sound on the stairs. All three turned their gazes upon Dr. Hargrove, who had just appeared at the top. He paused when he saw them, then shook his head sadly as he started down.

Audra awoke with a start and jumped out of her chair. She hadn't meant to fall asleep, but some strange urgency had awakened her. She needed to get back to her mother *now*.

Still groggy, she walked unsteadily to the door and stepped into the hallway. She stopped short, for Nick, Bertie, and McKee were all standing at the foot of the stairs. She must have made some small sound, for, as one, they all turned. Their faces wore expressions of shock that, when they saw her, turned to dismay. No one said a word. It all appeared to her like some unreal, frozen tableau.

Someone was coming down the stairs, and when she glanced up she saw that it was Dr. Hargrove. Her heart started pounding erratically. He was looking directly at her, and in his face, she read pity and sorrow. And suddenly she knew.

"No!" she moaned as she shook her head in denial. "No!" she screamed, and lifting her skirts, she raced past the other three before they could react. The doctor put out a hand to stop her as she neared him, but she batted it away and slipped around him.

Nick suddenly came to life and went after her. She was over half the way up by the time he got close and reached out to seize her, but she jerked away and continued up the stairs. "Audra . . ." He caught hold of her skirts.

"No! Let me go!" She tripped and fell to her knees, tried to scramble up and fell again as her skirts tangled about her legs. She clawed at the fabric wildly until she freed herself and leaped up again. She'd gained only two more steps before Nick's arm came around her waist and lifted her off her feet.

"Audra!"

"Let me go! Let me go, damn you! You can't keep me from her!"

She squirmed and kicked until he lost his footing and they both went down. Still he wouldn't release her. Entwined, they slid down several steps as she continued to struggle savagely, silently, her arms flailing, her breathing harsh, deep gasps, her eyes wild.

He ignored the stinging blows and finally managed to pin her down by pulling her beneath him and lying over her. "Audra! Listen to me! Please, sweetheart . . . !"

She squeezed her lids tightly and covered her ears with her hands. Her hair had come unbound and flew wildly about as she thrashed her head from side to side. "No no no no. *No!*"

Slowly, inexorably, he forced her hands away and pinned them between their bodies. He slid his fingers into her hair and cradled her face in his hands, raising it to mere inches from his.

"Audra, look at me!" he said forcefully.

She began to tremble uncontrollably. He kept repeating her name softly, but firmly.

Finally, she slowly raised her lids. Her gaze, haunted and dark, met his. "This isn't . . . one of my . . . my nightmares?" she asked, her voice hoarse, a whisper of sound so tiny, he had to almost press his ear to her mouth to hear it.

He didn't know what she meant by that; he was only relieved to see recognition in her eyes again.

"No," he said hoarsely. "She's gone. I am so sorry, my love, but your mother is gone."

She flinched, but said nothing. She only continued to gaze at him helplessly, her eyes pleading.

Gently, he smoothed the hair back from her face. Carefully, so carefully, he raised himself off her and lifted her into his arms. Still trembling, she folded into herself, curled against his chest, pressed her face into his shirt-front, and began to cry.

Everyone else was forgotten as Nick carried her up the stairs and into her room. Kicking the door shut behind him, he made straight for the armchair and sat down with her in his lap.

"Go on, sweetheart. Cry it all out. God knows it's past time." He held her pressed tightly to his chest as she sobbed, wishing there was some way to take her pain onto himself. Silently, he cursed the fates for not sparing her this, he cursed his uncle for all the past sorrow that had culminated in this, and he cursed himself for not being able to prevent any of it. She'd deserved none of it. Only a few days ago, she had been so gloriously happy. . . .

He didn't know—didn't care—how long it was before Audra's sobs finally quieted as she exhausted herself with her weeping. Her body ceased to be racked by shudders and became still. Nick lifted her chin slightly and saw that she was almost asleep. Yet her hands still clutched at his now-wet shirt.

He carried her to her bed, but as he gently set her down upon it, she wouldn't release him.

Her lashes flickered. "Nick, please stay. Please. Don't leave me alone. It hurts so to be alone." Her voice was ragged and low.

He bent over her. "I won't leave you, little one. I'm here and I'll stay as long as you want," he promised, his own voice husky with emotion.

Sighing, she released her hold on him and, turning her head into the pillow, closed her eyes.

Nick watched for several minutes. Finally satisfied that she was deeply asleep, he removed her slippers, folded the covers over her, and smoothed the tangled hair away from her face.

When he quietly exited the room, he wasn't at all surprised to find Bertie sitting in a chair next to Audra's door, quietly weeping. She composed herself when she saw Nick.

They spoke in undertones.

"She's asleep after crying herself into exhaustion. Thank God I returned when I did." Wearily, he rubbed his jaw. "I've promised to stay with her. Serena . . . ?"

"I'll see to it. Do you need anything?"

"Hot coffee now. A tray at dinnertime."

"I'll do it myself," Bertie promised.

Nick reentered Audra's room. He moved the chair close to the bed and sat down. Bending over the still figure, he dried her damp cheeks with his handkerchief and arranged her long tresses over the pillow. She'd been hurt so many times and in so many ways, but by God, he would see to it that it would never happen again! He couldn't bring Serena back. He couldn't return the years William had taken from her. But somehow . . . somehow . . . he would give her new memories and, if she would only accept it, love.

From the time he'd first looked into her eyes, even with that grubby little face, she'd touched him in some way. And with each new thing he learned about her, each hour he spent with her, it only intensified.

He'd never loved a woman before . . . hadn't been prepared for how powerful an emotion it was. Now he was terrified that Serena's death would destroy all he'd gained.

But as he sat watching Audra sleep, the compassion on his face was replaced by grim determination. Success had been within reach. Nick knew that he'd start over if he had to, because he was determined that she'd still be his—

in all ways. He wanted her body, but more than that, he wanted her heart.

The same heart that had just been broken again.

Serena was laid to rest next to Audra's father in the family cemetery on a small knoll next to the woods behind the house.

It all passed in a haze to Audra. She was only vaguely aware that there were many people present, that Bertie and McKee flanked her on either side. The one solid, reassuring presence stood directly behind her, and she tried to focus on him. Nick was standing so close that she had only to lean back to have his strength support her. At one point, when she swayed slightly, he shifted closer to her and cupped her elbows in his hands, supporting her unobtrusively.

She closed her eyes tightly. She felt drained . . . empty. It didn't matter—she wasn't going to cry again. She didn't have any tears left.

It was over, then. She'd tried so hard to keep her mother safe, and she'd failed. She'd borne William's presence, borne the humiliations and indignities he'd heaped on her, borne his disgusting friends. It hadn't mattered. Her mother was gone.

Now there was no one left who was hers. Now she was alone.

Nick's face remained impassive throughout the service, but he was becoming angrier by the minute. It was plain to him that some of those who'd come had done so not out of respect, but out of curiosity. Two women even had the nerve to whisper to one another behind their black-gloved hands as they cast speculative glances toward him and the slim veiled figure in front of him.

Damned gossipy busybodies!

Thank God Audra didn't appear to be aware of their rudeness. But then, she hadn't seemed to be aware of much of anything these last two days.

He'd spent the night of Serena's death on the chair in Andra's room, and when she'd awakened the next day, she'd only whispered a thank-you and asked him to send Bertie in. He hadn't seen or spoken to her since. Except for one hour of solitude spent beside her mother's body, she had remained secluded in her room, and wouldn't allow anyone inside but Bertie.

Upon Bertie's announcement that Audra had deferred the making of the arrangements for the burial to him, herself, and McKee, the three of them had conferred and done so. The only request Audra had made was that her mother be dressed in the gown she'd worn to marry Edward.

Nick almost regretted the decision they'd made to hold a reception at the Manor after the service. But they'd all agreed that Serena should be accorded the respect that was due her.

Reverend Trewer concluded the service and issued the invitation for the mourners to adjourn to the Manor. Nick's frustration was compounded when one dowager tried to waylay Audra as they left. Bertie managed to intercept her while Nick successfully spirited Audra away, but the woman arrived at the Manor right on their heels, her black cape flapping like the wings of a bird of prey.

Once inside, Audra made straight for the stairs, but Nick's hand on her elbow kept her beside him as he gave Bates a quiet order, then led her directly into the study. There, he had her sit. "I told Bates to bring tea. You'll have it quietly, and without any interference. Once you've finished, we'll see to your guests."

He didn't know what response to expect, but hoped for some hint of emotion. He was disappointed, for Audra only looked about the room vaguely—as if it were unfamiliar—looked at him as if he were a stranger, and in a flat, emotionless voice, said, "They aren't my guests. They abandoned us after Mother married William. I don't want to see any of them."

"Audra, I know you were hurt by their defection, but these are your neighbors. You have to live with them. I'll not have them gossiping about you."

"What do I care? They've gossiped about us for these last few years. It means nothing to me. They can't hurt me anymore."

Nick sighed. This wasn't the time to point out that gossip could indeed hurt her. Or to tell her that he had no intention of letting nosy neighbors place another burden on her slim shoulders.

"Who are you, Audra?"

She blinked, as if coming out of some trance. "What?"

"Who are you?" he repeated implacably.

"I . . . I'm Audra. . . ." Finally divining his intent, she straightened her shoulders. "I'm Audra Emily Sheffield, daughter of Edward and Serena Sheffield," she said more confidently.

Nick crooked a finger under her chin and smiled in satisfaction. "Exactly. I'd be very disappointed if Audra Emily Sheffield, daughter of Edward and Serena Sheffield, cowered in the study while the vultures hovered outside."

Her mouth opened, then snapped shut, and she lowered her eyes. For one moment, he was afraid she'd cry, and he braced himself. If she did, he'd be lost.

But when she lifted her face to him again, he saw only the determination and pride he'd hoped for. "I . . . I'll do it, only I simply can't face them alone. There will be polite murmurs of condolences, all false, of course. And there will be curious questions, all very nosy and very rude. I can't bear to be asked about Mother's life these last years. None of them have the right to know anything."

He reassured her. "I wouldn't think of allowing you to see them alone."

Audra nodded in silent gratitude.

The tea arrived. Nick poured it for her, then added a small measure of amber liquid. "It won't hurt you, and I think you sorely need it before you go out there," he said, responding to Audra's questioning look.

Audra drank it obediently and quickly. She wanted only to get the next hour over with, and there was no sense in delaying it. She was grateful that Nick was so understanding about her reluctance to face people. She knew she couldn't have gotten through the services without his quiet strength; now she needed him beside her to get through this ordeal. She was too numb to question why it was so.

Nick watched patiently as she finished her tea, stood to shake her skirts, then smoothed her hair back. More than anything, he would have liked to tell her to go upstairs to don her riding habit, then take her out on a long gallop. He thought that would do her more good than anything else. But she'd been ostracized long enough, and now, more than ever, she needed to reclaim her place in society.

She took a deep breath, indicating that she was ready. Nick offered her his arm.

The old buzzard had positioned herself right by the drawing room door, and pounced on them immediately. Resigned, Audra introduced her as Mrs. Eberly, the mother of one of the neighbors from whom he'd repurchased Sheffield land.

"My dear," the woman gushed, "I am so sorry about your sweet mother. How tragic for you, to have lost two fathers and your mother within such a short span of time. But how wonderful that you have a protector in Mr. Brannon, your . . . Oh, dear! What would you be, young man . . . Audra's stepbrother?" She peered at him through her lorgnette. "No, that isn't right. Stepcousin?"

Audra winced at the reference to "two fathers," but she managed to retain a stiff smile, even as Nick calmly corrected the old woman.

"Neither, Mrs. Eberly," he said, smiling disarmingly. "Audra was in no way related to my uncle, nor does she share a relationship with me. *Of any kind.* Excuse us, please," he added, and took Audra's arm to lead her to a group standing nearby.

Audra watched and listened, bemused, as Nick handled each guest who approached with charm and aplomb. It was hardly necessary for her to do more than nod once or twice, and keep a smile frozen on her face. He did everything else. She was unaware that they'd completely circled the room until they were back at the door, and into the hall.

Nick bent his head to her. "It's over. Are you all right?"

She tossed him a grateful look. "Yes. I . . . thank you, Nick. You managed to distract them beautifully," she added with a weak smile. "Now I'd like to go to my room. I . . . I'm very tired."

She did have shadows under her eyes. Ironically, they seemed to make her only more beautiful. It was her pallor that gave Nick the major concern. "Go on up then, sweet. There's nothing more you have to do, and you need to rest. Do you want Letty to come up?"

"No. I feel like I could sleep for days."

He walked her to the stairs, and watched as she as-

cended them wearily. He was still standing there when
Bertie came out of the drawing room and came to him.
"The guests are preparing to leave now that the object of
their speculation is gone," she said wryly. "Would you like
to help me see them out?"

Nick smiled wearily. "After you, madam."

The guests were sent off with so much charm and grace
that few realized that Nick hadn't committed himself to
any of the invitations thrust his way. And it wasn't until
they were on their separate ways home that some realized
that not only had they received no acceptances, but they'd
received no return invitations to visit Sheffield Manor.
Those of more intelligence knew they'd been adroitly ma-
neuvered, and cursed themselves for not having been
more sympathetic to Serena after her second marriage.
The most exciting person in the county was Nickolas
Brannon, and this was the first chance many of them had
to meet him.

Sick to death of smiling, Nick was relieved to see them
all go. He'd used caution in handling these people in order
to save Audra any more heartache. Her reputation could
be ruined simply by anyone knowing that he and she lived
in the same house. The gossips would give no credence to
the fact that he was her guardian. If anything, it would
only make matters worse.

He'd already taken a first step in attempting to halt the
talk. Yesterday, he'd written to his sister, Cleo, about the
situation and asked her to visit. Though they'd seen one
another at their father's funeral, he needed her to come
now.

Serena's death had complicated his plans. He'd gone
to London this last time in order to make arrangements to
extend his stay, because he'd mapped out a campaign to
overcome Audra's reluctance. To court her, as a woman
deserved to be courted, before asking her to marry him.

Now it would be even more difficult. He'd be lucky if any gains he'd made before Serena's death hadn't been irrevocably lost.

Cleo would help, but she wouldn't be able to stay long; she was very dedicated to her husband and didn't like being separated from him. At best, Nick hoped she would stay at least a month.

Audra awoke abruptly the next morning, wondering what it was that she needed to think about. Then she remembered.

It was true; they'd buried her mother yesterday.

Emptiness filled her, and sorrow pressed against her heart. She felt unbearably fragile and immensely weary and, for a time, didn't want to leave the bed. She wished she could pull the covers over her head and just lie here forever, not seeing anyone, not speaking to anyone. But she knew they wouldn't leave her be. God knew they'd tried to coddle her enough in the last days.

She didn't want to be coddled. She didn't want to be touched. If anyone touched her right now, she'd break into a million pieces.

All right, then. She'd leave before they could come to her.

Throwing off the covers, she ran to her wardrobe and jerked out the special riding habit Nick had had made for her and her riding boots. She dressed quickly, then tied her hair back with a scarf. She was out the door and running down the stairs in less than ten minutes.

When she got outside, she saw that it was very early—barely dawn. Not even the servants were stirring yet.

Fantasy greeted her with a soft nicker. Quickly, she threw her western saddle—another of Nick's gifts—on the mare and tightened the girth. Fantasy stood patiently while Audra jerkily adjusted the stirrups, then mounted her.

Once outside the stable, Audra prodded the horse insistently with her heels until the mare understood and took off, moving easily into a fast gallop.

They traversed miles together, jumping barriers Audra never really saw, fording streams, climbing hills. Instinctively pausing or slowing down long enough to let her faithful mount rest, Audra nonetheless refused to turn the horse around for hours. She felt no hunger; she never thought about the sun warming her shoulders, or the cool wind blowing through her hair, or the perspiration trickling between her breasts.

Her grief and rage beat in rhythm with the pounding of Fantasy's hooves, and when she finally turned Fantasy back toward the stable, they had still not abated.

Both horse and girl were exhausted, wet with sweat and grimy. Yet Fantasy whickered softly as Audra dismounted, and turned to nuzzle her, as if to say that she understood why Audra had driven her so. Audra hugged the horse briefly, then turned toward the house. She hadn't said a word to the gaping stable boys.

She entered the Manor and walked past an anxious Bertie and McKee as they stood speaking to a grim-faced Nick at the library door. Bertie took one look at Audra's face and placed a restraining hand on Nick's arm as he was about to step into Audra's path. They watched and waited as the silent girl went up the stairs, entered her room, and quietly closed the door.

"I think it would be best for you to leave her be for now," Bertie informed Nick sympathetically.

Nick's expression was worried. "My God, yesterday she looked like death itself. Now she looks ready to do murder!"

"Aye," McKee concurred. "I'll grant ye that. But 'tis

past time to deal with her grief. Not only her mother's death, but the grief of the last few years when yer uncle . . ." McKee hesitated.

"Go on," Nick prompted grimly.

"He dinna like the lass's spirit, ye ken? I once heard him brag to that scoundrel Norton that he knew how to teach his women to be meek and obedient. *His women!* Bah!" McKee's disgust was plainly evident. "Once Audra knew him for what he was, she would have defied him at every turn if it hadna been for her mother. Audra wouldna fight him, nor allow me to do anything, for fear he'd do worse harm to Serena." McKee looked ready to spew. "The lass came to fear him, and she had good reason."

Nick's expression darkened. "Did he abuse her?"

"Aye, he struck her the first time when she objected to his treatment of her mother. Then again . . ." McKee cut himself off, for he didn't think it was necessary for Nick to know that the second and last incident had occurred the night William died, when . . . "I saw the blood on her mouth, the mark of his fist on her face," he added grimly. McKee saw that Nick's eyes were burning fire at this revelation. 'Tis a good thing you are no longer alive, William Brannon, McKee thought.

But Nick's tone was calm and controlled. "You're saying she's held all that within all this time."

"Aye. If ye'd heed an old man's suggestions . . . ?"

Nick's brows rose as he waited.

"She needs to grieve in her own way. Give her time."

"But how will we know . . . ?"

Unexpectedly, McKee's eyes twinkled. "Oh, ye'll know. Believe me, we'll all know."

Nick nodded, resigned. Regardless, he planned to keep a close eye on Audra. He already knew she wasn't eating or sleeping well. He'd seen the light coming from under her door late last night.

She wouldn't appreciate it, but if he thought she was doing harm to herself, he had every intention of putting an abrupt halt to it, and damn the consequences to himself.

To everyone's consternation, Audra repeated her actions in the following days. She would rise early, ride for hours, come home exhausted, and retire immediately to her room.

She moved through the Manor like a silent wraith, not coming down for meals, avoiding everyone. She'd gone away in her mind, cocooned in her grief, using it as a shield from the rest of them.

Nick hurt for her, and he was completely frustrated by his inability to help her. He was further aggravated by the rumors and gossip making the rounds, just as he'd anticipated.

Audra's daily forays through the countryside didn't help matters. The rumors reaching him had it that she was half crazed by her grief; that she was racked with guilt because she'd been having an affair with him and it was this knowledge of her daughter's behavior that had killed Serena. Others claimed that it was the fact that he refused to marry her and kept her in her own home as his mistress.

Nick's hands were tied. He couldn't take on the entire countryside. Any overt attempt to deny the stories would add only more fuel to busy tongues.

Lord knew they all grieved with Audra, and for her. But she rebuffed even the slightest sign of caring or compassion. Only yesterday, he'd opened his door just in time to hear Audra shouting at a distraught Bertie to "stop hovering." He'd left his room in time to see the swirl of Audra's skirt as she spun away from Bertie, her cry still hanging in the air as she fled down the stairs. When the front door had slammed sharply, Bertie had turned back into her own room but stopped short when she saw Nick standing in his doorway. Though her eyes had revealed a mixture of sadness and exasperation, she'd smiled ruefully. "How can we be angry with her when she's hurting so much?"

"I know she's in pain," he'd agreed tersely, "but I feel so damned helpless. You know better than I do that she isn't eating enough to keep a bird alive. She's fading before our eyes." Bertie would bring her a tray, but more often than not, it returned to the kitchen with almost nothing eaten.

"She's a strong, healthy young woman. She'll bounce back. Remember what McKee told you."

So they all waited.

But the explosion, when it finally came, wasn't directed at any of them.

Chapter 12

*A*udra wrapped her arms around her legs and rested her chin on her knees as she watched Fantasy peacefully munching on new soft grass, wishing *she* had so few cares. The day was unusually warm, so her jacket lay beside her, and she had opened the top buttons of her blouse. The small clearing was delicately beautiful, with an abundance of wildflowers, the sun-dappled ground, and the soothing trickle of the stream. The only other sound to be heard was birdsong and the occasional chatter of a squirrel.

She'd ridden Fantasy hard the last days, for something had compelled her to traverse all of Sheffield land—as if she were not just saying good-bye to her mother, but to all that she had known and held dear all her life.

And she'd wanted to be left alone—to not have to think, not have to make any decisions, not have to *feel*.

But she did feel. She felt very lost, and very alone.

Fantasy raised her head, her twitching ears announcing

someone's approach through the woods behind Audra. The whinny of another horse only confirmed it. It could only be McKee or Nick.

She wasn't surprised. Despite her numbness, she'd been aware of their silent, constant scrutiny. And worry. She'd known she would have to face them, sooner or later. Resigned, Audra slipped her jacket on and went to stand beside Fantasy and wait.

The horse came into view, and Audra knew immediately that it wasn't one of Sheffield's. The rider's face remained in shadow for a few minutes until he cleared the trees. Recognition held Audra motionless for a moment; it was long enough for Silas Norton to spot her and dismount.

She was stunned at his audacity. It was a moment before she found her voice. "You're trespassing again, Mr. Norton," she said quietly and coldly. "This is Sheffield property! I want you to leave!"

Silas Norton's mouth twisted in an unattractive smile as he advanced. "Leave? After I spent the last three days searching these damned woods for you? I've waited a long time to catch you alone like this."

Alarm ran through Audra's veins, but she was determined to hold her ground. She wasn't afraid of him, and she was damned if she was going to bolt like a frightened rabbit. Still, her instinct cautioned her to tighten her hold on her crop and Fantasy's bridle.

Norton stood only a few feet in front of her, not even close enough to touch her, yet Audra was repulsed. "Then have your say and leave. What do you want? There's nothing here for you now that William's dead."

"You're right about one thing—William is definitely dead. And we both know how he died, don't we?"

Audra's heart began clamoring in her breast. All her senses were suddenly sharp and alert. *Calmly now, Audra.*

He can know nothing. Still, her voice trembled slightly. "Everyone knows. He was disappointed that his son was stillborn and he became drunk—very much so—and he fell. . . ."

Norton smiled slyly. "Well now, I'm not denying that he was drunk. You and I both know he was in that state more often than not. But you see, Audra, I was there— right outside the window."

"You're lying!"

"Am I? What if I told you that we'd planned on my coming with him to Sheffield, but that I was delayed and followed several hours later? That I saw the light in the library and was about to come in through the veranda when I saw the two of you? William was swearing at you. I almost interceded, you know. He had a nasty temper when he drank, too, didn't he?"

Yes, they all knew what William's temper had been like when he'd been drinking. So would Norton. "I still say you're a liar, Mr. Norton," she said bravely, "and I'm leaving now. I'm expected back. . . ." She turned her back on him, preparing to mount.

But Norton grabbed her arm bruisingly and jerked her around to face him. "Wait—you haven't heard the rest of my story. I said I almost interceded, but when he attempted to kiss you . . . well, I decided it would be more interesting to just watch."

Audra's face paled. Still, she tried to wrench her arm free. "You're merely trying to frighten me, and I don't frighten easily." His fingers were digging into her flesh, but she wouldn't give him the satisfaction of knowing he was hurting her. She thought about using her crop on him, but knew that wouldn't buy her enough time to mount Fantasy and ride off. She decided to brave it out. "Take your hand off me."

He only gripped her tighter, twisting her arm in the process. Audra bit her lip in pain.

"Damn, but you're as stubborn as William always complained. All right—he struck you when you fought him. Then he tore your robe. Oh, yes . . . I saw his face when he uncovered your breasts." Norton's eyes slid down to her chest, and when he licked his lips, Audra cringed. "Truth to tell, I felt the same way he looked. They were a sight to see."

That did it. Audra brought the crop down as hard as she could across his face and kicked him in the shin. Yelling in outrage and pain, he released her, and she whirled around to mount Fantasy. She had just gotten one foot in the stirrup when Norton seized her from behind again. Fantasy danced uneasily. Audra lost her grip on the bridle and dropped her crop.

"You little bitch! You'll pay for that!"

Surprised at the deceptive strength of his narrow body, Audra fought him, kicking and screaming as he pulled her backward. But when he thrust his fingers into the hair at the back of her head and jerked viciously, the pain was enough to still her.

It gave him time to capture her wrists and hold them in front of her. He pressed her so closely to him, she could barely breathe. When he freed one hand to slide it down her shoulder and over her left breast, she began to struggle in earnest again.

His fingers twisted cruelly. She froze, gasping as pain shot through her breast and arm. Tears stung her eyes. "Please . . ."

There was a shocking sound of fabric ripping. Norton shoved his hand down the front of her camisole, and Audra's flesh shrank at the contact of his fingers. "Please . . . Stop!"

"Ah, much better, Audra. I like to hear you plead,"

Norton said triumphantly. But he removed his hand. Audra closed her eyes in relief. "Good thing you don't have a poker handy, or you could rid yourself of me like you did William!" his voice panted into her ear.

Audra's stomach plummeted and she almost ceased to breathe. Oh, God! He *had* been there! He'd been there, and he'd seen!

"Who's the liar now? Shall I tell you the rest? You got away from William. He came at you again. You grabbed the poker and you struck him on his temple. Again, he came at you, but this time he lost his balance and fell and hit his head on the fireplace stones, didn't he?" Norton twisted her to face him and shook her roughly. "Which killed him, d'you suppose? Your blow, or the fall?"

Which killed him? God knew she'd asked herself that a thousand times. "William was . . . was pawing at me, and I was merely defending myself," she whispered hoarsely. "I didn't mean to cause his death! It was an accident. I swear!"

Norton pounced on that. "Then why, after you went to get him, did McKee pour just enough brandy at William's feet to make it appear that William slipped on it? That's what you and McKee hinted to the magistrate, isn't it?" he asked triumphantly. He shook her again when she didn't respond. "Am I right?"

"Yes! No! What difference would it have made?" she asked desperately. "It wouldn't have changed the fact that William was dead! If you knew all this, why didn't *you* go to the authorities?"

Norton smiled in satisfaction. "As you said, it wouldn't have brought William back. Besides, I can still go to them, can't I? Think they'd believe that your own stepfather tried to rape you? And my story would be even better than the truth. Maybe I saw that Scotsman help you kill William. I haven't forgotten how McKee threw me out of the

Manor when I wanted to see you after William's death." Norton's smile twisted, became an ugly sneer. "Or perhaps, something just may happen to that Scots bastard you're so fond of!"

He was practically holding her up now, because her legs had gone limp. This was a nightmare even worse that the ones she'd suffered after William's death. She and McKee had been so sure that no one would ever know. To find that this lecherous pig . . .

Audra slumped in defeat. "Oh, God! What is it you want?"

"Well now. That's more like it. Took long enough to convince you." He released her and took a deep, satisfied breath. "But that's all right, because I've never been one to rush. I've learned it's usually more rewarding to bide my time. As to what I want . . . I find myself damned short of funds now that William is gone. I was promised part of Cowan's settlement, but William—damn his blasted soul—left it with his bitch of a mistress, and she's disappeared with all of it."

Clutching the ends of her blouse together, prepared to flee if he put his filthy hands on her again, Audra faced him warily. "Then you know I have none of it. I have nothing . . . own nothing. William took it all," she said bitterly.

Norton's eyes narrowed speculatively. "True, but I understand that his nephew is a very wealthy man."

"But . . . but I can't ask Nick for . . . I can't do it!"

Norton smiled slyly. "From the gossip I hear in the village, you're already keeping his bed warm." His gaze traveled to her breasts, lingered, scanned the rest of her. "It shouldn't be too difficult to get him to share some of his wealth with you. Men like him can afford to be generous with their paramours."

"It's another lie! I'm not his . . . his mistress."

Norton shrugged. "Have it your way. I don't mind sharing you with him." He sneered.

"Sharing . . . I can't believe this. Never. Never!"

Norton took a menacing step forward and grasped her shoulders before she could prevent it. "I've wanted you from the first. William, damn his soul, wouldn't let me have you. Was saving you for something better, he said, but the truth was, he wanted you for himself." He tightened his hold. "Well, hell . . . I don't mind you giving it to Brannon as long as you *save* some for me." He leaned over her, his pale eyes glittering with a sudden fierce gleam. "And I'll take my first payment now." He crushed her to him and forced his mouth on hers. His tongue attacked, trying to probe through her clenched teeth.

Terror ran through Audra's veins, and she gagged as his breath filled her nostrils. He was bruising her unmercifully and her own hands were trapped between their bodies. She forced her mind to calm. She had to do something, or he would rape her!

Tensing her muscles, she brought her knee up as hard as she could. Norton bellowed and released her. Audra staggered back, glad at the sight of him bending over in obvious pain, hoping she'd damaged him permanently. God, but it felt good to strike back!

And then, unexpectedly, she was filled with a fierce rage at all of it—Norton, William, her mother's death. She was tired of feeling helpless. She wanted to fight back. To lash out.

With a hoarse shriek of exultation, she flew at Norton. He lifted his head in shock, only to have his jaw meet with her fist. The blow was powerful enough to almost knock him backward. She came at him again, to rake his face with her nails. She kicked out at him, her fists pummeled him unmercifully. And all the while, she was screaming like a banshee. Audra had gone completely wild. She was unstoppable.

Still enveloped in the pain her knee had caused, Norton threw his arms up to protect his face and crouched low, helpless to do more against her fury.

What did finally stop her was exhaustion. Audra dropped her fists and stepped back, panting heavily. Reality returned. He'd kill her! No—he'd rape her first, and then he'd kill her.

She bolted for Fantasy. One foot in the stirrup, hanging on to Fantasy's mane for dear life, she urged the mare into the stream. From the corner of her eye, she saw Norton's startled horse making for the trees, but Norton was already staggering after her.

Kicking out with her free foot, Audra forced Norton to back off. With one last effort, she made it into the saddle and kicked the mare's sides desperately. Fantasy plunged forward. Audra never looked back, though she could hear Norton screaming at her.

"You bitch! You little bitch! You'll pay for this! Do you hear me? I'm not finished with you!"

Audra nudged Fantasy up the opposite bank and over, then turned the horse to face Norton again. It was too much. She'd lived with William's threats for so long, and now Norton was doing the same. "You touch me or anyone in my household, and I'll *kill* you," she shouted furiously before wheeling Fantasy about again. Immediately they were on level ground, the mare broke into a gallop toward Sheffield, as if she knew that her mistress was frantic to return.

Audra rode low as they dodged trees and branches, until at last, they came to the path that led home. Only then did she dare to pause. She heard no hooves behind her, but she turned and scanned the trees anyway. He wasn't following her. Good! She hoped his mount had returned to whatever stable it had come from and left him on foot. She hoped he'd get lost in the woods and perish. She hoped . . .

Reaction set in. With her arms wound about the mare's neck, Audra wept helplessly into Fantasy's mane. Belly-twisting, racking sobs. Tears of relief, tears of sorrow. Deep, cleansing tears.

And when she was through, her rage was gone, and she felt strangely freed from misery. A pervading calm overcame her, instead. Wonderful, restful calm.

Audra lifted her head, took a deep breath, and took stock. She was wet and not a little muddy. Her blouse was torn. Holding the reins in her teeth, she buttoned her jacket and tried to wipe the mud off her skirt while debating what she was to do now.

Impossible as it seemed, Norton knew everything—even the fact that McKee had aided her. There had been no reason for the local magistrate to question their story, for even Dr. Hargrove and the servants had known that William had been drinking heavily that day. No one was surprised that he'd fallen and struck his head.

But what could she do if Norton went to the authorities and told them he'd seen her strike him first? She'd be branded a murderess! Hung by the neck until . . .

Audra shuddered. Thank God her mother would never see it. Dare she tell Nick? No. She couldn't bear to have him looking at her with loathing and condemnation. She'd killed his uncle, and though Nick had hardly known him, William had still been a blood relative.

She would tell McKee, though, for he was the only other person who knew what had really happened that night. Yet . . . oh, God! McKee would probably go after Norton and kill him, and then *he'd* be branded a murderer! What should she do?

By the time she and Fantasy arrived at the stable,

Audra had still reached no decision. Just as she was wearily dismounting, Rafe walked out. He stopped short, then rushed to assist her. "Holy . . . ! What happened to you? Are you hurt?"

Audra gave him a weak smile. "I'm all right, Rafe. I just took a little spill. I look a lot worse than I feel," she lied.

"You're sure?" At her nod, he took the reins. "I'll take care of your horse. You look like you'd be better off with a hot bath."

"Thank you, and Rafe . . . please see that Fantasy gets an extra handful of oats, will you? It wasn't her fault."

"Sure. I'll see she gets a good rubdown, too."

Audra limped to the house, still brushing at her skirt as she entered. Glancing toward the stairs, she saw Letty coming down the hallway toward her.

Nick paced the study restlessly.

This had gone on too long. It was time to take action.

He'd come to the end of his rope this morning after Audra had brushed past him with a cool "I prefer to ride alone" when asked if she'd like company. He'd held himself in check only by strong force of will, unsure which desire was greatest—to throttle her or to smother her protectively against his chest. Instead, he'd turned back into the study and slammed the door with such force the paintings shook, whereupon he'd broken his habit of not imbibing until late afternoon and poured himself an unusually large whiskey and downed it immediately.

Just when he'd thought—no, by God, when he *knew* Audra had been coming around, fate had played a cruel trick. She'd begun to trust him, but that blossoming trust had died with Serena. And Audra's pride wouldn't allow her to share her pain with anyone.

Nick sadly recalled the vibrant girl-woman he'd held in his arms the day he'd returned Fantasy's Lady to her. Her laughing face, upturned to his. Those fantastic eyes shining with joy.

His realization that he loved her. His decision to make her his wife.

She hadn't known it, of course, and he'd told himself that he could afford to wait. He'd wanted to woo her slowly and carefully, savoring each victory over her reluctance.

Damn! This had set him back too far.

More, he was worried sick about Audra, her brooding silence. . . .

His musings were interrupted by a scream and the clatter of a tray. What the hell *now*?

He opened the study door to find Letty and, surprisingly, Audra, on their knees retrieving broken china. Audra glanced up, saw him, and slowly got to her feet.

"What the hell?" Nick got to her in a few short strides. She was splattered with mud, head to toes. Her hair was a tangled mass about her shoulders. But it was the smear of blood on her face that his glance focused on.

Audra clutched the neck of her jacket. "I know I look terrible, but I just took a nasty spill into the stream and I'm really not hurt." She was speaking too fast, nervously, she knew, but she couldn't help it. Nick's face looked like a thundercloud, dark and menacing.

"Are you sure?" He grasped her arms and scanned her, his eyes narrowed thoughtfully. Audra was an excellent horsewoman—one of the best he'd ever seen. It was difficult to believe that she'd taken a spill in a placid little stream. And her eyes . . . damn it! Her eyes were swollen from crying.

"Don't look at me like that!" Audra snapped. "I tell you, it was nothing!"

Her sharp tone effectively canceled Nick's concern. "Come with me," he ordered brusquely and unnecessarily, for he kept hold of her arm and didn't release it until they'd gone into the study and he'd practically pushed her into a chair. "Sit there. I have some things to say to you." He walked around the desk without waiting to see if she followed his directive.

Audra wasn't up to fighting his grimness, so she dropped into the chair and obediently sat, facing him.

"There are two things I need to speak of," Nick began, his gaze holding hers. "The first is to inform you that my sister will be arriving shortly for a visit. Cleo is only a few years older than you. I think it will be good for you to have someone near your own age at this time, and—"

"And you think I'm a child, to be distracted by a new playmate?" Audra asked defensively.

"No, you're not a child," he said through gritted teeth, and Audra realized that he was holding his anger with effort. "But you've certainly been acting like one."

Audra's cheeks flamed at this.

"I'm not unsympathetic to your loss, Audra," Nick told her as he rubbed the tense muscles of his neck. "On the contrary, I was very fond of your mother, as were a number of others. They're suffering also, but you're only making it more difficult for them." He paused, and Audra had to look away from those amber eyes that were piercing her with their intensity.

"We've done our best to help you, and you've rebuffed us all," he continued. "Damn it, Audra, we understand your pain, and you have a right to be angry. But none of us are to blame for Serena's death. You have no right to be angry at us." Audra felt her cheeks go from hot to cold, and knew that she'd paled. It was true; she'd behaved abominably.

She recalled the woeful expression McKee wore lately,

each time he looked at her. Bertie's hurt face, as it had been this morning. Letty's tears, which seemed to flow so often lately.

Oh, God! She'd not meant to hurt any of them—not those who had cared for her and her family for so long and so faithfully. She winced as she recalled her coldness to them, the times she'd ignored their attempts to comfort her.

And there was Nick—who had done nothing to deserve her contempt. Who'd made her mother's last weeks comfortable. Happy.

She straightened her shoulders and turned back to face him with a bravado she didn't feel. "I'm sorry. You're right—I've been cruel and selfish beyond reason. I'm sorry if I've treated you unfairly. May I leave now, please?" She thought she saw admiration in his eyes before he nodded silently.

Gratefully, she left the room.

She began by seeking out Letty and Mrs. Murphy and tendering her sincere apologies to each. She had to go to the gatehouse to find McKee, for he'd picked up a cough and was feeling low.

"Aye, lass. 'Tis proud I am of ye again. I understand yer pain, but ye dinna have the right to inflict it upon others," he said sternly. "We have our own to bear."

"Oh, McKee," Audra cried, throwing her arms around him. "You cared for Mother. I know that. I truly am sorry. And I truly do love you." She kissed his ruddy cheek.

" 'Tis the only reason I dinna take ye over my knee," he replied gruffly, but he was smiling as she released him.

"McKee . . ."

"Aye, lass?"

Audra bit her lip. "Oh . . . nothing." She couldn't bring herself to tell him about Norton after all. If Norton had made his threats against only herself, she wouldn't have hesitated, but he'd also threatened McKee. Audra gave him a weak smile. "I'm off to find Bertie, and get my scolding from her."

"Wait, lass!"

Audra turned at the door. "What is it?"

"I have something for ye. I dinna remember until last night." McKee got up to rummage in the back of a cupboard, then put a heavy object wrapped in white cloth into her hand.

"What is it?"

"I dinna know. It wasna my business to look. Lass, your mother gave it to me about a year after she married William. She asked me to keep it for ye, and give it to ye if she . . . Well, 'twas so long ago, I forgot."

Audra studied the package. Whatever was inside appeared to be wrapped in several white handkerchiefs, and with a sense of shock, Audra saw that the outside one bore her mother's initials.

She slipped the bundle into her pocket, deciding to open it when she was alone. "Thank you, McKee," she said softly.

Bertie was the last. Like McKee, she accepted Audra's apologies with love, understanding, and shared tears. Audra felt unworthy once she'd completed this task, but she also felt a great burden lifted from her heart.

She knocked on the study door.

"Enter."

Taking a deep breath, she went in, carefully closing the door behind her. Nick was still at his desk and didn't even look up.

"Yes?" he asked.

Audra cleared her throat nervously. "I just want you to know that I've apologized to everyone for behaving so abominably after Mother died."

"Good," he replied. Then he merely glanced at her before resuming his writing.

For one moment, Audra gaped at him. That was all? After the lecture he'd subjected her to earlier, he was now dismissing her? Well, *she* wasn't finished. She waited. Still, he didn't look up. "I've only one person left to apologize to," she finally said quietly.

At that, he lifted his head, and frowned at her. "You said you were done."

"Not quite. I apologized to the others because I did wrongly blame them for Mother's death. But the one person I can't apologize to *does* deserve the blame. You see . . ." She faltered, swallowed, then went on, "I don't know how to forgive myself. It was my responsibility alone to keep Mother safe, and I failed. Tell me, Nick, how . . ." One large tear ran down her cheek. "How do I ever forgive myself?" Then, she spun about and fled.

Nick lunged to his feet. "Audra . . ."

But she was already gone. Seconds later, he heard the door to her room slam upstairs. Sinking back into his chair, he buried his fingers in his hair and cradled his head.

She'd stood there so beautifully proud, and yet so sincere as she'd made her admission, but he knew what it must have cost her to humble herself to everyone. Truth to tell, he'd been proud of her. No tears, no sulks.

God, he'd hated to rebuke her, but his stern directive had needed to be given. She was entitled to her grief. But she would have to learn how to cope with it in the living world. The longer she closed herself off, the more difficult it would be for her to get over her tragedy. And damned if he'd let her make herself ill with it.

When he'd glanced up, he hadn't been able to bear looking at her face for longer than an instant. It had taken all his willpower to sit still and keep from going to her.

He'd wanted nothing more than to hold her, to cradle her in his arms and soothe her bruised pride and heart.

But it was too soon. He would only have frightened and confused her with his tenderness. Better her anger; he knew how to handle that. It was her rejection that he couldn't accept.

Audra scrubbed tears from her cheeks as she paced back and forth in her room. She was convinced she hated Nick Brannon! First he'd given her a verbal thrashing, then when she'd done what he wanted, he'd as much as ignored her. She'd humbled herself before him, too. Even worse, she'd cried. Something she'd sworn never to do in front of another man.

Well, it wouldn't happen again. Ever. And she was tired of being ordered about by *any* man. She refused to put up with it—with *Nick*—any longer.

Then it occurred to Audra that there was no reason to. Though it had been her home all her life, there was nothing left to keep her at Sheffield. She could leave if she wanted.

Her parents were gone. There was no changing that.

Even if Nick let her stay at Sheffield forever, there was also no changing the fact that it was no longer her home. It belonged to him, and without her parents it was just a shell, empty except for the memories that haunted her. Perhaps, deep down, she'd known that already, and that was why she'd been driven to ride the land these last days. She'd been saying good-bye.

Though she didn't particularly want to leave Bertie and McKee, it wouldn't have to be for good. They'd understand, and perhaps someday, she could send for them to join her.

And there was one other pressing reason to leave. If she did, Norton would never find her.

Audra flopped onto the bed on her back, fingers interlocked behind her neck. Her ebony hair fanned out on the bed behind her as she thought and planned.

London, of course. She'd find a position with some respectable family, perhaps as a governess. She had an excellent education, after all. And if that wasn't possible, she could always be a companion. She'd read about wealthy older women—widows—who were willing to pay for someone to run their errands and play nursemaid. She certainly had the qualifications since she'd taken care of her mother's needs for so long.

And if worse came to worst, there was always Mr. Pemberly. He could help her find a position. Yes! She could do it.

Audra smiled to herself. Getting to London was no problem now that she had Fantasy back. How ironic that Nick would provide her transportation. Her only other requirement would be sufficient funds to keep herself until she found a position. What a pity she'd had to sell her emerald earlier. She had almost nothing left from the sale. Did she dare borrow from Bertie? McKee? No. Both would insist on knowing what she was planning.

Audra flopped over onto her stomach. "Ow!"

Something sharp had jabbed into her left hip. She flipped over again, reached into her pocket, and pulled out the white bundle McKee had given her. She'd forgotten all about it.

Sitting up, she carefully untied the knots of several tightly secured handkerchiefs. When she unfolded the last one, a gasp escaped her lips.

Sparkling up at her were the diamond choker and eardrops that her father had presented to her mother upon Audra's birth. She stared at them in disbelief. How had her mother managed to keep them from William? He'd taken the other pieces her mother had owned, for Audra had herself caught a brief glimpse of the jewelry on William's desk one day. When she'd boldly asked him what he was doing with her mother's jewels, William had told her it was no damned business of hers. And when she'd gone to Serena, her mother had told her only that she didn't want to speak of it. She'd never even mentioned the diamonds.

Somehow, her mother had managed to hide them and give them to McKee to keep safe.

Audra clutched the gems tightly. They were a gift from heaven that couldn't have come at a more opportune time.

Thank you, Mother, she breathed.

Chapter 13

$\mathcal{T}$he frantic drumming of her heart warned her that she couldn't continue. *Run! Go! You must keep on!*

Audra's lips formed the words silently, for she had no breath to voice them. *Run! Run, Audra!*

Shouts. Other feet pounding behind her.

Oh, God! They were gaining on her!

And then, suddenly, standing on a rise just ahead, a tall, shadowy figure, his face indistinguishable, but somehow, Audra knew that he meant safety. Security. If she could just get to him . . .

Another shout spurred her on. She pushed onward . . .

. . . and was brought up short so suddenly she staggered back. Blind with fear, she screamed and struggled wildly, until she realized that she had run into an unseen copse of trees, thick with underbrush. It was only her hair and skirts that were caught in the brambles. Desperately, she tore at them in an attempt to free herself. There was a hoarse cry of triumph nearby, the sound of boots coming her way.

God! They were upon her! She had to reach that silent figure!

She glanced over her shoulder and saw William's face leering at her. Terror lent her new strength; she tore free and turned to flee from him . . . right into other reaching arms. Silas Norton's arms.

Too late! Too late!

Desperately, she searched for the figure that had meant safety, but he was no longer there. She opened her mouth to scream, and . . .

. . . the sound of her own voice woke her, and the pounding boots became the wild beating of her own heart.

"Audra! Wake up, sweetheart!"

She was being shaken, and none too gently.

Fighting her fear, she raised her lids to see Nick's concerned face. Dazed and confused, she looked about and realized that she was in the hall outside her bedroom, and not in the woods at all.

Her relief was so great she threw her arms around Nick and clung to him tightly, moaning, still trembling. He calmed her, his voice a soft whisper. "Hush, sweet. It's all right now. I'm here." Nick lifted her easily to carry her back into her room.

"You're freezing," he said as they reached her bed. "I'll tuck you in and stoke up the fire." He tried to put her down, but Audra was still clinging tightly to him and wouldn't release him, so Nick twisted about to sit on the bed and hold her on his lap.

"What . . . ? I had another nightmare, didn't I?" she asked, her teeth chattering.

"Yes, and you were sleepwalking."

"Sleepwalking?" Audra shook her head to clear it.

"I've never sleepwalked before in my life!" she protested. "Where could I have been going?"

"I don't know. But I heard you shout my name, and I found you out in the hall." He gathered her closer and spoke into the mass of hair below his chin. "Audra. What do you mean . . . *another* nightmare?"

Audra tried to shrug it off. "Did I say that? I meant *a* nightmare." She wasn't about to tell him about the others—or that this one was different and the first she'd had since he'd come to Sheffield. Fully awake at last, she became aware that she was firmly ensconced on Nick's lap. "You can let me go now," she said, though she really wished he wouldn't. She felt safe and secure in his arms.

But Nick wasn't about to let her dodge his question. He reached over to pile the pillows high, and with Audra still on his lap, slid to the head of the bed to lean against them. He adjusted Audra so that her back was to him, then pulled her against his chest. Surprisingly, she didn't resist.

"Give me your hands," he ordered. She did, and Nick chafed them slowly, sliding his fingers between hers, rubbing until her hands were warm again. "Want to tell me about it?" His hands were now sliding up and down her arms, warming them, too, while he observed her carefully.

She shook her head adamantly, hair flying wildly about her face. Nick reached up to smooth it back. As he lifted the long tresses from her shoulder, his gaze became riveted on her upper arm, bare below the short, puffy sleeve of her nightdress.

Audra felt him suddenly still. She glanced over her shoulder, then froze, for his eyes had became glittering shards of ice.

"How did you get these bruises? Who gave them to you?"

Alarmed by the brittleness of his tone, Audra followed

his gaze. There on her arm were the bluish purple marks Norton's fingers had left. Too late, she attempted to cover them with her hand, but Nick pried her fingers away.

"Audra, I mean to know. Who were you with this afternoon? It wasn't just a spill from Fantasy, was it? Answer me!"

She slid out of his reach, stubbornly keeping her face turned away from him. It wasn't that she wouldn't answer; she was frantically searching for a plausible story. What could she tell Nick without relating the whole sordid mess? Lying had always been abhorrent to her, yet it seemed that since he'd come into her life, she was either living a lie or telling him one after another.

Truth to tell, she was sick of it.

She turned back to Nick, rubbing her bruises. "It was Silas Norton. He accosted me at the stream and . . . and made some insinuations. When I called him a liar, he became angry and manhandled me a bit."

Nick almost stopped breathing as he twisted her about to sit sideways on his lap. "Manhandled you? Was that *all* he did?" Nick's voice was steel now, his eyes ice-cold.

Audra bit her lip. "Why . . . I . . . What do you mean?" she hedged.

"Damn it Audra, you know what I'm asking! Did he force himself on you? Molest you? I want the truth!" he growled.

She blushed furiously, yet she was relieved that she could answer him truthfully. "Oh, no! No, Nick. I kicked him, and . . ."

"You what?"

"Well, I didn't exactly kick him. It was more like . . . uh, I used my knee. Hard. I daresay he's more bruised than I am." She fervently hoped it was true. Thank God Nick couldn't see the bruises on her breast nor the scratches on her shoulder!

A look of relief passed over Nick's face, but his mouth was still a grim line. "Audra, sweet, I'm thankful you have spirit. Another woman might have fainted." His eyes hardened again. "Now, about those insinuations. They wouldn't perchance have anything to do with the two of us, would they?"

Audra's face grew warm again. "I'd really rather not say. Please, Nick. It was just stupid gossip and Norton is the type who would revel in gossip of that kind."

Nick sighed. He had to keep reminding himself that for all practical purposes, Audra was really quite naive. That and the fact that she'd been so isolated the last few years made her innocence that much more touching.

"Audra, you fail to understand that it's not only Norton. I didn't tell you earlier, as I'd already upset you enough for one day, but the entire countryside is rampant with rumors."

"What are you saying? That everyone is implying that I . . . that you and I . . . ?" She was too stunned to continue.

"They are," he affirmed. "In fact, that's the real reason I've invited my sister to visit us. I'd hoped that Cleo's arrival would put a stop to it, but now I'm not sure. After all, Bertie's formidable presence hasn't stopped it. Damn! I'm afraid we can partly thank Rose for some of it."

"Rose? But why, Nick?"

"She was furious when you let her go. She swore she'd get even, and it appears she has. She's spread all sorts of vicious rumors about our . . . relationship. Unfortunately, it's only added fuel to the fire."

Audra was indignant. "Do you mean people have been gossiping about us? How could they possibly believe anything a dismissed servant tells them?"

"It isn't just Rose. I'm afraid you bear part of the responsibility yourself," Nick said wryly.

"Me? I don't understand . . ."

"By your pretending to be 'Agnes.' Rose has spread that story, also, and she's made it known that while you were playing the part of a maid, you never slept in the maids' quarters. It was enough of an insinuation to get tongues wagging."

Audra's initial shock turned to defensiveness. "Why should I care what they say about me now? It can't hurt me, and it will certainly no longer hurt Mother."

"I don't think you realize how such things have a way of ruining a reputation. Yours will be torn to shreds, if it hasn't already been."

"I don't care about rumors," she insisted. Then, before she could stop it, a yawn escaped her lips. She was so tired. She would think about all this tomorrow, when her head was clearer. Right now, all she wanted to do was sleep. She yawned again. "Sorry. May we talk about this tomorrow?"

Nick's expression softened at her request. "Of course." He slid off the bed and helped her under the covers again. "Go back to sleep, love."

Like a child, Audra closed her eyes and snuggled into the pillow. His voice soothed her. Strange. Hadn't she been angry with him earlier today? But he really did have a nice voice, she thought drowsily. Deep and resonant, yet even when he was angry with her, he never shouted. It seemed to her that he was taking pains not to frighten her.

She was almost asleep. Perhaps she was dreaming again, but she felt the lightest touch on her lips and a gentle pressure across her cheek. She felt as if she were a little girl again, and her mother had come in to see that she was safely tucked in and kiss her good night. Such a warm, secure feeling . . .

Audra lost the struggle to open her eyes, but her fuzzy brain registered a hint of tobacco and . . . a scent that now seemed soothingly familiar. It, too, made her feel secure. She didn't realize that her lips had curved into a soft smile before she gave in and passed into slumber.

She was stiff and sore the next morning, which reminded her all too clearly of Norton and his threats. She felt emotionally drained and loath to get out of bed. It seemed like nothing was going right in her life—nothing would ever go right again. It was as if a sense of impending doom was hanging over her.

What to do? Although she'd issued her threat to Norton with more bravado than intent, she knew with certainty that *his* threat wasn't an idle one. He was as vicious as William had ever been. He wanted something from her, and if she wouldn't deliver, he'd report her to the authorities.

For herself, she didn't know if she really cared anymore. But Norton had seen McKee pour that small amount of brandy on the hearthstones to convince the magistrate that there had been a reason for William to slip. McKee hadn't had anything to do with William's death, but that one action, done to protect her, had made him an accomplice of sorts.

Norton had threatened McKee. She dared not tell McKee for fear of what he'd do; she knew from past experience that McKee, usually the most mild-mannered of men, had a temper. Once, when she was a child, she'd seen him beset by two burly villagers who felt they'd had a grudge against him. McKee had knocked one unconscious and almost killed the other with his bare hands before Edward, summoned by a frightened Audra, stopped him.

If she told McKee about Norton's threats, she'd only endanger him further, both his life and his freedom.

What if she had no choice in the matter? What if

Norton, enraged at her escape yesterday, had already gone to the authorities? Even now, they could be riding to the Manor to arrest her and McKee. She shuddered at the thought.

How terribly embarrassing it would be for Nick. His sister was coming. What would Cleo think? Not to mention Bertie and the others! Audra giggled in nervous hysteria as a vision of them, all standing with mouths agape as she was dragged out of the Manor in chains, entered her head.

Suddenly loud voices broke into her reverie. She leaped out of bed and was tying her robe when her door was flung open and Letty appeared. The girl's eyes were wide as she clutched her apron to her mouth. "Oh, Miss Audra," she stammered, "it's McKee. Someone shot at him through the trees!"

Oh, God! McKee! "Where is he?"

"Mr. Nick helped him into the kitchen. . . ."

She bolted past Letty and down the stairs, stopping short only when she reached the kitchen and found McKee slumped into a chair. Audra leaned weakly against the wall and watched as Bertie ripped open his sleeve, which was soaked with blood. Mrs. Murphy was trying to coax him to drink the strong tea she'd poured.

"Christ, woman!" McKee growled as he pushed the mug away. "Dinna give me this watery tea! Bring me the bottle ye have hidden in yer cupboard! A mon needs something stronger."

"And how do you know what I keep in my cupboard, I'd like to know, Mr. McKee?" Mrs. Murphy sniffed. Nonetheless, she scurried to do his bidding and soon returned with the bottle and a glass.

Nick filled the glass before he sat down across from McKee. Bertie appraised the wound carefully. "It's not as bad as it looks, McKee. The bullet went through the fleshy part."

"Aye. I ken that." He emptied half the glass.

"How did it happen, McKee?" Nick asked. "Was it a poacher, or did you rile someone by poaching on *their* territory?"

The two men grinned at one another conspiratorially. Audra wanted to scream. How could they possibly joke about this? She wrung her hands together in helpless confusion, trying to sort the implications in her mind, afraid that her intuition of doom had become a reality.

"Canna say," McKee answered. "I dinna have no use for other men's property. And I canna say we ever had a problem with poachers at Sheffield. Those in need have always known they have only to ask, ye ken? And I was well out of the trees when the shot came. A poacher would have been shooting within, not out."

"Hmm. Perhaps. And perhaps it was only a stray shot. We'd better take a ride and check for any sign in the woods. Not you, McKee. You rest that arm. Rafe and I will go."

The men were so calm, so casual about it all. Audra could keep silent no longer. Not even her fear of exposure was worth McKee's life. "Nick, perhaps it wasn't an accident." Everyone looked at her as if she'd lost her senses. "I . . . I mean, what if it was someone with a grudge against Sheffield?" She could hear herself stuttering. How was she going to make them understand? Desperately, she turned to McKee. "It could have been Norton, don't you see? He was so angry when you threw him out!"

McKee considered as he watched Bertie put the last knot in the bandage she'd wrapped around his arm. "Aye, it could be. But I thought we'd seen the last of him. I dinna think that sniveling coward would come around agin."

Audra turned pleading eyes to Nick.

"He may not have been as frightened as you thought, McKee. Audra had a run-in with him yesterday. And shooting at you from out of the woods *is* an act of cowardice. Of course," Nick continued, "we have no proof that it was Norton. Still, let's not take chances. I'll alert all the men to keep their eyes open."

"Aye. But if I find that scum on this land meself, he willna mistake my message this time," McKee growled. "And if he ever comes near ye agin, lass, ye are to tell me. Do ye hear?"

Audra nodded.

Nick patted McKee on the shoulder. "Go easy today." He turned to Audra. "I'd like to speak to you."

"Now?"

"Now." Nick waited until she reluctantly came to him before moving aside to let her precede him. Once in the study, she walked straight to the veranda doors and stood there, gazing outside.

"What reason do you have to believe that Norton shot McKee?" he asked without preamble. "Did he make any specific threats against McKee yesterday?"

Audra groaned silently. She should have known Nick wasn't about to simply drop the subject. But if she admitted to Norton's threats, she'd have to also admit her part in William's death, and all the rest of the sordid story. Oh, God! Another lie. "No." The word was almost a whisper.

"Did he make any threats against *anyone*?" She wouldn't look at him. Nick waited, noting that she was twisting a lock of hair around her fingers. "Audra?"

Finally, she replied, "No. I told you, he made some nasty insinuations. That was all."

"All?" Nick's long strides brought him to her. He grasped her shoulders, forcing her to face him. "Bloody hell! I hardly call that *all* he did, when you have the bruises to attest otherwise."

Audra's eyes widened at his tone.

Seeing her alarm, Nick's voice gentled. "Sit down. Please." When she'd complied, Nick continued. "This brings up the point I wanted to make, and that deals directly with the insinuations Norton made." He hesitated.

Audra watched him in puzzlement. She'd never known him to be at a loss for words, but here he was, seemingly not sure how to proceed. She studied his profile, fascinated by a twitching muscle in his jaw. When he abruptly turned back to her, Audra quickly lowered her lids. Her head went up quickly again, however, for he'd taken her hand and was caressing her fingers. She found his touch soothing, so she didn't object.

"Audra, this proves my point about the gossip. For myself, it doesn't matter. It's merely a minor irritation. But for you . . . in your case, it matters greatly. Once a young woman's reputation is ripped to shreds, there's no repairing it."

"But I told you that I don't care. . . ."

"You may not think so now, but you will. And *I* care. And what of the others? Do you think they can ignore the ridicule that will fall upon them? McKee has already had more than one occasion to use his fists in your defense. What of his well-being?"

Audra was aghast. "But I didn't know! He never told me!"

"Of course not. He was protecting you."

"But I won't allow it! I'll not have him put in danger because of me. If more harm befalls him . . ." Audra fell silent. Her hair hid her face as she lowered her head in thought. What to do?

Nick wasn't happy taking advantage of her vulnerability, but he saw no other choice. He cupped her chin and lifted it so that she had to look at him. "I have a solution to this dilemma. Will you listen?"

At her nod, he released her chin, but retained his hold on her cold hands. "Good. I suggest marriage. The sooner the better," he said without preamble.

Surely, she'd misheard his words. Surely, he couldn't have just said . . . But Nick's eyes were boring into hers with such intensity that she knew he had!

Audra's first astonished reaction was to jump to her feet and flee, an action that was effectively prevented by Nick's tightened grip on her fingers. Her mouth dropped open, then closed with a snap. It was a moment before she could speak.

"You must be mad, Nick Brannon! That's your solution? Marriage? You know what I think of marriage—of becoming some man's property! Knowing that, you'd insult me . . . ?" In her agitation, she finally managed to jerk her hands free and leaped to her feet to stride angrily to the door.

Her shoulders were grasped from behind and she was spun about. Her long hair swung wildly, blinding her for an instant. When it fell back in place, Audra had only an instant to become aware of Nick's furious expression.

"An insult, you say? A man offers you marriage, and you call it an insult?" He shook her gently. "By God, Audra, I'll teach you what an insult is."

Forewarned, Audra raised her hands defensively, but in one swift movement, Nick jerked her robe open and pulled it down to her elbows, effectively rendering her immobile. In the next instant, she found her wrists imprisoned behind her back, and herself arched within the circle of his arms. Nick put his hand on one of her breasts, and fondled her with deliberate thoroughness. It was all Audra's shocked mind had time to register before his mouth cut off her gasp. Her senses, already whirling, de-

serted her completely. Mindless, helpless under the onslaught of his mouth and hands, she could do nothing.

Slowly, her bemused brain began to focus on what he
was doing with his mouth. Nick was crushing her soft lips,
as his mouth moved upon hers with fierce demand. He was
relentless, persistent, until he'd forced her lips and teeth
to open for him, and when they did, his warm, wet tongue
invaded and explored for an instant before he drew her
own tongue into his mouth. Audra sagged against him
helplessly.

Only then did he finally lift his head. His eyes, glittering with golden sparks, gazed into hers. "Consider yourself insulted," he said brusquely. Then his voice became
dangerously soft. "And just so you know the difference . . ."

Too late, she realized he wasn't finished with her yet.
She braced herself for another onslaught.

But this time, his kiss was tender, his lips soothed
where before they'd just bruised. And when he gained
entrance to her mouth, Audra's emotions seesawed wildly,
for this time his tongue wasn't an invasion; it swirled
against her teeth and tongue gently. His thumbs brushed
softly over her nipples. To Audra's shock, they peaked,
responding to his touch. Caught unawares, powerless
against shocking new pleasurable sensations, she moaned.

At her soft sound, Nick's head came up.

Audra stared back at him, caught helplessly by the
fierce blaze in his amber eyes.

After what seemed an eternity, Nick pressed his forehead to hers, then released her. But it was only long
enough to place a kiss upon the fabric covering her breast
and pull her robe together again before he gathered her
snugly back into his arms.

She became aware of his racing heartbeat under her
palm, then of his slowly moving hands as they followed

the contours of her back and the rise of her buttocks until his fingers splayed upon her and he pulled her roughly to his lower body. She gasped as she felt the angry proof of his manhood pressed against her stomach, and made an effort to pull away.

This time, he let her go. His eyes burned into hers.

"*That*, my sweet, is *not* an insult! It's merely proof that you're a beautiful, desirable woman." With those words, Nick turned to go to the sideboard.

Audra was still speechless. A tumult of thoughts and emotions raced through her mind, and she didn't understand any of them! By rights, she should have slapped Nick's face the moment he'd released her, but oddly, she didn't have the least desire to do so. In fact, she still felt so weak she was forced to grasp the back of the chair she thankfully found beside her. Her trembling hand covered her bruised mouth.

Nick struggled to regain his own composure as he poured his drink. Damn it! He'd lost his hard-won patience and manhandled her. Swearing under his breath, he was about to replace the top on the crystal decanter when he glanced up and saw Audra's gesture.

Quickly tossing down the drink, he refilled his glass and poured a small measure of the amber liquid into another. Carrying both glasses, he returned to her side, and curving her numb fingers around the glass, he ordered her to drink.

She obeyed without question. This time, the liquid fire went down her throat smoothly and easily.

Nick took the glass from her fingers and watched as a rosy hue returned to her cheeks. Only then did he again swallow the contents of his own glass. Still watching her closely, he set both glasses on a table.

Audra met his look and quickly lowered her lashes.

She was still trembling in reaction, and completely bewildered, because she didn't feel the least bit angry with him.

Nick finally broke the silence, his voice calm and even. "I would consider that we're now equal."

She lifted her eyes to him, deciding to meet his challenge. "I suppose we are, now that we've traded . . . insults," she agreed.

He almost smiled. Despite his deliberate crudity and roughness, she was still going to stand up to him. Still, he intended to see this matter resolved. "At least we agree on something," he said quietly. "Now, let's proceed with the original purpose of this discussion. If you'd but consider the matter objectively and clearly, you'd see that it's the perfect solution. In fact, it's the only solution. Audra." He raised his hands to forestall the words forming on her lips. "I know all your fears and objections. You made them more than clear to me on one occasion, if you recall. I realize that you still don't fully trust me. I can only hope that will come with time. However, we *must* put a halt to the gossip now, before more damage is done."

He was right, of course. "I know that, Nick. It's just that I . . . I . . . ." She faltered.

"I can only promise you, my dear, that I'm not another William. I won't leave you penniless or ill, nor will I rob you of your pride. To be frank, it's you who'll gain by this marriage, not I."

The same pride he spoke of kept her from allowing any hint of the humiliation she felt at his statement. He was, after all, only stating a fact. She had nothing, owned nothing. Even the robe she wore had been purchased by him. Still, she lifted her chin proudly. "That may be true. What, then, do *you* have to gain?" She grimaced. "Surely you don't profess . . . love. You must know that I'll never love anyone, ever. That path leads only to loss, as I've learned." She was proud that her voice was strong and steady. Still, her heart was hammering as she awaited his reply.

It seemed to take forever, but when he did, she could detect nothing in his tone. He sounded calm and unaffected. "No. I won't tell you that I love you. But Alex and I are required to entertain extensively, and most of our associates have wives. It would be to my benefit to have a hostess to aid us. As Alex is a cynic in regard to women, I doubt he'll ever marry. So you see, you would be a . . . partner, of sorts. In return, you'll never want for anything again."

Audra's eyes widened. "So this would be a . . . a business arrangement?"

"If that's the way you prefer to look at it."

She should have been relieved, but she wasn't. She would still be subject to Nick's will. Audra frowned. She wasn't sure she cared for that.

Nick noticed her expression. "You've had more than enough shocks for one day. I believe a woman is entitled to some time for consideration when she receives a proposal of marriage." His smile was rueful. "I'll allow you a few days to think about it. Is that satisfactory?"

Though his tone seemed matter-of-fact, Audra sensed a tension he didn't reveal, but she was too drained to think about it now. She was only thankful he was giving her some respite.

He was right—she'd had too many shocks in too short a time. More than even he knew.

She made up her mind that evening. There was nothing to do but to leave. If she stayed, she not only endangered McKee, she was in danger of losing herself, for if she married Nick, she'd never be her own person.

That morning's incident in the study frightened her.

She hadn't been prepared—hadn't expected that she could actually be physically drawn to any man, much less Nick Brannon. She was afraid of the feelings he aroused in her. He was too dangerous.

The entire situation was dangerous. Too many things had happened in too short a time, and she just didn't think she could deal with any more. It would be better for herself, for McKee, if she left. As for Nick . . . he'd be furious, she didn't doubt. He would probably even come looking for her. Or perhaps he'd simply brand her a coward—which she admittedly was—and wash his hands of her. Somehow, she doubted that.

Quickly, before she changed her mind, she packed as many things as she could into a satchel. She would have preferred to leave the clothes Nick had purchased behind, but she had to be practical. She managed to stuff a suit and two of the day dresses, a nightgown, and a few underclothes into the bag. Some of her favorite soap. She'd pack her brushes and combs in the morning.

The diamonds were wrapped in the handkerchiefs again, then went into the velvet bag that had once held her emerald pendant. She'd pin it securely inside her riding clothes in the morning.

When she'd made all her preparations, she washed, carefully brushed her hair and tied it back, and went down to dinner. If she didn't appear, Nick would probably come up to get her.

It was a difficult hour. She had to remind herself not to fidget, and she was too excited and nervous to eat. She pushed her food around her plate absently.

"Audra?"

Audra jerked and dropped her fork. Everyone was looking at her curiously, and she realized Nick had been speaking to her. "I'm sorry," she stammered. "I didn't hear

what you said." Was he looking at her suspiciously? Audra
gave him a tentative smile.

"I asked if you'd like to accompany us to the village
tomorrow? I want Dr. Hargrove to examine McKee's arm.
We won't leave until midmorning." He didn't add that he
wanted Audra with him so he could keep an eye on
her. . . .

Good, Audra thought! She could leave before they
did, and be through the village before they got there. "Oh.
Ah, I can't. I . . . ah, I have some sewing to do."

Bertie choked on her food. Audra glanced at her and
saw that Bertie was *definitely* giving her a suspicious look.
She knew only too well that Audra had no talent at all in
that direction.

"I . . . ah, I've been practicing," she told Bertie
lamely. And to Nick, "Thank you . . . for asking," she
mumbled.

"We'll forgo our ride tomorrow morning. And you
won't go riding about the countryside alone." It was a
statement, not a question.

"No. I won't ride about the . . . er, the estate alone.
In fact, I plan to sleep in tomorrow." Audra lowered her
head and hid a small smile. Things were working out better than she'd hoped. If both Nick and McKee were going
to the village, they'd probably be gone for a considerable
time. By the time they returned and found her gone, she'd
be in London.

Chapter 14

$\mathscr{N}$ick signed his name with a flourish to one of the documents Peter had posted to him, leaned back, and stretched his arms over his head. He'd been at his desk most of the morning, ever since he'd sent McKee on to the village with Rafe. Nick had stayed behind after he and McKee had decided that one of them would remain near Audra at all times.

Rafe and McKee were both armed, despite the fact that Rafe had been sent to Stanly yesterday and had returned with the report that Silas Norton *had* been staying at the village, but had packed and left in a hurry.

Nick rubbed the back of his neck. Audra's strange behavior at dinner the evening before still bothered him. And though he hadn't expected her for breakfast since she'd planned to sleep in, he hadn't heard her voice yet this morning.

He could understand why she hadn't been talkative last night; she was still grieving. Then, too, he'd shocked her to no end with his proposal, so it wasn't odd that she'd been distracted. What disturbed him, however, was that he could swear she'd been wearing an air of suppressed excitement—as if she had a secret.

Women! They would drive him to drink—this one in particular. Nick shook his head in helpless bemusement as he bent to his papers again.

The door to the study suddenly burst open. Nick leaped up in surprise as a slim woman in a green cloak rushed in and flew into his startled arms.

"Nick! Oh, Nick, how happy I am to see you!" Disengaging himself from the clinging arms, he stepped back to gaze down into the laughing face of his sister. "Cleo!"

Her laughter pealed out again at the surprise on his face. "Not *just* Cleo, dear brother. Richard, too. Aren't we a surprise?"

"I realize, my love, that you have the gift of making most men speechless, but your brother? Really. That is too much." The coolly amused voice came from a stocky blond man standing in the doorway. He came toward them, extending his hand to Nick. "How are you, old boy? I must apologize for our unorthodox arrival, but you know Cleo."

"Hello, Richard," Nick said as he shook the other man's hand. "I didn't expect you, too, but I'm pleased, just the same. As for the manner of your arrival . . . what else could I expect with this minx? I should have known."

"Oh, Nick, we'd hoped to arrive in time to surprise you at dinner last evening, but we received a surprise of our own, instead. We lost a wheel from our carriage and were forced to spend the night at a quaint little inn. I was in a fret to get here, but you know Richard. He told me in no uncertain terms to calm down, that evening was no time to be arriving unexpectedly anyway, and we'd simply have a good rest and come this morning. I put my foot down, however, when he suggested we send a message on ahead. I did so want to surprise you!"

Cleo finally paused for breath as the two men exchanged glances. Nick raised his eyebrows while his brother-in-law only grinned and shrugged his shoulders. The two men shared perfect understanding regarding this woman they were both so fond of.

Letty came to the door to ask Nick if his guests would require a late breakfast. Cleo answered for him.

"How lovely! Yes, thank you." She went on to endear herself to Letty with her warm smile and her apology for such short notice. Nick smiled again. People were always deceived by Cleo, who only came as high as Richard's shoulder. They were taken in by her small form and charm; it seemed to produce protective instincts in most people, yet they often never realized that they were the ones being managed.

"Cleo," he stated after a bobbing Letty had departed, "you never cease to amaze me. I don't understand it because I know you as well as I know myself."

She'd removed her cloak and handed it to Richard, who smiled fondly at her when she patted his cheek. Turning back to Nick, she gave him an impish grin. "But my dear brother, that is precisely why I always change my repertoire. You'd think me dull if I was predictable, and poor Richard would be bored to death within a week's time, wouldn't you, love?"

"Of course, my dear," Richard drawled. "You know my one true weakness. I dislike boring women intensely."

Nick laughed. Thank God they'd come. Lord knew he needed the distraction right now, and Cleo would be good for Audra.

"Nick, you're scowling. Are you very angry with us?"

Nick took Cleo by the arm and guided her to a sofa, where she perched in a flurry of skirts. "Of course not. I'm surprised that Richard accompanied you, however. How did you manage it, Richard? Isn't this normally a busy time for you?"

Husband and wife exchanged quick glances. Cleo's fell, and she proceeded to pick at imaginary threads on her skirt.

Richard Pendleton's quiet words belied a sparkle of anger in his eyes. "Actually, Nick, I no longer have an occupation to keep me busy. The truth is, your letter came at a most opportune time, for your sister and her husband are quite homeless and I am without employment."

"Do you mean to tell me that your cousin did as he's always threatened and sold his farm?"

"That's exactly what the old man did, I'm afraid. Found himself a new young wife who talked him into turning the farm into more tangible assets."

Cleo broke in. "Oh, yes—the type of assets she can wear around her neck and in her ears, and I've no doubt she's earned every carat."

"Now, Cleo, don't be catty," her husband scolded. "Cousin Leo has been telling me for years that he would sell the farm and the sheep someday. He had a perfect right, after all. Even if I am his only heir, the land wasn't entailed."

"That's neither here nor there, Richard. Why, who kept the farm running and earning Cousin Leo a nice tidy little profit, I'd like to know? You spent years building it up into what it is, and what did he do? Sold it and practically threw us out!" Cleo turned to Nick. "Do you believe that he gave us only one week to pack all our possessions—and I had to plead for that much time? Not only was it unfair, it was indecent!"

Nick pressed her firmly back onto the chair. "Now, Cleo, simmer down. No sense in getting upset all over again. It's done and you're here now. Time enough to plan for your future. Richard's an excellent manager with a solid reputation. His talents will be in demand."

"Exactly what I've been trying to tell her, old boy. Perhaps between the two of us, we'll be able to convince her."

Cleo pretended to glare at her husband, then burst into a spontaneous laugh. "Really, love. The two of you have tried that trick before, and it hasn't worked."

Nick groaned. "Don't we know!" He offered his hand and helped her off the sofa. "We'll argue about this later. Right now, your breakfast must be ready, and I seem to be famished again from all this verbal sparring. I see that I'll be forced to build up my energy with you around."

"Mmm, yes. Food!"

Nick looked at Cleo in surprise. "You never took that much interest in breakfasting before."

Richard and Cleo exchanged looks. "I suppose we'd better tell him," Cleo suggested. "After all, it isn't every day we have an opportunity to announce that he's about to become an uncle."

Nick looked from Cleo to Richard. Her eyes were sparkling with mischief, and Richard was wearing a rueful, but proud, grin. "But that's wonderful! When is this blessed event to take place?"

Cleo patted her stomach. "Not for six months yet, brother dear, so you have time to get used to the idea."

They entered the hall, laughing and joking, and met Bertie just coming down the stairs. Nick made the introductions, and Bertie welcomed them warmly. "It will be wonderful for Audra to have a woman near her own age here," she added.

Cleo agreed. "I do hope so. I would very much like it if Miss Sheffield and I could be friends."

"Perhaps you'll ask her if she cares to come down now," Nick suggested to Bertie.

Bertie frowned. "I was just up there. She's not in her room. I assume she's gone outside and will be in shortly."

Cleo's stomach suddenly growled. She laughed gaily, not one whit embarrassed. "May we eat? My stomach is begging. And while we're eating, Nick, you must tell us all about your neighbors."

"Neighbors?" he asked, puzzled.

"Why, yes," Cleo said coyly. "We met the most gorgeous creature—just before we turned onto your road, wasn't it, Richard? We assumed she must live nearby, though she had a portmanteau over the cantle of her saddle. It was rather odd, however. The young lady was wearing the most beautiful blue habit, yet she was riding astride."

Bertie gasped and looked at Nick. "You don't think . . . ?"

Nick's face darkened. "I *don't* think—I *know*. Damn it! I knew she was acting strangely."

Cleo watched in fascination as Nick stalked to the door and exited the room without another word. "Goodness! Was it something I said?" she asked no one in particular.

Audra moved off the road and to a small stream in order that Fantasy might drink. After dismounting, she dipped a handkerchief into the cool water to pat at her own face and hands, then paced near the bank for a few minutes to stretch her legs.

Fantasy lifted her head and whickered softly before coming to nudge Audra's shoulder. Audra hugged her. "You're right, girl. We've rested enough. You've been a sweetheart these last weeks. I worked you hard, didn't I? But I know you understand."

She'd been on the road again only a few minutes when

she thought she heard the sound of galloping hooves behind her. She looked over her shoulder, but the road
curved around a small grove of trees, and she couldn't see
anyone. Shrugging her shoulders, she turned forward
again.

The sound came again. Alarmed now, because the
other horse seemed to be moving very swiftly, Audra
glanced back again. What she saw caused her heart to stop
for an instant.

It was Ulysses—she'd know him anywhere—and Nick.
Even at this distance, she could see the blazing fury in his
eyes.

She kicked Fantasy. Hard. The mare, startled by this
unexpected treatment, threw her head and snorted, but
obediently jerked forward. "Faster, Lady! Faster!"

How had Nick discovered she was gone? How had he
discovered *where* she'd gone? Ducking her head low, she
urged the mare on. Fantasy couldn't match Ulysses'
strength and speed, but she was watered and rested, and
another quick glance showed that Ulysses was lathered
with sweat. Nick must have run him hard and long.

Hope was brief. In a very short time, she heard Ulysses
close behind her, and then he and Nick were abreast.
There was grim determination on Nick's face. Audra
urged Fantasy still more, but the mare was already giving
her best.

Audra knew it was useless, yet she wouldn't rein in.

In one fluid motion, Nick leaned over and grabbed the
reins out of her hands and hauled both horses to a sharp
stop. It happened so fast that Audra had to grope for Fantasy's mane to keep from tumbling right over her head.

Without a word, Nick guided both horses to a tree.
Audra chanced a quick glance at him. His face held a rage
so menacing, she shuddered and looked away.

Nick swiftly dismounted and looped the reins of both

horses around a low branch. He came around Ulysses' side and, before she knew what he was about, had clasped her waist and roughly pulled her off Fantasy's back.

She gasped when his strong fingers pressed into her ribs, and opened her mouth to protest. But his hands had already moved to her shoulders, which he gripped tightly.

"Just what the hell do you think you're doing! Where were you going, you damned she-devil?"

"Stop! Oh, please, Nick. Stop yelling!" she cried.

He released her so suddenly she collapsed to her knees. "You . . . you shouted at me!" she stuttered. "You actually shouted at me," she repeated in genuine surprise. And then she covered her face

Suddenly she felt her feet leaving the ground as he lifted her into his arms. She shrieked as he threw her across the front of his saddle. Ulysses snorted and threw his head at this unexpected burden and she almost fell off again. Frantically, she clutched his mane.

Nick released the reins of both horses. Swiftly, he sprang into his saddle, pulled Audra upright, and turned both horses toward Sheffield Manor. He clamped an arm around her waist, holding her tightly to him.

Audra tried to squirm away from Nick's hard chest. "You're hurting me," she protested stiffly.

"Keep quiet!" he growled. "And don't move, or so help me, I'll stop in the middle of the road and use the palm of my hand on that soft backside of yours."

Affronted, and not a little apprehensive, Audra straightened her shoulders and sniffed in disdain. So he wanted her to be quiet, did he? Well, that was easy enough. She didn't care if she never spoke to the brute again!

After stopping to water Ulysses at the little stream she and Fantasy had just left—a task which was accomplished in complete silence—they proceeded back to Sheffield

Manor in the same silence, both angry and unyielding. Audra attempted to maintain a dignity she didn't feel. She'd thought she'd seen Nick angry before, but that held no comparison to this cold rage. What would he do to her? He'd never dare harm her physically. If he even tried, McKee would probably kill him!

Nick was contemplating the situation very much along the same lines. What the hell was he going to do with the vixen? The appearance of the satchel and the direction she'd been heading proved she was on her way to London, just as he'd thought. How in hell had she planned to manage without friends or funds? He shuddered at the thought of Audra alone, hungry, and frightened in London. My God, he thought. She obviously didn't have the slightest idea of the dangers she'd face. The city was full of unwary innocents like her, and God knew they didn't remain innocent very long. The little fool!

By the time they arrived back at the stables, Nick's fear about Audra's fate in London had only sharpened his anger. He dismounted, handed the reins of both horses to Erin silently, and went to lift Audra down.

She braced herself, prepared to be dragged off Ulysses' back ungently. Instead, Nick came behind her and wrapped one arm around her waist, pulling her off backward. To her shock, she found herself being carried under one arm like some small child.

"Put . . . put me down!" She kicked vainly.

"When I'm good and ready," he said grimly.

Audra craned her neck to see who else besides Erin was witnessing her humiliation.

Off to one side, McKee sat quietly on his horse, watching. She looked away from his accusing eyes. Nick's long strides climbed the steps to the veranda, and she saw Bertie standing at the entrance, her arms folded and her face implacable. And behind Bertie—oh, good God! Two strangers! A man and a woman, both obviously surprised, but amused at her predicament. Letty in the hall, mouth agape. Bates, eyes averted and impassive.

Audra ducked her head. No help here, she could see.

Nick slammed the study door behind them with the heel of his boot before tossing her unceremoniously upon the settee. She landed on her stomach, and lay there, helplessly gasping for air while Nick proceeded to turn her satchel upside down and empty the contents on the floor. He went through them quickly, tossing her clothing and other items carelessly about.

"Is this it?" he asked dangerously. She looked up to find him standing over her with the empty satchel.

"Is *what* it?" she managed as she scrambled to sit up.

"Is this all you were taking with you?" At her hesitant nod, he demanded, "Where were you going, Audra?"

"Somewhere. Away. To—to London," she clarified quickly when he took a threatening step forward.

"With only these few possessions? Just how the hell did you propose to keep yourself? Or have you so lost your senses that you hadn't even planned that far?" A sudden thought darkened his face. "Were you meeting someone there? Answer me, damn you!"

"Of course not," she sputtered indignantly. "That is, I wasn't meeting anyone, and yes, I made plans. I don't need anyone to take care of me. I can do it myself, contrary to your opinion. I have money—or I would have had, just as soon as I could sell . . ." Too late, she broke off.

"Sell what? There's nothing of value in that bag, Audra," he prodded with steely determination.

Damn! He wouldn't relent until he knew every detail of her planned escape. With a sigh of defeat, she stood and turned her back to him to unbutton her riding skirt. Reaching down the front, she unpinned the bag she'd so carefully hidden within the waist of her drawers. When she turned around to drop the bag into his outstretched hand, she was blushing profusely.

Nick opened the bag and shook the contents into his palm. "Very nice pieces. Where's the rest of it?"

"The . . . the rest?" Audra stammered, perplexed.

"The jewelry! I want all of it, Audra. Every piece. Yours, your mother's. Now!"

"But . . . but there is no more. That's all of it."

"I'll strip you myself if I have to. Believe me, I don't give a damn about preserving your maidenly modesty." His voice was steel, his eyes blazing golden fire. He meant it.

Audra almost stamped her foot. "There is no more, damn you!" She'd had enough. First, she'd been manhandled, then humiliated in front of everyone, and now he was threatening to strip her! "I've already sold the emerald that was a gift from my father. This is all that Mother managed to keep. William took the rest—every last piece, not that there were many to start with. I don't know if he gave them to his mistress, or sold them. My God! Do you think that I'd have let Mother live in such desperate straits if there had been anything left to sell? Do you?" Audra sank to the settee, hands over her mouth, eyes brimming with tears.

A muscle twitched in Nick's cheek, but he remained unmoved. "Where's the jewelry my uncle bought you and your mother?"

Audra raised shocked eyes to his.

"I saw the bills, damn it! I know all about them. Just as I know about the little arrangement my uncle made with Lord Cowan. So where are the jewels William bought to help attract the Earl?"

Audra's face turned white, then fiery red. Her chin shook, her mouth twisted. Nick expected her to break into sobs, but to his astonishment, she broke into unrestrained laughter, instead.

"You want . . . the jewels? Those lovely . . . little pieces that William gave to Mother and me . . . ?" She struggled for control, finally succeeded, and leaped to her feet to come to stand before him. "Wait! Wait right here. I'll get them for you." Her face was contorted with a combination of suppressed laughter, anger, and shame. She backed away from him, toward the door, her fingers fumbling with her scarf. "Wait," she said again. Her mane of hair whipped about as she spun on her heels and ran out of the room.

Nick heard her steps running up the stairs, then doors slamming on the second floor before she came running down again.

She'd gathered something into her scarf, and now she leaned over the desk and opened it. A small, gleaming pile of necklaces, ear screws, and rings fell onto his desk.

"There!" she said triumphantly, pointing to the jewelry. "There's all that *valuable* jewelry your uncle so *generously* gifted us with." She snatched a crystal paperweight from the desk and before he could stop her, brought it down with force upon the shining heap. Hard. Then again.

He reached her in two strides and snatched the paperweight from her hand in time to stop a third blow. He looked down. Most of the jewelry was now just a pile of ground glass and dust.

Slowly he turned to face Audra. She was sitting on the settee again, as stiff and still as a frozen statue.

"Paste," she said tonelessly, her eyes almost cobalt blue as they met his astonished gaze. "All paste and glass. That's how much William Brannon thought of his wife and stepdaughter. I have no doubt he bought real jewels for his mistress, but these were for show. Just as I was. He invited his friends here, especially old men with money, and he forced me to play hostess. I was his bait, you understand. He used me! Can you possibly have any idea what it was like to be used like that? I doubt it—you're a man, after all. You have no idea how sickening, how degrading and shameful it was to be ogled by lascivious eyes, cornered and pawed and . . ." She shuddered and covered her eyes.

"Don't," Nick pleaded hoarsely. "You don't have to . . ."

She was on her feet in an instant, her hair in wild disarray as she flew at him, slamming into him with enough force to rock him on his feet. "Damn you! *Damn* you!" she cried. "You wanted to know. Now you'll hear it . . . the entire sordid story." Every other word was punctuated with a hard slam of her palms against his chest, his arms, his shoulders, forcing him to step back with each blow—not so much by her physical strength, but simply by the force of her fury. "He stole everything . . . do you understand? *Everything!* He sold the livestock, then the land—Sheffield land, not his, damn you—and then"— now her fists pounded into him with each word—"after there was nothing left, after he'd used everything of value—including me—he sold me! *Sold me* . . . to that filthy, lecherous old man, as if I was no more than a . . . a . . ."

By now, she was unstoppable, an eruption of anger too long suppressed, of hurt too long contained, of humiliation too long forced upon her. Sobbing, she flailed at him hysterically, striking any place she could reach. Blows bounced off his chest, his jaw. Another struck his left ear. He stood stoically, arms limp at his sides, and accepted each one without feeling any pain but hers. He wished he could take more of it from her.

When at last she staggered and collapsed against him,

still panting harshly but subdued and spent, it took all his willpower to keep from gathering her into his arms. He desperately wanted to soothe away the pain and the shame, to kiss her and stroke her hair. To tell her that she was more precious than she could ever know.

She'd rebuff him, he knew, but he was even more afraid that she'd look at him with disgust, as she must have looked at Lord Cowan and William's other friends. Those stupid bastards who hadn't recognized a genuine gem, such as she was.

He hoped his uncle rotted in hell.

Audra stirred and took a deep, gasping breath.

He stepped away carefully, walked to his desk, and placed Serena's diamonds in a side drawer. His hands were shaking as he locked it. The key went into a pocket of his waistcoat.

"I'll marry you, Nick."

He turned slowly, his heart leaping to his throat. It took all his effort to stay still and keep his voice calm. "What did you say?" he asked carefully.

She was standing near the door, her back to him. "I said I'd marry you," she repeated quietly. "But please . . . don't ask me any questions right now. I'm very tired, and I need to be alone."

With that, she was gone, leaving Nick wearing a stunned expression as he stared at the closed door.

Chapter 15

$\mathcal{A}$udra awoke feeling stiff, but strangely rested for the first time in weeks. Not only rested, but purged of much of the uncertainty and pain of the past. The lump was still in her chest. It would always be there whenever she thought of her mother, she supposed, but it seemed smaller. She could swallow around it.

Then she bolted upright. Blazes, she'd told Nick she'd marry him! Oh, if only she hadn't been so worn out, so tired of struggling and . . . Resigned, Audra lay back against the pillows. The truth was, she just didn't have the energy to fight him anymore.

Besides, what choice did she have but to marry him? How else was she going to be safe from Norton's threats? How else could she protect McKee? If she married Nick and went to America with him, Norton would no longer be able to touch either her or McKee.

Audra frowned. She couldn't rid herself of a little niggling feeling that what she was doing wasn't really fair to

Nick. Yet, he'd practically *demanded* that she marry him. Perhaps that made them even.

Or did it? She didn't doubt that he'd also demand a full marriage. She'd sworn that she'd let no man ever control her in the way William had her mother, and yet she was now facing that very prospect.

Still, if she was to be completely honest, she had to admit that she wasn't afraid of Nick, even after his recent shocking displays of temper. And she certainly wasn't disgusted by him. On the contrary, she found his kisses . . . thrilling. At times, she'd even found it wonderfully reassuring to be held close to him.

He was, after all, *very* attractive. And there were so many other things she liked about him. The way his eyes glittered when he looked at her. The way his mouth curved when he smiled, the sound of his laugh, his purely masculine scent. . . .

Audra jerked straight up as someone knocked on her door. She pushed her sleep-tossed hair back from her face and attempted to control her vivid recollections as she called for the person to enter.

The door was pushed open tentatively, and a woman's smiling face peeked around it. "Ah, so you're awake at last! I've been all impatience the last half hour, wanting to come in and speak with you, but Richard absolutely *insisted* I must wait 'til a sensible hour. Poor Richard! He despairs of me ever being sensible!"

With this rush of words, Cleo reached the bed, from where Audra was observing her with astonishment. Setting down the tray she carried, Cleo pulled a chair close and proceeded to seat herself, fold her hands demurely on her lap, and reveal an impishly innocent smile on her face.

Audra couldn't help but laugh. Nick's sister looked

much like a child about to be reprimanded, yet sure that her punishment wouldn't be harsh.

Cleo copied Audra's laughter with her own. "I'm Cleo," she said unnecessarily. "Good morning, Audra Sheffield."

Audra smothered another laugh. "Good morning, Cleo. Do you know that you look like Nick when you laugh?"

Cleo pulled an exaggerated face. "Goodness! Really? I've been likened to several persons, but I must say, I'm flattered to be told I resemble my charming brother. Most people have no idea we're related, you know."

"I can see why. It's only obvious when you smile or laugh. Nick has the same charming manner. Sometimes."

"Ah, yes. Most men do. Sometimes."

Both women enjoyed another laugh.

"More of our charming men later." Cleo casually turned to the tray. "You must be starved after such a long sleep. I've brought tea for both of us. I do hope you don't mind, Audra, but I thought it would be a lovely way to become acquainted. I so want us to be friends. I don't have many close lady friends, and, of course, none at all here. How do you like your tea?"

"Sugar and lemon. No milk, please," Audra said shyly. "I've never had *any* lady friends. I'd like it very much if you would be the first."

Cleo handed her a cup and saucer, then sat back to sip her own tea. "Good. It's settled, then. We'll be friends as well as sisters."

"Nick told you?"

"That you're to be married? Yes. I must say, I despaired for years, but now that he's made the decision, I approve most heartily." Cleo's eyes made frank appraisal of Audra's face and hair. "You're very beautiful, you know. Even more so than I expected."

"Expected? I'm afraid I don't understand."

"Nick has written often since he's been here. Of course, he's mentioned you. Several times, actually."

"Oh." Audra pondered while she sipped her tea. Finally, she asked hesitantly, "Did he . . . did Nick say that I . . . that he thought I was . . . beautiful?"

Cleo smiled sympathetically. "I think his exact words were that you are the most *exquisite* creature he has ever seen."

"Oh!" Audra softly exhaled, then lowered her head so that her hair would hide her blush. And the fact that Cleo's revelation gave her a deliciously warm feeling inside.

Cleo pretended to not see Audra's confusion. She poured more tea into Audra's cup, then offered the sugar bowl to her. "Nick said you'd had a nasty fall off your horse two days ago. Are you still very bruised?"

"Not very. I was a little shaken, however." Audra hesitated fractionally. "About that little scene yesterday . . ."

Cleo raised her hand. "You don't have to explain. I'm only thankful Nick didn't throttle you. He's not the most patient of men, as you've probably already learned."

Audra's eyes widened. "Oh, but I wouldn't have blamed him, Cleo. I haven't always been very nice to him. The truth is, he's been extraordinarily patient with me. Even when I haven't deserved it, such as pretending to be Agnes."

"Agnes?"

Audra blushed. "I played a terrible trick on Nick. . . ." She went on to tell Cleo of her little charade.

Cleo listened, speechless, until Audra was finished. "And Nick didn't shout and blister your ears? I can't believe it—he's always been such a perfectionist. And he absolutely will not tolerate being made a fool of. Hm." Cleo eyed Audra speculatively. Her brother had made it sound as if this marriage was one of convenience. Now she wasn't so sure. "Well," she said, grinning, "it's all rather exciting—a wedding, a runaway bride who pretended to be a maid. I must say, Audra, it's far from the quiet country life I expected."

Audra's laughter pealed out. "I suppose it is. Things haven't been boring at Sheffield since Nick arrived." She sobered. "And I must apologize for not coming back down to meet you."

Cleo didn't answer immediately, only continued to look at her shrewdly. Audra was somewhat disconcerted to discover that Cleo's gaze was almost as piercing as Nick's, though Cleo's eyes were a soft brown and not tawny gold.

"It's quite all right," Cleo finally said. "You needn't apologize. I think I know what you've been going through, Audra. I lost both my parents, though I was much younger when my mother died. Father loved us very much, but he was rather busy, and Nick left home when I was ten, so I, too, felt very alone."

Audra realized that Cleo really did understand the loss she felt. It must have been even more traumatic for Cleo to lose her mother at such a young age. And though Audra had no siblings, as Cleo had Nick, she'd had Mc-Kee.

Cleo patted her stomach and smiled gently. "Now that I'm about to have my own child, I plan to make certain that this one has brothers and sisters. That way, he—or she—won't be alone."

"You're having a baby?"

Cleo nodded.

"Oh. Aren't you frightened?"

"Of having a baby, or becoming a mother?"

"Of having it. My . . . my mother had a terrible time, and she was never well after. . . ." Audra closed her eyes, remembering with a pang the perfectly formed still-

born boy who would have been her half brother. There
had been only Audra and Mrs. Murphy to bathe and dress
the tiny body. Just before they'd laid the baby in the min-
iature casket McKee had made, Audra had pressed her
cheek to his and wept because he'd never grow into a boy.
It hadn't mattered that William was the father—she
would have loved her brother, regardless. She would have
taught him to climb trees and ride. . . .

"Audra?" Cleo was calling her name softly.

"I'm sorry. I was daydreaming."

"You're forgiven. As to your question—of course, I'm
afraid. But women have been having babies forever, and
doctors are much more advanced nowadays. And Richard
had promised to be there when it happens. As long as he's
with me, I can handle anything. Well, almost anything,
except spiders. I can't abide spiders!"

"Neither can I!"

They smiled at one another in perfect harmony, and
Cleo rose to leave. "Nick told me I was only permitted a
half hour with you, and that if I couldn't limit my tongue,
he'd come and remove me forcibly, if need be," she said,
laughing. "He says you're to have a hot bath to rid you of
your aches, and we'll await breakfast. But hurry, Audra.
I'm so eager for Richard to meet you. You'll adore him.
Most people do. He can't help it, but he's actually more
charming than either Nick or I!" Laughing, Cleo exited,
with a final wave to Audra.

Audra had to gather her courage to come downstairs, for
she didn't know what to say to Nick about her appalling
lack of control after he'd brought her back to Sheffield.
Would he look at her with disgust and condemnation?
Should she apologize?

When she saw that he was waiting for her at the bottom of the stairs, she hesitated. But when he looked up at her with only concern in his eyes, when his mouth curved into a relieved smile, she knew it would be all right.

He took her hand as she met him on the landing. "We have some time before breakfast," he told her. "I'd like to speak with you privately for a few moments, if you don't mind."

She had a moment of trepidation, for though he was still smiling, his eyes were somber. Still, he was squeezing her hand reassuringly, so she nodded and let him lead her into the study.

Once there, he surprised her again by seating her in a chair, then standing before her, his hands clasped behind his back.

"I promise I'll only ask once. But I need to know. Why did you try to run away, Audra?"

He deserved her honesty. "I was confused. It all seemed too much." She swallowed painfully. "Mother dying . . . McKee being shot . . . you."

"Me?" he prodded.

Her lids fell. "Yes. You asking me to marry you."

"Is the thought of being married to me so repugnant to you, little one?" he asked gently.

"No," she replied truthfully. There was something she needed to say to him. As embarrassing as it was, she needed to know. Her head lifted. "Except . . . this marriage. You don't mean for it to be . . . That is, I don't know if I can . . . " She faltered, her cheeks a furious bloom of color.

Nick sighed. He'd been afraid of this. "I damn well *do* expect it. I know you, Audra, better than you know yourself right now. If I allow you to put this off, if I allow less than a marriage in the fullest sense, you'll continue to find excuses, or to defy me. I don't want any discord between us. Therefore, we'll begin as I intend for this marriage to go on. Do you understand?"

"Yes." Despite the quiver that went through her, she was relieved to have it out in the open. At least she wouldn't have to torment herself, wondering.

Her eyes widened as Nick sank to his knees before her, but he only stroked her cheek with the back of one hand. "Be sure, sweetheart. I won't allow you to change your mind."

She met his gaze head-on. "I won't. I've given my word."

His mouth curved. It was such a sweet smile, she couldn't help returning it.

"All right," he said calmly. "Tomorrow we'll meet with the minister. I'll see about a special license. The wedding will be a very small, very quiet affair out of respect for your recent bereavement. I realize I'm asking you to break all the rules, but I've noticed that you're not wearing mourning. . . ."

"Mother wouldn't have wanted me to," she said quickly. "She refused to let me wear it after Father died."

"Good, because I've planned an intimate betrothal dinner a couple of days from now. It will be a way to announce our intentions and put a stop to the gossip. I'd like you to wear the ivory gown I gave you."

Audra's smile faltered. Everything was happening too fast. "You've planned a dinner. You've dictated what I'm to wear. Am I to assume that you've already chosen the wedding day, and what I'm to wear then, also?" she asked sweetly.

"Yes, of course," Nick said carelessly as he began to pace. He was too engrossed in his thoughts and plans to notice the warning glints in her eyes. "We'll be married a week from today. I'll send Peter instructions regarding your gown. I'll also have him book our passage to the States. I should have sailed weeks ago, as it is."

Audra fumed silently. She was tempted to tell him he could go to Hades, but she'd given her word that she'd marry him. Still, she hadn't expected for things to happen quite so soon. Worse, it seemed that she was to have no say in anything. Didn't he realize that she would at least like to be *asked*? Blazes! Were all men this dense?

Then her lips curved in a secret smile. Perhaps it was time to remind Nick Brannon that she was no child, but a woman with a mind of her own.

She stood and faced him. "Well, then. It seems you have everything taken care of," she said quietly, and smiled sweetly to allay his suspicions. "Now . . . what about breakfast? I'm starving."

Nick glanced at her strangely, but when he saw her smile, he came to her and offered his arm. "Breakfast," he agreed.

Richard was indeed charming. He greeted Audra by kissing her hand, and he did it with such naturalness and aplomb that she didn't feel one bit uncomfortable.

The two hours the four of them spent lingering over breakfast and coffee was a complete revelation to Audra. Even to her inexperienced eyes, see could see that Cleo and Richard were devoted to one another. They spent an inordinate amount of time teasing one another, but always with intimate smiles and private messages passing from one pair of eyes to another.

Audra couldn't help but glance at Nick from time to time, wondering what he thought of this behavior, but apparently he didn't see anything at all extraordinary about it. Once, he even caught her eye and winked at *her*!

Over the next two days, Audra observed Richard and

Cleo closely. She was so bemused, in fact, that she failed to notice that all this time, Nick was carefully observing *her* with a small, satisfied smile on his face.

Cleo was funny and sweet, and for the first time in years, Audra *did* have a companion of her own age. The two of them spent time visiting and laughing, and Audra was distracted enough so that her encounter with Norton was pushed to the back of her mind.

The household was in a mood of excitement about the upcoming nuptials. To Audra's disgust, Bertie and McKee expressed no surprise at all, only delighted approval. There was a short meeting with Reverend Trewer, who, instead of chastising them for ignoring the social dictates of a decent mourning period, expressed his approval of the nuptials so heartily that Audra knew that Nick hadn't exaggerated about the gossip.

The guests were gathered in the drawing room. Champagne had been poured, but the air of celebration was slowly being replaced by a slight tension. The bride-to-be hadn't yet made her appearance.

Cleo wasn't deceived for one minute by her brother's insouciance. Nick was smiling as he listened to Reverend Trewer expound on the virtues of his congregation, but Cleo clearly recognized the dangerous glint in his eyes. She almost held her breath when the Reverend's wife, oblivious to the budding tension, blurted out the question they were all dying to ask.

"Goodness, Mr. Brannon. What in the world is taking your betrothed so long?"

Nick smiled tightly, but replied smoothly enough. "I assume she wants to look her best. You must excuse her, Mrs. Trewer, but I understand that affianced women are sometimes a bit nervous."

"I do understand. Why, when I was to marry the Reverend, I . . ."

"Excuse me, madam. I see that my sister has need of me."

Cleo, having heard this exchange, managed not to look surprised. At Nick's almost imperceptible signal, she followed him out the door to the hallway. He turned to her the moment they were out of earshot, his back to the stairs. His genial air had disappeared. "If that little minx got it in her mind to abscond again, I'll break her neck when I get my hands on her—*after* I paddle her delectable little backside with my bare hand!" he said through gritted teeth.

Cleo wasn't fooled. Nick was more worried than angry.

"I'll go up and see what's taking Audra so long," she offered. "Perhaps she needs some help. . . ." Cleo's eyes widened as she glanced over Nick's shoulder. "Ohh . . . my . . . *Lord*!"

Nick spun about.

The woman descending the stairs was *not* the one he'd expected. He'd specifically asked her to wear the ivory evening gown he'd purchased for her. All day he'd envisioned her in that pure gown, all innocence and allure.

This woman was a temptress, a seductress wearing a ruby gown that was cut so low it was almost indecent. He could tell that she was wearing a corset beneath it, for her breasts were pushed high, and bounced with each step. He gritted his teeth. There was absolutely no doubt in his mind that she'd deliberately dressed to provoke him.

Where had she gotten the gown? It looked vaguely familiar, but he knew damned well it hadn't been among the clothing he'd purchased for her, because he'd approved every item himself.

Masses of hair were piled upon the back of her head, heavy enough to force her to hold her head unnaturally and make her pert nose appear to view the world with disdain.

Which was just the expression she turned on him, the little minx!

He was so relieved that she'd appeared at all, anger was replaced by amusement. Relief, too, because her rebellion meant that she'd recovered some of her spirit.

She reached the bottom of the stairs and swayed toward him, smiling sweetly. He wasn't deceived. Her every move, every action spoke defiance. Her eyes remained glued to his.

"Good evening, Nickolas. Cleo. I do hope I'm forgiven for being so late, but I never *dreamed* it would take so long to transform myself into the kind of woman I knew you *preferred*, Nick," she purred.

He almost smiled, despite himself. But he wasn't going to let her off that easily. He took her hand and, instead of kissing the back of it, turned it over and kissed her palm.

Audra was slightly taken aback, but recovered quite nicely, he thought. "And it was worth all your efforts, sweet. Delia's gown looks much better on you." He'd finally recalled why the gown looked familiar. "I only hope the good Reverend will appreciate it as much as I do," he said smoothly.

She jerked her hand free. "Reverend Trewer! Nick! You didn't tell me you invited him!" Audra's eyes were wide with dismay.

"And Mrs. Trewer, of course," he said innocently as he tucked her arm under his and drew her toward the drawing room. "And let's see—Dr. and Mrs. Hargrove, and of course, our nearest neighbors, the Eberlys."

Audra planted her feet. This wasn't going the way she'd planned, damn him! She'd hoped to make it clear to him that she wasn't going to allow him to control her. But who would have thought he'd invite Reverend Trewer and his prim little wife, and . . . Oh, Lord, that nosy bat Mrs. Eberly? And Mrs. Hargrove. Audra loved the doctor dearly for his care of Serena, but his wife was second only to Mrs. Eberly as the biggest gossip in the county!

"Nick, I . . ."

"Something the matter, sweet?" Nick looked down at her, his expression one of complete innocence.

"If you don't mind, I think I'd like to change . . . my gown," she said weakly.

"Why didn't you say so?"

And with that, he simply picked her up in his arms and headed up the stairs. Audra remembered the company in the drawing room just in time to stifle her screech of outrage.

"I'll tell them you'll be down shortly," Cleo called from below, and waved gaily. Audra had completely forgotten Cleo was witnessing the entire humiliating incident. She lowered her face to Nick's chest and groaned. Pins spilled out of her hair. It came loose and fell to drag against the carpeted stairs.

"Nick! Put me down!"

His only reply was to tighten his hold on her.

Nick carried her into her room and let her slip down his arms and onto her feet. "You've got six minutes," he announced.

"Six! I'll never get changed in six minutes! I'll need Letty to help, and . . ."

Nick thrust his fingers into the bodice of her gown. Audra stood, frozen with disbelief as he ripped it from her body and tossed it aside in disgust. "Destroy that," he ordered brusquely. "Where's your ivory gown? In here?" He was already opening the door to her closet. "Get rid of that damned contraption you have on. I don't want any corset leaving marks on your body."

As his back was still to her, she thought it might be a good time to obey. But her fingers fumbled with the fastenings. Nick suddenly appeared and, brushing her fingers aside, pulled the laces free himself. "You don't need this," he said, as he stripped her mother's corset from her and threw it after the ruined gown.

Audra, mortified and not knowing what part of her she should conceal first, stood unmoving in her lacy camisole and petticoats. She remained frozen until Nick slipped the ivory gown over her head and turned her about to button it. She felt like such a fool. She was standing in her bedroom, letting Nick disrobe and dress her like some dressmaker's dummy, and making no objection whatsoever. "I . . . I thought perhaps the red gown . . ." She faltered.

"No. That one's only for me to see."

"Oh."

"Where's your hairbrush?"

She gestured toward her dressing table. He got the brush then stood behind her to pull it through her hair. It was too much!

"I'll do it!" she said, snatching it out of his hand. She went back to her dressing table, needing to get away from him. She didn't want him to brush her hair; it was too intimate an act. Which was a ridiculous way to feel, considering that he'd just stripped her and dressed her!

She brushed furiously, trying to pretend he wasn't there, but when she couldn't resist a quick glance in her mirror she saw that he was very much still in the room. He was leaning against her closed door, arms folded over his chest and one ankle crossed in front of the other. She meant to look away immediately, but for the first time she noticed how handsomely dressed he was himself.

He was wearing a beautifully tailored cutaway coat with matching vest. His shirt was pristine white silk and his trousers were cut so perfectly that she knew they'd been tailored just for him. His shining hair was carefully brushed back, though Audra would have preferred to see the usual lock of hair over his forehead.

She was immediately remorseful. He'd dressed carefully. This party meant something to him, and she'd tried to spoil it. Suddenly, she felt incredibly stupid and childish.

She put the brush down and went to stand before him, her eyes fixed on his cravat. "Nick," she began, "I'm sorry I tried to ruin the evening for you. But I was so angry because you'd made all these plans without asking, even telling me what I would wear. I realize now that it was childish. I should just have told you how I felt."

There was a long moment of silence. Audra wanted to peep at his face through her lashes, but was too afraid. She watched his legs straighten, instead.

Her chin was lifted gently. "No. I'm the one who's sorry. You're right. I should have asked you, not told you. Forgive me. I was overly eager to have things settled between us."

Her eyes went wide. "You were?"

One corner of Nick's mouth twisted wryly. "Very much so." He stroked her cheek with the back of his knuckles.

Audra's eyes went storm-dark blue with emotion. Could it mean that he cared for her, just a little? Why it should matter, she didn't know. Only the thought that he might gave her a warm, fuzzy feeling in her stomach. She was too shy to ask him. Instead, she returned his smile. "Thank you for not being angry," she whispered.

"We'll discuss gratitude later," he told her as he took her arm. "Right now, we've got guests, and they're probably hungry enough to be chewing on the furniture."

* * *

The last of the guests had just been seen out after a delightful dinner party. Richard watched Cleo stifle a huge yawn, and suggested it was time he got her to bed.

Nick took Audra's hand. She gave him an inquiring look.

"Come with me, sweet. I have something I want to give you."

Bemused and more than a little curious, she let him lead her into his study and to the desk. "Stay right there," he ordered as he dropped her hand and went around the other side. She watched as he took a key from his pocket and unlocked the drawer he'd secreted her mother's diamonds in. She thought he was going to return them to her, but instead, he pulled out a jeweler's box. Two jeweler's boxes.

Nick came back around and took her hand again. "Come along," he coaxed, and led her through the doorway into the library and to the fireplace. She was about to pull her hand from his and sit in the little chintz chair, but he clasped her hand tighter and shook his head. "Over here," he said, and led her to the large chair, where he promptly sat down and gave her hand a little jerk.

She landed exactly where he'd wanted her—in his lap. Her soft exclamation of surprise turned into a sputtering laugh. "Nickolas Brannon! You could have simply asked!"

He chuckled deeply. "And give you the opportunity to deny me? Oh no, my sweet. You've been opposing me for far too long."

"Perhaps you should have chosen a different woman," she shot back. "One who is silent and demure and only knows how to say 'yes, Nicky' and 'no, Nicky.' "

Nick rolled his eyes. "If you ever call me Nicky, I'll probably wring your delectable little neck," he threatened.

Audra laughed again, for he was glowering at her in

exaggerated fierceness. But her laughter died out, for his expression was slowly changing to one of serious intensity.

"Audra, sweet . . . before we go any further, we need to clear up some matters. What would you think of asking Richard and Cleo to stay on while we're in America? He's an excellent manager. Sheffield will be in good hands, I promise you."

"Richard does seem to be very knowledgeable, and Cleo loves Sheffield. Yes. I'd like that."

"Good. The other question is whether you'd prefer to live at Sheffield after we're married?"

"Do you mean I have a choice?"

"Absolutely. I still intend to take you to the States for a honeymoon journey. I want to show you the country of my birth, but we don't have to live there if you'd rather not. It will be necessary to clear up a number of business matters, first, but if you don't like America, then yes, I'm willing to return. Alex and I will work something out."

He saw that he'd surprised her. Did she think that he'd intended to drag her away from all that was familiar, all that she loved so dearly? "Will it be so difficult to leave, little one?" he asked gently.

"No. Oh, no!" she replied quickly. "I'd already decided that the memories here are too painful. Besides, you've made me so curious about America. I'm eager to see it. I'd love to go." She gave him a smile that melted his heart. "Thank you, Nick, for giving me the choice."

He grinned. "You see, I *can* learn to defer to my wife."

"I'm not your wife yet," she reminded him.

"But you will be in just a few short days," he said, staring down at her.

Audra's stomach quivered as the golden flames in his eyes burned brighter and hotter, until the heat seemed to flow between them. It became difficult to breathe. She felt

as if she was melting slowly—dissolving right into him—
into his lap. . . .

Nick saw immediately when Audra became aware of
his arousal. The dazed look in her eyes changed to one of
alarm. Blushing delightfully, she glanced away and stirred
restlessly, which almost brought a groan to his lips. She
was so damned innocent, she didn't even know that her
movements were inciting him only more! He struggled for
control, not wanting to frighten her.

In a few days they would be married, and he could
wait. If he frightened her now, she'd doubtless spend the
next days worrying and not sleeping well, and her wedding
day would be ruined. And, he admitted ruefully to himself,
he sure as hell didn't want her worn out by that evening!

He reached for the smaller of the boxes he'd dropped
between his thigh and the chair. "I meant to give this to
you before dinner, but I'm afraid I was a bit distracted
. . . by a minx in a red gown." He smiled to show her
he'd forgiven her. "Give me your hand."

Audra obeyed, and before she'd realized it, Nick had
slipped a ring onto her finger. "Oh! Oh, Nick! It's beautiful," she cried as she held her hand up to let the stones
catch the light. "Are they diamonds? Yes, of course, they
are," she answered herself. "And the emerald . . . it
would have matched my pendant perfectly." She turned
back to him, surprise and delight written on her face. "Oh,
I don't know what to say!"

He grinned in satisfaction. "Say 'thank you,' Audra."

"Oh! Of course! Thank you!"

"There's something else." Her eyes widened in anticipation. "Close your eyes and lower your head," he ordered,
and was amused to see that she obeyed immediately, her
pretty nose wrinkled in impatience, like a child's. "Don't
you dare look," he warned.

Audra felt his hands brush her ears before something

cool touched her skin, just below her throat. Nick gathered her hair to one side, then his warm fingers touched her nape before he spread her hair over her shoulders again.

"You may open your eyes now."

She did so, and straightening, felt the cool stone against her skin. She glanced down eagerly.

Nick watched the expressions on her face go from delight to disbelief to surprised joy as she turned to him.

"Nick! It's my emerald!" she exclaimed, clutching the jewel tightly. "Oh, Nick . . . how did you know?"

"McKee. When he told me about Fantasy, he told me about the emerald, and how you had to sell it. Thank God the jeweler had the sense to hold on to it, in case you came back for it."

"He did?"

Nick nodded. "You can thank your father for that."

"My father? I don't understand."

"Do you know Mr. Purdy—the village chemist?" She nodded. "It was your father who helped Mr. Purdy go into business. Purdy became successful, and now owns a number of apothecary shops in several different villages. So successful, in fact, that he was able to help his relatives, including his cousin who was a jeweler's apprentice, open his own shop in London."

"Oh! How like Father to do something so generous."

"It's a wedding gift. I'm giving it to you now because I thought you may want to wear it on your wedding day."

"Yes, I would. Oh, Nick, it's the most wonderful gift you could have given me! I don't know how to thank you!"

He gave her a long considering look from under his thick lashes. "I don't think a thank-you kiss would be out of order, considering that we're to become man and wife," he teased.

Well. At least she wouldn't have to stand on tiptoe this time, for they couldn't get much closer than this, Audra thought. She closed her eyes and leaned forward. She'd meant to put her lips to his just briefly, but they seemed to linger of their own accord. He smelled so good, so familiar, and he was warm, and his arms were going around her waist, and it just seemed natural to lift hers, too, and curl them around his neck.

He wasn't moving, and he was holding her only loosely. She felt perfectly comfortable, so when he murmured against her lips, she responded automatically.

"Open your mouth, sweetheart."

She should have anticipated it, but she wasn't prepared for his moist tongue as it invaded her mouth. It twisted and twined about hers, as if savoring the taste of her. It was so sensual, so erotic, she trembled. Nick pressed her closer to plant little nibbling kisses on her face and neck. He bent her over his arm, his lips were warm on her skin, and it felt so wonderful she wasn't the least bit alarmed.

She wasn't even aware that he'd loosened the front of her gown until his thumbs slid erotically over the tips of her breasts. Her nipples puckered in response, making her gasp. Immediately, Nick's mouth replaced his thumb. Audra was too shocked to protest as he suckled through the silk fabric covering her, and by the time it occurred to her to do so, his mouth was drawing new, strange feelings from the depths of her being, and unexpectedly filling her with a longing she'd never before known. She wanted desperately to find what it was she yearned for, to fulfill it. She arched toward him and drew his head closer. She heard Nick groan, and felt his teeth graze her nipple.

He was above her, and around her, surrounding her with scent and sensation and, unbelievably, she didn't feel threatened at all. She just wanted to be closer, to have this wonderful feeling go on forever. She pressed her hips into his.

"Oh, God! Don't move, sweet," Nick suddenly groaned. His voice was filled with such raw pain, it alarmed her. She immediately stilled and opened her eyes to look at him as he raised his head. His eyes were closed tightly, and his breathing was a harsh sound in the quiet room. There was a fine bead of sweat on his lip and more of his hair had fallen over his forehead. This time, Audra did reach to brush it back.

Nick's burning golden gaze met hers. "Oh, God!" he said again, and this time it sounded like a prayer. Gently, he placed his hand against her cheek and pressed her face to his chest. She could hear the frantic drumming of his heart.

For the first time, Audra realized that it was *she* who could rouse his emotions. *She* who could make him lose that steely control. *She* who had some unfathomable power over him.

It was a heady discovery.

She was rather pleased about it.

Maybe being married to Nick wouldn't be such a bad thing, after all. If only it didn't involve . . .

She must have sighed, for Nick's breath touched her cheek as he lowered his head to look down at her. "Something wrong?" he asked softly.

"No. Yes. Nick . . ."

"Yes, my love?"

Audra took a deep breath and lifted her flushed face, but quickly hid it again.

"Something *is* wrong!" he said in alarm, twining his fingers in her hair and gently pulling her face away to peer down at her.

"No! It's just that I need to say something to you, and

I can't do it when you're . . . when you're looking at me
. . . like that."

He saw that she was very serious. Deciding it best to
humor her, he tucked her face against his chest again.
"What is it?" he teased gently as he stroked her hair.

"It's just that . . . well, it stands to follow that there's
to be a . . . uh, a wedding night. You've already made
that clear . . . but I've just realized . . . " She knew she
was chattering terribly and snapped her mouth closed.

Nick waited patiently, but she didn't resume. "Is it
that you don't know what to expect, Audra? You *do* know
what goes on between a husband and a wife?"

She raised her head to look at him indignantly. "Of
course, I do. I'm not stupid! This used to be a breeding
farm, after all—we bred the finest sheep and horses in the
county!" He was suddenly grinning from ear to ear, and
his chest was rumbling suspiciously. "Nick Brannon—
don't you dare laugh at me!"

He tried to straighten his mouth, with little success.

"Oh, all right! I know I can't compare animals with
people, but after all—the concept is the same. Isn't it?"

Now he did burst out laughing. Audra finally had to
laugh herself, but she quickly sobered. "I'm serious, Nick.
And it isn't the . . . the act itself I'm so concerned
about. Well, it *is*, but it's really . . . " Finally, she hid her
face again and just blurted it out. "I assume you want an
heir, and I'm afraid . . . that is, I don't want to become
pregnant."

Nick took a deep breath. So that was it! Damn! He
should have foreseen this. Should have realized that her
mother's experiences had affected her deeply. Truth to
tell, he didn't want her pregnant either—not yet, anyway.
He wanted her to himself for a time. She was only twenty.
Time enough to overcome her fears and change her attitude.

"Audra," he said gently as he lifted her chin. "Look at me. Having an heir isn't that important to me. Shh," he prompted as she began to speak. "Now, I don't want you to be embarrassed; I'm only trying to plan ahead. May I ask you some personal questions?"

Puzzled, she nodded.

He proceeded to ask her a number of questions about her intimate bodily functions, and she was mortified, but she stuttered through until he was satisfied.

"I think there's little likelihood that you'll became pregnant in the days immediately after our wedding, sweet. There's no reason for us not to enjoy our lovemaking to the fullest."

A little thrill ran through her at his use of the word "lovemaking." Still . . . "But, Nick . . ."

"No buts. There *are* ways to prevent it," he informed her.

"There are?"

His mouth quirked at her astonishment. "Yes, there are. You won't even have to worry about it. I promise I'll take care of it. Will you trust me to do that?"

His heart turned over as she studied him. Did she still have reservations about him? God knew she'd never had much reason to trust men. But he *would* take care of her. He'd promise whatever she wanted—as long as she stayed with him. There was no way in hell he would ever let her go.

"Yes. I trust you, Nick." And she gave him a radiant smile as she wrapped her arms around him and snuggled up to his chest.

Nick laid his cheek against her hair and held her tightly against him. Eyes closed, he breathed a prayer of thanks.

She was so young. Her girlhood had been arrested at a time when she should have been blossoming, learning to become a woman. But by marrying him, he'd be able to give her that now—give her the freedom to spread her wings, give her the time to discover who she was and the woman she could be.

And most significant of all, he'd teach her to love him.

Chapter 16

One recent morning, when Cleo had been feeling low and had invited her into her bedroom for morning coffee, Audra had seen an unusual red mark on Cleo's neck, near the top of her low-cut nightdress. Audra was positive Cleo hadn't had the mark before. Had Richard made it?

He was such a nice man; he didn't seem the kind to hurt anyone, but for all Audra knew, all men changed while they were making love. Audra wanted desperately to ask Cleo what marriage was really like, but was too embarrassed, in part because Nick was Cleo's brother.

How could she tell Cleo about the strange feelings Nick's caresses roused in her? Like that warm and buttery melting in her stomach? Or the tingling in her breasts? Or even disappointment sometimes—like the night of the dinner when Nick had set her on her feet, given her a chaste last kiss, and bid her good night?

She'd been tempted to push him a little further, just to

see if she could break through that perfect control of his. Just to see what he'd do. But strangely enough, he hadn't kissed her since.

What were men really like while in the throes of passion? she wondered. When Nick's kisses intensified, his eyes would gleam with that strange light and—she couldn't help it—her emotions seesawed between fear and longing for him to continue. It was confusing. It was frustrating.

She tried to tell herself that it would all come out right. Women didn't *die* from being married, after all!

But on the day of her wedding, she still had doubts.

Two days before, a carriage had arrived from London with a shy young man who was introduced to her as Nick's assistant, Peter Winters. And with him had come boxes and boxes of new clothing for both her and Cleo, including Audra's wedding gown.

It was the most beautiful gown she'd ever seen. Made of white satin, the bodice, long sleeves, and short train trimmed only with Valenciennes lace, it was pure in its simplicity. The square neckline was a frame for the emerald pendant. Her mother's wedding veil, adorned with honeysuckle from the garden, was perfect with it.

Nick had insisted that, despite the hasty wedding, it was necessary to do things correctly, and so the closest neighbors had been invited to attend both the ceremony and the wedding breakfast. He wanted to dispel the rumors once and for all, he explained. To that purpose, he'd also let it be known that the wedding was being held so shortly after Serena's death only because he had to return to America and wanted to take his bride with him.

"There," Cleo said, as she made the last adjustment, then stood back. "Oh, Audra! You look positively ethereal."

Letty nodded, her face alight with approval.

"Your mother's veil is the 'something old,' the gown is the new, one of the garters you're wearing is blue . . . you need something borrowed, Audra. I know . . . Letty, run and get one of my lace handkerchiefs!"

"And a sixpence for your shoe, Miss Audra. You need one of those, too," Letty reminded them as she slipped through the door.

"There's one on my dressing table," Audra told her future sister-in-law. "Cleo, are you certain I look all right?"

"Absolutely," Cleo said as she handed Audra the sixpence. "Are you excited?"

"No," Audra admitted with a small laugh. "But I'm nervous. Cleo . . . " But Letty had already returned with the handkerchief. Audra sighed. It was too late to ask Cleo now. She should have garnered her courage and done it days ago.

When Cleo and Letty finally agreed that she was ready and left her alone for a few minutes, Audra stood in front of the mirror, staring at her reflection.

The woman staring back seemed a stranger.

She'd never envisioned herself thus, yet here she was, dressed in bridal white—and feeling like a lost lamb ready for slaughter.

She touched the veil, then the pendant at her neck for good luck, took a deep breath, and squared her shoulders. She wasn't really alone, after all. Somehow, she knew that her mother and father were with her.

Nick watched Audra come down the aisle on McKee's arm and thought she had never looked more beautiful. Her raven hair was loose, pulled back at her temples and held in place with pearl-studded combs. The purity of her gown only heightened the blush of her skin. Her blue eyes were pinned upon him as she walked up the aisle of the small church—somewhat apprehensively, he thought.

She was everything he'd envisioned, dressed in her bridal white. Innocent, but alluring. Beautiful, but shy. She took his breath away. He felt his body stirring, but tamped it down. God forbid he'd make a spectacle of himself at his own wedding!

He smiled and took her hands as she came to him. They were ice-cold. He squeezed them reassuringly, and was relieved when she gave him a tentative smile in return.

Audra had been surprised to find that the little village church was almost filled. She recognized many of their neighbors. This was a small, private wedding?

She saw Nick, tall and handsome in his formal cutaway suit and vest, and experienced a moment of pride that he was waiting for *her*! And when he greeted her with a warm smile and a squeeze of her hands, she was able to relax enough to speak her vows clearly and without faltering.

Nick slipped the simple gold band onto her finger, and Reverend Trewer pronounced them man and wife. Nick took her gently by the shoulders and kissed her rather more fervently than she'd expected, leaving her blushing and flustered. The guests seemed to find it appropriate, however, for she heard noises of approval.

They exited the church and found that practically the entire village had come out to send their blessings with the bride and groom. Nick led her to their carriage through a throng of well-wishers. He sat close beside her on the way back to Sheffield Manor, holding her hand and making small talk, amusing her with impersonations of some of the gentry who had been at the wedding. He seemed to divine her nervousness, and his attitude was one of relaxed carelessness.

The servants were all waiting outside the Manor. Even Bates dropped his stiff attitude long enough to wish them well. Just before the guests arrived for the breakfast, Audra excused herself. Nick stood at the study window, watching as she walked to the small knoll between the house and the woods where the family cemetery was and knelt at her parents' graves.

McKee and Bertie came into the room and joined him. They observed Audra silently as she placed her bridal bouquet upon Serena's grave.

"It's more difficult than she thought it would be, I think—preparing to leave the only home she's known," Nick said without moving away from the window.

"Aye," McKee agreed, his voice not quite steady. "But she canna go back, only forward."

"Yes. It's time for her to spread her wings," Bertie agreed, mopping at her eyes with an already sopping handkerchief.

Nick turned to look down at them both. "You could still change your minds and come with us."

McKee shook his head mournfully. "Sheffield needs me more than Audra does right now. The lass understands that. Besides, she has ye now, doesna she?" McKee's look was acute.

Nick nodded. "That she does." He turned to Bertie. "What about you? The change would be less difficult for her."

"She needs to learn to trust you fully, and you need time to teach her. Besides, I abhor water, Nick. I turn green just watching the swans swimming in the pond in front of the house. I would only be a nuisance."

Nick laughed. "We'll both miss you two. Still, I've promised Audra we'd return, but it may be months. Perhaps even a year."

McKee tried to speak, but choked up. Giving Nick an

awkward pat on the shoulder, he left the room without saying anything more. Bertie managed a quick hug. "I'll make you a promise, Nick Brannon—if you're still in the States when you and Audra are expecting your first child, send for me. It will be the only thing that will make me brave the waves and come."

"I'll hold you to that," Nick replied.

When Audra returned to the house, the drawing room was full of people. Where had they all come from? It was easy to pick Nick out, for he was inches taller than anyone else in the room, which was probably how he found her immediately, also. A number of the guests saw her, too, and cheers of "a toast, a toast" went up.

"How are you holding up?" Nick asked as he came to her.

"Wonderfully!" she announced with a gaiety she didn't feel.

"They've been waiting for your arrival to begin the toasts." Nick lowered his head to rest his cheek against hers. "I think I should warn you," he whispered into her ear, "that Mrs. Eberly is waiting to pounce again." His voice contained a hint of laughter.

Audra turned wide eyes to him. "Really?" she asked innocently. "Is she wearing her black vulture cape?"

"Unfortunately, this one is an atrocious shade of purple." He rolled his eyes expressively.

Audra couldn't help but giggle. Nick gave her an appreciative look. "There! That's better. I was beginning to think you'd forgotten how to smile. Come along," he said as he tucked her arm into his. "Let's get this over with."

Someone handed her a glass of champagne. They stood in the circle of guests while toasts and jovial com-

ments went about the room. Nick bore it all with good
cheer, a much more relaxed Audra smiling beside him.

The breakfast was a buffet rather than a formally
seated affair, so the newly married couple were constantly
surrounded by well-wishers. Everyone seemed to want to
speak to the bride, and though Nick brought her a plate of
the sumptuous food, Audra never did find the time to eat
it. And then, somehow she got separated from Nick, and
she lost track of him.

The breakfast almost over, Nick was on his way to the
study, for a puzzled Cleo had come to tell him that a late
guest had arrived and had requested a private meeting
with him. She'd shown him into the study, she informed
Nick.

He'd looked for Audra, but when he'd spotted her,
she'd been surrounded by a group of women and, from all
appearances, safely occupied. He'd had to smile at the
slightly dazed look in her eyes.

He entered the study with a mild sense of irritation at
this interruption. It was almost time for him and Audra to
leave, and he was eager to have her to himself again.

The man was standing, looking out the open veranda
doors, but turned as Nick closed the door. Nick saw that
he was young, slightly built, and had light hair and eyes.
Nick didn't know him.

The stranger was wearing a mocking smile that unaccountably set Nick on edge. Nevertheless, he was a guest,
so Nick extended his hand politely. "You asked for me?
I'm Nickolas Brannon."

The young man seemed somewhat taken aback at having to look up at Nick, but he recovered quickly and took
Nick's hand. "Norton. Silas Norton."

Nick dropped Norton's hand immediately. So this was

his uncle's nefarious partner. The man who'd probably
shot McKee, and who had manhandled Audra. He felt
anger boiling up within himself, threatening to spill over,
but he managed to keep his tone cool and noncommittal.
"Norton," he acknowledged. "I believe you've made a mistake. You weren't invited to this wedding."

"An oversight on Audra's part, I'm sure," Norton said
confidently. "She and I are . . . friends, after all. But it
doesn't matter, for I really came to see you, not Audra."

Nick walked to his desk and removed a cheroot from a
box. He took his time lighting it, not bothering to offer
one to Norton. "You'll call her Mrs. Brannon," he said
mildly. "And it wasn't an oversight. My *wife* tells me that
she dislikes you immensely."

His words didn't seem to faze Norton, for the man only
adjusted his cuff, looked up, and smiled smugly. "A lie, of
course. Audra . . . *pardon me* . . . Mrs. Brannon is a
very good actress. But then, William trained her beautifully."

"Did he now?" Nick asked quietly as he peered over
the smoke of his cheroot. "For what purpose?"

"He had big plans for her," Norton said. "Originally,
he intended to marry her off to someone of wealth, thus
ensuring his own future. The only problem was . . . William couldn't keep his own hands off her." Norton
shrugged carelessly. "There was nothing to do but alter his
plans and settle for second best." When Nick made no
reply, Norton continued. "Ah, I see you already know
about Lord Cowan. Then you must also know that the old
fool insisted on certain . . . requirements, shall we say?"

Still, Nick remained silent.

"But as I said, Audra's very good at acting. Those shy,
innocent looks, you know. That delightful blush." Norton
glanced up to gauge Nick's reaction.

Outwardly, Nick still showed no emotion, but his eyes

had narrowed to mere slits. He was holding on to his control by only the slimmest of threads.

"She's so good at it, in fact, that she even fooled William. He never guessed how much she hated him. She agreed to the arrangement with Cowan to get away from William. Of course, it helped that he'd promised her part of the settlement money. But then he up and died, and the money disappeared. She was furious until she learned about you. When she discovered that you were even wealthier than Cowan, she made her own plans. In one fell swoop she found a way to get the wealth she's always wanted, plus revenge on William. It *was* her coup de grâce—enticing you into marriage. Clever little minx, our Audra. Oh, pardon me again. *Your* Audra, now."

Unknown to both men, Cleo had just stepped into the study after receiving no reply to her hesitant knock. Upon seeing her brother's expression as he stared at the stranger, she stepped back into the hall and beckoned a footman and calmly gave him an order. The footman nodded and disappeared down the hall, while Cleo slipped into the study again and quietly closed the door behind her.

Nick would have thrown Norton out minutes ago, but he knew damned well that the man had come here for a purpose. "It's only consideration for my guests that keeps me from knocking that smug smile down your throat, Norton. You didn't come here simply to give me a litany of my wife's history. You have exactly one minute to tell me what it is you really want, and at the end of that time, I'm throwing you out!"

Norton puffed up with pleased satisfaction. "I see you're a man who likes to get right down to business." Without invitation, he seated himself in the chair in front of the desk. "I've researched you, Mr. Brannon. You're an important man—both here and in the States. You have a reputation to uphold. I assume it could do you irreparable harm if word should get out about the rather loose morals of your new bride. . . ." He hesitated deliberately, and when Nick said nothing, he shrugged. "However, we're both gentlemen. I'm positive we can come to an amicable agreement. . . ."

Nick tossed his cheroot into the fireplace. "Your minute is up, Norton. Get out!"

Silas Norton blinked, then heedlessly pushed on. "Oh. Did I neglect to mention that your bride and I have been lovers for years?" He laughed crudely. "Hell, I've had her here, at Sheffield, dozens of times. I've even had her in the woods, after you came. Tell me, was she as eager for you as she was for m—"

In two strides, Nick was upon Norton and had grabbed his collar. "Repeat one word of what you've just said to anyone else," he grated, his voice steel, "and it will be your last." He didn't bother to wait for a reply as he lifted the man off his feet.

Norton struggled. "Wait!" he sputtered. "I haven't told you the rest. Did you know that your little bride is also a mur—"

He was cut off as Nick roughly propelled him to the door. Cleo sidestepped quickly, and opened the door just in time for Nick to shove Norton into the hall.

Nick expressed no surprise to find Bates, flanked by two sturdy footmen, waiting. But his eyes were glittering with suppressed fury. "Mr. Norton is leaving, Bates. Take him through the back door. See to it that he's not allowed back into Sheffield Manor. Ever."

The two footmen each grasped one of Norton's arms, and with Bates following, steered the unwelcome guest toward the back of the house. Norton twisted his head about. "You'll be sorry, you know!" he shouted. "You're a fool if you think you'll be able to keep her. Once she gets what she wants from you, she'll come back to me!"

Cleo, recovering from her initial shock, came to stand beside Nick, her eyes wide and distress written all over her pretty face. "Nick," she said as she touched his arm. "Don't believe those vicious lies. Audra isn't like that. She couldn't possibly be."

Nick took a deep breath. "The guests?" he asked shortly.

"They're milling about outside, waiting to see you and Audra off. The coach is ready, and she's gone upstairs to change. Nick . . ."

He abruptly turned away. "I'll be out shortly, then."

"Nick . . ."

But the door had already been firmly closed, and Cleo was left standing in the hallway, alone.

Bertie was in Audra's room, waiting to help her change. They'd saved this special time for themselves, but not to say good-bye. Audra had already said her private and painful farewells to both Bertie and McKee last night, and they'd all agreed not to repeat those wrenching scenes.

Audra's things had been packed into trunks days ago, and were to go to London with Rafe and Letty. Though their ship wasn't sailing until tomorrow morning, she and Nick were boarding tonight. He'd explained that it would be simpler than booking into a hotel, then having to rise early the next morning to board. Audra had eyed him suspiciously when he'd told her that, for the gleam in his eyes told her he had another purpose.

"Have Rafe and Letty left?" she asked as Bertie helped her into her traveling suit.

"Yes. Poor Letty was in a tizzy, though," Bertie said.

Audra laughed. "I know. She's been torn between excitement and apprehension ever since she agreed to come with us. I can't tell how much of her excitement is due to going to America and how much is due to the fact that she'll be spending weeks in Rafe's company."

"Mm," Bertie murmured as she adjusted Audra's jacket. "And how about you?" Bertie's sharp gaze met hers. "You don't appear to be as reluctant to leave Sheffield as I thought you'd be."

"Oh, no. I'm excited, too! Father and I always planned to visit the States when I got older, but . . ." Audra managed a crooked smile. "Well, now I'll be able to see it with Nick. Anyway, he's promised that if I don't like it, we'll come back. And though I'll miss you both dreadfully, I'm relieved that you and McKee will be here to look after Sheffield and help Richard and Cleo."

"That we'll do. Now . . . let me take a look at you. Perfect!" Then Bertie frowned. "But what's this? You're too pale, child."

"Oh, it's nothing. Just . . . I'm just nervous, I guess."

"Nervous about . . . ?" Enlightenment hit as Audra's pale cheeks suddenly bloomed with color. "Oh! Audra, did your mother ever speak to you about . . . er, about intimacy between a husband and a wife? Do you know what will happen?"

"No. That is, no, Mother never did. But yes, I know *what* to expect, Bertie. It's just that I don't know what to expect with Nick. It's so confusing, don't you see? My parents adored one another, but William . . ." She shuddered in revulsion. "William was cruel and abusive to Mother. What if Nick . . . ?"

Bertie leaned forward to give Audra a fierce hug. "You're right. There is a difference. Your parents were madly in love with each other, while William—from what I can gather—never knew what love was. But Nick does. He's in love with you, child."

* * *

Audra closed her eyes and leaned back gratefully against the seat of the coach. "Heavens, I'm glad that's over. Are you?"

When there was only silence, she opened one eye and peered at Nick, who was sitting opposite her. He was observing her closely, and his face was drawn into harsh lines.

Bertie had to be mistaken. He certainly didn't look like a man in love. Not that she'd really know, of course, but somehow she had the feeling that it should be the same look he'd given her as she'd walked down the aisle toward him. A warm, almost possessive look. A look that seemed to say that he was proud and happy to be marrying her. Oh, if only he would look at her like that tonight! If he did, she knew she'd have nothing to fear.

But what had Cleo meant with her enigmatic remark, made as she'd given her a farewell hug? *"Whatever Nick says or does, only remember that he loves you."* It was shocking enough to have been told by two different people, in the space of only minutes, that her new husband loved her. But Cleo's whispered words had seemed too much like a warning.

"I . . . I want to thank you, Nick. For the flowers and the breakfast and . . . everything. It was lovely." She forced a small laugh. "I didn't even mind old Mrs. Eberly."

He remained mute, but his lips curled into a tight smile.

She felt her cheeks warm. "You're tired," she said uneasily. "I am, too. I'll just keep quiet and try to nap." She closed her eyes tightly, wanting to block out the look on his face.

Why was he so cold? So silent? Why was he looking at her as if he'd never seen her before?

* * *

Ah, there it was, Nick thought as he watched Audra's lids flutter. That hesitant manner that bespoke innocence. That charming blush.

Audra Emily Sheffield Brannon!

So lovely. So young and seemingly fragile. So seemingly innocent.

Was she? Or was she a shrewd, calculating wanton?

It had been obvious that Norton had an agenda, but whatever the man's motives were—greed, jealousy—whatever he'd hoped to gain didn't really matter. If she'd lied, Nick thought grimly, if even a fraction of what Norton had told him was true, his dreams would be gone. Crumbled. Disappeared into dust and air.

She had been all his dreams. He'd wanted her—body, heart, and soul—and he'd planned to teach her how to love him in return, slowly and patiently and with his own love to lead the way.

Nick crossed his arms and finally closed his own eyes. It hurt too damned much to look at her.

Yet he couldn't stop Norton's words from replaying in his mind.

Had Norton been Audra's lover? She *had* admitted to meeting him in the woods. No, that wasn't right. She'd claimed that Norton had attacked her, but Nick knew she wouldn't have told him even that if he hadn't discovered the bruises on her skin. Had she told the truth? Or had it been a lie to cover the result of rough loveplay?

And William . . . Nick couldn't forget the day Audra had tried to run away to London. She'd blurted out truths about William—"*He used me. Used me, then sold me.*" He was almost afraid to discover what she'd really meant.

But he had to know. Whatever it was, he had to know *tonight.*

Chapter 17

*A*udra sat in front of the dressing table studying the stateroom through the mirror while Letty rearranged her hair. She could see almost all of their quarters, for it was really a compact suite which, despite its size—or lack thereof—was as luxurious as any found in a hotel. There was a large combination sitting room–bedroom, and a separate dressing room. Two beds occupied most of the space between the two portholes.

Nick had accompanied her straight here. When the purser had opened their door, she was delighted to discover the room was filled with flowers of every description. When she'd expressed her thanks to the purser, he'd explained that the flowers had been ordered by Mr. Brannon. Embarrassed, she'd turned to thank Nick, but he had already disappeared without a word. He'd been gone the two hours she and Letty had spent unpacking, but he'd returned some time ago and was now in the dressing room making his own preparations for the evening ahead.

Though the connecting door was closed, Audra was only too aware of the proximity of his presence.

When she'd explored the little room, it had been a slight shock to find Nick's shaving paraphernalia on a small washstand, his brush and comb next to it. It had immediately brought home the inescapable fact that she would be spending the night—and many others—in this cabin with Nick.

She was becoming more and more apprehensive with each minute. How could she not be when those beds were so nicely framed within the mirror before her? When her husband was so grim and so silent?

He'd hardly said a word to her since they'd left Sheffield. To her surprise, she really had fallen asleep in the coach and hadn't stirred until the noise and bustle of London had awakened her. Whether Nick had slept or not, she didn't know.

As if thoughts of him had conjured him, the dressing room door opened and Nick came through. He was once again beautifully dressed. "We're having dinner in our cabin tonight, Letty. Once it arrives and you've seen to the table, you may have the rest of the night off. I believe you've already found your accommodations?"

Audra blushed at the implications of an intimate dinner, but Letty was delighted. "Yes, thank you, Mr. Nick. I'm sharing with several other ladies' maids. They're friendly and we're all quite comfortable."

"Good."

Audra sat with her hands in her lap, not quite knowing what to do with them or herself. She was so relieved when Nick finally spoke to her and asked if she wanted a glass of champagne that she turned to him eagerly. "Yes, please."

He brought it to her. She waited, holding the stemmed

glass awkwardly, thinking he might toast her, but when he silently went to sit in an armchair to drink his own champagne, she sat quietly and sipped slowly. It was a relief when dinner arrived a short time later. Letty bustled about, directing the placement of the plates and cutlery and food. All too soon, it was ready, and Audra and Nick were once again left alone in the cabin.

Whether it was the effect of the champagne or not, Nick suddenly turned amicable. He seated her, then proceeded to fill her plate with morsels of food. Audra pushed it about her plate absently, managing to chew and swallow only bits of it. She was sure it was all delicious, but she couldn't taste a thing. She was too busy trying to keep up with Nick's sudden inconsequential chatter, and too nervous at his sudden turn of temperament.

"Aren't you hungry?" he finally asked.

"What? Oh . . . not really." A quick glance at his plate showed that he hadn't eaten much more than she had.

"Have you had enough?"

"Yes, thank you." Why were they suddenly so polite with one another?

Once again, they waited in silence until the table was cleared. Once again, she sat in a chair feeling awkward and naive. She prayed he wouldn't be silent again. *Anything* would be better than that! Well . . . almost anything!

"Could we . . . could we take a walk about the ship?" she asked nervously as the door closed behind the waiter.

"It's dark out. I'll take you around tomorrow."

But the ship has lights, she wanted to say. It has public rooms and other people. . . .

"We had another guest today. One you never saw," Nick suddenly said in a casual tone.

"What?" She looked up, startled to see that he was standing right before her. "Who?"

"An old friend of yours. So he said."

Audra frowned in thought. "I can't think who it could be. All the neighbors were already there. Why didn't he ask for me?"

"Because I preferred that he not speak to you. In fact, I more or less threw him out."

Her eyes widened. What man could she possibly know who was so obnoxious that Nick would actually toss him out? The only person who came to mind was . . . No! It couldn't have been!

"Ah, I see comprehension in those beautiful eyes of yours. We had a little discussion, your friend Silas Norton and I. I must say, he was a veritable font of information."

Audra was suddenly glad she'd eaten so little. Her stomach was coiling painfully. "Nick, I . . ."

Abruptly, he was leaning over her, his hands on the arms of her chair effectively trapping her, his face only inches from hers. "I warned you, did I not, to never lie to me again?"

"I didn't! That is . . ." She began playing with a loose strand of her hair.

Nick reached down and pulled the strand from her grasp. Twisting it around his fist, he shook it in her face. "You give yourself away each time you lie. Did you know that?"

"Nick, I'm sorry. I . . ."

"How many times did Norton come to Sheffield?"

"I . . . I don't know. He came often with William," she answered helplessly. She couldn't understand what difference that made.

"How many times did you meet him in the woods after I came?"

"I . . . I'm not sure. He was there twice, I think."

"Are you and he lovers? The truth, Audra. I'll know if you're lying!"

Audra's face twisted in revulsion. "*Lovers?* You're as mad as he is if you think I'd let him touch me!"

He stared at her intently. "Why would he lie about that?"

"How would I know? He's as devious as William was."

"And Lord Cowan?"

"What about him? I met him only once when William brought him for dinner. I excused myself as soon as I could. I didn't like the way he looked at me. As to that sick arrangement William made with him—I only learned about it on the night William died."

Nick almost sighed in relief. So far, she'd disclaimed a good part of Norton's story. And she was telling the truth. Though there was a touch of fear and confusion in her eyes, she was meeting his gaze openly and without guile. And she hadn't touched her hair again. But there was still one other question to clear up. "What," he continued, "were you really doing at the Crown and Arms in town?"

"I told you! I came to London to find Nickolas Brannon. You! Only I thought you would be your father. I . . . oh, you know all this. Why are you questioning me so?" She made an attempt to get up, then gasped as Nick placed a hand on her chest and pushed her back.

"I want to know," he said grimly, "what your real purpose was. Was it to intrigue me? Rouse my interest so that I'd follow you back to Sheffield, where you could put your plan to entrap me into place?"

"You *are* mad!" Audra sputtered. "How could I do such a thing? I didn't even know about you then."

"Didn't you? Why did you really marry me, Audra?"

"I married you because . . ." Audra flushed guiltily. How was she to tell him she'd wanted to escape Norton?

Oh, she should have known this was all going to come back to haunt her!

"Never mind." Nick's tone was flat. "I can see the answer in your face. How many . . ." Nick's words were clearly enunciated. "How many lies *have* you told me, Audra? Which of them was the first?"

"The first . . . ?" Nick was shooting too many questions at her. Confused, Audra rubbed her now aching head. He had to mean William. William's death. "I never lied to you about William, I just never told you," she said helplessly. "You never asked me about that. Nick, you must believe me. It wasn't really my fault. He was drunk and . . . and he attacked, and he . . . it just happened." If she'd only told him about William from the beginning, this wouldn't be happening now. Nick wouldn't be so furious. She deserved whatever he did to her, except . . . Oh, God! He wouldn't turn her in to be hanged, would he? "What are you going to do, Nick? Are you . . . are you going to send me back to England?" she asked haltingly.

Nick straightened slowly, still staring at her, unable to speak. Oh, Christ! So now he knew all of it. William had raped her.

The rage and pain was almost more than he could bear. Rage against William, pain for her—for what she'd had to bear—mixed with his own pain.

So now he knew. William had raped her and because of that, she'd plotted to take her revenge on a Brannon— on *him*. Damn her! Norton was right. She was a damned clever actress.

Audra flinched. For an instant, she'd thought Nick was going to strike her. His expression was absolutely terrifying. He looked as if he wanted to strangle her. For a fleeting moment, she thought she'd prefer that. If he sent her back . . . Her head was suddenly filled with the images of her nightmares—a scaffold, a noose, and William, laughing. God! *Did* they still hang women?

She leaped to her feet and flung herself at Nick, clinging to him fiercely. "Please. Don't, Nick. Don't send me back. I'll do anything you want, but don't send me back."

Nick hadn't expected this. He'd thought that she would be only too happy to leave him—for a price, of course.

Well, she'd be the one to pay.

Gripping her wrists, he slowly removed her arms and held them at her sides. "Anything, eh? How convenient. This is, after all, our wedding night." The smile he gave her was more a grimace. "It's time, my love, to go to bed."

Audra quailed. For a moment she thought that she might faint. Then pride came to her aid. God knew she'd carried the guilt of William's death long enough. She deserved whatever punishment Nick meted out. He could do whatever he wanted to her.

"Light the bedside lamps. Both of them," Nick ordered coldly as he locked the cabin door.

Her hands were shaking, but she managed it. When she finished, she glanced fearfully at him. He'd extinguished the candles on the table and was leaning against the door, arms crossed, one ankle in front of the other. He pointed to a spot in front of the beds, and she went to stand there, the light behind her, and faced him.

"I own you," he said coldly. "You and everything you have on, from the pearls in your hair to the tips of your prettily slippered toes. Take it all off. I want to see if I got my money's worth."

If he saw her flinch, he didn't show it. She didn't know how she managed to do it with him standing there, so silent and cold, watching as every button came undone, as each ribbon was loosened. She had to struggle with a few buttons, but he didn't offer to help and she was only relieved. Finally her clothing was pooled at her feet. Naked within the glow of the lamps, her hands clenched at her sides and her eyes glued to the floor, she simply waited.

"Now take your hair down. Slowly."

It fell around her shoulders, partially covering her breasts. She left it, thankful for some concealment. But he wouldn't allow even that. She heard his slow footsteps as he came to stand in front of her, brooding and still, and then his hands reached out to gather her hair in his fists. His fingers brushed her neck, her ears as he pushed her long tresses back over her shoulders. She forced herself to remain still, to keep her shoulders stiff, though she wanted desperately to cover her nakedness, to hide herself from him.

She watched his shoes as he walked slowly to her left; they disappeared as he went behind her, then came around her right side and stood before her once more.

"Beautiful," he murmured. "So beautiful . . . and so damned deadly. You'd take a man's soul, wouldn't you, and give it to the devil?"

She'd been numb since the moment he'd told her of Norton's visit. Now, at last, she was coming back to life. And to anger. He was looking her over like some prize filly! How dare he? Damn him!

The sound of her palm hitting his cheek echoed in the silent room. The blow was hard enough to rock him on his heels.

"I may be naive about some things, but I know what a whore is," she hissed. "Don't you ever, *ever* treat me like one again."

With those words, she turned and, despite her nudity, walked in as slow and dignified a manner as possible to one of the beds. Ignoring her nightgown and robe, which Letty had carefully arranged over it, she slipped under the cover, pulled it up to her chin, and turned her back on him.

Cupping his stinging cheek, Nick stared at the back of her head. He hardly believed what had just taken place.

How the hell had she managed to put him in the wrong and make him feel like the worst kind of cad?

Bloody hell! He *was* a cad, and worse.

William had abused her. He was sorry for that. No young girl deserved that kind of suffering. No wonder she'd been so vehemently opposed to being a mistress or a wife. She'd probably been disgusted each time he'd touched her. She must have wanted revenge pretty damned bad to suffer his attentions, and then to marry him.

But had he really given her a choice? William had left her nothing. She'd sold her emerald and had been about to sell her mother's diamonds. And he'd taken them from her. Like William, he'd pushed her into a corner and left her no means of escape.

What difference did it make why she'd married him? If it was for his wealth, he had plenty of it. If it was for revenge, she had it coming. If he had to pay for his uncle's sins, so be it.

The hell of it was that he still loved her, and damned if he'd ever allow her to divorce him and leave. He'd give her no reason, no excuse to do that. The marriage had to be consummated. Not that it wouldn't have been, anyway, but he'd planned a leisurely seduction—a gentle and considerate initiation.

But that was no longer possible. Right now, she didn't just hate William. She hated all men. Including him.

She was probably going to hate him a lot more before this night was over.

Nick sighed. Best to get it over with.

* * *

Trembling in reaction and trepidation, Audra lay with her eyes tightly closed. Frankly, she was astonished that she was still tucked under the covers. She'd expected him to come after her. He'd been so furious when she'd slapped him!

Why, oh why, had she let her temper get the best of her again? Lord, she'd never struck anyone she cared about in anger before. True, he had no right to humiliate her as he'd done, but it was partly her fault. She should have told him about William.

Audra's breath caught in her throat as she listened to the sounds Nick made. She could tell by the rustlings of cloth that he was removing his clothing. Perhaps he'd just climb into the other bed and . . . But she felt her bed give on the other side. Her heart began beating so frantically, she thought it would explode.

When Nick moved to her and she felt the smooth warmth of his naked skin against hers, she couldn't keep from flinching, despite her resolve. She kept her eyes tightly closed as his fingers threaded through her hair. He pulled her around to face him.

His warm breath was upon her face as he silently looked down upon her. She could hear and feel his every breath, quick intakes and longer expulsions, as if he had just run a great race.

She was prepared for violence, so when his fingers softly caressed the angle of her cheek, she was so startled by the gentle touch that her eyes flew open.

His expression was one of grim determination. He looked like someone who was about to swallow bitter medicine. Only she was the medicine. "If you do this," she warned, "I'll hate you forever."

"Yes." His smile was one of self-mockery. "I know. But it has to be done. You understand that, don't you?"

She didn't understand, but she read regret in his voice

and in his eyes. He seemed almost . . . hurt. Hope raised its head. Her eyes suddenly brimmed, and she shook her head fiercely to get rid of the tears. "Nick, please . . ."

"Don't, damn it! Don't say anything. And for God's sake, don't fight me. Give me your mouth, Audra. Pretend you don't find my kisses distasteful."

His kiss was anything but. Audra closed her eyes as his mouth possessed hers, fierce yet tender. His familiar scent—one that had begun to mean security to her—filled her nostrils. His tongue traced her lips, probed between. Without conscious thought, she opened to Nick.

He continued to kiss her, his lips tracing the line of her jaw, nibbling on her ear. . . . Oh, if only he would just keep holding her and kissing her like this! She didn't mind his mouth pressing kisses over her, as he was doing now. And his hands . . .

Audra suddenly realized that Nick's hands were roaming over her naked body. His fingers skimmed over her neck, her breasts, down her belly . . . and to the juncture of her thighs. She stiffened, stunned not so much by his touch as by the unexpected warmth that flared beneath his trailing fingers. Embarrassed and confused, she tried to push him away. But he was too heavy.

Suddenly, shockingly, his mouth was on her breast and his fingers were sliding between her legs. He rubbed his thumb against her intimate flesh, and slid one long finger lower. . . .

Audra gasped as strange heat and moisture flooded her. Her eyes opened wide in shock. "Stop! What are you doing?" she cried.

"It's all right," Nick murmured. "It will be all right, now," he said as he parted her legs and pushed her knees up. He knelt between her bent knees, his face determined, his nostrils flaring. Audra's gaze moved lower, and found his full arousal. She stared in fear. He was so large, so hard, and he was going to . . .

All her resolve, all her determination not to plead, flew away at the realization of his male superiority. She heaved upward to wrap her arms about his neck and cling for dear life. "Nick," she whispered, closing her eyes again. "Please don't hurt me."

"I won't," he assured her as he smoothed the hair back from her face. "I promise. Just relax. Lie back down and relax," he coaxed as he gently pushed her back against the pillows.

Relax? He was insane. Utterly insane. Her muscles were frozen in fear.

Nick was fighting his own battles. When had his cold determination to consummate this marriage become a desperate need to possess her, to make her know that she was his, and his alone? To become forever a part of her and she a part of him?

Perhaps, in time, he'd be able to rid her of her fear and loathing of this act. But it wasn't going to happen tonight, even though she wasn't fighting him. In fact, she'd been soft and pliant as he'd kissed her. He'd readied her as best he could. The only consideration he could give her now was to get this over with, before she froze up on him again.

"Audra! Look at me! I want you to look at me and remember only my face. . . ." He slid his hands under her buttocks to pull her hips to him. Rearing back, he plunged forward and entered her in one powerful thrust.

Audra screamed.

Somewhere, in the foggy recesses of his mind, Nick heard, and realized that something was terribly wrong. That he'd just broken through a genuine physical barrier.

He told himself he should draw back, but it was already too late, for his body was being governed by a multitude of emotions and passions too great to contain. The

best he could do was wrap his arms about her and whisper
her name as he thrust again. And again . . . then spilled
himself into her.

Nick's shout wasn't one of triumphant fulfillment, but
of anguish. Lowering his head onto her breast in defeat, he
knew that he'd just concluded the greatest debacle of his
life.

When he was finally able to, he raised his head to scan
her face. She was crying, great sobs that racked her body.
He slid out and off her, and smoothed the hair away from
her wet face.

His own anguish forgotten, he had a powerful urge to
comfort her. "Audra. Sweetheart . . ."

She turned away from him swiftly, presenting him with
only her naked back. "Go away. I thought you were different from other men. You promised you wouldn't hurt me,"
she sobbed brokenly, "but you did. You *wanted* to hurt
me."

There was nothing he could say. He'd disbelieved her,
wrongly accused her, humiliated her, and broken a solemn
vow he'd made to never hurt her. He touched her shoulder, but she swiftly curled into a small ball. "Don't touch
me," she said fiercely. "If you ever touch me like that
again, I swear I'll kill you!"

Audra wanted to hate Nick. At that moment, she
wanted to hate him as fiercely as she'd ever hated William.

And she wanted to turn to him and have him hold her
and soothe her with soft words and caresses, as he had in
the past.

Her emotions were seesawing wildly. It was too much
to think about now. "Just go away," she whispered.

She heard Nick's softly muttered curse, then felt the
mattress shift as he left. The covers were pulled over her.
There was a rustle of cloth. The light dimmed as he

turned off the lamps, and a door closed softly. Then there was only silence.

He'd planned on getting drunk. Very drunk. Drunk enough to drown his self-loathing. But the brandy bottle and the filled glass sat untouched on the dressing room table beside him.

God almighty! He was thirty-two years old. He'd been making love to women for half his life. How could he have misread the signs and botched things so badly?

William hadn't raped her. He may have tried, but he hadn't. When Audra had said William had "used" her, she'd meant exactly what she'd said—that he'd used her as his hostess. His bait. The prize he'd dangled before his wealthy friends.

And Silas Norton? Bloody hell! He *would* kill Norton if he ever got the chance. The clever bastard had mixed just enough truth in with the lies to confuse the whole matter.

The last of Nick's doubts had disappeared when he'd seen the proof—the bloody stains only too evident upon the white sheets.

Audra was still crying. He could hear her through the closed door. Each sob pierced him deeper. He'd accused her of stealing his soul, but he'd tossed it away himself when he'd taken her so carelessly.

He sat, unmoving, feeling dead inside. Wondering how the hell he was going to make it up to her.

Hours later, he was still awake when he heard Audra calling his name. Heart pounding, he threw open the door and rushed into the room. He'd left one dim lamp burning beside the bed and he saw her, tossing and turning restlessly. She was having another nightmare.

He slid into bed beside her and gathered her carefully

into his arms. She didn't resist. Instead, she quieted, then snuggled up to him, her cheek and the palm of one hand resting against his chest. He felt his heart splinter into a million pieces. He had deliberately caused her pain and humiliation, yet she called for him to save her from her nightmares.

She murmured in her sleep. "Shh," he soothed. "It's all right, love. Go back to sleep." She didn't move when he wound his other arm about her and pulled her closer. Nick held her like that, close against his heart, for the rest of the night.

Sometime past sunrise, Nick finally stirred. Audra was still wrapped in his arms.

He wanted nothing so much as to kiss her awake, to stroke that silky expanse of skin that wasn't covered. Her hair was fanned out over the pillow, and a strand of it lay on her cheek. He lifted it, carefully pushing it behind her ear. Audra made a small sound, tucked her fist under her chin, and slept on.

Slipping out of bed, he knelt on the floor and watched her sleep, trying his damnedest to tamp down the rising desire of his body. She looked like a child. In some ways, she *was* still just a girl, but he'd always been aware that she had a woman's lush body and a temperament that promised a passionate nature.

He'd desperately wanted to ignite that passion, to teach her the joys of his body and her own. To watch her eyes glow with rapture. To hear her cry out his name.

But he'd probably blown all chance of that to hell.

Of course, he could just take her. He knew men who had no consideration for their wives, who used them only as a receptacle for their passions. But she would hate him for it. Even more than she hated him now.

He could probably overcome that, but he wanted more than her reluctant compliance. He wanted her to give herself to him fully and freely, without any reservations on her part.

Nick sighed. It was probably—no, it was *definitely* going to be the most difficult thing he'd ever done in his life, but he was going to keep his hands off her and try to teach her to trust him again. If he had to start over, he would. He would go slowly. He would first acquaint her with the close intimacy that resulted from two people living together and sharing a bedroom without actual physical intimacy.

He just prayed it wouldn't take a long time—and that it would even be possible.

Audra groaned as the sound of clattering china penetrated her consciousness. Keeping her eyes tightly closed, she lay still, wondering why she felt so odd.

She would never drink champagne again, for her stomach was rolling. Actually, her entire body seemed to be rolling.

Her eyes popped open. She *was* moving! Or rather, the great ship was, for she could feel its almost imperceptible swaying. She sat up quickly, then groaned and sank back onto the pillows.

"Good morning. Or perhaps it would be more appropriate to say good afternoon."

At the sound of Nick's voice, Audra ducked under the covers. Oh, Lord! How terribly, horribly embarrassing!

And then she remembered what had happened the previous night. The covers went farther over her head.

The bed gave momentarily as he carefully seated himself near her knees. "You can't hide under there forever, my love. You may as well come out and face the world. And me. Just as I must face you."

At the humility in his voice, Audra cautiously lowered the sheet to the tip of her nose and peered out at Nick. His golden eyes looked sad and weary, but they were watching her carefully. He was freshly shaven and, she was relieved to see, fully dressed. That lock of hair had fallen onto his forehead again, making him look young and perfectly harmless.

Did he turn into a monster only at night? Only when he had a woman in his bed? She flushed, and hid under the covers again. "Go away. I don't want to speak to you. I don't even want to see you," she said miserably.

She heard Nick sigh. "I'm afraid you have no choice. We're on a ship, Audra. I booked late, and like it or not, we must share this stateroom. Come on out from under there now," he pleaded quietly.

At that, she did sit up, but she carefully kept her face averted and the cover pulled to her chin.

"Look at me, sweetheart."

He'd used the endearment like a caress. It made her angry. She turned to him, her eyes brimming with tearful accusation. "Don't call me that! You have no right!"

He raised his hand to brush away a tear, but let it drop again when he saw her flinch and reached to the foot of the bed, instead. "Here's your robe, and I've brought hot coffee and croissants." He tugged on the covers until she finally, grudgingly accepted the robe, and then he politely turned his back. "We'll talk afterward."

Audra managed to wriggle into the robe and wrap it about herself. She tied it, then sat up and plumped the pillows and raked her fingers through her hair self-consciously. Oh, Lord! She must look absolutely terrible!

"You look adorable. Here, drink this."

She accepted the cup and saucer, took a tentative sip,

then another, and felt better. Nick sat back down and placed a plate on her lap. "Eat this."

Despite the fact that she'd expected to choke on it, the warm pastry melted in her mouth, and her stomach felt less queasy after she'd swallowed it. She ate the rest of it, then sipped on her coffee, trying to ignore him, trying to ignore the fact that her hands were unsteady, making the cup rattle against the saucer.

Nick watched silently as she ate and drank, refusing to look at him all the while. When she was finished, he took the china from her trembling hands and set it all back onto a tray. Then he turned to face her.

Audra knew he was looking at her. She commanded her body to be still and not fidget throughout his silent perusal. Finally, she heard his deep sigh.

"Won't you look at me, love?"

He'd said it differently last night, she remembered. In fact, he'd ordered her to look at him when he . . . Her face turning bright pink, Audra shook her head frantically.

"All right. I don't blame you. It's difficult for me to face you this morning, also. In fact, it's probably the hardest thing I've ever done in my life. I can't tell you how sorry I am. I know I hurt you. I can try to explain away my atrocious temper, but I won't, for I've promised to be patient. I can try to excuse myself by saying I was under a gross misapprehension, but that would only compound my guilt. I should have given you a chance to explain. For that, I'm more guilty and sorrowful than I can say. I can't tell you how much so. What happened last night was not at all what I'd intended for your wedding night."

She knew that was true. It had to be. Otherwise, he wouldn't have gone through all the trouble of filling the stateroom with flowers and ordering an intimate dinner. He'd wanted to stage a romantic setting. For her.

"You have a right to refuse to forgive me," Nick was saying. "I don't even have the right to ask you to do it. What I do ask is that you at least consider it."

That brought her surprised glance up.

"I deeply regret the pain I caused you. But you should know that it won't happen again."

Relief washed over her. Hope flared in her eyes.

But Nick was shaking his head slowly. "Let me finish, love. You must know there would have been pain, anyway, as it was your initiation, sorry as it was. But I have some rather strange notions, one of them being that marriage is a lifelong commitment. So I'm telling you now that I still expect this to be a marriage in the fullest sense of the word, eventually. Am I clear on that point?"

"You said 'eventually,' " she whispered.

"Despite my despicable actions of last night, I'm not a monster. You've had some bad shocks. You've been under considerable strain these past weeks. I think you need to regroup, to heal some wounds, and that's what I'd like this . . ." he frowned and his lips curved wryly, ". . . honeymoon trip to be for you. A relaxing time. Little one, I'm not about to ask anything of you that you're not yet prepared to give. If you can agree to what I've just said, and if, someday, you can find it in your heart to forgive me, I'll leave it up to you to decide when you're ready to make this marriage . . . complete. And I can only promise that it will be better next time."

She blushed a bright red at his last statement and looked away, torn between embarrassment and anger. Ha! Fat chance of that happening! When hell freezes over, she thought.

Yet she considered.

It hadn't been as bad as she'd expected. In fact, there had been a short time last night when his caresses had made her feel warm and breathless and oddly eager for his touch.

She glanced back at Nick. He seemed so calm, so matter-of-fact, but his eyes told a different story. She could read the earnestness, the regret, and . . . yes . . . the hope reflected in those amber eyes. But Nick wouldn't beg. He would explain logically, and he would ask. But he would never beg.

She could understand that. She knew all about pride, for she had never begged William—not even for her mother. Pride had been all that stood between being herself, and being nothing.

It was obvious that Nick had already forgiven her for causing William's death. And he hadn't asked for her outright forgiveness. He'd asked only that she consider it.

Nick waited silently. Expectation . . . dread . . . hope . . . his emotions were seesawing. Still, he was convinced he knew Audra as well as she knew herself. She was innately fair and generous. Would she find it in her heart to extend that generosity to him?

When she finally sighed softly, his heart started tripping in excitement. She was going to give him a chance to redeem himself! Thank you, Lord, he breathed.

"You promise not to . . . to try . . . ?"

"I promise," he said solemnly. "Not until you indicate that you're ready for that part of marriage."

"Then . . . yes," she whispered.

Was that relief she saw pass over his face? She wasn't sure, for he leaned forward and planted a quick kiss on the tip of her nose. "Thank you, my love. Now . . . I'm going to send Letty in to help you bathe and dress, then I'll be back to take you on the promenade deck. The fresh air will be just what you need."

Audra didn't argue, but as Nick left the cabin, she sank back against her pillows and pursed her lips in thought.

How odd that she hadn't been furious! Hadn't lashed out at him—told him what a cur he was. Nick *had* hurt her last night. The physical pain had been the least of it.

So why was it so difficult to hate him?

Nickolas Brannon—who up until last night had treated her with consideration. Who had taught her to laugh again. Who had taught her that it was possible to trust again.

Yes, he was proud, he was stubborn, but so was she.

He could also be tender and caring. Funny. And forgiving. He'd not castigated her for the trick she'd played on him, pretending to be Agnes. And now that he knew about William, he'd not blamed her.

Could it be . . . were Bertie and Cleo right? Did Nick love her?

Audra shook her head in frustration. Why try to understand it all now? He'd given her time. He'd given her this journey.

She would wait, she would observe, and she would use the time to discover all that she could about this man who was now her husband. She would try to sort through these confusing and conflicting emotions he caused, and learn what it was that *she* felt for him.

Chapter 18

$\mathcal{N}$ick stood quietly in the doorway of the private rail-road car observing his wife. Audra was comfortably curled up in a large lounge chair, entirely engrossed in the novel she was reading.

He'd been doing a lot of that since their wedding night—watching but not touching.

He'd set his course on a deliberate campaign to regain Audra's trust and, hopefully, earn her love. It hadn't been easy. His greatest fear had been that he'd fail in curtailing his own burgeoning desire for her. He was painfully aware that it only increased each day they were together. The nights were the worst, when he tossed and turned rest-lessly, desperately fighting desire, fighting the longing to slip into her bed, to take her into his arms and make passionate love to her.

But his patience was paying off. He was beginning to see rewards. They were becoming familiar with one an-other, and she was much more visibly relaxed in his company. He didn't think she was even aware of it herself, but slowly, cautiously, she *was* beginning to trust him again.

And she delighted him continually. She was the rarest glowing gem—like the emerald she wore at her throat. Each day, he discovered new facets to her.

Nick straightened and approached Audra. "We'll be arriving at Union Station in just a few minutes."

Audra started in surprise as Nick's voice came from behind her left ear. Turning her head, she found him leaning close, his arms crossed over the back of her chair. "Good Lord! You startled me," she gasped, her hand resting on her racing heart.

His eyes crinkled as he smiled down at her. "Sorry, sweet. Alex will be meeting us. I thought you may want to freshen up."

"Yes, I would. Thank you," she responded with a tentative smile of her own, which quickly changed into a small frown as Nick stepped back. She watched as he walked to the door with the long, smooth stride that was so familiar to her.

Audra's initial relief that Nick hadn't yet tried to claim his husbandly rights since their wedding night had swiftly disappeared. Their first few days together had been awkward. Out of necessity, they were often in the stateroom at the same time, but he'd always been careful to give her time and privacy to attend to her personal needs. He made no overt moves toward intimacy. In fact, he hardly ever touched her.

It wasn't that he ignored her. On the contrary, he always treated her with a consideration that she found touching. He was solicitous to a fault; all her needs were taken care of before she ever had to ask. Around others, he acted as if they were a happy, if somewhat reserved, newlywed couple.

Why, then, did she feel so—alone?

She'd loved the ocean voyage, for it had been the first time she'd sailed. There had been a mad social whirl on board—cards and games, dancing and wonderful dining.

Boston had been quaint and interesting. Nick had taken her to meet Alex's sister, Leslie, who was living with an aunt while attending an exclusive girls' seminary. Aunt Lorna had been only too happy to accompany Audra on shopping expeditions, which Nick had encouraged as he was busy with his business interests. Thanks to the two of them, she now had a fairly extensive wardrobe.

Nick and Alex's private railroad car was luxuriously appointed. Audra lacked for nothing, including companionship, if she so desired, for there were other ladies traveling on the train.

But they were mostly elderly, and she was tired of discussing the same dull topics. Her initial fascination with the scenery had palled, for once they'd crossed the great Mississippi River, there was only the sameness of the vast prairie which stretched on forever. She missed the rolling green countryside of England, stately trees, and cool air. Everything west of the Mississippi seemed to be treeless, brown, and arid, and it was so *warm*.

Audra was tired of traveling, she was bored, she was homesick, and most of all, she was lonely.

She missed Nick's touch. She missed his caresses and his kisses. She wanted desperately to be held and reassured, to have him look at her as he had at Sheffield Manor, with eyes brightly warmed with tenderness or . . . or even glowing with desire.

It was strange; sometime during this journey, the old fear that he would want her again was beginning to be overshadowed by the fear that he might not want her at all.

It had been a shocking revelation, once Audra had

admitted the truth of it. Only she wasn't sure what to do about it.

Audra sighed. Perhaps things would improve once they reached their destination. They'd spend the night in Denver and take a private coach to Central City on the following day.

Audra was nervous about meeting Alex, for she wanted to give a good impression. Nick always spoke of Alex with such warmth and affection that it was obvious to her that the men were not only partners, but the best of friends.

Audra stood in the car above the steps, waiting as Nick hopped down onto the platform to greet the man who awaited them.

"It's about time you got home, old son." Alex grinned and slapped Nick jovially on the back. His voice was even more accented than Nick's, Audra noted, but with a charming drawl. As tall and lean as Nick, he had hair almost as black as her own, and his eyes—his eyes were a startling cat's green.

"Good to be back, Alex," Nick responded. "I've missed . . ."

His words dropped off as Alex brushed right past him and came to the bottom of the steps. He stood looking up at Audra and boldly appraised her.

"Ma'am," he addressed her in a soft drawl, then swept her a courtly bow. "You are the loveliest bouquet of spring flowers I have ever seen." Audra blushed, which Alex seemed to find fascinating. "May I offer my assistance?" he asked, and raised his arms to help her down. She was about to accept when Nick suddenly swept in front of Alex.

"I'll thank you, Alex, to keep your hands off my wife,"

Nick said easily as he grasped Audra's slim waist to swing her down over the steps and set her on her feet beside him. His arm stayed around her waist possessively. Alex's face showed only an instant of shock before his mouth curved into a wide smile, and his eyes showed approval. She knew immediately that she was going to like Alex Benedict, very much.

"By God, you've done it this time, Nick. When you cabled me to tell me you were bringing home a bride, I expected . . . well, hell. I *didn't* expect her to be a young . . . er, a dewy English rose."

Nick grinned proudly as he turned to his wife. "Audra, love, I warn you. Don't pay any attention to a word this man says. He's a born flatterer. He'll charm you and dazzle you with words, but he's completely untrustworthy when it comes to women."

Alex took Audra's hand and squeezed it. "He's the liar, of course. It's a pleasure . . . a very *great* pleasure, to meet you, Mrs. Brannon."

Audra gave him a radiant smile. "Please. It's Audra."

"I give you leave to get acquainted while I check on our baggage, Alex. Use a little restraint, please. Try to remember that she's married to me, *old son*," Nick said, laughing. He was already walking off.

"I enjoy reminding him that he's older than I am," Alex explained. "I don't suppose you'd consider that I'm much more suitable?"

Audra couldn't help laughing. "I'm afraid it's too late, sir. I'm already a married woman."

Alex shrugged. "A man can but try."

"I would wager, Mr. Benedict, that you *try* all the time."

"Ah, a discerning woman. Already she recognizes one of my weaknesses."

They spent the night in a small hotel, and Alex took

them to dinner. Audra found him a delightful companion. He was very courtly and amusing, his drawl fascinating. They found mutual understanding, for his story was similar to hers. The son of an old Georgia family, Alex had been raised in privilege and wealth. He had come home from the War Between the States to find his parents both dead and his sister living on the goodness of a neighbor, for the Benedict plantation had been destroyed and the land sold to a carpetbagger. Audra could sympathize, and fully understood that the losses he'd suffered accounted for the cynical air he wore like a shield.

For his part, Nick was fully aware that his wife and best friend had already developed a rapport, and he was glad for it.

The journey the next day went quickly, despite the fact that Audra didn't think they would *ever* reach the beckoning mountains. But once they entered the narrow road commonly known as the "Casey," Audra became a bit queasy at the sight of steep slopes. It dampened her excitement and she stopped poking her head out the window.

She felt better and was relieved when they finally reached the outskirts of visible settlement. Nick and Alex laughed at her confusion and tried to explain that what she was seeing were actually several different towns. "But where does one start and the other begin?" she asked, frowning.

"No one's sure," Nick said, laughing. "They've merged into one big, messy settlement."

And not a very pretty settlement, Audra saw. Again, there were few trees, and there didn't seem to be any orderly layout of the muddy streets. The buildings appeared to have been tossed higgledy-piggledy, in any crazy manner. They were even clustered up the side of hills, and she was astonished to see that some were on stilts. Audra fervently hoped their house wasn't one of them. She didn't think she'd feel very secure walking about on floors that weren't on firm ground.

It was all very confusing, very busy, and absolutely fascinating.

The new Teller House hotel was surprisingly delightful. Though it looked like a warehouse from the outside, it was beautifully appointed inside. The dining room easily held a hundred guests, and there was a smaller, adjoining one called the "ladies' ordinary." There was also a courtyard with a glassed-in conservatory filled with potted plants and vines. There was even an elevator!

The second floor contained a music room and a ladies' parlor. Their own suite was fairly large and well appointed, with walnut furniture and a Brussels carpet.

Audra's enthusiasm was increasing. "Oh, Nick!" she exclaimed. "It's all perfectly lovely." She was eagerly looking out the window of their third-floor suite. "I've never been in really high mountains." She turned to him eagerly. "When will we be able to go into them? I mean . . . *really* go up into them?"

Nick grinned at her enthusiasm. In fact, he was relieved. She'd become so listless on the train that he'd begun to worry that she was regretting leaving England and Sheffield Manor. "As soon as I catch up on business and you've settled in, I'll take you to the ranch," he promised. "Rafe should have our horses stabled in town by now, so we'll be able to ride out."

It was a promise that Audra was looking forward to seeing fulfilled.

They were meeting Alex for dinner again, but it was still hours away, and once their luggage had been brought up, Audra found that she was exhausted. Nick left to meet

Alex at their offices, so Audra had her bath, then donned her robe and climbed into bed.

When she awoke, it was near dusk, and Nick was sitting at a desk lit by one lamp, head bent over the paper he was writing on. She watched him for a time. That wayward lock of hair had fallen onto his forehead again, and she wished she had the courage to go to him and brush it back.

What would he do if she did? Would he reject her, or would he . . . ? She had a sudden yearning to have him pull her onto his lap again, and cuddle her and tease her with soft words and that look that he used to give her—as if he wanted to devour her.

She caught her breath, for Nick had turned in his chair and was just sitting, observing her in turn.

Nick had tried to concentrate on his letter, pretending that Audra wasn't asleep only a few feet away, but it was impossible. When he finally gave in to temptation and turned to look at her, he saw that she was awake, lying quietly, staring at him.

Her cheeks were still tinged with rosy color and her eyes soft from sleep. Her mane of hair was spread across both pillows. One side of her robe had slipped low on her shoulder. Even from here, the faint scent of roses assailed him.

Fierce hunger flared in his groin. God, but she was so damned desirable! Why in hell had he ever made the decision to wait? With care and tenderness, he could overcome her objections and join her right now, in that bed.

He was still waiting for an overt sign from her. Often, he'd catch her watching him, a puzzled expression on her face. And now—just in the last week or so—he could swear it had been replaced by longing. If he wasn't mistaken, he wouldn't have to continue this torture much longer. He just had to fight his growing desire.

He forced himself to stop thinking about it.

Audra saw Nick's expression change. He'd been looking at her as if he'd wanted to eat her for dinner, but now his face had become unreadable again.

"I would like," he said slowly, "to ask you a favor."

"Yes." Her voice was breathless.

"Alex is very shrewd, and I have many other business acquaintances here. You're going to be a surprise to them, but they'll all want to meet you. This is really a small settlement, and everyone talks. There are no delusions of love between us, I know, but I don't want everyone gossiping about us. I'd prefer that they all believe that our marriage is . . . normal. Will you do that for me?"

Audra felt a pang of disappointment. Truth to tell, she was just the tiniest bit peeved with him and his casual attitude, for she was becoming weary of being treated as if she were his sister.

Now he wanted her to play the part of loving wife, did he? "Of course, Nick," she replied sweetly. "If it means so much to you, I daresay I can manage to play *my* part."

Nick threw her a suspicious look, but she only smiled at him.

"Thank you," he replied.

Audra continued to smile innocently. She didn't have much experience, but it couldn't be too difficult to flirt with one's own husband, could it?

Audra found that she was famished, yet she was still so enthralled with her surroundings she could only nibble between exclamations of delight. She asked so many questions of Nick and Alex that they laughingly pleaded for a halt.

She gave in gracefully and concentrated on her meringue dessert. "This is marvelous. Nick, darling, you really should try some," she cajoled, and offered him a spoonful.

Nick swallowed it, along with his smile. He couldn't help but be amused at Audra's attempts to fulfill his request. Her comments and questions to him during dinner had been interspersed with so many "darlings" and "dears" that he was afraid the game would soon be up with Alex. The minx was deliberately baiting him again.

It had been a long time since they'd had a contest of wills. He realized that he regretted that, very deeply. He'd enjoyed their little skirmishes. What harm would it do to relax tonight and play her little game?

Taking her hand, he teased it with his lips. She appeared a little taken aback at first, but when her eyes began sparkling with mischief, he smiled with satisfaction.

Audra laughed gaily as she slowly traced his jaw with her fingers. "Darling! Whatever will Alex think of us?"

Nick drew her hand to his lips to nibble on her fingertips. "He'll think that we're newlyweds, still on our honeymoon. Which we are, *darling*." Over her hand, his eyes gleamed with mischief.

"Just pretend I'm not here," Alex said, stifling an exaggerated yawn.

Audra blushed furiously and tried to withdraw her hand, but Nick wouldn't allow it. Her fingers tingled as his sharp teeth nipped them. Damn him and his laughing eyes! And damned if she'd let him win.

She leaned toward him. "But, dear," she cooed softly into his ear, "there are others watching." She had just noticed a very attractive brown-eyed blond woman pause in the doorway as her escort—an older, rather corpulent gentleman—spoke to the headwaiter. The woman's gaze scanned the room, until it fell on Nick. Without a word to her escort, she bore down on their table.

Alex turned to see what had caught Audra's attention,

but Nick was still too busy playing with Audra's fingers to notice that the attention of his dining companions had turned elsewhere.

"Oh, hell!" Audra heard Alex mutter. Immediately she knew who the woman was. Brenda. The woman Nick had spoken of in England.

"Nicky! Darling!" Startled, Nick dropped Audra's hand and raised his head—only to find himself suddenly wrapped in another woman's arms and fervently kissed.

What the hell . . . ? In all the time he'd known Brenda, she'd never been this affectionate. Particularly in public.

Audra watched avidly, wondering what Nick would do, telling herself she didn't *care*, yet she was inexplicably relieved when, after throwing a quick glance her way, he gave Brenda only a perfunctory kiss on the cheek.

Alex leaned closer to murmur into Audra's ear. "Tell me, Mrs. Brannon—are you a playful kitten, or a ferocious mountain cat? For I must warn you, the female entwining herself around Nick has claws."

Audra dragged her eyes away from her husband and the woman who was still clinging and whispering to him, and met Alex's eyes with her own storm blue ones. "I think, Alex, you're about to find out."

His eyes showed instant approval.

Nick finally managed to extract himself from Brenda's grasp and stood courteously. "Hello, Brenda," he said blandly.

"Darling, why didn't you wire and let me know you were returning? I would have met you in Denver." Brenda stood between Nick and Alex, and though she hadn't shown any awareness that her escort had caught up to her and was standing awkwardly behind her, she snapped "El-wood—a chair" so imperiously that the poor man became flustered. He looked helplessly around, until a waiter saw his predicament and brought a chair from another table.

Elwood slipped it under Brenda. "You don't mind if we join you, do you?" Brenda asked, and sat down without waiting for a reply, while throwing Elwood a look that clearly told him to find a seat, too. Audra, feeling sorry for him, patted the empty chair next to her. "Please. Do sit down, Mr. . . . ?"

"Culbertson," Brenda answered for him. "Elwood Culbertson. This is Nickolas Brannon, Elwood. A very *dear* friend." She waved her hand carelessly. "And Alex Benedict. How nice to see you again, Alex dear," Brenda said without enthusiasm.

"Can't say the feeling is mutual," Alex replied baldly.

"You're ever so gallant," Brenda replied sarcastically. "How you earned your reputation as a womanizer, I'll never know." She gave Audra a cool glance. "Forgive me, dear. I hope you're not insulted that we've ignored you. I'm Brenda Farrow. I assume you're Alex's latest conquest?" she asked bluntly. Her look clearly said that she didn't think that was a desirable position.

"Actually, Brenda," Alex drawled with obvious satisfaction, "Audra isn't my conquest, though if I'd met her first, I daresay I would have given Nick a run for his money."

Brenda glanced at Nick, who suddenly looked extremely uncomfortable. "What does Nick have to do with . . . *her?*" she asked.

Audra gritted her teeth at the insulting way Brenda had emphasized "her." She was going to pay for that. And for the insulting insinuation that she was Alex's newest paramour.

Nick cleared his throat. "I wrote you, Brenda, about my impending marriage. Audra is my wife."

Complete silence fell. Finally, Brenda laughed uncertainly. "I did receive your letter. But I assumed it was just a joke. One, incidentally, which I didn't find at all amusing!" Her glance fell to Audra's left hand. Her eyes narrowed when she saw the magnificent emerald next to the matching gold band on Audra's finger.

"I rather think it is," Alex said to no one in particular.

Brenda threw Alex a hateful look before searching Nick's face. "Tell me it isn't true, Nicky. You can't possibly have married this . . . this *child*. I know your tastes, and you prefer a more sophisticated *woman*," she breathed, and placing a possessive hand on his arm, she gave Audra a defiant look. "Nick and I understand one another so well, you see. Perhaps he's neglected to inform you that I'm one of his oldest and *very dearest* . . . *acquaintances*."

Audra was furious. How dare this bold blonde treat her like a nonentity and flaunt her past relationship with Nick? "But it is true, Miss Farrow. I *am* Nick's wife," she said with a deceptive calmness as she reached out to lift Brenda's hand from Nick's before dropping it as if it were a loathsome insect. "Obviously you don't know him as well as you think, for if you did, you'd know he wouldn't joke about such a thing. As to his preferences . . . perhaps he's realized the true definition of a 'woman.' It's possible that your ideas are *outdated* and lack *freshness* and vitality." Audra paused to deliberately scan Brenda from her hair on down, before she met her gaze head-on. "For I can certainly see that you must be one of his *oldest* . . . friends."

Alex didn't even attempt to stifle his chuckle. Audra chanced a glance at Nick and found he was staring at her with something that looked like awe. She gave him a sweetly innocent smile.

Mr. Culbertson cleared his throat. "I say," he began, "would anyone like another glass of . . . ?"

"Be quiet, Elwood," Brenda snarled.

Audra felt sorry for the poor man as he sank back into his chair. "It's sweet of you to offer, Mr. Culbertson," she said, smiling at him. "But it's been a long day and I'm rather tired. Nick, *darling?*"

Nick seemed relieved, and quickly got to his feet. "It *has* been a long day. Alex, I'll see you in the bar in a few minutes."

Audra smiled at Nick as she took his proffered arm, relieved that he was still playing the part of a loving husband. What had started out as a joke to her had now become extremely important.

"Thank you for the dinner, Alex," Audra said with a warm smile for him. "It was lovely."

Alex bent over her hand. "It was *my* great pleasure, Mrs. Brannon." His eyes twinkled as he looked down at her. He lowered his voice so that only she could hear his words. "You're the first *ferocious* kitten I've had the opportunity to meet, you see. You were magnificent."

Poor Mr. Culbertson looked like a lamb strayed from his flock, while Brenda's face wore an expression of cold malice. Audra had a moment of regret, for this was her first day in Central City, and already she'd made an enemy. Somehow, she didn't think Brenda Farrow would simply concede victory. She was positive she was going to hear a lot more from the woman.

She met Alex's glance again as she and Nick left the dining room, and he winked at her.

Brenda glowered at Audra's back as she and Nick left.

An amused smile quirked at the corners of Alex's mouth. "You'd be wise to sheathe your claws, Brenda," he told her mildly, "for I think this kitten has some rather sharp ones of her own."

"Oh, shut up, Alex!"

* * *

Nick saw Audra to their suite then excused himself to return to Alex. Audra wanted to ask if he planned on seeing Brenda again, but pride kept her silent.

She hadn't been able to tell what Nick had felt about seeing Brenda again, for except for his initial awkwardness—which was so unlike Nick it made Audra smile—his demeanor had been completely neutral. Was he in love with Brenda? He certainly hadn't acted like a man in love, but Audra wasn't sure. What did she know about love, after all? And if William and his friends were examples, men didn't have to be in love to desire a woman.

She pondered as she sat at the dressing table brushing her hair. She didn't want Nick to desire Brenda. But how was she, Audra, going to prevent that? He was a man, after all.

Her troubled musings were interrupted by Nick's return. He seemed surprised to find her still up, but went to sit on her bed.

"What do you think of Central City?" he asked casually.

Audra looked at him in the mirror. "It's so different, Nick. But I'm excited. I can't wait to see the house and explore the shops. Not that I want to purchase anything, of course," she added quickly. "I'm just curious." She was nervous, and dropped the brush. Before she could twist around to reach it, Nick was there to collect it. To her complete shock, instead of handing it back to her as she'd expected, he stepped behind her and proceeded to brush her long hair himself.

"You can purchase whatever you want, sweetheart. In fact, tomorrow I'm going to open an account for you at my local bank." He went on to give her some specifics, including the fact that he intended to give her an allowance. The amount made her gasp.

"Nick, I'll never be able to spend that much!" she protested.

"Whether you do or don't is up to you. It's yours to do with as you want. Don't fight me on this, love. Except for Cleo, I've never had anyone of my own to spend my money on. It would make me happy."

She saw that he was sincere, and thanked him with a beatific smile. Nick's hand suddenly stilled. They stared at one another in the mirror. Audra's heart tripped.

Abruptly, he handed the brush back to her and turned away.

"Thank you," Audra said in a small voice.

Nick very seriously replied, "You're welcome," then disappeared into the dressing room. Audra quickly discarded her robe and practically leaped into bed. She pretended to be asleep when he climbed into his own bed, but she apparently hadn't fooled him, for he softly murmured, "Good night, my love."

She didn't reply, but she lay awake a long time afterward.

Why hadn't he kissed her? He'd wanted to. She'd seen it in his eyes, in the way the corner of his mouth had twitched.

What, she wondered, had Nick read in *her* eyes?

Had he been able to see that she'd wanted it, too?

They moved into a house the next day.

Though it wasn't anywhere as large as Sheffield Manor, it wasn't quite as small as Nick had indicated, either, and Audra was positively enchanted with it. Perched on the side of a hill, but thankfully without stilts, it looked like a fairy-tale cottage from the outside with its intricately carved bargeboard trimming that was popularly known as "gingerbread." Inside, the rooms were more spacious than Audra expected. The lower floor was composed of a roomy kitchen with a scullery and another little alcove off the side, a dining room, a parlor, another smaller sun parlor, and a small study. The second floor contained three bedrooms, only two of which were furnished. A narrow flight of stairs revealed two tiny, charming bedrooms hidden under the eaves. One would be Letty's. Though it appeared too small, the other was already occupied by the cook and her son.

Mrs. Gilly was a robust, pink-cheeked Cornish woman whose husband had died shortly after they'd come to mining country. Her eyes sparkled, and her smile seemed perpetual. Audra had a difficult time following her strange, quaint speech, which was interspersed with "thees" and "thous," but she managed to endear herself to Mrs. Gilly by suggesting that the warm little alcove next to the kitchen be converted to a bedroom for her son, Joey.

Joey was a gangling boy, just in the awkward stage of puberty. He had a charming grin, and a mop of black hair that kept falling into his eyes. He blushed furiously when his mother fondly brushed it back with her hand. Audra gladly agreed to accept his offer to " 'elp wi' the 'eavy work and the 'orses 'n such."

Audra was relieved to see that the furniture was of warm oak and not the heavy dark walnut that she had noticed seemed to be so prevalent in these parts. There was a small patch of grass behind the house. It was too late this year, but Audra already knew she'd fill it with flowers and some vegetables come spring.

"It's not at all like the Manor, is it?" Nick said ruefully.

"Oh, Nick, I think it's charming. I love it. Really I do."

"I know it's small, but space is at a premium in Central City, and of course, I never realized that I'd be looking for a house to bring a wife to. I've always made do with hotels."

Audra looked at him, head tilted. "It will do wonderfully," she assured him quietly. But her heart was filled with relief. His comment proved that he'd had no intention of marrying Brenda. The realization made her happy.

"I didn't usually spend all that much time here, anyway. There's the ranch, and both Alex and I have purchased a fair amount of property near Denver. It's already becoming the center of the area—supplying all the merchandise and equipment to keep the mining towns going. It's growing fast, and I've drawn plans for the sizable mansion I plan to build there. Someday I'll show them to you, for you may want to make some changes. It'll be rather large, but not as large as the one I owned in Boston."

"I didn't know you once had a home in Boston."

"I turned it over to the Children's Society when I decided to relocate out here. It's an orphanage now."

"Oh." Audra realized that there were still many things she had to learn about this man she called her husband.

"I hope that you'll learn to like this country as much as I do, and that you'll be very happy here. I think you'll like the ranch. I'd like to take you there soon."

"I'd like that. And Nick, I already like this country, for it's absolutely beautiful. It's all so new and strange to me, but in a nice way. It's exciting—being part of a growing city and society."

"I'm glad you feel that way."

When Audra went upstairs, she found that Letty had already unpacked most of her things and put them away in the larger bedroom. "Are you sure this is my room, Letty?"

"Yes, Miss Audra. Mister Nick says you're to have the large one. He's just across the hall from you."

Audra blushed. She'd suspected that Letty already

knew that she and Nick didn't spend their nights in the same bed.

But Letty had concerns of her own. "When do you think I'll see Rafe again, Miss Audra? I miss him already," Letty said mournfully. Rafe had already gone on to the ranch.

Audra laughed. "It's only been two days, Letty. Besides, Nick says we're to go to the ranch soon. I'll ask if you can come along."

Audra left Letty to her unpacking. She couldn't resist a look into Nick's room. Like him, it was neat and orderly, for he'd already put his personal things away. She wandered in, going to his gentleman's dresser to idly pick up his shaving brush and sniff it.

It smelled like him—very male, and very familiar to her now. She missed the nearness of that scent.

Audra stretched out on her back on Nick's bed, arms outflung across the coverlet, and wished she was still sharing sleeping quarters with him. On board ship, she'd discovered that he left the dressing room door open as he shaved in the morning, and she could lie quietly in bed and watch. The first time he'd peered at her in the mirror, she'd been mortified to be caught staring, but he'd only smiled at her and asked her what her plans were for the day. Thereafter, she'd usually sat in bed, drinking her morning tea while he shaved. She'd become used to their shared intimacy.

She'd missed that morning ritual in Boston, too. On the train, he'd again shared her quarters but not her bed. She'd welcomed the return of those shared mornings.

Audra sighed. Now, once again, it appeared they were to be separated.

And once again, the thought filled her with desolation.

Chapter 19

$\mathcal{A}$udra left the mercantile and smiled when she saw Joey waiting with the buggy. He'd been her faithful companion for the two weeks since she and Nick had moved into the house. Audra spent her days with Joey exploring the "Gulch," as the area was called. He either drove the buggy or proudly sat on his own pony, which Nick had bought for him so that he could accompany Audra whenever she felt like riding Fantasy. As a result of their forays, she now knew her way around the stores and most of the strangely laid-out streets.

"Wait, Joey," she said after he'd helped her into the buggy. "I want to see what's down this street," she instructed, pointing down Pine Street. "Go on," she urged, as Joey hesitated.

"Be a church," Joey mumbled.

"A church? I'd like to see it."

"That hain't no real church, ma'am. I mean, the Catholics use it, but hait's jest a two-story building. Nowt much to see," he said hopefully.

Audra glanced at him. Strange. He was usually so eager to show her things, and now he seemed reluctant.

"Well, I'd like to see it anyway."

It *was* only another nondescript frame building, but the street continued. "Let's go to the end, Joey. I see some interesting-looking houses there."

But Joey was already turning the buggy around.

"What are you doing, Joey?"

"Cain't take thee no farther, ma'am."

"Why not?"

Joey's ruddy face was even redder. "Them's sportin' houses, ma'am. Ain't no a place fer a lady," he insisted.

"Sporting houses? But what . . . ? Oh!" Joey's stubborn reluctance and obvious embarrassment made it easy to ascertain exactly what "sporting houses" were.

She was silent the rest of the way home. Did Nick avail himself of the diversions the houses offered?

Was it possible? He was gone most of each day, but they always breakfasted together and he was home each night. Alex had been a dinner guest several times, and they had dined at the Teller House twice. But the other evenings had been shared ones of reading or playing chess next to a cozy fire. To an outside observer, their life would seem perfectly normal.

But, of course, it wasn't, for they shared little else. Each night they walked upstairs together, separated, then went to their respective rooms. They didn't even share a good-night kiss.

She had her freedom, including a substantial allowance. The lump that had burned in her chest since her mother's death was slowly dissipating. Why, then, did she feel so bereft and so lonely? She could fill her days, but her nights were empty.

She pondered the rest of the day, but in the end, it took only one unexpected instant. She and Nick were sitting before the fireplace that evening when she happened to glance up at him. The glow from the fire lit his face and burnished his hair gold, and she suddenly recalled that night at the inn in London. Her mind replayed all that had taken place since then, and she thought about how she loved the curve of his mouth when he smiled, and the way his eyes crinkled when he laughed, and even that unruly lock of hair that insisted on falling onto his forehead all the time.

She was suddenly engulfed by an unfamiliar tenderness and a desperate longing to be in his arms, to be held and kissed as before. The emotions were so strong that she moaned softly.

Nick glanced up at her questioningly. "Is something wrong?"

Eyes wide, she shook her head, mumbled something about being tired, and excused herself. In her room, she sat on her bed, hands folded on her lap, helpless against the feelings washing over her.

Oh, God! Was it possible?

She couldn't love him! She couldn't! Love meant domination and subjection. It meant giving herself up to another's will.

But this is Nick. The voice came, unbidden, into her head.

I can't! I can't be in love with him!

Why can't you? came the voice again. *Are you going to be a coward about this, Audra?*

Falling onto her side, Audra curled up into a ball, her arms wrapped about her knees.

When had it happened?

When she'd seen that he was doing everything in his power to keep her mother healthy and happy?

When he'd returned Fantasy to her? Or her father's emerald?

When he'd first kissed her at Sheffield Manor and held her so tightly that she'd felt safe and secure?

It didn't matter. Perhaps she'd even loved him all along. And if loving him meant physical subjection, she could stand that, too. At last, she could admit that she was even ready for it. Audra laughed quietly, joyously, to herself.

Just how, she mused, did one go about enticing one's own husband?

She began in subtle ways. She changed her perfume and dressed with the utmost care. She began coming down to share breakfast with him clad only in her nightgown and robe. Whenever Nick glanced at her, she held his gaze as long as she dared. When he read to her in the evening, she would lean over his chair to see the passage. She even resorted to finding excuses to knock on his door at night.

Nick's responses were no different than before.

At the end of a week, Audra was beginning to think that she'd have to resort to throwing herself at him, naked, but she couldn't quite find the courage to take that step.

On Saturday evening, she was distracted from her purpose. As Alex's guests, she and Nick attended a comedy at the Montana Theater. Afterward, they went to the Gilpin Restaurant at the Teller House for a late dinner of oysters and champagne. Audra was having a wonderful time. She'd never seen a real theatrical performance before. Still giddy with laughter, she drank several glasses of champagne. She only realized she'd imbibed so much when her face began to feel warm.

"Is my face flushed?" she asked Nick. Alex had excused himself and left the table some few minutes before.

Nick looked at her. Her eyes were sparkling, her lips

curled into a smile. "Now that you mention it, your cheeks are very rosy. And your mouth looks . . . very kissable."

"Oh!" She looked away, seemed to consider this for a moment, then laughed breathlessly. "Then perhaps," she said hesitantly, "I need some air. What do you think?"

Nick's heart skipped a beat as he gazed into her eyes. She met his look boldly, almost defiantly. He wasn't mistaking the invitation he saw there.

Thank God! He'd almost lost his mind this past week. Her efforts had hardly gone unnoticed. He'd been by turns confused, amused, aroused, and cautious. He'd wanted her to be damned sure.

Without a word, he took her arm and led her to the conservatory. Once there, he didn't stop, but found a dark corner and turned her to face him.

Audra stumbled. "Oops! Nick, it's dark—"

Her words were cut off by his mouth. He kissed her with unrestrained abandon, hungrily, his arms wrapped urgently around her. It felt so damned good to have his arms about her again. It had been too long.

Audra curled her own arms about his neck and arched forward to take his kiss.

He parted her lips and teeth with his tongue, probing eagerly.

"Audra, sweet . . ." His groan filled her with sweet satisfaction. She sighed.

His mouth left hers and found her cheek, her throat. "Let's go home," he whispered urgently against her ear.

Audra pressed herself closer against him. "Yes. Let's."

"Oh, there you are, Nicky!"

Nick groaned in frustration and released Audra.

Brenda was making her way toward them, followed by the hapless Mr. Culbertson.

"Nick, you simply must come with us," Brenda announced without preamble. "You promised Elwood that you'd meet his friend from New York." Brenda barely glanced at Audra. "Sorry to take Nicky away from you, dear, but Elwood's friend is very wealthy, and he's looking for investments." The victorious gleam in Brenda's eyes told Audra that she'd seen them kissing, and she wasn't one bit sorry to have interrupted.

Nick's eyes met Audra's apologetically. "Sweetheart, it will only take a few minutes."

She gave a small shrug. She certainly wasn't going to interfere in Nick's business dealings. Besides, he said it would only be for a few minutes. "It's all right, Nick. Alex will keep me company."

After fifteen minutes had passed, Audra began to fume. Nick wasn't even looking her way. The only glimpse she had of him was the back of his head as he sat at Brenda's table with Mr. Culbertson and two other men.

She began to tap her fingers on the table. She spoke with Alex, and couldn't remember what either of them said. She laughed, and she couldn't recall why.

How could Nick do this to her? For the first time in weeks, he'd acted like he wanted her. Like she was his *wife*, not just the woman who slept in the next room. Oh! She'd been so close to achieving her goal. Yet what was he doing now?

Ignoring her. Completely.

They were in Audra's bedroom, where Nick had followed after she'd stomped home on foot, all the way up the hill, refusing to use the buggy, refusing his help even when stones cut into her soft slippers. At one particularly rough point, he'd tried to take her arm to help and she'd struck him with her reticule and told him to leave her alone.

He'd trailed the rest of the way a careful distance behind her.

Now she was standing before him, hands on her hips. "Explain! Explain how you can kiss me, then turn about and ignore me for hours!"

"I've already explained it was business. And it wasn't *hours*. It was only one hour, damn it!"

"Aha! You see? You don't know. It was exactly one hour and twelve minutes." Audra turned away and reached behind herself to unbutton her gown. "Leave my room. I'd like to go to bed." She fumbled with the last few buttons. "Oh, damn!" she cried as one popped off.

"Well, that's hardly *hours*," Nick said mildly as he grasped her shoulders and spun her around to take over the buttons himself.

"Well, it certainly felt like hours to me!" Audra flung over her shoulder. "I felt like . . . like an abandoned wife."

"Will you hold still, damn it! I can't get these buttons . . . Oh, the hell with it!"

In frustration, Nick grabbed the neck of her dress and ripped it open. Roughly, he spun her back to face him again, and her gown slithered from her shoulders to land heaped about her feet. She was too angry to do much more than kick it out of the way.

"I didn't abandon you. I left you in Alex's care while *I* took care of something important."

"Important? Ha! What does that make *me*? Inconsequential? A minor annoyance?"

"Hardly. Admit it, love. You're really angry because you wanted to get me into your bed."

Audra's jaw dropped. Then she gasped in guilty outrage. "Oh! Oh, you are *such* an insufferable egotist!" She suddenly realized that Nick had torn her dress. "Nick! You ruined my gown! Oh, damn you!" Angrily, she grasped his lapels and shoved and tugged until his jacket came off. Defiantly, she threw it across the room.

He ripped open the ribbons of her petticoats and drawers, gave them a yank, and they, too, slithered off her hips and fell about her ankles.

She retaliated by jerking his cravat off. Then she ripped his shirt open from the collar down. Buttons flew every which way.

Both of them were panting now.

His long fingers reached inside the bodice of her camisole, ripped it down the front. She stood, bare breasts heaving with indignation.

She reached for his trousers and the backs of her fingers brushed against him. His body's sudden reaction brought her to her senses, and she hesitated.

"Don't stop now. This is becoming interesting," Nick mocked.

She stared at him, still panting, but her anger had been replaced by shock, for she was suddenly all too aware that she was now naked except for her silk stockings and high-heeled slippers. She covered herself with her hands.

"No? Well, I'll do it myself—this time."

Mesmerized, she watched as Nick hopped from foot to foot, pulling his shoes and stockings off. And then his trousers were suddenly gone, too, and he straightened before her, naked.

Splendidly naked. Audra gasped. Her stomach quivered. Her entire body quivered. She was suddenly filled with a myriad of emotions—fascination, fear, anticipation. . . .

And for the first time, she recognized what she was feeling as true desire. She wanted this man—this wonderful creature standing before her as beautifully formed as any Greek statue. Only he was real. He was flesh and blood, and heat and male. All wonderfully male. Oh, Lord! A fully, hugely aroused . . . male.

She hesitated, met Nick's warm look with a wide-eyed one of her own. "I . . . I don't think it . . . You . . ." Her face flamed.

Nick saw Audra's eyes darken to midnight blue. Enough, by God! He wasn't about to let her talk herself into fear. He wasn't going to wait any longer to have her.

He gently pulled her to him with his hands splayed against her buttocks, and pressed himself against her heated skin.

"It's just *me*," he murmured against her hair. "It's only that part of my body that needs to join with yours. I'm starving for you, sweet Audra." His voice fell, hoarse and thick with desire. "Don't think about it. Don't think—just feel." Grasping her wrists, he placed her arms over his shoulders. "Come closer. Do you feel me?"

He was sliding smoothly against her, skin against skin, and when he arched her closer, a shocked gasp escaped her lips. He was so warm, so hard . . . Audra trembled. If she just didn't *think* about it . . . She closed her eyes and let her body take over, let each nerve ending and each pore soak up his heat, his musky scent. . . .

"You'll find, my sweet wildcat, that we'll fit together perfectly. No pain, only pleasure. I promise."

His palm smoothed the way from her waist, over her hip, glided to her abdomen, cupped her . . . his fingers suddenly, shockingly parted her flesh. Audra's knees weakened. She clung to Nick helplessly as his fingers glided back and forth, building a tension within her that was so great she thought she would faint. She whimpered softly.

His mouth moved to her ear. "I think," he murmured, "that I've just discovered how to make a wildcat purr."

Her legs gave out. Nick caught her and carried her to the bed, where he dropped her without preamble.

He wanted desperately to fling himself upon her soft body and sink into her. Yet he also wanted to gaze upon her, fill his eyes and his senses with the sight of her like this—her glorious hair spread about her, and those long legs still encased in black stockings . . . Nick slid onto the bed, and knelt between her legs.

She made a self-conscious effort to draw her legs together.

"No! Don't move," he ordered gruffly. "I want to look at you. All of you. Every inch. My God, but you are beautiful!"

Audra froze. She should have been dying of embarrassment. But it was difficult to think of such things as modesty when he was looking at her body with eyes so hot that her skin felt like it burned wherever they touched. Her own eyes were drawn to that part of him that jutted so proudly, so eagerly. . . . She wondered if she dared touch him there.

As if he knew, he took her hand and placed it on himself. Audra gasped. Never . . . never had she imagined that flesh could feel so unyielding, yet so soft. Her hand tightened. Nick groaned.

Immediately, she released him. "Did I hurt you?"

The sound he made was half pain, half laughter. "God, no!"

Their gazes locked. They stared at one another until Nick finally grasped her right leg and lifted it. Slowly, he rolled down the stocking, following with his lips as he went. He repeated the process with the other stocking.

His hands slid up her legs and met between her thighs. She gasped as he parted her, gasped again as his thumbs gently played circles upon her most intimate flesh.

Nick's eyes met hers, and he was gratified to read desire. She was all woman. Soft and curved. Yielding, yet demanding. Hot, moist . . .

Not yet. Lord give him strength, not yet! He kept one hand cupped between her thighs as he sank carefully onto the bed beside her, afraid of rushing her. But to his astonished joy, she suddenly threw her arms around him and pulled him down on top of her, and he felt control slipping away. It didn't help that her arms and legs were winding about him, and that she was making little smothered gasps that were driving him insane. He moved over her and then forced himself to stillness, breathing deeply for control. He was going to try to do this slowly, carefully. If it killed him, he would try.

He pulled away slightly, and when Audra made a murmuring sound of protest and attempted to bring him back to her, he took her arms from around his neck and, entwining his fingers with hers, pressed their joined hands to the bed.

Audra stared at him, disappointment filling her. "Nick . . . ?"

"Not yet, my sweet. I ruined your wedding night . . . I intend to make this one perfect for you."

"But, Nick . . ."

"You don't even know what I mean, do you? Well, I'll make you a promise. Before this night is over, you'll know exactly what I'm speaking of. I'll be back in a moment."

Despite his earnest appeal, Audra saw that he wasn't as calm as he pretended. His face was terribly flushed, his voice trembling. Desire struggled with tenderness as he left her momentarily, and tenderness won. She smiled softly when he came back to her, and let her body relax. "Then teach me, Nick."

At her soft invitation, his nostrils flared, his eyes flamed brightly. Still, he held himself in check. His face came closer to hers, and just as she thought he was going to kiss her, his mouth brushed butterfly kisses along her cheek instead. He trailed a path to her ear, back across her nose, and took the same path on the other side of her face. He nibbled at her throat leisurely. "Ah, that's it, love. Open your lips—give your mouth to me."

And she did. His lips and tongue played havoc with hers until she was on fire again, and longing for more.

Nick's fingers found her breast. At first, he played his teasing game there, also, slowly brushing his fingertips back and forth until her nipples peaked and her breasts began to ache. Excitement began in her stomach, then moved lower. His hand moved down and slid up and down her thigh in slow, teasing circles. She stirred restlessly.

"Do you like my touching you?"

"Yes," she whispered hoarsely.

"Do you like it when I kiss you . . . here?"

He brushed her hair aside and pressed a kiss onto the crest of one breast.

"Oh, yes!"

"And this . . . do you like this?" His mouth covered her nipple, and his tongue flicked it. He began to suckle gently, and when she arched her back slightly, he nipped softly. Then his hot mouth moved to her other breast.

Audra was melting slowly, feeling the same sensations she'd felt earlier, only this time, they were even more intense.

The hand that had been stroking her thigh slipped between her legs. Nick watched her face as his fingers parted her and began to stroke her there. "You're beautiful, my love. Every inch of you is smooth silk and honey."

She moaned helplessly, and it seemed to drive him on, for he slid two fingers into her and began to move them in a rhythmic motion as his thumb pressed down upon the sensitive nub. She was immediately flooded with heat and moisture. Tension coiled within her. "Oh! Nick . . . Nick, help me!"

He responded by spreading her limbs and coming

down over her. His voice was low and hoarse, and so filled with desire she could barely understand him. "Now, my sweet Audra. Now I'll show you what it's like to be truly loved."

And he proceeded to do just that. He proved to her that he could be a tender and considerate lover as he slowly and carefully entered her, bringing her body to a new level of consciousness.

Audra's eyes went wide with astonishment. There was no pain. There was only a wonderful fullness that made her ache for more. There had to be more! Audra clutched at him frantically, pulling him closer, wrapping her legs around him. She didn't know what was expected of her, but her mind accepted that she wanted this as desperately as Nick obviously did. And then she was too busy trying to assimilate all the other sensations she was experiencing. Confusion, wonderment, pleasure, and a desperate hunger for something she couldn't even begin to comprehend.

And then, all thought fled as Nick began to move within her, slowly, almost reverently. "Oh, Nick . . . Oh, Nick!"

"That's it, my love. Let your body take what it so badly wants and needs. Give over to me. Let it come." And he began to stroke faster, then with more intensity as he demanded and took, worshiped and gave . . . and all the time, he whispered words of praise and endearments as he urged her on until she lost all inhibitions and all conscious thought, and only touch and sound and scent cocooned her. And all of it was Nick.

And then, there was a burst of pleasure so keen Audra fleetingly thought she was dying, and all she could do was repeat his name, over and over, in a litany of splendid awe.

* * *

Wrapped in each other's arms, they were lying side by side against the pillows, her cheek pressed against Nick's hard chest. She was listening to his heart, which, like hers, was still beating a rapid tattoo. He was stroking her hair tenderly while her fingers swirled his chest hair in idle circles. She breathed deeply through her nose. She felt like crying. She couldn't help it—he smelled and felt so good and she was so blissfully happy.

She felt Nick stir as he looked down at her. "Are you happy, love?" he asked her, almost as if he'd read her thoughts.

"Mmm. Deliciously, deliriously so." She laughed softly. "To think that I was convinced this was all a one-sided affair, with the woman doing all the giving and the man all the receiving." She felt his chest rumble, and raised up on one elbow to fling her hair back from her face and glare at him in feigned anger. "Don't you dare laugh at me, Nick Brannon," she warned. "How was I to know?"

The smile that had been curving his mouth abruptly disappeared as he reached up to brush back a strand she'd missed. "I consider myself extremely fortunate that you didn't. Thank you. You've made *me* very happy, my love."

Audra's pique evaporated immediately. She snuggled up against him again. "This must have been what it was like for my mother and father," she said dreamily. "There were times when they seemed to have eyes only for each other. I felt . . . left out, somehow." She smiled against Nick's shoulder. "Now I understand. This *joining* is a celebration of sorts . . . of love, isn't it?"

Surely, if Nick loved her, he'd tell her now. He was very still, and when he finally spoke, his voice was low and hoarse. "Most definitely."

Audra felt a pang of disappointment. She so desperately wanted to hear him say the words and to be able to tell him that she loved him. But he stayed silent. She pressed on. "Do you know what the most wonderful part of it is?"

"What, my love?"

"When you're inside me, warm and hard, you touch my heart and my soul and we're one. I feel complete. I'm not alone anymore. I'll never have to be alone again," she said shyly.

Nick didn't reply, for he was trying to swallow the lump in his throat.

Again, Audra was disappointed. All right. So maybe Cleo and Bertie had been wrong. Maybe he wasn't in love with her. Not yet, anyway. But, oh! He would be! She'd make him love her!

Then she remembered Brenda, and frowned. She propped herself on one elbow. "Nick . . . ?"

"Hm?"

"Have you and Brenda ever . . . *you know?*"

He blinked in surprise, almost grinned, but then saw that she was completely serious. "No. Brenda and I have never . . . *you know.*"

She glared down at him. "Good! Because I couldn't stand it if you ever took a mistress, or if you ever go to upper Pine Street. I'll kill you if you ever go there," she announced breathlessly, her eyes dangerously narrowed.

How the hell had she ever found out about Pine Street? Nick wondered. "Audra, I give you my word. I have never taken Brenda Farrow to bed, I have absolutely no desire to, nor do I have any desire to keep a mistress, nor do I have any inclinations to visit Pine. Ever."

"You swear?"

He cupped her neck and brought her face to his. "I don't want any other woman," he whispered against her mouth. "The only woman I want has hair that smells like roses and skin . . ." His nose and lips nuzzled her neck, under her ear. ". . . skin that smells like . . . love. I want only *you*, Audra."

She smiled against his cheek. "I believe you."

"Thank you," he said simply as he released her.

But instead of lying down again, Audra stayed as she was, while her fingers made idle circles around his nipples. Nick caught his breath.

"Nick . . . ?"

"Another question?"

"An easy one. Are we always going to have spats before we make love?"

"Certainly not. Are we having one now?"

"Nooo." She stared down at him. "What do you mean . . . *now*?"

Nick slid her hand down his belly, then lower. "Does this answer your question?"

Audra's eyes widened, then darkened.

"Oh! Oh, my goodness! I should say . . . it . . . does."

Chapter 20

$\mathcal{T}$he next day they hurriedly packed a few essentials and had Joey take them to the stables, where they collected Fantasy's Lady and Ulysses. Then they went to inform Alex of their plans.

He groaned and complained about being left at the office, but Audra could tell that he didn't really mean it, for when Nick's back was turned, he winked at her. Nick stopped to have a word with their accountant, Samuel Bentley, and Alex walked Audra outside. "You look extremely pleased with yourself, kitten. It's a good name for you. If you had four paws, you'd be licking cream off your whiskers."

Nick joined them just as Audra's laughter pealed out. From the corner of his eye, he glimpsed a man at the end of the street abruptly whirl about in their direction, but he was too fascinated by his wife's merriment to notice more than the sudden movement. By the time he took a better look, all he saw was the back of a tall, slim man with light hair disappearing around the corner.

For just an instant he wondered who the man was; he thought he looked familiar. But Audra came to him then and took his arm, and he forgot the man immediately.

They rode to the ranch for an extended honeymoon. Letty and Mrs. Gilly would come the following week, but for now, they wanted to be alone.

The two-hour ride took them twice that long, for they stopped a dozen times to lean out of their saddles and share breathless kisses. Finally, in a burst of desire, Nick pulled her out of her saddle onto his lap and guided the horses into a copse of trees, where he tied them and lifted her down. Carrying her beneath a towering pine, he spread the blanket he'd brought and made passionate love to her. Afterward, lacking any sleep from the night before, they napped until Nick woke Audra with soft, gentle kisses which soon became a mutual hunger that had to be appeased once again. Their picnic lunch took forever as they teased and fed one another. Finally, deliciously sated, they got to the ranch.

Just in time, for they found a worried Rafe organizing a search party. When they hadn't arrived when Nick's message said they would, he explained, he'd worried that one or both of them had been injured and needed help.

Nick did his best to explain their delay—other than telling Rafe the truth—but he was hampered by Audra, who covered her mouth in a vain attempt to stifle her giggles at his lame and stammering excuses. Rafe finally caught on, and when he left them, he was grinning as broadly as Audra, to Nick's consternation.

They had four weeks of happiness and laughter on the ranch. It was a new world for Audra. Though he was careful to keep his promise to her—that of preventing a pregnancy—Nick rid her of all other inhibitions and taught her to revel in her femininity, and they were both happier than they'd ever been. They went for long rides into mountains where the trees were beginning to turn into wonderful colors, and they swam in ice-cold streams, and they made love wherever they went.

Sometimes it was like the roaring mountain river, wild and passionate. And other times Nick worshiped her with reverence, in a dappled clearing under blue sky. They were oblivious to everyone around them, engrossed in each other and the richness of the love they shared.

At the end of that time, they reluctantly returned to Central City, for Nick felt he could ask no more time from Alex, who had been managing their business affairs on his own for months now.

Once back, they settled into a routine. It was the longest time Nick had ever been in one place; usually he was the one who traveled. This time, Alex would take his turn in New York and Boston, while Nick stayed and handled the business from Central City. He wanted to spend the winter with Audra.

One night, after he'd closed and locked up the office, he walked to the Teller House, where he was meeting Audra for dinner. "Has Mrs. Brannon arrived yet, Soames?" he asked the desk clerk.

"No, sir."

"Let me know when she does. I'll be in the bar."

"Sure thing."

He had time for one drink before Soames came in to tell him that Audra had come and was waiting for him in the dining room.

"Hello, sweetheart," he greeted her as he leaned over her to give her a quick kiss. He would have preferred to lift her to him, kiss her passionately, and keep her nestled next to him, but it was a public hotel, after all. "How was your day?" he asked as he took the seat across from her.

"Wonderful, Nick. I had some of the ladies I've met in

for a real English tea today, and they were thrilled. Mrs. Gilly makes the best saffron cakes."

Nick smiled at her. It was a relief to know that she wasn't bored or, worse, homesick. She'd never said so, but now he wondered if she was just keeping it to herself. "Audra, sweet . . ."

Her gasp alarmed him. She had turned horribly pale. Nick jumped up and went to her side. "What is it, love? Are you ill?"

"No, I . . . Yes. I have a . . . a sudden headache. I . . . please, Nick, can we go home? Now? I'm not hungry and I . . . I need to lie down."

"Of course we'll go." Nick signaled to a waiter and hurriedly gave him instructions. "They're bringing the buggy. Can you walk?"

Audra only nodded.

Solicitously, he placed an arm around her waist and helped her out of the dining room. He was so concerned, he didn't even notice when he brushed past Brenda Farrow and her escort. Nor was he aware that they were both watching him and Audra avidly.

Nick was worried about Audra, for not only had her nightmares returned, she was pale and listless, and she refused to go out, saying only that she preferred to be alone with him. Against her protestations, he sent for Dr. Byers, who examined her privately while Nick paced the hall outside their bedroom. Afterward, the doctor reported that Audra seemed perfectly healthy.

"Can she be pregnant, Doctor?" Nick asked bluntly, though he knew it was highly unlikely considering the care he'd taken to prevent such an occurrence.

"I doubt it. I didn't do an internal examination, but I

questioned her carefully. She has no symptoms. Your wife is English, isn't she?" Dr. Byers asked.

Nick affirmed that she was. "Well, she's probably just a little homesick. I didn't find anything physically wrong with her, Mr. Brannon. I'm only recommending more fresh air and good, wholesome food. Summer is fading, and I've found that people who aren't used to the mountains sometimes become slightly depressed at the thought of winter coming on. Something to do with the feeling of being closed in, I think."

Nick raked his fingers through his hair. Alex was in Boston and wouldn't be back for at least another two weeks. As soon as he got back, Nick decided, he'd take Audra back to the ranch for a few days. She'd loved it there.

To his relief, when he mentioned it to Audra she seemed to recover her energy and her usual exuberance.

Nick was trying to catch up with some of his paperwork in preparation for leaving. He looked up as the door to his office opened, then stood as Brenda breezed in. Without invitation, she perched on his desk and played idly with a paperweight.

"I'm inviting you to take me to a late lunch, Nick."

"I can't, Brenda. I have too much to do."

"Oh, pooh! You have two clerks to do that for you. I haven't seen you for ages." She gave him a coy smile, reminiscent of the ones she used to give him when she wanted something.

"Audra and I've been out at the ranch," he said warily, "and we'd like to go back shortly."

"Oh. I see. You know," Brenda began conversationally, "you were really cruel to me. After all we meant to one another, it was an unpleasant shock to find out you were married."

Nick was well aware that Brenda had been expecting him to propose to *her* someday. He'd actually considered it. She would have made an exemplary hostess, and the perfect wife. Bedding her wouldn't have been a hardship, either; Brenda was beautiful in face and form. But something had always held Nick back. There was a coldness about her that bothered him.

Thank God he hadn't made the mistake of marrying her. He couldn't imagine any other woman in his life besides Audra.

Still, he felt a twinge of guilt. "I sent you a letter explaining the circumstances. I'm sorry if you didn't receive it until after I got back from England." He had also sent her a very expensive diamond bracelet which she'd never acknowledged, even though it was on her wrist right now.

"So you did. Well, I didn't handle it very well. I'm afraid that, based on our past relationship, I expected more than you were apparently willing to give."

Nick squirmed uncomfortably. "Brenda, I'm sorry . . ."

"No, no! Don't apologize, Nick. I'm the one who should apologize. I had no right to make those assumptions. And I had no right being so catty to Audra. I truly want to make amends, Nick, and I want you to believe that I've turned over a new leaf."

Nick's glance was filled with suspicion. Brenda never apologized for anything. She expected things always to go her way, or not at all. "Apology accepted."

"Good! I feel so much better. Now, what about that lunch? That isn't too much to ask, is it? Besides," she pouted, "you owe me at least this little favor."

Nick sighed. He didn't see how he could refuse without being downright rude, and he'd just as soon avoid any unpleasantness. In a town this small, it was inevitable that they'd attend the same social functions. What would an innocent meal hurt?

Though it was rather late for lunch, the dining room was still half full, and the waiters were busily clearing tables. Nick allowed Brenda to inform the headwaiter that they would wait in the conservatory until their table was ready.

"Come along, Nick. We'll have a glass of wine before we eat."

She led the way, silent for a change. They had just stepped through the doorway when she turned back. "Oh, dear. I'm afraid it's already occupied. Oh, dear, Nick! I'm so sorry . . ."

Peering behind Brenda, he saw a man and woman standing together in a shadowed corner. The woman's back was to him, but it took Nick only a second to realize that she was his wife.

The man stepped forward, into a shaft of sunlight, and reached out to grasp Audra's arms and pull her into an embrace. A jolt of shock went through Nick as he recognized Silas Norton.

His vision blurred by a red haze, Nick took a step forward, but stopped abruptly. It took every ounce of control he had to keep from dashing to Norton and beating him to a bloody pulp.

Without a word, he turned and brushed past Brenda.

He fought his rage all the way home, reminding himself that he'd almost ruined things once before by jumping to conclusions. This time, he'd wait for Audra to explain what Norton was doing in Central City, why they were having what appeared to be a very intimate meeting in the secluded conservatory.

And why Norton had, wrapped around his hand, her

mother's diamond necklace and her own precious emerald pendant.

Audra didn't even try to hide her disgust and revulsion as she pushed away from Silas Norton. He'd grabbed her so swiftly, it had taken her a moment to overcome her shock. "Don't ever try that again, Silas. Ever! I'll kill you if you touch me again!"

Norton only smiled. "I don't doubt that you would try. Too bad. There's a certain glow about you now. I do believe you're even more desirable as a married woman." He reached out to touch Audra's cheek. She flinched and slapped it away, and he laughed.

Audra tried desperately to conceal her anxiety. "You'll get nothing more from me, Silas. Except for my wedding rings—which I will *never* part with—I've given you the only things I own of any value. It will pay your passage back to England and keep you in style for a long time. In return, you'll not spread your lies here, nor anywhere else. But understand this—I'm not buying your silence for myself. You can't hurt *me* by telling anyone about William. Nick already knows all of it, and he's the only one who matters to me."

"Which is why you want to protect your husband." Norton sneered. "You're afraid that his business will be ruined if his associates find out his wife is a murderess. . . ."

"Stop it! Stop calling me that!" Audra was trembling now. God! She'd thought she'd escaped her past. That Norton had actually followed her to America was unbelievable. Or would have been, if he weren't standing right before her, wearing that horribly smug expression. "We have an agreement, do we not?" she asked tightly.

"So we do. But remember—you can always call on me

if your marriage starts to pall. I could teach you things you've never imagined."

Audra paled. "Keep away from me, Silas. Keep away from both of us." Whirling, she fled out of the conservatory.

She made it to the ladies' powder room just in time to be violently ill.

Nick leaned against a wall, sipping at a glass of tasteless champagne as he watched Audra at the other end of the room. It was intermission at the Montana Theater, and his bride was encircled by several admirers, all of whom seemed to be enraptured by her. How could he blame them? Audra was dressed in a sapphire gown that perfectly matched her eyes, the pearls he'd given her entwined in the soft chignon of her hair and around her throat. She'd made no excuse for not wearing her pendant, and he hadn't asked for one.

But he was dying inside. He'd waited, wanting to trust her, wanting to give her the chance to tell him about Norton. He'd desperately hoped and prayed that she would come home and tell him it had all been a mistake. That Norton had accosted her. Even that he'd tried to seduce her and she'd refused. *Anything* that wouldn't have meant she'd wanted that embrace!

But Audra hadn't said a word to him about meeting Norton at the Teller House. When he'd inquired about her day, she'd said only that she'd run several errands. "I did go to Buell and Burlington's to order stationery, and Leiter's to purchase some material for new aprons for Letty and Mrs. Gilly." And then, almost as an afterthought, she'd added, "Oh, yes, and I stopped at the Teller House to speak to the chef. That was all."

All week Nick had watched her closely—brooding,

worrying, wondering. Nights, he made love to her with desperation born of fear. She was as genuinely, as sweetly responsive as ever.

It confused the hell out of him.

A feminine shriek suddenly pierced the noise of the crowd. Nick turned and found Audra standing near the doorway. Nick's gaze went past her—and found Brenda, her hair soaked, liquid dripping down her gown. Beside her stood—Silas Norton!

The anger that had simmered just below the surface all week suddenly exploded. In a few long strides, Nick reached Audra and grabbed her arm. The empty champagne glass fell from her fingers and shattered. Ignoring the broken crystal, he pulled Audra to where Brenda and Norton were standing.

"Nick!" Brenda wailed. "Did you see what she did to me? She . . ."

Ignoring Brenda, Nick thrust Audra aside. Norton never saw his fist coming. He was unconscious before he hit the floor.

Brenda screamed. Nick spun back to Audra. She was frozen, her hand over her mouth, her eyes wide in dismay. Did he read guilt there, also?

Grasping her arm again, Nick faced the crowd. "Ladies. Gentlemen. I'm afraid you'll have to excuse us. My wife isn't feeling very well." Murmurs of sympathy turned into shocked gasps and a stifled titter or two from the ladies as Nick tightened his hold and dragged Audra down the hall.

Her face flamed. "Nick! What are you doing? Stop! You're making a spectacle of us."

"It appears to me, madam," Nick said in icy tones, "that you've already managed to do just that."

"She called me an English slut, damn it! I . . ."

He just kept pulling her along. "Be quiet, Audra, or I

may be tempted to have our discussion right here—in sight and hearing of everyone present. It won't be pretty, and it may affect the ladies' sensibilities. We both know it shouldn't affect yours as you don't have any."

Audra was too frightened to retort. Her mind was whirling. Oh, God! Norton had promised to leave. But he'd lied, because here he still was.

And Nick was furious. She dared say nothing, for she'd never seen him this coldly furious. Not even when she'd tried to run away. Not even on their wedding night. What would he do?

He was coldly silent as he drove them back to the house. Leaving the horse standing, he unceremoniously pulled her off the buggy and practically pulled her inside, past a wide-eyed Letty, and up the stairs.

The door to their room slammed shut behind them. Nick still had her wrist in a viselike grip, and he dragged her to the center of the room then just as carelessly flung her away, so that she staggered backward and fell into a chair.

Gripping the arms of the chair, he effectively trapped her as he leaned over her. Each question was punctuated by another movement toward her, until she was shrinking back from him. "Why is Norton here? Did you send for him, Audra? Did he come running so that he could get the benefit of your new status as Mrs. Brannon?"

"No! I didn't send for him. You know I despise him!"

He leaned closer. His eyes were full of fury. "I warned you once never to lie to me again. You despise him, yet you gave him your mother's diamonds and your emerald. You despise him, yet not enough to keep from kissing him. You despise him, yet you met him behind my back."

Audra paled. "I didn't kiss him! He *tried* to kiss me and I wouldn't let him. And I met him only twice, Nick. I swear it! The first time was to find out what he wanted.

And the second time was when I gave him the jewels. He threatened to tell everyone about my past. It would have hurt *you*—your business! I couldn't let him do that."

Nick focused on only one thing. "What about your past?"

"You know about it! Norton told you, back in England. About William and—"

"I thought," Nick cut in, his voice deadly steel, "that we'd already ascertained that everything Norton told me was a lie. Are you now saying it wasn't?" Nick's face was as pale as hers, and there was a small line of perspiration above his upper lip. She'd been a virgin. There was no doubt about that. But there were other ways . . .

"No! Yes!" Audra threaded her fingers into her hair. "Stop this, Nick! You're confusing me! I don't know what to tell you anymore. I gave him the jewels on the condition that he leave. I would have given him anything to keep him from ruining you."

"Anything, Audra?" Nick's voice was ice. "*Anything?*"

Audra gasped. "Nick! I didn't mean . . . I could never have . . . You don't really believe that I'd . . . ?"

Nick stepped away from her. "I don't know what to believe anymore," he said, his voice flat. "I thought you'd finally learned to trust me. I thought you were completely honest with me. I thought you finally learned to . . ." His voice dropped off.

"Love you? I do, Nick! I not only trust you, I love you."

Nick only stared at her.

"It's true, Nick! I swear it," she said desperately.

His tone was as bleak as his eyes. "Do you know how long I've waited to hear that from you?" He laughed sardonically, but his mouth was still a grim line. "Tell me, dear *wife*, is that why you married me? Because you love me?"

Guilty color suffused Audra's face. "No. It isn't. I didn't love you then. Or if I did, I didn't know it." How was she to explain it to Nick without hurting him further? How could she convince him that she did love him, now, fiercely. "All I know is that I love you now. Nick, please believe me—"

But he'd been watching her, reading the consternation on her face. He cut her off by straightening and moving away. "It no longer matters," he said wearily. "How can I believe anything you tell me when you constantly keep secrets from me? When you refuse to give me your complete trust?"

"Nick, I said I was sorry, but please, understand. Norton was my problem, not yours. Ever since William my life has been controlled by others. I wanted to handle Norton myself. I *needed* to do it myself." But Nick had picked up his hat and was walking to the door. Audra jumped to her feet. "What are you going to do?" She was afraid for him. Afraid that he'd go after Norton.

"I'm leaving."

"Leaving? For how long? Where are you going?"

He turned back to her and his eyes were as cold as his smile. "I don't know. Does it really matter?"

"Of course it matters. Damn you!" Audra stamped her foot in frustration as Nick opened the door. "Come back here, Nick Brannon! Don't you dare leave this house. If you leave, I'll . . . I'll . . ."

Once again, he turned back. "You'll what? Go to Norton? Give him anything he wants? Or has he already had it all?"

"No! I'll . . . If you leave, I swear I'll go back to England."

Too late, the feral gleam in his eyes warned her. She should never have challenged him in the mood he was in!

Nick's long strides brought him back to her. His fingers

sank into her hair and curved around her head as he jerked her to him. "You'll not leave. I told you once that I was particular in my tastes. Right now, I have no *taste* for you. I can hardly bear the sight of you. But I'll be back, if only because you're preferable to going to Pine Street."

"You're mad! If you think for one minute that I'd submit . . ."

"Submit?" He laughed scornfully. "You forget, my dear. I know how to make your body sing. I know how to make you writhe with passion." Nick was torturing himself as much—no, more—than he was her, but he couldn't seem to stop. "I know how to make you moan and beg me to take you. I know how to make you whisper my name . . . plead for me to . . ."

"Stop!" Audra pulled his fingers away and covered her ears with her hands. It was all true, damn him! But for him to make a mockery of what had once been shared between them, of what had been the happiest moments of her life, was unbearable. Yet his hurtful words still penetrated.

"When I can stand the sight, the feel of you again, I'll be back. And I'll have you if I want." His mouth tightened cruelly. "Do you understand, Audra?"

His cold indifference infuriated her. Her palm itched to slap that smug expression off his face, but she wouldn't give Nick the satisfaction of knowing how much his words hurt.

Damn it! She was sick and tired of always being in the wrong! Tired of having to apologize. If he didn't believe she loved him, so be it. It was his loss!

Her eyes clashed with his. "Oh, I understand perfectly, Nick," she said coldly. "Understand this—*you* are a bastard! And someday, you're going to regret all this, but it will be too late. You'll have lost more than you know."

Nick shrugged indifferently. "You may be right about

my being a bastard," he said as he headed for the door again. "You're wrong about one thing, however—I already regret the mistake I made in asking you to be my wife. It was probably the sorriest thing I've ever done!"

Fury lent her wings. She flew to him, grabbed the back of his jacket, and spun him around to face her.

"How dare you? How dare you talk of love and trust? You've never admitted any love for me. You say I've never learned to trust you. Well, trust is a two-way street, you idiot. Where's your faith in *me*? Why do you believe others' *lies*, but not in *me*? You're a hypocrite, Nickolas Brannon. I'm sorry I ever loved you. You don't deserve it. Do you hear me, you foolish man—you don't *deserve* me! Go, then! I'm well rid of you! Get out of my room! Get out of my house! And don't bother to come back, because I won't be here!" And with that, she furiously threw all her weight at him. Unprepared, he lost his balance, staggered backward through the doorway, and slammed into the wall at the other side of the hall.

He recovered, looked up in astonishment. Audra was framed in the doorway, panting in fury, eyes spitting blue fire. He took a step forward. The bedroom door slammed in his face.

It was just as well. A crash followed close behind. It was the unmistakable sound of china shattering against that same door.

Audra was sitting in the little sun parlor, chin in hand, unenthusiastically gazing at a stack of invitations to Thanksgiving celebrations which had arrived in the past few days. She poked at them idly, until the top ones slid off and lay askew.

It had been a month since she and Nick had that final argument, and she hadn't seen him since. At first, she'd been at a loss as to how to reply to the invitations, for Nick wasn't even communicating directly with her. Then, after several days of feeling sorry for herself, she'd decided that she wasn't going to sit home and brood, thereby giving Nick the satisfaction of thinking that she missed him one whit. Luckily, some of his friends' spouses were genuinely cordial, so she had taken advantage of their invitations and offers of accompaniment and attended every soiree, every luncheon and dinner, every dance she'd been invited to.

But it had all become senseless and hollow without Nick beside her. She missed his little side comments, his touch on her hand, the way he would look across a room and unerringly find her to signal a silent message with an arch of his brow.

She hadn't responded to these last invitations. She wasn't exactly sure what a Thanksgiving holiday was anyway, though she knew it was coming up in a few weeks. She didn't feel sociable these days, and she was already dreading the thought of Christmas. Despite William's lack of interest, they had always decorated the Manor and celebrated the holidays. She missed England, she missed McKee and Bertie, but most of all, she missed Nick.

Even more, she desperately needed him.

Audra pressed her hand over the small bulge of her abdomen.

Immediately after Nick had walked out, she'd been violently ill again. Initially, she'd blamed it on her state of mind. But when her stomach persisted in doing morning acrobatics, when she'd felt so exhausted she found herself dozing all the time, she'd gone to Dr. Byers. The news had been a shock, for there had been no signs. Even he had been surprised.

How could she have known? Her monthly flow had never ceased during the three and a half months of her marriage. Besides, she'd trusted Nick to protect her from just such an occurrence.

Still, she couldn't really blame him. What happened on their wedding night had been—unanticipated.

But she was so afraid. She didn't want to be. She tried not to be. But the memory of her mother's screams during childbirth haunted her dreams, even now.

She could go to Nick. She had, in fact, almost done so even before she'd learned about the baby. But she was too proud and too stubborn to go to him now. If he came back, it had to be because he wanted to. It would have to be for *her*, not for any obligation he felt toward her.

Audra knew it was going to be almost impossible to keep the baby a secret. Nick would find out eventually, but she'd keep that from happening as long as possible.

Nothing and no one—not even Nick—was going to prevent her from taking *her* child to England.

Chapter 21

"Your wife has forwarded a financial request, Mr. Brannon. Naturally, I replied that I was required to bring it to you. She asked me to convey her wishes to you immediately, sir."

"Well, what are they?"

Samuel Bentley cleared his throat nervously. Nick had brought his wife to the offices of Brannon and Benedict to introduce her to the staff. Samuel, the clerks, and the secretary had all been charmed by Mrs. Brannon. Now, they all knew that something had gone awry, for Mr. Brannon had moved back into the Teller House almost two months ago, while Mrs. Brannon was living in their home with only the servants. His employer's mood had been dark and forbidding since, and everyone treaded carefully around him. Even Mr. Benedict.

The partners were barely speaking, ever since Mr. Benedict had returned from a trip three weeks ago, stormed into Mr. Brannon's office, and called him a "stupid, stubborn, goddamned son of a bitch." Everyone had heard it, since he'd been shouting.

Today was the first time any of them had seen or heard from Mrs. Brannon, although it was Samuel's responsibility to deposit what he considered a very generous sum into the account he'd been ordered to set up for her. He'd been surprised when she'd sent the note to him instead of Mr. Brannon, and asked him to relay her request to her husband.

"Mrs. Brannon has asked for an appropriate amount to furnish the remaining upstairs rooms in the house. She also requests an increase in her personal allowance. She didn't offer any specifics; only that she wished to hire additional staff."

Nick's eyebrows rose.

"The sums she requested aren't that excessive, sir," Samuel hastened to explain. "I have the figures here if you . . ."

"There's no need to see them. Give her whatever she asks for, whenever she asks for it. Mrs. Brannon doesn't need to explain the particulars. Is that clear?"

"Absolutely." Samuel released a silent breath of relief as he gathered his papers to leave.

"Just a moment, Samuel. Double her household allowance. See to it that any wages are paid out of that and allow Mrs. Brannon whatever she wants for personal expenses. Make it clear to her that her allowance is strictly for her personal use and that she's not required to pay any wages from it."

"Very good, sir."

"And Samuel . . . It's snowing hard. Let's close up early today."

"Thank *you*, Mr. Brannon!"

Samuel left, whereupon Nick cleared off his own desk,

donned his heavy coat, and locked up. On the way to the Teller House, he pondered Audra's unexpected request.

From the time he'd first gone to Sheffield, Audra hadn't asked him for a cent. Not once. On the contrary, when he'd purchased a new wardrobe for her, she'd been upset. He very clearly recalled her oath to never be dependent on any man. Yet, now she was asking for an increase in her allowance. She must have felt a dire need in order for her to *humble* herself. At least, knowing Audra, he was sure she'd see it that way.

It wasn't that she hadn't spent any of her allowance since he'd moved out. Despite the fact that he hadn't returned to the house, as he'd threatened, Nick was well aware that Audra had become quite the social butterfly, attending every public function that the county offered. She never went alone, but was always accompanied, ironically, by his business associates and their wives.

Then, almost a month ago, she'd inexplicably dropped out of the social scene. At first, Nick had worried that she was planning to return to England—which would have forced him to take some action, because he couldn't stand the thought of never seeing her again—but she was still residing at the house.

It was puzzling. Or was it? Perhaps this request proved that she'd determined that his pocketbook was as good a route to revenge as any.

Yet he couldn't really believe that. He'd never known Audra to be petty. A liar definitely, an adulteress, possibly. But never petty. What did he care how much of his wealth she spent? If she wanted to throw his money away on carpets or lamps, or even frivolities, so be it. He could afford to indulge her every whim. As long as he didn't have to see her, watch her with other men. . . .

He jerked upright. There *was* one thing he wouldn't tolerate. Damned if he'd allow her to give any of his money to Norton, who was still in Central City, living in this very hotel. Nick had never confronted him again; he merely kept an unobtrusive eye on the bastard, to discover whether or not Audra was meeting him.

To Nick's relief, she hadn't and she wasn't. In fact, as far as he could tell, Norton spent most of his time losing his money—the money he'd gotten from the sale of the jewels, no doubt—in the gaming dens. The rest of the time he was usually escorting Brenda or some other woman about town.

Nick was biding his time. Norton would soon run out of money, and Nick was convinced he'd go after Audra again. Then, and only then, would Nick interfere and take steps to get rid of Norton once and for all . . . and clear up this mess with his wife.

Nick entered the Teller House and headed for the elevator. Soames, the desk manager, saw him coming and held the door open.

"Good evening, Mr. Brannon. I'm on my way up to the third floor. Going to your room?"

"Good evening, Soames. Yes, I am."

God, he was tired of this! Each evening, he came back to the Teller House, went up to his room to change, came back down to have his dinner. He couldn't even have that in solitude, for Central City was always receiving visitors from the East, and he was entertaining either them or his business acquaintances. How he missed the quiet, intimate dinners he and Audra used to share.

The nights were the worst. He'd lie in bed, remembering how *she'd* looked in bed, so utterly beautiful and so damned vulnerable. When they'd been together, he'd wake each morning and lie quietly watching her sleep, filled with wonder that she was really his.

Damn it! A man's pride was worth only so much. If he had to, he'd get on his knees and beg her to take him back. Whatever she'd done or not done, it wasn't worth this nagging pain and miserable loneliness. He may as well admit he still loved her, would always love her.

Soames was speaking to him. "Will you be having dinner in, Mr. Brannon?" he asked just as the elevator stopped at the third floor and the doors opened.

Nick sighed. "Yes, I—"

He was cut off by a sudden, sharp retort. Slightly muffled, the sound was still unmistakably that of gunfire. He and Soames exchanged startled looks. Just then, the sound was repeated.

Soames stepped out of the elevator, Nick right behind him.

At the end of the hall, Nick saw the back of a woman as she turned the corner to the rear stairs. All he had time to notice was that she was wearing a dark cape or cloak of some sort.

Two of the doors opened and guests poked their heads out.

"Did you hear where the shots came from?" Nick asked.

"Near the end of the hall," a short, bearded man said. "Don't you think so?" he asked the couple standing in the doorway across.

"Yes," the woman replied. "We'd just opened our door to leave when we heard the noise."

Nick and Soames raced to the end of the hall, stopping at a door which was partially open. Nick looked at Soames inquiringly.

"The English gentleman's room. Mr. Norton."

Nick felt his heart lurch uncomfortably as he stepped back to allow Soames to enter first.

"Oh, Lord!" he heard Soames exclaim in a horrified voice.

Nick pushed his way past the clerk.

The room was in disarray. Clothes were strewn about and the bed covers were a tangled mess. But what caught Nick's eye immediately was Silas Norton. Or rather, his body.

He was lying on the floor beside the bed, wearing only trousers and an unbuttoned white shirt. At least, it had been white at one time—now there was a shocking splash of red over his heart. His eyes were staring sightlessly at the ceiling.

"You'd better get the sheriff," Nick said calmly. "I'll keep everyone else out."

Soames nodded and turned to leave. By now, there was a crowd of people standing in the doorway, all trying to peer inside. Nick followed Soames to the door and, without a word of explanation, closed it. Then he turned back to the room and began a swift but methodical search, ignoring the body on the floor. He'd seen too many dead men in the war, including some of his own crew, to be squeamish about this one.

He was relieved to find no articles of women's clothing strewn amongst Norton's. He'd almost concluded his search when he spotted a pair of men's shoes at the bottom of the armoire. He quickly upended them. A heavy object fell into his hand, and he closed his palm around it tightly. He didn't have to look at it to know that it was an emerald pendant. He slipped it into his pocket just as the sheriff came through the door with his deputy and Soames.

Sheriff Cox nodded at him. "What've we got here, Nick?"

"Appears to me he was shot through the heart, Sheriff. What did Soames tell you?"

"Just that there were two shots, and you both came running up here and found him." The sheriff pulled Norton's shirt aside. "Come and look at this, Nick. What do you think?"

Nick took his time to study the two small holes, less than an inch apart, which were visible in Norton's chest. "Small caliber," he said.

"Uh-huh. Let's turn him over and have a look-see."

There was no blood on Norton's back, and no exit wounds. "Very small caliber. I'd say it could even have been a derringer," Sheriff Cox surmised. He let Norton's body slide back onto the floor. "Know anything about him?" he asked Nick.

"Just that he's British. Don't know what he was doing here," Nick said shortly.

"Well, from what I've heard, he wasn't too well liked. Heard he claimed to have some money to invest, though. Tried to push his way into a couple of mines, but no one would have him. Spent most of his time gambling. Have many visitors?" he asked Soames suddenly.

"Not that I know of. Not up here, anyway. He didn't spend much time in the hotel, Sheriff."

Nick released his breath. Soames had been on duty the day Audra had met Norton in the conservatory, but if she'd ever come to his room, Soames wasn't saying. He was either worried about Nick's reaction, or he was telling the truth. And he obviously hadn't seen the woman running away.

"Uh-huh. Well, I may want to talk to you both later. You can go, for now. Soames, get those people out of the hall. The coroner will be coming up the back way soon."

Nick changed his mind about going to his room and followed Soames downstairs, where he detoured into the bar. He found a solitary table at the far corner and curtly ordered a bottle of brandy. His expression was warning enough to the other patrons. No one came near him for the next hour.

He'd hoped to numb his mind so he couldn't think about Audra and Norton—to forget he'd ever seen them together. But he couldn't, and the brandy seemed only to make his thinking sharper. After one glass, he shoved the bottle aside and sat musing it all over in his mind. He knew, he simply knew that Audra wasn't capable of murdering anyone. There was also the fact that because of the way her father had died, Audra hated handling pistols.

Yet the emerald was burning a hole in his pocket.

He picked up the bottle to refill his glass. At that moment, a hand reached out and took it from his grasp. Nick lifted his head to see Alex looking down at him with narrowed eyes.

"You have a choice, Nick. You can sit here and finish off this bottle, or you can go home and give your wife the help and support she so badly needs from you."

"What the hell's that supposed to mean?"

"It means, old man, that Audra needs you. She sent for me, but she needs her husband. She's in her parlor right now, being interviewed by Sheriff Cox as a suspect in Norton's mur—"

Nick shoved back his chair with such force that it fell over. Alex grinned as he poured a measure of brandy into Nick's glass, lifted it, and saluted the door through which Nick had just exited. "Here's to you, friend," he toasted before emptying it in one swallow.

And about time you went to her, he thought as he followed. He'd been tempted to punch his best friend in the jaw—had been tempted several times since he'd returned and found that Nick and Audra were no longer living together. Been even more tempted ever since he'd gone to see her, living in that little house of hers like a hermit.

Once he'd discovered her reason, it had been all he could do to keep his mouth shut. But he'd made a promise to her, and she'd threatened to never forgive him if he told Nick about the baby.

Alex expected she'd have to tell him herself, now.

Nick didn't bother to ring the bell. It was still his house, damn it! He barged inside and headed directly for the front parlor.

The room was filled with people, all of whom fell silent as he suddenly appeared in the doorway, but his eyes went directly to Audra. His mouth tightened. She was sitting in a chair, separated from the rest like the accused facing a jury, except for Letty and Mrs. Gilly, who both hovered behind her. Though the fire was burning and the room was overly warm with all the occupants, Audra was covered to her chest with a crocheted blanket, and she was as pale as a ghost.

Her eyes widened with surprise when she saw him. He waited, and when he saw her expression change from dismay to dawning relief, he went to stand directly behind her and place his hand on her shoulder. When she grasped it tightly with shaking fingers, he was shocked to find that her skin was ice-cold. Absently, he covered her hand with his other one and began massaging her fingers. "I understand you're questioning my wife, Sheriff."

"Well, er . . . yes. It's routine, you understand. I have to question everyone who had any kind of . . . acquaintance with Norton. And you see, Soames, here . . . well, he recalled that he saw a woman leaving the third floor just as the two of you came up. You don't happen to have seen her, did you? The woman, that is."

Nick's heart thumped uncomfortably. "If I had, I would have told you, Sheriff."

"Of course. Of course."

"May I ask why you've brought all these other people into our house?" Nick's voice was dangerously grim. Although he'd been surprised to find Brenda sharing a settee with her father, he didn't show it. Nick nodded at Mr. Wilson, the district attorney, and a younger man he recognized as a deputy. There was Soames, of course. He also saw that Alex had just followed him in, and was now leaning casually against the door frame.

"The sheriff was considerate enough to ask to hold this session here, Nick, as I've caught a chill and wasn't up to going out." Audra sneezed delicately into her handkerchief. "He was just about to ask me how well I knew Silas Norton, weren't you, Sheriff Cox?"

The sheriff cleared his throat. "Yes, ma'am. Miss Farrow, here . . ." He indicated Brenda, who was sitting across from Audra. "She says you were, er, good friends in England."

Nick quickly stepped in. "As Miss Farrow has never been to England, and never knew either my wife or Mr. Norton until only a few months ago, I rather doubt she would be an expert witness to that effect. I believe that would be considered hearsay. Am I right, Mr. Wilson?"

The district attorney straightened. "You are. However, I would advise your wife that it would be in her best interests to answer the sheriff's question."

"It's quite all right, Nick," Audra said. "I have no reason to refuse." She looked Sheriff Cox in the eye. "Miss Farrow is either mistaken or a liar, Sheriff." Audra ignored Brenda's gasp of indignation as she continued. "I did know Mr. Norton in England. However, he was not a personal acquaintance, but rather an associate of my stepfather's. He came to our home on several occasions with my stepfather. I can tell you unequivocally that, despite Miss Farrow's assertions, Mr. Norton was *not* a friend of either mine or my mother's. Frankly, I detested the man."

"Aha! You see!" Brenda said eagerly. "She admits it! I told you . . . I told you I heard her threaten to kill him!"

Nick felt Audra's fingers jerk, and he squeezed her hand reassuringly.

"Mrs. Brannon . . . ?" the sheriff prodded.

"I did say that, yes. However," Audra continued calmly, "I did *not* kill him. I saw him, only twice, here in Central City. The first time was soon after his arrival, and after he'd sent me a note. He was most insistent about calling upon me. I preferred he not do so, and I met him at the Teller House to tell him so. He refused to accept that, and I was forced to meet him once again to reinforce the fact that I did not wish to renew his acquaintance under any circumstances. Unfortunately, it was at this meeting that he tried to force his attentions on me, and yes—I told him if he ever tried such a thing again, I'd kill him." She shrugged. "It was one of those things said in the heat of anger. Fortunately, however, that was the last time I saw Mr. Norton privately."

"You never met him in his room at the Teller House?"

"No, sir. I did not. I only ever met him in the conservatory. I never even knew his room number. I believe Mr. Soames will verify that I never asked for Mr. Norton's room number."

"Mrs. Brannon is telling the truth, Sheriff," Soames confirmed. "She asked me to send someone to tell Norton that she was below. She never went upstairs either time."

"He's lying! Can't you see that? Why does everyone protect her? Why, she's nothing but a little British tramp who . . ."

"Now, Brenda . . ." George Farrow began to protest weakly.

"Sheriff Cox!" Nick's forceful words drew everyone's

attention. "I will not stand for my wife being insulted in her own home. If Miss Farrow can't conduct herself in a more genteel manner, I must ask that she leave. Immediately!"

"And I," said Soames indignantly, "don't appreciate being called a liar. You know me, Sheriff. Have you ever found me to be dishonest?"

"Well, now, can't say as I have," the sheriff agreed. "Tell me, Miss Farrow, just where were you when you heard Mrs. Brannon make this threat?"

"Why, right outside the conservatory. They were inside . . ." Too late, Brenda realized the trap.

"I see," the sheriff drawled.

Brenda opened and closed her mouth several times, but remained silent.

"I apologize, Mrs. Brannon." The sheriff contemplated for a minute. "One more question, please—can you tell me where you were three hours ago?"

"Certainly. As I mentioned, I haven't been feeling well. Letty and Mrs. Gilly can both verify that I haven't left the house today except to step out the back door for a few minutes of fresh air." Audra smiled at the sheriff ruefully. "As they've been cosseting me and pouring tea down my throat the entire day, I've hardly had a minute to myself."

Both women were nodding furiously.

"Soames, what else can you tell us about the woman you saw at the hotel right after Norton was shot?" Mr. Wilson asked.

Soames considered. "Not much, sir. She was wearing a dark coat and a scarf . . . or maybe a hood of some kind. Anyways, it looked to me like she had something over her head, but she ran around the corner and down the back stairs too fast for me to see anything else. She was real quick."

Sheriff Cox scratched his chin. "The servants use those stairs all the time, but none of them saw anyone."

Alex straightened up and came forward. "Did you say the woman was running, Soames?"

"Yes sir."

"Fast?"

"As I said, she moved real quick-like, Mr. Benedict."

"Audra . . . ?"

"No, Alex!"

Nick frowned. What the hell was going on here? Some message had just passed between his wife and his best friend, and he wasn't privy to it. Whatever it was, Audra didn't want the rest to know. All right. He'd find out later. Right now, he intended to protect her at all cost. "Perhaps you should ask Miss Farrow what *her* relationship with Norton was, and why she seems so anxious to implicate my wife. I'd be very interested in knowing the answer to that, myself," he told the sheriff.

"Well now, Mr. Brannon. I was just about to get to that."

Everyone turned to look at Brenda. "Silas was just a friend. Everyone knows that I have a lot of male friends," she protested. "And he told me he knew Au . . . Mrs. Brannon quite well in England. When I heard that you suspected a woman, why, naturally I felt bound to do my civic duty and inform you of the threat she'd made. I had no reason to think Silas had lied about his *relationship* with Mrs. Brannon, particularly when everyone knows that Nick moved out of this house right after Silas arrived."

"I think, Brenda, that you'd do well to keep my wife and our personal affairs out of this matter," Nick said warningly.

"But, Nick, dear—what *is* anyone to think? You attacked Silas at the theater and left right after. It does seem rather a strange coincidence, wouldn't you say?" Brenda asked in exaggerated innocence. "And she . . . your wife admits that she hated Silas." Brenda shrugged carelessly. "Perhaps the fact that he insulted the two of you made her angry enough to put two bullets through his heart."

Letty and Mrs. Gilly both gasped at this blunt accusation, but the reaction of some of the men interested Nick much more. In the doorway, Alex suddenly straightened. The sheriff and Mr. Wilson both stared at Brenda. Suddenly, Nick realized what had just occurred. He bent low over Audra, and whispered into her ear. "Only a little longer, love. I think this little play is about to come to an end."

"Miss Farrow," the district attorney began, "perhaps you'd like to explain just how it is that you know Mr. Norton was killed by two bullets to the heart?"

"Why . . . why . . . everyone knows! Goodness, Mr. Wilson. Everyone at the Teller House was speaking of it."

"You're wrong, Miss Farrow," Sheriff Cox corrected. "Everyone knew he was shot, but the only people who knew just where and how many times are the coroner and all the men present here, with the exception of you, Mr. Farrow," he announced with a nod to Brenda's father. "We intended to keep that quiet for a time. Now, would you like to tell us again how *you* obtained that information?"

Something else just occurred to Nick. "Where's the fur coat you were showing off last week, Brenda?" Nick asked.

Brenda's brow creased. "My fur?"

"Yes. The one Mr. Culbertson gave you. I saw you wearing it at the Teller House. As I recall, it had a hood. Perhaps you'd like to model it for Sheriff Cox?"

"Really, Nick," Brenda replied coyly. "I hardly think this is the time. Half the wealthy women in the Gulch own furs. You know how dreadful the winters can be."

That was certainly true enough.

"Forget the coat," Alex said as he came up behind Brenda and snatched the reticule she'd been holding carefully in her lap, "I'm more interested in knowing when the last time you used this was." He shook the bag, and a small, lethal-looking derringer fell into his other hand.

"So what? Everyone knows I carry a derringer for protection. Why, with all this riffraff working the mines, a woman can't be too careful." She shrugged carelessly.

"I agree," Alex said smoothly. "Were you accosted today, by any chance?"

"Why, no! I haven't had an occasion to use it at all lately, I'm thankful to say." Brenda turned to Sheriff Cox. "I must say, that's all due to you, Sheriff. You're doing an excellent job. If you weren't, I daresay a lady wouldn't be safe in Gilpin County."

"So you've had no occasion to use your derringer lately?" Alex persisted.

"If I had, I would have probably used it on you, Alex!" she replied with an angry glare.

"And you haven't lent it to anyone else?"

"Certainly not! It was another gift from an admirer."

"In that case, perhaps you'd like to explain how it is that it's been fired. Recently," he added, and handed the weapon to the sheriff.

Brenda's eyes widened as Sheriff Cox sniffed at the barrel of the derringer, nodded, then passed it on to Mr. Wilson, who repeated the sheriff's actions before handing it to Brenda's father.

Mr. Farrow sniffed it derisively, but his expression changed immediately to one of alarm, particularly as he saw the nods exchanged by other men who'd handled the weapon. He held the barrel to his nose again. The weapon fell into his lap as he looked bleakly at his daughter.

"Father! What . . . ?"

"Alex is right, Brenda. This gun has been fired recently."

Brenda's eyes revealed sudden panic as she looked from one to another desperately, realizing that she'd been caught in her own trap. "Well, perhaps I . . . It wasn't . . . I didn't . . ." she floundered. Suddenly, she changed tactics and her face took on a woeful expression as she turned to her father. "He tried to assault me, Daddy. I was only protecting myself." Brenda sniffed delicately. "You believe me, don't you?"

George Farrow patted her shoulder awkwardly and glanced at the sheriff. "You see, Sheriff . . . this can all be explained."

Alex snorted derisively. "Perhaps the women in this room would like to believe you, but the men know better. You've been sleeping with Norton ever since he got here, just as you do with all new arrivals," he said bluntly. "That's your habit, isn't it? Enticing the men, particularly the wealthy and important ones. And when you tire of them—or them of you—you go on to the next one. Is that what happened? Norton get tired of you?"

Brenda's demeanor took another startling change as she jumped up furiously. "How dare you? How dare you insult me like that?"

"Believe me, it wasn't hard," Alex drawled. "Sheriff . . . I do believe you've been questioning the wrong woman."

The sheriff nodded. "Yup. I do believe you're right. Miss Farrow . . ."

"It's not true!" Brenda cried. "Silas would never have left me. He wouldn't! He loved me, I tell you! He would have come back to me. . . ." Brenda halted as she saw that none of their faces showed even the slightest hint of belief. Her father's was red with humiliation. But the worst—the worst was Nick's wife. Hers displayed only pity. Brenda let out a scream of rage and flew toward Audra. "It's all your fault, damn you! First you took Nick from me and . . ."

Alex and Nick got to Brenda first.

She struggled briefly, but subsided as they released her to Sheriff Cox. Lifting her chin defiantly, she glared at them. "You'll never be able to prove a thing, you stupid bastards! My father will never allow you to take me to court, and even if you do, I'll plead self-defense. I'll say that Silas tried to rape me. No jury would dare convict me."

"That remains to be seen," Sheriff Cox said as he handed Brenda over to his deputy. He turned to her father. "I'm sorry, George. But I think we'll have to adjourn to the courthouse and let these folks get back to their lives. Nick. Mrs. Brannon . . . hope you feel better soon, ma'am. Sorry to put you through all this."

Audra gave him her hand. "I understand, Sheriff Cox. Forgive me for not seeing you out, but I'm suddenly very fatigued. Nick?"

Brenda protested all the way. Her father followed dejectedly.

When Nick got back to the parlor, Alex was sitting beside Audra, holding her hand. Nick wasn't able to hear their conversation, but he was aware that it suddenly broke off when Audra saw him. He felt an unexpected pang of jealousy.

"Nick, what will happen to Brenda? I feel terrible about this. If Norton hadn't followed me here, she would never have been forced into this situation. Isn't there something we can do?"

"You want to help her? After all she's done and tried to do to you?" Alex asked incredulously.

"Oh, Alex. We don't really know what happened. But I do know that Silas Norton was a disgusting man. Perhaps he didn't deserve to be shot, but it could be that Miss Farrow was pushed to her limits. Or perhaps it was an accident. It's a frightful thing . . . to think that you're responsible for the taking of a life."

Nick and Alex exchanged a glance. They both knew that, only too well, but how could Audra possibly have any idea?

"I expect that Brenda will be invited to leave the territory," Nick said. "She's right, you know. Without a witness, no one will be able to either prove or disprove that she shot Norton in self-defense."

"I agree. And by attempting to blame his death on Audra, Brenda has just effectively ended her own social standing in this community," Alex said dryly, and patted Audra's hand comfortingly.

Nick's face tightened at this gesture. "If you don't mind, Alex, I'd like to speak to my wife . . . alone," he said tersely.

Alex raised a brow at Nick's tone, but stood to leave. Bending over Audra, he gave her hand a reassuring squeeze. "Guess I'll tag along to the courthouse. I think George could use some support right now. Take care of yourself, kitten," he said softly.

"I will, Alex. Thank you so much for . . ."

"Think nothing of it. You know where to send word if you need me," he reminded her, and, giving Nick a warning glance, he left.

Immediately after Alex was gone, Audra became restless and uneasy. Nick watched silently as she smoothed her hair back, adjusted the blanket on her lap, and fiddled nervously with her hands. She was still pale, and for the first time, he noticed the hollows in her cheeks. It appeared she'd lost some weight. Nick frowned at that. "Have you had Dr. Byers in?" he asked abruptly.

Audra seemed startled. "What? Oh, for my chill? Yes,

he's been here. Several times, in fact. I'm perfectly healthy. Don't bother to concern yourself," she said stiffly.

Her frigid tones told him all too clearly that she'd still not forgiven him. Still, he needed to know.

"I'm going to ask you this only once, Audra. And I'll never ask you again. Were you and Norton ever lovers?"

She made a move as if to throw the blanket aside, then apparently thought better of it as she sank back into the chair and pulled it higher, instead. Her eyes flashed angrily, but her tone was calm. "I'm not going to answer that, Nick. I've taken enough of your accusations and your insults. Besides, as you pointed out not so long ago, you don't know whether to believe me or not. Why should I even try to convince you?"

"Damn it! Just a simple yes or no will do!"

"Sorry. You're not going to get either from me."

Two long strides brought him to stand before her. He bent over her, clasping her chin in his hand and forcing her to look directly at him. Audra thought she saw a flash of pain in his eyes, but it was gone instantly. Instead, his golden gaze burned into her as Nick released her chin, and used his thumb to wipe away a tear. "Perhaps you don't have to," he said softly. "Perhaps I already have my answer." Audra felt something fall into her lap just before he straightened and turned to stride out of the room without a backward glance. She heard Letty's murmured response as he said something to her, then the sound of the front door closing behind him.

She looked down into her lap.

Her emerald pendant blinked up at her.

Chapter 22

$\mathcal{N}$ick stomped out of the house, his teeth still clenched, unaware of his surroundings, not looking where he was going.

Damn! She was the most frustrating woman he'd ever known! All he'd wanted was an unequivocal no. Just one word. Why the hell did she have to be so bloody damned stubborn?

Oh, hell! Who was he to talk? Hadn't he decided, only a few hours ago, that he'd throw his own pride aside to get her back? He should have stayed. It didn't matter that she wouldn't answer his question. She was his wife, he couldn't stop loving her, and not being with her was tearing him apart. So, maybe he should just turn back and . . .

"Ohh!"

He'd bumped against another woman coming from the opposite direction. Heavily bundled against the cold, she was awkwardly trying to retrieve the parcel he'd knocked out of her arms.

"I beg your pardon!" Nick got the package and handed it back to her. "I'm very sorry. . . ." His eyes widened in astonishment, for the eyes peering back at him over the heavy scarf were familiar. In another second, recognition froze him into shock. The last person he'd ever expected to see in Central City was . . .

"Bertie? Roberta Hauson?"

Bertie pulled the scarf aside. "Hello, Nick," she acknowledged.

"I'll be damned. What are you doing here? When? Why?"

Bertie hesitated for only an instant. "Audra asked me to come. I've been here two weeks now."

"But why didn't you wait until spring? Winter's not the best time to be here. We're very much closed in during the winter."

"I don't mind that. Besides, I was told that crossing the Atlantic in early spring was much worse." She shuddered. "Though how it could possibly have been worse . . . it makes my stomach roll just to think of it." Bertie's gaze held his. "You *do* recall my saying that I can't abide water, don't you, Nickolas?" she asked carefully.

Nick's eyes narrowed. Was Bertie trying to tell him something? "I thought that you were going to be nurse to my new nephew."

"I stayed long enough to help find a younger nurse. As Cleo and Richard are hoping to give you more nephews, perhaps even a niece or two, we agreed she needed someone younger." Bertie laughed. "I'm getting too old to run after an entire brood. I prefer to look after infants."

Nick frowned in puzzlement. He'd gotten Cleo's news of the birth of her son only a month ago himself. But the baby was now only three months old. Hardly a toddler.

"I see." They continued to stand awkwardly. "You know about what's just happened with Silas Norton?"

"Yes. I was in the kitchen for a time while you were all there. Audra didn't want you to see me. I'm sorry, Nick, but it's rather cold out here, and she's waiting for me."

Nick frowned again. That didn't make sense. Why didn't Audra want him to know Bertie was here? "Yes, of course. Well, let me know if Au . . . if you need anything over the winter, will you?"

"Yes. I will, Nick. Good-bye."

Nick watched as Bertie briskly walked away and turned into the walk to Audra's house. Just before she opened the door, she swung about to look back at him. Then she entered the house.

He continued on his way slowly, lost in thought. Bertie's actions had been strange. Something was going on here, but damned if he knew what.

Why hadn't Alex mentioned Bertie's arrival? Not that they'd spoken of anything but business matters recently, but Nick knew full well that Alex was still a frequent visitor at the house. Come to think of it, Alex had been acting strange lately, too. And what secret message had passed between him and Audra earlier?

Nick's feet crunched loudly in the quiet air as he walked slowly, still pondering. Not for one minute did he believe that Bertie was too old to be a nurse. She had more energy than a woman twice her age. And when he'd asked her to come to America with them, she'd refused, saying that she couldn't abide water—that boating made her deathly ill, and that only dire circumstances would force her to board a ship. But then, she'd added, *"Perhaps when you and Audra have children, I'll come and be their nurse. . . ."*

Nick's footsteps stopped. Oh, Christ! Was it possible? Audra had been covered by a knitted blanket, claiming she'd taken a chill. She'd been bundled up damn near to her chin. . . .

* * *

Bertie's greeting only confirmed his suspicions that she'd been expecting him. "I have to give you credit, Nick," she said after letting him in. "You returned sooner than I expected, but you're still a couple of months too late."

There had been no decision to make. He remembered only too well what Audra had admitted to him just before their marriage—that she was frightened to death of having children. She needed him. It was as simple as that. "Where is she?" he asked.

"Upstairs." Bertie touched his arm. "She's stronger than she thinks she is, physically, but old fears are hard to defeat."

He nodded. "I know. That's why I had to come back."

He took the stairs two at a time and opened the door quietly.

She was gazing out the window, her long curtain of hair draped over one shoulder as she slowly stroked her brush through it. A stab of pain went through Nick. He'd once done that for her.

Her bare toes peeped out from beneath a white, full-length nightgown. She looked as he'd remembered her, before he'd taken the gown off her. . . .

He knew when she became aware of his presence. He saw her quick intake of breath, and the hand holding the brush stilled and fell to her side. She turned slightly, and looked over her shoulder at him.

One lamp gave off enough light to reveal her profile. Her gown draped over fuller breasts, then fell softly over a definitely rounded stomach. Self-consciously, she folded her hands over herself and stared at him.

Nick didn't move from the doorway. "Why didn't you tell me?" he asked quietly.

"And have you demand to know who fathered my baby? No, thank you." Her chin lifted proudly.

Nick's face remained impassive, but he winced inwardly, for the question had crossed his mind. How could this baby be his? The only time he'd failed to take precautions had been that cursed wedding night. He'd been damned careful since, making sure his seed didn't spill into her, and he knew for a fact that she'd had her monthly courses at the ranch. There had been several days during their stay there when she had been too embarrassed to let him touch her.

They'd had only three weeks together after that. For the life of him, he couldn't recall if there had been any curtailment of their lovemaking during that time. It seemed to him that they had always been making love.

So if the baby was his—and he admitted that there *was* a slim possibility that his precautions hadn't worked—she had to have gotten pregnant right after the ranch. But that was only two months ago. Cleo had been three months pregnant and hadn't looked it. Then why was Audra already showing physical signs?

He couldn't get it out of his mind that Norton had to have been in Central City before they'd ever gone to the ranch. Had Audra first met Norton then?

He couldn't ask. Seeing her like this, so terribly vulnerable, he couldn't bring himself to attack her verbally. Instead, he pulled the cord to summon a servant. Audra's eyes widened, but she remained silent. As did he.

"Yes, Miss Au . . . Mr. *Nick*!" Letty corrected when she saw him standing near the bell cord.

"Send Joey to the Teller House with the buggy. Go with him. Have Mr. Soames let you into my room. I want you to pack my things and bring them back here."

"Yes, *sir*, Mr. Nick!" Letty spun about. They could hear her running down the stairs.

"You can't move back now! There's no room," Audra objected.

"Really? What's happened to the other bedrooms?"

"Bertie has one, and the other . . ." Her voice fell off. "I had the other converted into a nursery," she admitted.

So that was what the extra allowance was for! "Well then," Nick said casually, as he loosened his tie, "I'll just have to share your room, won't I?"

Her mouth dropped. "But you can't!"

"Can't I? Think again, my sweet wife. You *are* still my wife? You haven't divorced me and forgotten to tell me, have you?"

"Of course not!" Audra stamped her foot in frustration. "Then may I ask how long you intend to stay?" Her voice was frigid.

"Until you've had the child, Audra. I realize there's a possibility it could be mine. I intend to face my responsibilities in this incident."

Audra gaped at him. "*Possibility? Incident?* Why, you . . ." She threw her hairbrush at him. He ducked, and when he straightened she was at the bed reaching for a pillow to fling at him. He dodged it, but not the next one. Nor the next. He batted his way through a cannonade of pillows until he was able to grasp her shoulders. She jerked away and fell backward onto the bed, kicking at him. Sidestepping to avoid her feet, Nick pulled her to a sitting position. He grasped her wrists tightly, holding them before her.

"Enough! I'm sorry. I didn't mean for it to sound like that." She was panting heavily, enough to alarm him. "For God's sake, stop fighting me, Audra. Please. We need to come to an understanding."

"Understand *this*, I don't want you here! You have no right to push your way back into my life. This is *my* baby. I don't need you and I don't want you, so . . . so get out!" Oh, God! If only he hadn't had that guilty look on his face when she'd accused him of questioning the baby's paternity. It had hurt, more than anything else he'd ever said or done.

Nick shook his head slowly. "I know you don't want me, Audra. Nevertheless, I'm staying. I want to take care of you—to see you through this, if you'll only let me." He released her wrists.

Stormy eyes met his. Her face contorted.

Oh, hell! She was going to cry. "Audra . . . sweet . . ."

"Oh! This is too rich! I can't believe this! You accuse me of being unfaithful, and you *think* there's a *possibility* that the child may be yours, and you want . . ." To his utter amazement, she began laughing. Her shoulders shook. Tears rolled from her eyes as laugh after laugh pealed out. Astonishment turned to alarm as he saw that she was becoming hysterical. He grasped her shoulders again. "Audra . . . stop this!"

But she continued alternately to laugh and cry until he pulled her tightly to him. "Stop it, I say! You'll harm yourself, or the baby." That seemed to penetrate, for she stilled abruptly. She pulled free, sliding away from him to curl up against a bedpost. Holding the last pillow protectively over her stomach, she stared up at him, her eyes darkened with emotion. He waited.

"You'd stay with me, even if the baby wasn't yours?" she finally asked.

"Yes."

"Why?" she whispered.

Nick replied carefully. "Because you need me. Oh, I know you have Bertie now. But she can't be your strength. Bertie can't give you courage or keep you safe through the long nights and help you through the nightmares. But I can . . . if you only let me."

Audra turned her face away and laid her cheek against the pillow. How had he known about the nightmares?

How was it possible that he always knew what she was feeling? And why, oh why, couldn't he just love her? Or trust her?

She was so tired—she was *always* tired these days—and her back hurt again, and she was lonely, and she was afraid of being afraid. And now he was upsetting her again.

But oh, what blessed relief! In spite of everything, she knew she could lean on him, that he *would* be her strength. It wouldn't have to be for long. Just until the next frightening months . . .

"Audra, look at me."

His voice was quietly demanding. She lifted tear-filled eyes to meet his gaze.

"I'll stay as long as you need me. And then—then, once your baby is born, and you've recovered, I'll step out of your life. You can go back to England, if you want. I promise I won't ever bother you again."

"You'll let me go? With our . . . my baby?"

"You have my word."

She searched his face carefully, but saw no condemnation, no anger. In fact, she could almost convince herself that she saw her own pain reflected there. She desperately wanted to throw herself into his arms, and have him hold her as he used to. But she held herself carefully, tightly, away from him.

Let him stay. It was his child, after all, and he owed it to her. But she was never, ever going to ask him for anything. She would die, first. And once the baby was born, she *would* leave, and never have to see him again. He'd promised.

It would kill her to leave. But better to do it that way than to die slowly, by degrees.

"All right," she said wearily. "You can stay."

* * *

Nick swiftly made his arrangements. He held a conference with Alex, and, to the delighted gratitude of their staff, they decided to close the office until mid-January and give their employees a two-month paid holiday. Alex was going east to spend Thanksgiving and Christmas with his sister and aunt, and once he returned, he would reopen the office and take over the work.

Nick and Audra spent their own holidays quietly, and by the time they welcomed in the new year, Nick knew that he'd always be grateful for these months. No matter what happened, he wouldn't be racked with the guilt of abandoning Audra when she needed him.

For it was obvious that even Bertie's presence hadn't allayed her fears. Though the child in her womb grew, she was too thin. She was pale, she was nervous, and she was subdued. Yet she never voiced her fears.

Privately, Bertie admitted that she, too, was worried. "Dr. Byers says that she's healthy, physically, but I'm afraid that she's working herself into near hysteria. No matter how I try to reassure her, she just looks at me with those great eyes and says nothing. It breaks my heart, it does, Nick. We have to do something."

Nick met with Dr. Byers himself, and received assurances that his wife was indeed healthy, and would remain so if she exercised carefully, and ate well. Nick cabled Alex and had him send fresh fruits and produce from the East to tempt Audra's appetite. He encouraged her to eat until she complained that she knew what a stuffed goose felt like. He still wasn't satisfied. It seemed to him that she carried most of her weight in her womb.

He pampered her, he rubbed her back and her feet, and made sure she rested. They played chess. He taught her how to play poker. He read to her and amused her with stories of his sailing days. Other times, they simply had quiet conversations, but by silent accord they never discussed the past. Nor the baby.

He insisted that Bertie prepare only the softest cloths and sheets and towels. And by the time the buds on the trees had turned to new leaves, Nick had developed a close friendship with Dr. Byers, whom he considered bright and a progressive thinker. And he questioned the young doctor after each visit and examination, until he'd learned as much of birthing babies as the doctor cared to tell him. Bob Byers was amused by Nick's persistence, and he answered each of Nick's questions good-naturedly.

And that was how Nick finally learned that the baby was his.

They'd been discussing Audra's progress. Nick expressed his concern about the large size of the baby, and was seeking reassurance. "How much more will this baby grow in the next three months?" he asked anxiously.

Dr. Byers looked at him strangely. "Not three. Less than two," he said.

Nick looked at him as if he'd lost his mind. "Are you sure?"

"Of course I'm sure, Nick. I'm the doctor. Remember?"

"You must be mistaken, Bob. I mean . . . in late fall you told me she wasn't pregnant. And I've been damned careful."

Bob Byers's expression was one of chagrin. "Contrary to what I just said, doctors do sometimes make mistakes. I should have done a more complete examination then, but your wife assured me that . . . well . . ." Bob grinned at him. "I'm afraid your precautions were all for naught. After carefully considering all your wife told me, she and I have determined that she became pregnant on your wedding night."

"Damn it, Bob! It's not possible. She's had monthly courses since. I know that for a fact."

The doctor sighed. "She had what she *thought* were her monthly courses. It sometimes happens. Believe me, Nick. I questioned her very carefully. My examinations, and all the physical signs, indicate that this baby is coming in about six weeks. Your wife has a slender build, and the baby may actually be small. But take my word for it—it will be here then, and it will be full term."

And Nick believed him. He finally realized that the night he so regretted—their wedding night—was the night he himself had so carelessly impregnated Audra.

He said nothing to her, but he doubled his efforts to cosset her. In fact, over the next weeks he succeeded in distracting Audra so well that she sometimes felt like screaming with frustration and ordering him to leave. She probably would have, except for one thing that he did. . . .

He was beside her each night to hold her when the dreams came.

Blessedly, they weren't the nightmares of old. Instead, her dreams were confusing and distorted, filled with vague images and an endless search for something, or someone, she could never identify. They weren't as frightening as the old ones, but she always awakened with a sense of desolation and longing that dissipated only once she felt Nick's arms wrapped around her.

So when she was awakened one night, not by a dream but by a vague feeling of something being not quite right, Nick was immediately alert.

"Bad dream?" he asked as he pulled her to him.

Audra shifted to fit more comfortably against his chest. "No, I'm just . . . Oh, Lord!"

"What is it?"

"I'm not sure. Light the lamp, please, Nick."

The breathless quality of her voice put him into quick

motion. When the lamp was lit, he turned back to see Audra peering under the covers. She looked back up at him with wide eyes, her cheeks pale. "Something's happened. The bed's soaked. I think that means . . ."

Not for nothing had Nick consistently questioned the doctor. He sprang out of bed and was immediately at her side, leaning over her. "I know what it means. How are you feeling?" he asked urgently.

Audra wrinkled her nose. "Fine. I mean, I don't feel any different . . . just slightly wet and uncomfortable."

He lifted her out of the bed and set her down in a chair. Pulling the quilt off the bed, he tucked it around her. "Stay there. I'll go wake Letty and Bertie." He headed for the door.

"Nick . . ."

He was back at her side immediately. "Yes, sweet?"

"Don't you think you should put something on, first?"

Nick, who hadn't slept in anything other than his skin for years, looked down at himself, and realized that he was stark naked. He grabbed his robe off the foot of the bed and donned it as he exited.

Audra smiled to herself. It was astonishing, but she felt strangely calm, as if she were only an observer and not an actual participant. The primary participant, at that!

Nick rummaged for clothes and went into the next room to dress while Letty changed the bedding and Bertie helped Audra into a fresh nightgown. He was back in only a few minutes, his hair still sticking up every which way, to carry her back to bed. "Are you sure we shouldn't fetch Dr. Byers?" he asked Bertie as she fluffed up the pillows behind Audra.

"It's far too early. Audra only has a slight backache. Let's give it a little more time."

Nick was on the bed in a second, massaging Audra's

lower back firmly but gently. "What else can we do?" he asked tersely.

Bertie's reply was short. "Wait."

"I can't! I can't do it anymore, Nick!"

"Yes, you can, love. I'm here to help you." But lacking the calmness of his tone, Nick's eyes were pleading as he turned to the doctor. "It won't be much longer now, will it, Bob?"

Dr. Byers glanced up. "It's progressing very nicely, Nick."

Nick thought that was probably the understatement of the year. Audra had been in labor for thirteen hours, and she was exhausted. He'd managed to keep her calm for most of that time, but she'd lost her composure some two hours ago, and was now at the end of her endurance.

His worry only increased as the next contraction came, only short minutes after the last.

"Oh, God! Oh, God! I'm going to die, aren't I?"

"No, you're not going to die, damn it! Don't even think it. You're going to have a healthy baby and you're going to be fine. Tell her, Doctor."

"Your husband is right, Mrs. Brannon. Listen to him."

But Audra was past the point of listening. Nick tried to coax her through the contraction, but she had a tight hold on his shirt, and she was tugging at him. "Nick—you have to promise me something," she pleaded, her face still contorted with pain.

"Anything, my love."

"Promise me . . ." she panted. "If I die, promise that you'll never tell my baby that his mother was a murderess."

Bertie and the doctor's heads jerked at that. Nick knew that the shock written on their faces was also reflected on his. Audra was obviously confused by the pain. "Audra . . . sweet . . . you didn't kill Norton. Brenda did."

"No! Not . . . not Norton. *William!* You won't ever let my child find out, will you?"

She was still breathing hard, though the contraction had receded. Instead of lying back against her pillows, she clutched Nick's hands more tightly and leaned toward him. "You have to promise me, Nick!"

"Anything, my love. Anything you want. Tell me, sweet," he urged, freeing one hand to wipe her sweat-drenched face with a damp cloth. "Tell me about it."

"But you know! Norton told you!"

"I want *you* to tell me."

She closed her eyes tightly. "That night . . . the night my mother gave birth to a stillborn son. William got roaring drunk. He locked himself in the library. Late that night, I went downstairs . . . Oh, God, Nick. Hold me! It's starting again!"

This time, when the pain lifted her up off the pillows, Nick climbed into the bed behind her to support her against his chest. It seemed to help, for she wasn't straining as hard. He coaxed her gently, encouraging her while she panted through the pain.

When it was over, she rested her head weakly against him. "Finish telling me about William," Nick urged quietly as he smoothed her tangled hair from her face with one hand while he held her fingers tightly with the other. He was completely oblivious to the others in the room; all his concentration was on his wife.

"I . . . I went downstairs. I was so furious . . . he'd put Mother through so much pain. Oh, God . . . now I know what it was like!" Audra took several deep breaths. "I told him I wouldn't allow him to touch her again. He laughed, and then he told me about Lord Cowan . . .

about how he'd sold me. He raved about how worthless Mother was, and then he began to say that *I* could give him a son. Lord Cowan was old and foolish, he said. He wouldn't know whether the child was his, but he wouldn't want a bastard anyway, and William said it would be easy for him—for William—to adopt the child. *His* child. Oh, God," she panted. "Hold me, Nick. Here comes another one."

Goddamn William Brannon to hell! Nick wasn't aware that tears were streaming from his own eyes as he held her, willing all his strength to go to her, holding her, urging her until the pain was over and Audra slumped in his arms. "What happened, love?" he asked softly.

"William . . . grabbed me. He . . . he kissed me, and he ripped my robe, and he tried to . . . Oh, God, Nick. It was horrible. And all the time, he was saying disgusting things, and I was so frightened. I finally got away from him, but he came after me, and I grabbed the poker, and I . . . I hit him with it! Oh, Nick!"

"You couldn't have hit him that hard."

"I didn't think I had, for he came after me again. But he lost his balance, and he fell and hit his head—the same place where I'd struck him—and . . ." Audra buried her face against Nick's chest. "I ran to McKee," she whispered hoarsely. "He said it wasn't my fault. But I'll never know, will I? Then Silas Norton—he was there . . . outside, watching. We didn't know that then. Later . . . after you came . . ." Audra told him about Norton, how he'd threatened to turn her in, how he'd told her she would be hanged. And how he'd threatened McKee.

Jesus! Was this what she'd been guilty of? This—and not . . . ?

"You did nothing. McKee was right—it was an accident and you're not responsible. Audra, is that why you gave Norton your emerald? Because he threatened to tell everyone about William?"

"Yes! I thought he'd told you on our wedding day. I thought you already knew. But when he followed me— us—here, I was afraid that it would ruin your business if it was known around Central City. I gave him the diamonds and my emerald, and I told him it was all that I owned . . . that I wouldn't give him anything of yours. He promised to leave. Only he didn't, and you were so angry when you found out."

"Audra, sweet . . . he never told me about William. What he *did* tell me was that you and he were lovers, and though I found out it wasn't true, there was that time I saw him embracing you. . . ."

Audra's shriek this time wasn't one of pain, but of outrage. She tried to twist away from him, but her position made it impossible, so she swung her fist over her head as hard as she could, striking Nick over his right eye.

"Ouch! Stop it, sweetheart!" Nick caught her wrist just as it came flying back toward him. "You'll only injure yourself."

"You . . . you thought I *welcomed* it? Oh! Oh, God! It's coming again!" Her breathing was starting to come in shallow little gasps again. Nick could actually see her abdomen begin to contract.

"Mrs. Brannon, I want you to gather your strength and push this time. Hard." Dr. Byers's calm voice came from the foot of the bed.

Audra ignored him as she railed at Nick. "How could you, damn you! Oh!" She paused for another deep breath, then continued without interruption. "Oh, to think that . . . I could kill you for that, Nick! Oh!" All the fury she had intended to direct at him was instead focused on the unrelenting demands of her body. There was only the pain and the absolute necessity to rid her body of its cause. "Ohh!"

"That's it," Dr. Byers coaxed. "Take a deep breath now, and push."

Audra's nails dug into Nick's hands. She screamed.

"Congratulations, Mr. and Mrs. Brannon. You have a beautiful, healthy daughter."

Nick tiptoed into the bedroom. Audra was still asleep, as was the baby in the cradle next to the bed. He bent over it, gazing down at his daughter.

His daughter! How could he ever have doubted it?

She had a thick mop of sandy hair, and her eyes were already a bright blue. She was going to have her mother's eyes, as she already had her pert nose and his chin. Nick softly brushed the tip of his finger across the fuzz on the baby's cheek. He was filled with so much love for this little creature, he was almost bursting with it.

He turned back to the bed and found Audra watching him.

"How are you feeling?" he asked softly as he moved to kneel beside the bed.

Audra yawned widely. "Still tired. Sore." She shifted into a more comfortable position and her eyes went to the cradle. "Oh, Nick. Isn't she beautiful?"

"Yes, and so are you." Nick tenderly brushed a strand of hair back behind her ear before taking her hands in his and studying her fingers. "When we were married, I promised to love and cherish you forever. I've done a lousy job of it. I can't tell you how I regret that. Or that I doubted you, even for an instant." Nick brought her hands to his face. "But I'm particularly sorry for putting you through this after I'd promised to take care of you."

"Then you do believe she's yours?"

"Of course. I think I knew all along. I was just too damned stubborn and proud to admit it. I'm sorry. I went a little crazy. It just hurt so damn much, thinking that another man had touched you. I wanted to hurt you back. I'm sorry," he repeated helplessly. "I failed you, my love. Can you ever forgive me?" His eyes pleaded.

"I can forgive a lot of things. I can forgive the fact that you deliberately humiliated me, even the fact that you thought I'd let another man make love to me. . . ." Audra broke off. Waving her hand at the cradle, she added, "I can even forgive you for thinking I would foist another man's child off as yours." Audra pulled her other hand free. "But what I find so hurtful, Nick, is this: that you taught me to trust you, after I'd sworn never to trust another man. But somehow, in the teaching, you lost your trust in me." Audra closed her eyes. "I need some time," she said wearily. "Please leave me now. I'm tired."

He stood and looked down at her, but she'd turned her face away. If she hated him now, it was no more than he deserved.

Had ever a man been as stupid as he? Over the last weeks during the quiet times he'd spent with Audra, his mind had been freed of the jealousy and hurt that he now knew had blinded him. Watching Audra, worrying over her, he knew that she would never have had a careless affair. Her apprehensions regarding pregnancy had been vivid enough to keep her from it.

All this time, all she'd been guilty of was believing that she was a murderess, and that he hated her for it.

His sweet Audra—a murderess! It was preposterous!

It didn't excuse him—that he'd loved her so much, he'd let his pain at her supposed betrayal overwhelm him. It didn't make him any less guilty. Guilty of destroying her trust in him. Guilty of destroying that innocent wonder in her eyes. She would never look at him again in that way.

And even if, by some wondrous miracle, she forgave him, he didn't know if he could ever forgive himself.

Audra stayed in bed for the rest of that week and most of the next, simply because no one would let her get up. Nick would come in several times a day to check on her and the baby, Marena—a combination of her mother's name and his mother's, Maryanna. He ate dinner with her each night and sat silently as she nursed their child before their bedtime.

So when she hadn't seen him all of one day, she slipped into her robe and slowly made her way downstairs. Bertie met her at the bottom of the stairs. "You shouldn't be on your feet. Besides, he's gone," she announced. "He left letters for you on his desk in the small parlor."

There were two envelopes on the desk, both with her name scrawled on them in Nick's bold handwriting.

My sweet Audra:

If you decide to return to England, I have no right to stand in your way since I promised to set you free after the baby was born. I've not been good at keeping my promises to you until now, so I'm determined to keep this one. But I cannot bear to watch as you leave. I only ask that you let me support you and Marena, and that you let me see my daughter whenever I come over.

I thought I was giving you a new life. I'd hoped you'd be happy with me, but I've only given you misery and pain. I don't want to hurt you anymore.

I shall be in the mountains for the next several weeks, checking our business claims. If you need anything, ask Alex.

I'll always love you. Always remember that.

> *Good-bye, my love.*
> *Nick*

Audra was stunned. He'd done it again—made a decision for her, assuming that she'd be happier without him. How could one man be so blind? Didn't he know that without him, she was incomplete?

She opened the second, larger envelope and gasped. It was the title to Sheffield! Made out to her, and dated— Oh, God! The day of their wedding. He had given Sheffield back to her; she could have stayed in England if she'd wanted. But he hadn't given her the deed until now. Why?

The answer was clear. . . . Because he was afraid she wouldn't leave England with him. He was afraid she would turn him down if she had Sheffield back, and he'd never see her again. He cared for her. He came to her aid, even when he thought she'd taken a lover . . . even when he thought she was carrying another man's child. He loved her. Despite everything, he'd loved her longer and stronger than she'd ever loved him.

Audra clutched the deed to her heart and let the tears flow freely. "You fool, Nick," she whispered. And then she laughed joyously. "Oh, you wonderful, adorable *fool*!"

Chapter 23

$\mathcal{N}$ick was weary to the bone, and badly in need of a bath and a shave, but it could wait for another hour. He wanted to catch Alex and let him know he was back. Once Alex left the office for the day, it was hard knowing where he'd be off to.

Nick greeted the staff, then poked his head into Alex's office. "Thought I'd let you know I'm back."

Alex looked up from straightening the papers on his desk. "Nick! Damn, it's good to have you back! I was beginning to think you'd gotten lost in the high country."

"No such luck," Nick said ruefully, rubbing the stubble on his face. "Just that some of the passes are still damned deep. I'm ready for a bath and a bottle of good brandy." Nick hesitated. "Ah, you don't happen to know if . . ."

"The house is empty."

"Oh." Nick's heart dropped to his feet. All his time in the mountains, he'd tortured himself with memories of Audra as he'd fought his desperate longing to turn around and come home to her and Marena. But he'd known he had no right to expect her to stay. "Well . . . I'll just go check in at the Teller House," he told Alex. Wearily, he turned to leave.

"You might want to check your desk first. There's some important correspondence on it. I think there may even be a letter from England." Alex grinned when Nick instantly disappeared from his doorway.

There was indeed a letter, but hope fell again when Nick recognized the handwriting as Cleo's and not Audra's. Carelessly, he dropped it back onto the desk, then abruptly bent over to peer at it again. It was addressed to Mr. and Mrs. Nickolas Brannon. Now why would Cleo address it to both of them if Audra was at Sheffield Manor? He'd been in the mountains for two months— more than enough time for Audra to get back to England.

He sat down and ripped open the envelope.

My dearest brother and Audra,

Richard and I are so pleased to learn of the birth of your daughter, and send all our blessings. Our own little Tony is doing well. . . .

Nick impatiently skimmed over the next page, which seemed to be a litany of his nephew's wondrous achievements. Then, the last paragraph caught his undivided attention:

I saved this for last, for I am so overwhelmed at your unexpected gift, words almost fail me. We received the deed to Sheffield in yesterday's packet. Audra, my dear sister, we cannot begin to tell you what your generosity means to us. That you could gift us your beloved home is absolutely the most wondrous, unselfish act! You must know, of course, that Nick has offered to

*purchase half of England for us in the past. Richard's pride would
not allow that, and I supported his decision. But he recognizes
that Sheffield is a gift from the heart, and therefore accepts most
humbly. I think you must know what it will mean to us to have a
home of our own and security for our future and our children's
future. Mere words are inadequate to express our astonished gratitude and our love to both of you.*

Nick sank into the chair, barely comprehending that
the balance of Cleo's letter went on to assure Audra that
the house and property would be well loved and tended,
and to express invitations to visit at any time. None of it
was as important to Nick as the paragraph telling him
what Audra had done.

He was speechless with shock. What could it mean
that Audra had deeded over her beloved Sheffield? And if
she wasn't there herself, then where in hell was she?

Resting his elbows on the desk, he pushed his fingers
into his hair and closed his eyes in defeat. She'd gone
away—she'd taken their baby and gone to a place where
he couldn't find her.

"Here, old boy. I think you're ready for this." Nick
looked up to see Alex perched on the corner of his desk,
holding two full tumblers. He automatically accepted the
one Alex held out to him. "To homecomings," Alex offered.

Nick knew damn well that Alex had come into his
office for more than a drink and a toast. But he said nothing until he'd lifted his glass in salute then emptied it. He
set the glass down and looked up at Alex. "You know
what's in Cleo's letter?" he asked, indicating the envelope
with the English postmark. Alex nodded. "You helped
Audra do this, didn't you?"

"She asked me to."

"Where is she?"

"She didn't tell me where she was going."

"Alex . . . Goddamn it!"

"Now, hold on. I said she didn't tell *me*, but she told you."

"This is no time to play games, man!"

Alex held his hand up to cut Nick off. "She said to tell you she'd be waiting at the place where she'd spent the happiest days of her life. I have no idea where that is, but I think you . . . do."

Nick was already on his feet and out the door. Alex followed, and was just in time to see his friend running down the street toward the stables.

"Is everything all right, Mr. Benedict?" Samuel had come to stand beside him.

"Hell no, Sam," Alex replied in a thoroughly disgusted tone. "I'm stuck in the office again."

And with that, Alex shoved his hands in his pockets and sauntered away, whistling gaily, leaving the baffled accountant to stare at his back.

Nick didn't feel his weariness on the ride to the ranch. All he felt was anticipation, and renewed hope. Audra had told Alex that she'd be waiting. For *him*.

He made the ride in record time. The ranch seemed normal, the men busy as usual, though they stopped their work long enough to greet him. Bertie was just going upstairs and turned in surprise when he burst into the house. Her face creased into a welcoming smile when she saw him.

"Where's my wife and baby, Bertie?" he asked without preamble.

"The baby's upstairs, sleeping. Audra just went out riding. She's usually gone for only an hour or two. I don't know which one you want to see first, but either way, I'd suggest a bath and a shave." Her eyes were twinkling at him.

Nick rubbed his scratchy chin. "You're right," he said ruefully. "How long will it take for you to . . . ?"

"We always have hot water. You go on up and shave, and we'll get your bath ready."

But he couldn't help but peek into the room next to the master bedroom, where he knew he'd find his daughter. She was lying on her back, cooing at a brightly painted wooden butterfly someone had hung over her cradle. When he bent over her, Marena's eyes focused on him immediately, and her little fists waved erratically. Nick was astonished to see how much she'd grown. Her hair was now a thick, soft golden brown, the same as his. He slipped a finger into one fist and was gratified when Marena curled her fingers around it and held on tightly.

"You're as beautiful as your mother," he whispered softly.

Marena smiled at the sound of his voice and gurgled.

"And she's got both her parents' disposition." Bertie's voice came from the doorway. "Stubborn as they are."

Nick reluctantly tugged his finger from the baby's hand and turned to face Bertie. "Let's just hope she turns out to be smarter than her father is."

Bertie grinned at him approvingly. "I'd say, if there's hope for the father, then there's hope for the child. Come along, Nick. Your bath's ready, and your wife has waited for you long enough."

In a meadow filled with columbines, Audra lay on her back and closed her eyes. If she tried very hard, she could almost imagine that Nick was beside her, that they were lying together as they'd done so many times before in this same place.

This was her favorite site on the ranch. She'd been so happy here, where he'd taught her what loving really was. Taught her what it was to be a woman loved and a woman loving; shown her the wonder and rapture of shared passion; given her the renewed joy of living.

The only other gift he could give her now was himself.

It had been so long, and she was so lonely. If it weren't for Marena, she didn't think she could stand it much longer. She wouldn't! If Nick wasn't back soon, she'd pack the baby up and go search for him. Blazes! She'd carry Marena on her back if she had to. She didn't care where or how far. She'd find him, somehow.

Fantasy whinnied softly. Almost at the same time, a shadow fell over Audra's face.

She opened her eyes.

He was standing at her feet, his stance wide, his arms hanging loosely at his sides. The sun was directly behind him, and she couldn't see his face clearly. But she didn't have to.

Audra lifted her arms and smiled lovingly.

"What took you so long, my darling Nick?"

"Are you sure about Sheffield Manor?"

They were lying face to face, sated and wonderfully content after their tumultuous and satisfying lovemaking, on the blanket Nick had pulled from behind his saddle. Their clothing was strewn haphazardly around the meadow, and all that touched their skin were rays of warm sunlight. Near the stream, Ulysses and Fantasy shuffled as they contentedly munched on the grass.

Audra answered Nick's question with conviction.

"Absolutely. I've never done anything more right in my life. Except loving you, of course."

"I've waited a lifetime to hear you say that."

"It's true. You told me never to lie to you again, after you returned Fantasy. I haven't, Nick, and I won't now. I love you and I don't want to live without you. I couldn't bear it. That's the truest thing I've ever said in my life."

He pulled her closer still, held her so tightly she couldn't breathe, but she didn't bother to complain. "I don't deserve you, love. And I don't deserve your sacrifice," he murmured against her cheek.

"Nick," she said earnestly, tugging at his hair to pull his head back, "giving Sheffield up wasn't a sacrifice. It doesn't matter to me anymore. The only thing that *does* matter is being with you. I want to live where you live. Our children's roots will be here. Sheffield Manor is just bricks and stones. It's just a house, Nick. *You* are my home. My home, my heart, my life. You and Marena."

"My God!" Nick breathed. "Do you know how humble you make me feel?" He squeezed her tightly. "I love you. Are you sure?"

"Yes. Besides, Sheffield is still in the family. I know Cleo and Richard will take good care of it, and we can always visit."

"As often as you want. I promise."

Audra pursed her lips and tilted an inquiring look at him.

"What?"

"Don't you think you should check with Alex before you make that promise?" she asked, laughing. "The last time I saw him, he seemed somewhat . . . restless."

Nick rolled his eyes. "The hell with Alex. The hell with everyone. Right now, I only want to look at you, and taste you again, and . . ." He stroked his palms over her cheeks and down her neck, but hesitated fractionally just at the crest of her breasts. Nick's fingers cupped one reverently and squeezed gently. He watched, fascinated, as a bead of liquid formed on the nipple. "Your breasts are fuller."

"Yes." Audra's face was tinged with pink. "Your daughter has a voracious appetite."

"So do I, my love." Nick bent his head and licked the moisture. Immediately, a small rivulet ran down Audra's breast.

She squirmed uncomfortably. "Nick . . ."

He lifted his head and looked at her. Audra was struck by the wonder in his eyes.

"It's the milk of love, sweetheart. Don't be embarrassed." But he left her breast and began nuzzling kisses onto her neck.

"Have you seen her?"

"Yes. She's breathtakingly beautiful. Like her mother." Nick's voice was muffled against her.

"Thank you for the compliment, my love."

"Thank *you*." Nick's head came up. His eyes were clouded. "I'm sorry you had such a difficult time, sweet. I would have spared you—"

Audra's fingers over his mouth effectively cut him off. "No. There's no reason to say it. I realize now that my fears were overblown. I'm not my mother, Nick. I'm stronger and healthier than she was, and we'll have more babies. In fact"—her mouth curled impishly—"we may just have started another."

Nick turned pale. He groaned. "Not yet, I hope. I'm not ready to go through that again."

Audra grinned. "*You're* not ready?"

"Definitely not. Besides, I want you to myself for a time." His gaze burned into hers. "I'm going to be extremely greedy, my sweet Audra. I'm going to adore you and cherish you. I'm going to love you like no other woman's been loved before. I'm going to devote my life to loving you," he promised.

"Then, Nick darling," Audra said, trembling laughter in her voice as she pulled him down to her again, ". . . do you think you might perhaps start now . . . ?"